*Secrets*

*Satisfy your desire for more.*

## *Hot on Her Heels* by Mia Varano

Private investigator Jack Slater dons a leopard-print g-string to investigate an exclusive male strip club, the Lollipop Lounge. He's not sure if the club's sexy, hard-driving owner, Vivica Steele, is involved in the scam, but Jack figures he's just the Lollipop to sweeten her life.

## *Shadow Wolf* by Rae Monet

A half-breed Lupine from the Alagon slums challenges a high-ranking Solarian Wolf Warrior. When Dia Nahiutras tries to steal Roark D'Reincolt's wolf, does she get an enemy forever or a mate for life? Only their sensual journey across the universe will tell.

## *Bad to the Bone* by Natasha Moore

She's a good girl who wants to be bad, and he's a bad boy who wants to be good. At her class reunion, Annie Shane sheds her good girl reputation through one wild weekend with Luke Kendall. But Luke is done playing the field and wants to settle down. What would a bad girl do?

## *War God* by Alexa Aames

Estella Eaton, a lovely graduate student, is the unwitting carrier of the essence of Aphrodite. But Ares, god of war, the ultimate alpha male, knows the truth and becomes obsessed with Estelle, pursuing her relentlessly. Can her modern sensibilities and his ancient power coexist, or will their battle of wills destroy what matters most?

# Mia Varano
# Rae Monet
# Natasha Moore
# Alexa Aames

Volume 24

# Secrets

*Satisfy your desire for more.*

**SECRETS** Volume 24
This is an original publication of Red Sage Publishing and each individual story
herein has never before appeared in print. These stories are a collection of fiction and
any similarity to actual persons or events is purely coincidental.

Red Sage Publishing, Inc.
P.O. Box 4844
Seminole, FL 33775
727-391-3847
www.redsagepub.com

SECRETS Volume 24
A Red Sage Publishing book
All Rights Reserved/July 2008
Copyright © 2008 by Red Sage Publishing, Inc.

ISBN: 1-60310-166-0 / ISBN 13: 978-1-60310-166-7

Published by arrangement with the authors and copyright holders of the individual
works as follows:

HOT ON HER HEELS
Copyright © 2008 by Mia Varano

SHADOW WOLF
Copyright © 2008 by Rae Monet

BAD TO THE BONE
Copyright © 2008 by Natasha Moore

WAR GOD
Copyright © 2008 by Alexa Aames

Photographs:
Cover © 2008 by Tara Kearney; www.tarakearney.com
Cover Models: M. Nichole Sylvester and Jimmy Thomas
Setback cover © 2000 by Greg P. Willis; GgnYbr@aol.com

Printed in the U.S.A.

Book typesetting by:

Quill & Mouse Studios, Inc.
www.quillandmouse.com

# Contents

# Hot on Her Heels

by Mia Varano

*To My Reader:*

If you feel lucky, indulge your fantasies at the Lollipop Lounge in Las Vegas where men wear g-strings and women stuff them just to see them bulge. But beware. That hottie with hard body may have secrets he's not willing to share—unless you ask nicely.

# Chapter 1

Vivica Steele ran the palms of her hands along the smooth slabs of muscle on the new guy's freshly waxed chest and inhaled his fresh, soapy scent. Her fingertips tingled as she stuffed down an insane desire to grab the bulge in his tight black polyester pants. Even here at the Lollipop Lounge in the middle of the Vegas strip, too much fondling could land her smack in the center of a sexual harassment lawsuit, although this one might be worth the risk.

She flicked his silver nipple ring. "You'll do, but lose the body jewelry. We don't want to frighten the sweet little old ladies who come in here for their eightieth birthdays."

She grinned as she watched his Adam's apple bob. He cleared his throat. "Sweet little old ladies come to the Lollipop Lounge?"

"Yeah, and you better cater to them instead of the hot young things because the old broads tip better, in cold, hard cash."

Two types of men worked at the Lollipop Lounge. Gay men who loved showing off their well-toned bodies, and straight men who loved getting laid every night. Judging by the way this one eyed her assistant, Chanel, earlier, not to mention the pure masculinity that emanated from his hard body in suffocating waves, she pegged him as the latter.

She glanced at the application on her desk and raised a brow. "Your name's Jack Savage?"

He nodded. "Yes, ma'am."

Subservience. She liked that in a man. Perching on the front edge of her desk, she crossed her legs and took inventory of his black hair, dark eyes, and olive skin that rippled with solid muscle across his chest and belly.

"Well, Jack, you aren't on the docks anymore. Maybe we'll call you Fabrizio."

His gaze lingered on her thighs, and she uncrossed and re-crossed her legs Sharon Stone-style just to mess with him. He had to learn to control his libido around the boss. She never sampled the Lollipops.

His dark eyes smoldered as they trailed to her face, and his distractingly sensuous lips lifted at one corner. "Fine. You can call me Fab."

What made her think one little "ma'am" from his lips signaled subservience? Maybe he said it just to mess with her.

Two dollops of heat scorched her cheeks, and before they could spread, she jumped from the desk and turned her back on him. If she planned to keep him at the Lollipop Lounge, she had to slap him down. Nobody toyed with Vivica Steele. Not anymore.

"Does this mean I have the job?"

She spun around and almost toppled back against her desk. He'd taken one step closer, and now towered above her, his body heat nearly singeing the ends of her lashes. She dug unsteady fists into the desk behind her and drew her shoulders back until her breasts, clad in powder blue silk, almost brushed his bare chest. Bad move. Her nipples crinkled in response to his proximity.

"You'll start out as a waiter. All our Lollipop Boys do. If you show me you can strut your stuff among the tables, I'll put you on stage. Then you can make some real money. Fair enough?"

Jack held out his hand. "Fair enough."

As they sealed the deal, his long, powerful fingers enveloped her hand in a warm clasp, sending rivers of sweet honey coursing through her veins.

This had to stop, right here, right now. She squeezed his hand hard, but he only grinned and squeezed harder. She ground her teeth together and yanked her arm back. When he released her hand, she resisted an urge to flex her fingers to revive her circulation.

Time to wipe that boyish grin off his face and show him she had complete control of the situation. She gestured toward the black Lollipop Lounge trousers Chanel gave him for the interview. "One more thing before we take you on. Remove the pants."

The lazy sweep of his long, dark lashes over his eyes and his lazier grin lanced her belly with disappointment. He didn't look the least bit uncomfortable. Either she just lost her ability to figuratively grab a man by the balls, or Jack enjoyed her games. Instead of unbuttoning the fly and pulling down the zipper, he ripped the pants off his body and tossed them to the floor.

"Might as well make use of the Velcro."

Nothing fazed him. She hadn't run into many men lately she couldn't grind beneath her heel. While it exhausted her, it allowed her to keep the upper hand. Maybe she just met her match.

Her gaze dropped to the leopard print pouch nestled between his muscled thighs, and her breath hitched in her throat. That kitty cat looked ready to pounce.

Crossing her arms, she clenched her jaw, and everything else, as her eyes wandered up and down his chiseled frame.

He struck a pose and flexed his muscles. "So do you think I got what it takes for the stage?"

For the stage and her bed, but he didn't have to know that. She shrugged. "Turn around."

He obeyed her command, displaying a set of broad shoulders that whittled down to narrow hips. The g-string disappeared between a pair of tight buns, and she bit down on an impulse to pluck it from its hiding place.

Apparently, she didn't bite hard enough. She smacked her palm against his backside and met pure muscle. His smooth skin clenched beneath her touch, and she tweaked his flesh between her fingertips.

The door to her office swung open, and Chanel hovered on the threshold, her eyes wide. Vivica stepped back from the tempting hunk of male positioned in front of her, heat burning her cheeks. Busted.

"Jack was just showing me his, ah, attributes for the stage."

Chanel zeroed in on Jack's crotch, and then she glanced over his shoulder toward Vivica. "Are you hiring him on as a dancer?"

Vivica folded her hands in front of her before they could lead her into any more trouble. "Of course not. He'll wait tables first just like anyone else, but he's eager to hit the stage and wanted to show me his wares."

Actually she demanded to see his wares, but he hadn't exhibited any shyness about revealing all. Would he rat her out now to her assistant?

Jack shifted to the side and stood between her and Chanel wearing nothing but his g-string and a smile. His pouch bulged, but he didn't bother to hide it. In fact, he seemed to enjoy it.

He grinned. "Just thought the boss should see what I have to offer the clientele."

He didn't tell the truth about how he happened to be standing in her office half-naked. Why? Could this be someone she could count on? She squashed the thought before it could lead her into any foolishness.

Chanel circled him once. "You have a great body, Jack, and attitude to match. The women will love you."

He nodded, his dark hair brushing his shoulders and falling over one eye. "I hope so, but I understand I have to learn the ropes and prove myself first."

Vivica spun around and swept his application off her desk. "Good.

Chanel will take you back to her office to fill out some paperwork. You can start tonight, but we'll do a background check, and you have to submit to a drug test. If anything turns up, you'll be fired. Any problems with that?"

His dark eyes narrowed. "You do a background check?"

"Do you have anything to hide?"

"No, ma'am, just surprised."

"We run a tight ship here, Jack, and expect all our employees to meet certain standards."

He held up his hands. "No problem."

She gave Jack's application to Chanel, who opened the door and beckoned him to follow. Before he walked out of the office, he bent over to retrieve his slacks, giving Vivica a full view of his muscled buttocks. Then the door slammed behind them.

Vivica let out a long breath and sank to the chair behind her desk. He enjoyed teasing her, but he'd soon learn she didn't indulge in the Lollipops. Although his attitude attracted her to him, as it signaled a certain strength, and she longed to lean on someone for a change.

While some of the Lollipops tended to be somewhat effeminate, Jack exuded pure, potent masculinity. His application indicated that he waited tables in L.A. while taking acting classes, as well as singing and dancing lessons. Obviously, his acting career flopped. Guess he figured he could use those dancing lessons to earn some cash in Vegas.

She stared out the window at the Vegas strip below. How many dreams of fame and fortune turned to dust in L.A. and Vegas? At least Jack Savage didn't have stars in his eyes. He didn't look like he'd allow anyone to take advantage of him, but then men had the upper hand in that area.

After her rocky start in Vegas as a naïve seventeen year old, she never allowed anyone to take advantage of her either. She turned the tables. She exploited men now and loved the delicious sense of power it gave her—most of the time.

She made it on her own, in her own way, and she'd never let her guard down again. She'd never let some man control her. They only pretended to care until they got you in their clutches.

She dashed a tear from her cheek. Why did Jack Savage dredge up all these old memories? Must be the way he stood his ground, her liberties skimming off him like beads of water on a freshly waxed car. Her actions didn't intimidate him, embarrass him, or make him angry, like so many other men. And while it intrigued her, she didn't like it. His attitude threatened her sense of control.

Her office door flew open, and Chanel stormed into the room, her dark eyes flashing. "What's wrong with you, girl?"

Vivica pushed back from her desk and lifted her chin. "What are you talking about?"

"Don't play the innocent with me. I saw you handling the help."

Chanel didn't miss a thing. Vivica bit her lip. "He's an employee, not the help."

"Cut the semantics. You had your hand on his ass, not that I blame you. He's a hot property, but you just left us wide open for a lawsuit."

He hadn't given the impression he objected to her fondling. She came out from behind her desk. "Did he threaten a lawsuit?"

"No. In fact, he followed me into my office wearing that g-string, and didn't even put his clothes back on to sign his W-2. He's a cocky SOB, and I mean that in all the right ways."

Vivica giggled. "He didn't try to hide his erection in here either."

"Well, his erection subsided substantially after he left your office, but he's packing something in that pouch, and it ain't a baby kangaroo."

Doubling over with laughter, Vivica clutched her stomach. Leave it to Chanel to brighten the situation. They started a friendship when they both worked in the chorus line at the Costa del Sol Resort and Casino. Chanel had connections in this town, and she matched Vivica in grit and determination.

Chanel wiped her eyes and plucked a tissue from Vivica's desk. "Seriously, what were you thinking?"

Vivica shrugged. She had no idea. The man had her firing on all pistons, and not just the sexual ones. When she looked in his eyes, she saw someone she might be able to trust. "I don't know. It's like you said. His cockiness irked me, and I just want to show him who's boss."

"We all know who's boss, and if this Jack's game, I don't see why you shouldn't enjoy a Lollipop once in a while. God knows I've had my share."

Did she even have the ability to enjoy a man again? She had to hold the reins with a tight fist at all times, and lately she'd been getting tired of the fight. Could she hand over those reins to someone like Jack? "Don't worry. I won't slip again."

Someone tapped at the door, and Vivica called, "Come in."

Jack stepped into the room wearing faded jeans and a denim shirt with the sleeves rolled up to his elbows. "Excuse me, ladies. I left the form for my drug test in Chanel's office, and the door's locked."

Chanel said, "Come with me. I'll get it for you."

"So you'll be here tonight at nine o'clock, Jack?" Vivica held her breath as his dark eyes burned into hers.

Then he winked. "With bells on."

He backed out the door, and Chanel turned to Vivica and matched Jack's wink.

Chanel clicked the door firmly behind her, and Jack followed the sensuous sway of her hips down the hallway to her office. Business at the Lollipop Lounge must be good judging by the plush offices above the club.

Chanel stood in the doorway while he claimed the form from her desk. Obviously, she didn't want to leave him in here alone. Afraid of what he might discover?

She smiled and nodded as he thanked her. Then he jogged down the stairs, feeling her eyes pinned to his back, or lower. Vivica and Chanel treated men like slabs of beef. He couldn't believe the way Vivica ran her hands over his body, tweaking his nipple, pinching his ass.

Did these other guys put up with that? As he pushed out of the club's front door and met a gust of hot air, he snorted. They probably loved it. Who wouldn't want that woman fondling his body? Her cold, blond iciness couldn't conceal the fire that burned beneath the freeze.

When she slapped his ass, his body responded the only way it knew how, but he couldn't allow her to think his erection embarrassed him. That kind of thing wouldn't embarrass a Lollipop, would it?

God, if the guys on the force could see him now, he'd never live it down — reduced to a Lollipop Boy. He yanked open the door of the little rental car with clenched teeth. Hell, it paid the bills, and then some.

He slouched in the front seat and dug his cell phone out of his pocket. He punched in Ben Crawford's number. Ben picked up after the second ring.

"What do you have for me, Jack?"

Jack drew in a deep breath and exhaled. "I'm in. Vivica Steele and the boys of Lollipop Lounge just met their match."

# Chapter 2

"That's great, Jack. I'm glad I trusted my wife's instincts about you. Did the nipple ring help?"

Jack winced, remembering the pain he endured to get that thing on. For sheer torture, it almost beat out the body waxing. "No, she didn't like it."

"Oops, I guess Bobbie Jo's instincts went awry on that one. Did you get the tattoo she suggested?"

Bobbie Jo had suggested a number of alterations to his body to ensure he landed the job at the Lollipop Lounge, but he drew the line at permanently marking his body. "No, I didn't get the tattoo, and I'm glad. I don't think it would've gone over any better than the nipple ring."

Ben exhaled. "Bobbie Jo wasn't sure. She's only been to the place once for a girlfriend's bachelorette party. So you met Vivica Steele?"

"Yeah, I met her."

"What's she like?"

Jack recalled the texture of her smooth hand as he grasped it in his, staring into those smoldering blue eyes. He shifted in his seat to accommodate his tightening crotch. The woman acted like a drug on his senses. He'd have to learn to control his response to her if he hoped to get this job done. "She's a hard-ass businesswoman."

Ben laughed. "So I understand. Do you think the rumors Bobbie Jo heard are true? Does it look like she might be involved?"

Vivica treated the Lollipop Boys like pieces of meat, and maybe she added a little seasoning by allowing them to con elderly women out of their money and jewels. Did she set them up? Did she take a cut? Her hard-as-nails demeanor sure made it easy for him to imagine her involvement, even though her eyes with their hint of wariness, made him want to reach out with a soothing touch. He said, "She might be. That's what I'm going to find out."

"Did you meet any of the other men there? Any luck finding Rock?"

"Not yet, but I start tonight."

Ben thanked him and assured him that he'd have his money tomorrow, with the promised bonus for securing the job at the Lollipop Lounge.

Jack tossed his phone onto the seat next to him and closed his eyes. Ben had forked over a lot of cash already to recover his mother's jewels, and for good reason. His sixty-five year old mother refused to go to the police out of embarrassment.

She'd met a handsome young dancer, Rock, at the Lollipop Lounge and returned again and again to stuff bills into Rock's g-string. But that didn't satisfy Rock, who had his eye on a bigger prize. Rock started dating Sadie Crawford, who gave him her trust and free access to her home. After Rock ended the relationship, Mrs. Crawford's jewelry disappeared along with him.

Ben hired Jack to get the jewels back, and Ben's wife, Bobbie Jo, provided the lead. She'd heard through the grapevine of a few other regulars at the Lollipop Lounge who began relationships with the dancers only to discover expensive items missing from their homes once those relationships bit the dust.

Was the whole club a set-up for a bigger take than the nightly receipts? If so, Vivica Steele had to be involved in the scam, and if she'd been duping old ladies, he couldn't wait to bring her down—despite the little girl lost look in her eyes.

⁂

Jack reported for duty at the side door of the Lollipop Lounge in jeans and a t-shirt, his uniform for the evening tucked under his arm.

He joined the other Lollipop Boys in the locker room, the dancers claiming one side and the waiters clustered on the other—definitely a caste system at work. Ben had informed him Rock graced the stage as a dancer, and Jack's eyes flicked to their corner.

A few of the dancers met his gaze boldly, and the others ignored him. He'd have to make it clear from the get-go that he swung one way and one way only.

He already wore the leopard-print g-string under his jeans, so he replaced his jeans with the tight black slacks, securing the Velcro closures. He pulled on a pair of black silver-tipped cowboy boots and grabbed the last piece of the uniform from his assigned locker.

He scowled at his reflection in the mirror as he buckled the silver-studded black leather collar around his neck.

"Don't look so grumpy. The ladies love the collar, and when the ladies approve, the ladies tip big."

Jack spun around, folding his arms over his bare chest. The guy stood so close, Jack could smell the mint toothpaste on his breath. He narrowed his eyes and growled, "Not interested, buddy."

The blonde held up his hands. "I pegged you as a straight guy the minute you walked in here. Just offering some friendly advice from one relatively new Lollipop to another."

Jack rolled his shoulders. "Whatever. Why the collars? Are we supposed to be Vivica Steele's slaves?"

"A lot of guys here wouldn't mind that, although she doesn't mingle. I take it you met Viv?"

"Yeah, what's her story anyway?" He'd dug around but hadn't turned up much on the mysterious Ms. Steele. Seemed she'd arisen from the desert a fully formed creature, or goddess.

The man shrugged. "She used to dance at the Costa del Sol, she and that delicious chocolate kiss, Chanel. Vivica started the business, hired Chanel as her assistant, and opened this place four years ago."

A showgirl. That explained Vivica's lean, lithe body with those endless legs. "Looks like they've been successful."

"They are, and they're good about spreading the wealth. The crowd here is strictly champagne wishes and caviar dreams. Play your cards right, and you can make a lot of dough."

He planned to make a lot of dough, but not from working at the Lollipop Lounge. He stuck his hand out. "Thanks for the info. The name's Jack."

"My name's Derek, but the ladies call me Dick."

Jack dropped his hand, and Derek laughed. "Don't worry. I'm not interested in hitting on straight men. Did Viv and Chanel tell you about the hundred dollar tip rip?"

"No." This sounded bad.

"The first woman who tips a waiter a hundred gets to rip off his slacks."

That explained the g-string underneath the slacks. Jack swallowed. "Does that happen a lot?"

Derek laughed again. "By the end of the night, we're all prancing around in our pouches, boots, and collars."

Jack pasted a smile on his face. "That's great. I could use a hundred dollar tip."

Derek sauntered away and approached another waiter, placing a hand on his shoulder.

He'd have to cultivate Derek's friendship. The guy liked to talk and seemed to know everyone, maybe even Rock.

Jack finished his prep by rubbing warm oil on his upper body. He had to play the part and play it well. Succeeding at this job would land a bundle in his already burgeoning bank account and might just put him over the top to buy that ranch in Idaho.

He wandered into the club. Its plush red velvet cushions, mirrored walls and ceilings, and glittering bottles lining the bar made him feel as if he'd just entered a palace of pleasure. His heart pumped in time to the pulsing dance music, and then sped up a few more beats when he caught sight of Vivica in a short, white halter dress skimming her curves. Her silky, silvery blond hair shimmered around her shoulders as she darted from one end of the club to the other, inspecting every last detail before the doors opened.

She had to have smarts to transform herself from Vegas showgirl to Vegas business owner. Why screw it up with illegal activities?

She almost bumped into him at the bar, clutching his bicep to steady herself. "Sorry, oh, it's you. Finding everything okay?"

Her gaze dropped from his face to his collar, a smile curving her full lips. Did she want to make sure she had him properly shackled? He flexed his bicep. "I'm working section seven, lucky seven."

Dropping his arm, her delicate brows rose. "Are you hoping to get lucky tonight?"

"This is Vegas, baby, and I'm always hoping to get lucky."

"Just remember the rules. No touching the ladies, but they're allowed to touch you within reason."

"Is that why you grabbed my ass this afternoon, just testing the merchandise?"

A pink flush washed across her porcelain complexion. "I—I, yes, that's it."

"Did I pass inspection?" He wanted to fluster her, get her on the ropes, get under her silky smooth skin.

She straightened her shoulders, the V of her halter dress widening to display a delicious curve of supple breast. "Yeah, you did, and I see you followed my orders regarding the nipple ring. You're now the perfect Lollipop, collar and all."

She obviously didn't stay flustered for long. Inhaling her floral scent, he leaned in close and brushed her soft earlobe with his lips. "I'm nobody's slave boy, Vivica."

His warm whisper curled her toes, but before she had a chance to respond, he sauntered past her to pick up his drink tray and order pad.

She sucked in her bottom lip. Jack puzzled her. He had all the smooth moves and lines of a male stripper, but with an edge of steel. A strange combination for a man in this environment. He probably wouldn't last long. A man had to swallow his pride at the Lollipop Lounge, and for Jack that would be a huge gulp.

The glittering doors to the club swung open, and the women streamed into the bar, chattering, laughing, and ready for anything. And the Lollipops delivered every night.

She and Chanel paid the waiters minimum wage and the dancers not much more, but the men made up for the low salaries in tips and perks.

Still fifteen minutes until show time, and the noise level rose to a cacophonous din. The booze and the laughter flowed in section seven, by far the liveliest corner of the room.

Chanel sidled up to her and draped an arm across her shoulders. "Our new Lollipop makes quite a first impression, doesn't he?"

Vivica had been tracking Jack's progress more than she cared to admit. Now her eyes followed him on one of his many trips to the bar. When he served the women in his section, he laughed and joked with them, even allowing them to fold bills in the waistband of his pants. But when he returned to the bar, he appeared strangely isolated from the hilarity around him. Jack seemed to have substance beneath the finely-toned exterior, unlike most of the Lollipops.

As he balanced his tray on one hand and placed another drink order, he turned his head toward her. His jaw formed a hard line, and his dark eyes kindled with some emotion she couldn't identify. Then his lips broke into a smile and he winked.

She blew out a breath. Everyone had demons. Even Lollipops got the blues. Jack strutted back to his tables, his muscular buttocks clenching beneath the smooth fabric of his pants.

Chanel sighed. "Hot stuff."

A few minutes later cheers and whistles rose from section seven, and the women started chanting, "Tip rip, tip rip, tip rip."

Vivica checked her Rolex. Still five minutes before the show started–a record for a tip rip.

Someone must've filled Jack in. He vaulted onto a table, waving the hundred over his head. A silver-haired woman in sequins positioned herself in front of him, grabbed the waistband of his trousers, and yanked.

The pants ripped away from Jack's body, leaving him exposed in his cowboy boots and pouch. The women screamed and reached for him. He turned his back on them, flexed his muscles, and clenched and released his butt cheeks. Then he spun around, thrust his pelvis forward a few times, and jumped from the table.

Chanel laughed. "That man's got attitude to spare. Good hire."

Was he? Vivica could only nod as threads of desire zinged up her thighs and pooled in all the right places. No Lollipop ever had this effect on her before. Her hands trembled as she smoothed them across the bodice of her dress, brushing her peaked nipples. Her breath hissed between her teeth. Maybe she could allow herself one little taste, but only if she could maintain the upper hand.

Thankfully, the room darkened and the show began. The dancers on the stage moved much more suggestively than Jack had, but they all left her cold.

Jack possessed more than just sex appeal, but the raw power of his body weakened her knees and moistened her panties. Who was she kidding? He'd never allow her to have control, and for that reason she had to put him off limits, no matter how much she wanted to get to know the man beneath the g-string.

After the show, the Lollipop Lounge opened its doors to male clientele, which signaled the time for her to retreat to her office and review the receipts for the evening. On the curve of the stair, she turned to survey her little kingdom. Jack hovered on the edge of the dance floor, holding his drink tray aloft, his pouch stuffed with bills. A woman reached for him and turned him around. While she slipped money in the string that snaked up his buttocks, his dark eyes met Vivica's, burning her with their intensity.

Shivering, she climbed the rest of the stairs and slipped into her office. What would it be like to make love with that man? When she slept with someone, she called the shots. She dictated the time, the place, and the pace. So far, nobody complained. Except her.

Even though holding all the power made her feel comfortable and safe, it didn't fulfill her on another level. She longed to let go, allow someone else to take charge, but the idea filled her with a terror greater than her desire.

She shook her head and accessed the club's database. They had a program that tracked their clients' attendance, their ages, how much money they spent at the club, and even their spending habits. She wanted to know something about every woman who walked through the club's doors and make her experience at the Lollipop Lounge everything she dreamed. Vivica

15

had become an expert at fulfilling everyone else's fantasies.

When someone tapped on her office door, she jerked her head up. Better not be one of the customers. This part of the club was strictly off-limits. She called, "Come in."

A tall, thin man entered the office and snapped the door behind him. He settled his shoulders against the door and smiled.

Vivica froze. Blood rushed to her head, and she clamped a hand over her mouth against the nausea rising from her gut.

"Vivian Sorenson, as I live and breathe, or should I address you as Vivica Steele? I like it."

She dropped her hand and placed her palms flat on her desk. Her heart raced, but she forced a long, deep breath into her lungs. "Don't address me at all. Get out."

Clicking his tongue, he shoved off the door and dropped to the sofa. "Is that any way to treat an old friend? You never did show proper gratitude to the man who saved your pretty ass."

She'd known this day would come—and she'd dreaded it. Standing up, she put on her best sneer. "You saved my ass from the frying pan only to fling it into the fire."

"You could've been a contender, Viv. I would've transformed you into one of Vegas's top dollar hookers, and that's saying something for this town."

Her hands curled into fists, her nails biting into her palms. "Get out before I call security."

He pushed up from the sofa and ambled forward until he faced her across the desk, the stench of booze on his breath. He placed his hand on the phone. "You have a sweet deal going on here, and I want a piece of the action. You owe me, sweet cheeks."

She flinched at the name. He'd dubbed her "sweet cheeks" the first day he met her in that bus depot. She licked her lips, her eyes darting to the phone covered by his large, bony hand.

"I don't owe you shit, Charlie."

He shook his head. "What language. You used to be so sweet and innocent."

Sweet, innocent, and stupid. "Until you corrupted me."

"What's a little corruption between friends? You could've been the top dog, or should I say, pussycat, in my kennel."

She gripped the edge of the desk. She had to stay cool, had to get security up here, or get Charlie out. Knowing Charlie, he wouldn't stick around for insults. Smirking, she let her gaze wander over his unfashionable suit.

"Looks like your kennel went to the dogs."

He roared and threw the phone across the room where it cracked a mirror. Then he lunged across the desk. She screamed and stumbled back into her chair.

As Charlie grabbed for her, the door burst open. Jack loomed on the threshold and ground out, "What the hell's going on?"

Charlie straightened up. "Nothing for you to worry about, Lollipop. Go jerk off another dancer."

A dark, dangerous cloud rolled across Jack's face, and he clenched his fists. "Get away from her, and get the hell out of this office."

Even half-naked, Jack looked menacing, but Charlie had never backed down from a fight in his life. "Or you'll what, strike me with your dick?"

In two steps, Jack devoured the space between them and gripped Charlie's throat with one hand. He shook him back and forth until Charlie's eyes bulged from their sockets.

Vivica could smell the pungent odor of fear pulsing from Charlie's body, and she screamed, "Jack, no. He's not worth it."

Jack released Charlie, and then planted his fist against Charlie's nose. Charlie clutched his face and collapsed to the floor, spouting blood, and Jack drew his arm back and delivered another punishing blow to Charlie's mid-section.

Vivica scrambled for the phone and punched in the extension for security. In the few minutes it took them to arrive, Charlie resembled a bloody heap of rags on the floor.

Two security guards hauled him to his feet. "Do you want to call the cops, Vivica?"

"No cops. Just get him out of here. Use the back entrance."

They dragged him out of the office, and Jack stood in the middle of the room rubbing his fist like a conquering hero. He'd probably just rescued her from one of Charlie's beatings. From the moment she'd met Jack, she'd hoped she could count on him. She just didn't figure he'd prove her instincts right so soon.

She pointed to his hand. "Are you all right? Let me get you some ice for that."

The finger she pointed shook as much as her voice. She needed help more than he did. He just suffered from physical pain. Her troubled blue eyes reflected a deep, soul-searing pain. One he could relate to only too well.

He said, "Sit down."

She stopped in her tracks. "What?"

He rubbed his sore knuckles. "Sit down. I'll get the ice myself."

Her eyes claimed half her pale face and those lush lips trembled. She stood rooted to the floor, so he took her arm and guided her to the sofa. She sat down mechanically, all signs of the tough chick gone.

He grabbed some ice from the freezer of the little fridge in the corner, and wrapped it in a couple of paper towels. He sank down next to her. As his shoulder brushed hers, she jerked and clamped her hands between her knees.

He wedged the ice against his knuckles and threw his arm across the cushions behind her. "Who the hell was that?"

She drew in a shaky breath and expelled it slowly. "Nobody. He's a nobody."

Okay, he didn't expect the boss to confide in him, especially since he still wore this damned uncomfortable g-string, but he did just save her ass. "For a nobody, he sure punched your buttons."

She grimaced, and then tossed her head, sending her hair shimmering over one shoulder. "He doesn't concern me. Why aren't you on the floor working?"

The tough talk didn't fool him. Her leg bounced, and her mouth quivered with every word. His arm dropped to her shoulder, and he pulled her close until he could see the pulse throbbing in her throat, emitting a whiff of her feminine scent with every beat.

Her lashes fluttered and her full lips parted. He claimed her mouth with his own, his tongue edging just inside her lower lip. She shuddered, drawing his tongue into her warmth. He pressed his body against hers until the ripples of fear that coursed through her subsided. Then he buried his tongue deeper into her mouth, and she closed around it, sucking it, drawing strength from it.

His cock hardened as he pushed against her hip, and he slipped his hand along her silken thigh.

She gasped and placed both hands against his shoulders, shoving hard. Her chest rose and fell as she blinked. "What the hell do you think you're doing? I don't toy with Lollipop Boys."

Her lips, moist and swollen from his kiss, gave lie to her words. Her gaze dropped to his erection straining against the thin fabric pouch of his g-string. Her eyes widened before she jumped from the sofa. "I'm sure you can get one of your fans downstairs to take care of that for you. Just don't do it inside the club."

He wanted her to take care of it here and now and drop the bad-ass attitude. He pushed up from the sofa and thrust his hips forward. Let her get a good look at what she'd just turned down. He had the satisfaction of seeing her swallow, and he grinned. "Thank you, ma'am. I may just do that. Parking lot okay?"

She dragged her gaze to his face, her own blooming pink roses. "Excuse me?"

He gestured to his aching cock. "Is it okay if one of my fans relieves this in the parking lot?"

She shrugged and turned her back on him. "Whatever."

Her slim frame straightened as if she shoved a rod of steel down her spine. Despite her words, she needed him. And he wanted to be there for her. He took a step toward her, and then spun around and slammed out of her office.

*Chapter 3*

Jack cranked up the air as he tooled down the flat desert highway, leaving the crowds and traffic of downtown Vegas behind him. This job was proving to be harder than he expected, with an emphasis on hard.

Last night after the tip rip, he'd sashayed around the Lollipop Lounge half-naked with women stuffing money into his g-string, their fingers whisper-close to his erect cock, which stayed that way because of Vivica's blue eyes tracking his every move.

In his former life, that scenario would've constituted his dream job, but by the end of the evening his balls ached with unrelieved arousal. He almost followed Vivica's advice about finding satisfaction in the parking lot when the club closed, but he took care of it himself in the privacy of his hotel room, the memory of their warm kiss fueling his release.

She'd succumbed to him for a moment, but just a moment. Then she clamped down. She must take her edict about not fraternizing with the hired help seriously. Good thing someone did.

It wouldn't do his career any good to be accused of getting his rocks off on the job... again. Even though P.I.'s had a lot more leeway than cops, nobody wanted to hire someone more interested in getting screwed than in screwing over the suspect.

Was Vivica a suspect? Maybe a few of the Lollipop Boys, including Rock, worked freelance. That's what he had to find out instead of getting involved with Vivica Steele and her problems.

That slimeball in her office last night had terrified her, although she tried to hide it beneath the hard-as-nails veneer. What kind of power did a loser like that hold over her? Maybe he had something to do with the thefts.

He jammed his foot on the accelerator. Never mind Vivica Steele for now. Just find Rock and the missing rocks.

He rolled up to the huge stone gate protecting a community of multi-million dollar homes edging a lush golf course. Someone must have been paying a helluva water bill to get grass that green in this desert wasteland.

The security guard checked his name against a list, and the black, wrought-iron gate edged with gold swung open.

Clutching a cigar between his fingers, Ben waited on the porch as Jack cruised to a stop in front of the white mansion that glimmered like an oasis. Ben squinted at the little rental car. "I would've paid for something more comfortable, Jack."

Jack slammed the door and strode up the steps to shake Ben's hand. "I'm a struggling actor hoping to make it big as a male stripper. The car suits the persona."

Ben nodded. "You're right. I guess that's why you're the P.I. Come on in. Bobbie Jo has drinks waiting on the terrace."

Jack followed Ben across the marble tiles of the massive foyer. They stepped down into a great room with cathedral ceilings, and Jack's flip flops almost disappeared into the plush peacock blue carpet.

"Bobbie Jo, Jack's here."

Bobbie Jo skipped in from the terrace through the cut-glass French doors, a pair of short shorts hugging her hips and a cropped-off t-shirt clinging to her perfect fake boobs. She pressed them against her husband's arm as she grabbed his hand.

She grinned. "Hi there, Jack. I heard you got the job." Her dark, flashing eyes raked his body. "I never doubted it for a minute."

Jack glanced at Ben, contentedly sucking on his cigar. Did he realize his wife had just checked him out? Ben's smile remained in place, if a bit frozen. Maybe he indulged his young wife's flirtations.

Jack cleared his throat. "No thanks to the nipple ring."

Bobbie Jo pouted a pair of collagen lips. "Benny told me the dragon lady made you remove it. Too bad."

"Dragon lady? Do you know Vivica Steele?"

"Not really. She danced at the Costa before I got there, and I heard a few stories about her. I also understand she runs that club with an iron fist, and if she ordered her employees to scam her customers, they'd do it. There's also the money."

"Money?"

"My friend's husband is president of the Bank of Las Vegas, and she said Vivica's been making some huge deposits lately." Bobbie Jo put her finger to her lips. "That's confidential info. Don't tell anyone I told you."

Benny curled an arm around her waist and patted her hip. "Sit down, Jack. Bobbie Jo, get Jack a drink."

She walked to the bar, the contours of her ass visible in her tight shorts.

She looked over her shoulder, batting her long lashes. "What would you like, Jack?"

"Beer's okay." He pulled a chair up to the table and sat down, crossing an ankle over his knee.

Ben dropped to the chair across from him. "How'd it go last night? Must've been great cavorting with those women, all sexed up from the show."

Remembering his permanent hard-on and aching balls, Jack clenched his teeth behind his grin. "Yeah, great." Like being sixteen again.

Bobbie Jo put his beer in front of him, leaning over so that her breasts bulged out of the top of her low-cut t-shirt. She ran the tip of her tongue along her lips. "Did you get a tip rip? I'd tip you a hundred to see your g-string."

Jack's gaze slid to Ben's smiling face. He must put up with her for what she put out in bed. "I learned the names of all the dancers. Not a Rock among them, but a few matched his description. I also made contact with a talkative waiter in the know. I'm confident I'll find Rock or someone who knows where he went."

"I have every confidence in you." Ben swirled his martini. "Prescott Turner recommended you highly. He got his painting back without a whisper of scandal, and I'm sure you'll do the same for my mother's jewels."

Bobbie Jo sank to Ben's lap, curling her arms around his neck. "If Jack gets the jewels back, will your mother consider giving half of them to you?"

"I don't think so, baby. She's leaving those to my sister. I'll buy you new jewelry. Now let me run upstairs to get Jack's money."

When Ben left the room, Bobbie Jo ambled toward Jack with her hands on her swaying hips. "Tell me the truth, Jack. Did you work that club in your g-string all night?"

Her heavy perfume choked him, and he pushed back in his chair. He didn't need his client's wife coming on to him. "No."

Crouching down, she rubbed her hands along his thighs. "For a private investigator and former cop, you're not very truthful."

He gripped her wrists. "For a new wife, you're not very faithful."

She leaned forward until her breasts almost brushed his chin. "Ben knows why your department fired you."

"I told him myself. I don't lie to my clients."

"You lied about the tip rip. A man like you wouldn't last ten minutes in that place with your slacks intact."

Bobbie Jo played dangerous games. He lifted a shoulder. "I don't lie about the important things."

"Like coercing a witness in a drug case?"

He shoved her hands from his thighs and jumped up from the chair. "Never happened. The witness lied. The department wanted to get rid of me for a different reason."

She stood up to face him. "Your own wife didn't believe that story. Or should I say 'ex-wife?'"

Ben's sweet smelling cigar announced his return. "I hope you don't mind that I told Bobbie Jo about your situation, Jack. You know I believe you. Never would've hired you otherwise."

Jack stepped around Bobbie Jo. "I don't mind. I heard from my attorney last week, and he told me he might have someone from the department willing to talk. Even if he does, I'll never get my job back. I don't want it now."

Ben slapped a thick manila envelope into the palm of his hand. "You don't need it. And this is just for getting into the Lollipop Lounge. There will be a lot more when you recover those jewels."

Jack thanked him and escaped into the dry heat of the late afternoon. Ben and Bobbie Jo had a weird vibe. She came onto him hot and heavy, and her rich husband either didn't notice or didn't care.

The colored lights of the Vegas strip twinkled and flashed, luring unsuspecting fools with a promise of warmth and gaiety. As a seventeen-year-old runaway dazzled by the prospect of a new life, Vivica had fallen under the spell of those lights.

When she'd left the last in a series of foster families, nobody had cared. Nobody had looked too hard for her. Her father had broken his promise to rescue her from the system where he dumped her after Mom died.

Running into Charlie Champagne at the bus station had seemed like fate. Even his name suggested fun and excitement, and he delivered at first.

When Charlie showed up last night, he still had the power to pluck a chord of terror in her heart, and yet somehow he seemed smaller than she remembered, insignificant. Maybe he just shrank in comparison to Jack.

Jack could put any man at a disadvantage, and not just by his size and strength. His calm, confident demeanor suggested a self-assured, capable man. She felt safe with Jack, at least physically. Emotionally he represented all kinds of danger.

Her reflection stared back at her, and she almost didn't recognize that woman with the huge eyes and soft, full lips.

She turned from the window and strode back to her desk. The man rescued her from Charlie and all of a sudden he was Sir Galahad in a g-string. An out-of-work actor hoping to find fame and fortune as a male stripper probably didn't stash a suit of armor in his closet.

At least his background check came back squeaky clean. No arrest record, no drugs in his system, no employee termination. Jack's record was as shiny a new penny, and if he performed on the floor every night like he did last night he'd be earning lots of those pennies.

He'd slipped right into the routine and the rhythm of the club, and the ladies, young and old, loved him. His Adonis-like body fueled his popularity, and the bulge in his pouch fueled his customers' fantasies. And her own?

Did he hook up with one of those customers last night? Her hands clenched. She could've had him right here in this office. Had him? No, nobody had Jack Savage. He'd take what he wanted on his own terms, and she could never allow herself to be with someone like that, could never give up her hard-earned control.

Despite her assertions, wings of anticipation fluttered in her belly as she descended the staircase into the club. Her gaze swept through the room, settling on Jack hunched over the bar, straddling a bar stool and chatting with the bartender. His form-fitting black pants hugged his powerful thighs, and his muscled back glistened with oil. He deserved a chance to audition for the stage—maybe tonight after hours.

Jack spun around on the barstool, catching her watching him. Damn, as if the man needed anymore reassurance that she found him irresistible. He shoved off the barstool and swaggered up to her. She clutched her hands behind her to make sure they didn't stray.

He drew in close until she could smell the light sandalwood scent of the body oil. "How are you doing?"

The sincerity of his tone surprised her. What, no smartass comment? No come-on? "I'm fine. Why wouldn't I be?"

"So you recovered from your run-in last night with that little weasel?"

Did he just call her worst nightmare a little weasel? She laughed, the sound loosening the tight knot in her gut. "I recovered a long time ago."

He smiled, his expression so sweet it loosened another knot. He ran his hands up her arms and cupped her elbows. "Good. Maybe you should lock your office door when you're up there alone."

"I have security for that." Did he really care about her safety? His warm touch on her bare arms weakened her knees, and she swayed toward him before pulling back.

"They didn't do a very thorough job last night. Good thing I crashed that conversation."

She didn't want him to think she actually needed him. Narrowing her eyes, she shrugged out of his grasp. "You never did explain why you went up there."

"I saw that guy going upstairs, and I didn't like the look of him. Looked like a cheap hustler."

She jerked her chin toward the doors of the club swinging open. "Speaking of hustlers, you better get your tight buns moving."

His dark eyes burned into hers before he turned back to the bar to grab his drink tray.

She spoke like that to all the other Lollipop Boys, why didn't it work with him? He wore his composure like a shield. Even while women pawed at him, he maintained his dignity.

It attracted and frightened her at the same time. Maybe she needed to dig a little deeper than the standard background check. Maybe she needed to call Buck O'Hannigan.

Why did Vivica have to be so hostile? She must be hiding something. If she had some of the Lollipop Boys working for her on the side, she'd want complete control over them. Maybe she and that guy last night had a partnership, and he just witnessed a business disagreement.

He made noises in the locker room tonight about wanting to make more money, and he commented on the obvious wealth of some of the club patrons. He had to throw those lures out there in the hope that someone would bite.

Gritting his teeth, he smacked the drink tray against his thigh. Time for another ball-bruising night.

He sauntered up to his first table, winking, smiling, and gyrating his hips. The women shrieked and one hooked a finger in the o-ring of his collar and pulled him closer to whisper her drink order in his ear. God, he hated this shit, but he had to make it look good.

After the woman ordered, he grabbed her hand and kissed it. Then he made his way to the next party, a group of rowdy young women. He approached the new table and almost dropped his tray. Bobbie Jo Crawford, dressed in a tight red dress, winked at him. Did she have Ben's approval to be here? He didn't like it when clients took matters into their own hands.

He took their order, which consisted of two pitchers of margaritas. He just hoped the booze wouldn't loosen her tongue, or she could blow this entire operation.

He carried the two sweating pitchers back to the table along with a tray of salt-rimmed glasses. After placing a glass in front of each of the women, he poured the drinks. As he poured Bobbie Jo's drink last, she grinned at her companions. "What do you think, ladies? Hasn't this Lollipop done a great job?"

His belly clenched as he stared into Bobbie Jo's shining eyes. Then she reached into her glittering little bag on the table and drew out a hundred dollar bill.

The women screamed and chanted, "Tip rip, tip rip, tip rip."

Damn Bobbie Jo.

As she patted the tabletop, she purred, "Come on up here, big boy."

The other women in the club craned their necks to watch, and even Vivica stopped at the corner of the stage.

Bobbie Jo waved the hundred in his face, while the women amped up the volume. Jack grinned and vaulted to the tabletop. Raising his arms above his head, he pumped his pelvis forward.

Bobbie Jo stood up, clutching the bill in her left hand. With her right, she reached forward and shoved her fingers into his waistband. She gave a hard tug, and the Velcro holding his pants together ripped. She peeled the rest of the Velcro open and whipped the pants from his body.

The over-heated air of the club pressed against his bare legs and backside. With his arms still raised, he spun around on the table, thrusting his hips forward.

Vivica watched him from across the room, her lower lip caught between her teeth, her eyes luminous. Desire jolted his crotch and his cock stiffened.

The women around the table squealed and giggled as his erection filled his pouch. Before he jumped down, Bobbie Jo pulled him forward by the string of material clinging to his hip. With his crotch level with her face, she tucked one edge of the folded bill into his pouch, her fingertips skimming his hard cock.

He crouched in front of her, thighs spread open. "Why, thank you, ma'am."

The women screamed again and patted his buttocks as he leaped from the table. When he got to the bar, Derek slapped him on the back. "That's two nights in a row you got the first tip rip. You must be raking it in. Are you interested in scoring really big?"

Jack's heart thumped against his chest. "Maybe. What do you have in mind? I already told you, I don't do any Brokeback Mountain shit."

Derek dropped his hand. "Nothing like that. Meet me in the parking lot when the club closes."

His first big break. The sooner he got this job over, the better. He couldn't take much more of this nightly teasing, especially with the alluring Vivica Steele around adding fuel to the inferno.

A few hours later, the last of Bobbie Jo's party staggered out of the club. Bobbie Jo and her friends kept him hopping all night. They stuffed so many bills into his pouch, he had to dump the money in his locker and start over.

He planned to donate all his earnings from the Lollipop Lounge to some worthy charity. His clients forked over a lot of money for his discreet investigations, and once Ben paid him for recovering his mother's jewels, he'd have enough for that ranch.

That's what tortured him the most about losing his job as a cop, even more than the desertion of his wife. It destroyed his work with the kids, the ones who were jumped into joining gangs, the ones who wanted a way out. His boot camp for troubled youths just might be the fresh start those kids needed—the one he needed too.

The last of the patrons deserted the club, and he sat at the bar and tallied his receipts.

Vivica, her short black dress swirling around her thighs, perched on the stool next to him. "Word spreads fast in this town."

He dragged his eyes away from her shapely legs, one crossed over the other, swinging back and forth. "Oh?"

"That rowdy table you had tonight requested your section before they even got here."

He raised a brow. Did she find that odd after he'd been here just one night? He knew how the word spread, courtesy of Bobbie Jo. "Maybe they heard someone else worked that section before me."

She shook her head. "Nope. They requested you by appearance—the tall bronzed god with the longish dark hair and killer smile"

Bobbie Jo better be careful. He flashed the killer smile. "That's me. I must've waited on one of their friends the night before."

"Those women always know what goes on at the club. They're regulars, especially the petite hottie in the red dress with the fake boobs.

He drew in a quick breath. Bobbie Jo came here on a regular basis? How come nobody bothered to let him in on that little detail before?

Her eyes narrowed. "Are you surprised?"

More than she could ever know. "I guess not. They seemed to know the drill."

Why hadn't that occurred to him before? Did Ben realize his wife frequented the Lollipop Lounge? What else did she hide from him?

"Anyway, this is your lucky night."

He finished counting the money to cover his receipts and snapped a rubber band around the roll of bills representing his tips. He held up the roll to Vivica. "Looks like it is."

She nodded. "That's what I mean. The ladies obviously love you. Maybe it's time to give you a shot at the stage."

"Thanks. When do I audition?"

"Now."

His suddenly sweaty palm clutched the role of bills. As much as he wanted to stay right here and dance for Vivica, he had a meeting with Derek in the parking lot. "Now?"

"Yeah. You, me, and Chanel. Select an outfit from the wardrobe and meet me at the stage in ten minutes."

He didn't want to make her suspicious, so he grinned. "I'll be there."

Through narrowed eyes, Vivica watched Jack hurry to the locker room. He seemed hesitant. Any other waiter would be chomping at the bit, especially after working here for only two days, but Jack differed from the other Lollipops in every way.

After dismissing Sean, her night watch security guard, Vivica poured herself a club soda. Jack emerged from the locker room wearing black pants and shirt, a black, red-lined cape, a bolero hat, and a black mask over his eyes.

Chanel glided downstairs and circled Jack. "Zorro, you look rico suave. You have my vote."

She beat a path to the front door, and Vivica's breath hitched in her throat. "Where are you going? I told you we had an audition."

Chanel waved. "He already has my vote, and I have a date."

She bit her lip as Chanel swept out the front door. She didn't want to be left alone with Jack. She didn't trust him... or herself. "Maybe we should postpone this."

Jack tipped his hat over his left eye. "I'm ready to go right now, se-ñorita."

Did he set this up? Tell Chanel to leave? *Don't be ridiculous.* She still had control over this situation.

She strode to the announcer's booth and dimmed the club's lights. Then she flicked on the swirling stage lights and queued up a song. She called out, "Ready?"

"Yes, ma'am."

That "ma'am" business didn't fool her a bit. She flipped the switch to start the music and dragged a chair to the edge of the stage. The slow, sinuous strains of a Latin beat filled the room, and Jack weaved into the spotlight.

He moved his body to the rhythm, swiveling his hips and rolling his shoulders. He swept the hat off first and tossed it in her general direction where it landed on the floor. The black cape swirled around him as he whipped it over his head and flung it off stage.

The form-fitting black shirt and pants molded to his muscular frame as he arched his back and dropped to his knees. She'd seen better dancers, but Jack knew how to move his body with an athletic grace and power that oozed pure testosterone.

He ripped the shirt from his body and threw it at her. She reached out to block the shirt from hitting her face, clutching at its silky folds. His light sandalwood scent clung to the shirt, and she dropped it as if it scorched her hands.

He pumped his chiseled chest and caressed his pecs. Vivica sat forward in her chair and ran her tongue along her dry lips.

Jack turned his back on her, reached down and ripped off the Velcro pants. He flexed his buttocks a few times before spinning around. The lights bounced off his gold lamé pouch, which swelled with his erection. Her nipples tingled, and to keep from touching them, she wedged her hands beneath her thighs.

His pelvis undulated, his bulge straining against the thin material barely containing it. The black mask hid half his face, but his eyes gleamed and his lips turned up in a smile.

She gulped. Could she stop this now? Did she want to? He dropped to the stage and pumped his hips, imitating the sex act. She felt each thrust and pressed her thighs together, squirming in her seat.

The music ended with a flourish, and Jack skidded across the stage on his knees, coming to a rest in front of her, his thighs spread.

His chest rose and fell, a trickle of sweat inching down his flat belly. As steam rose from his body, Vivica couldn't distinguish her heavy breathing from his.

Her gaze tracked down to his crotch. The tip of his cock peeked out from the edge of his pouch, a bead of moisture gleaming in the light.

She took it as an offering. She reached forward and traced the outline of his shaft captured by the glittering material. He groaned, his hips bucking. She teased her fingers to his head and ran the pad of her thumb along the pearly drop, and then sucked his manly essence from her finger.

He ripped the g-string off and lunged forward. His cock extended straight out, the pulsing veins visible beneath the smooth surface. He rasped, "Please, Vivica. I've been like this all night."

She couldn't deny him when he asked so politely. She dipped her head and sucked him between her lips. He moaned and drove into her mouth. Her mouth encircled him, her tongue pressing against his throbbing shaft. She cupped his balls, running her finger back toward his tight hole.

He gasped. "That's right. Slip it in."

He wanted her to enter him? She just planned to tease him with the prospect. He opened his legs further, and she nudged her finger inside his hole.

Grunting, he plowed into her mouth, gagging her with his length and breadth. He nestled his fingers in her hair to move her head to his driving rhythm. He murmured, "Oh yeah, baby, please me. Take me in."

His grasp tightened as he impaled her mouth over and over, the blunt head of his cock pounding the back of her throat. She couldn't turn her head, couldn't move. His buttocks trapped her hand, pushing her finger deeper inside him.

He manipulated her into satisfying his every need. Just when she thought she'd suffocate, he cried out, pumping his hot seed down her throat.

She swallowed every drop, had no choice. He lifted his body off of her finger and slid out of her mouth. That stupid mask still hid his face, and she reached up to snatch it off.

He caught her wrist in a vise and then kissed her palm. He perched on the edge of the stage, hanging his legs over the side. He pulled her up, trapping her between his thighs and wrapping his arms around her waist. Her breasts rose and fell as he nuzzled them.

She molded her body against his, getting lost in the sensations that fogged her brain. Placing her hands on his heaving shoulders, she didn't know whether to push him away or draw him closer. He'd turned the tables on her, but she didn't feel used.

He pulled her closer and sealed his mouth over hers. The kiss consumed her, lighting a fire in her belly. Just when she felt ready to melt, his lips trailed across her jaw, and he nibbled her earlobe.

He slipped a hand up her dress. "Your turn."

Did she want a turn? She'd never felt so close to losing all control. She pinned his hand between her thighs. She couldn't allow him to feel her wet panties. Didn't want him to know how much pleasing him turned her on.

She placed her palms against his damp chest. "I think that's enough for tonight."

He blinked and sat back on his heels. "Do I get the promotion?"

She gulped the rest of her club soda, grabbed her bag, and headed for the staircase. "You need to work on that dancing a little more."

# Chapter 4

Jack slumped in his rental car with his cap pulled low on his forehead. The heavy gates swung open. Nope, not her. Bobbie Jo drove a Mercedes, not a Jag.

He felt like a rat tattling to her husband, but he didn't want Bobbie Jo and her libido interfering with his work. What if one of Rock's friends recognized her and linked her to him? She could blow his cover sky-high. Seemed that wasn't the only thing she wanted to blow.

She'd practically grabbed his cock right out of his pouch in the middle of the club. As much as the offer tempted him, he was glad he reserved it for Vivica. He'd enjoyed dancing for her last night, and she had too. Her reluctance to let him reciprocate puzzled him, but then everything she did puzzled him.

The obvious answer to her skittishness had to be her involvement in the robberies. God, he'd hate to see her go to prison, but if she headed up a ring of thieves who preyed on women's fantasies, she deserved everything she got. Didn't she?

A red 350 SL zoomed out of the gates. Jack watched it zip around the corner before wheeling up to the security gate.

Ben welcomed him with the inevitable cigar wedged between his fingers. "News already, Jack?"

"Rock doesn't work at the Lollipop Lounge anymore, and one of the waiters invited me to learn more about ways to increase my profits at the club."

Ben clapped him on the back and propelled him into his office. "That's great. What did he have to say?"

"The club's closed on Mondays, so we're meeting tomorrow night after the show. If I can infiltrate the scam, I have a good chance of meeting Rock or at least finding his connection."

"Well done, Jack. I knew you were the man for the job."

"There's something else." Jack shoved his hands in his pockets.

Ben raised his brows but didn't meet his eyes. "Yeah, I figured you didn't come all the way out here to tell me you have a meeting."

"Ben, your wife showed up at the club last night."

Ben's jaw tightened before he took another puff on his cigar. "Is that right?"

"She came with a group of female friends." Jack didn't want to mention that they had mauled him. If Ben didn't want to admit his wife regularly patronized the Lollipop Lounge, he didn't want to force him into it.

Ben sat behind his mahogany desk and brushed off an imaginary speck of dust. "I knew she went out with friends, but she didn't give me the details. She's a lot younger than I am, Jack. She just needs to blow off steam now and then."

If the guy didn't care if his wife boozed it up with her girlfriends at a male strip joint and man-handled the Lollipop Boys, he didn't either. "Maybe you could tell her to blow off steam somewhere else. I don't want anyone to connect the two of us."

"You're right. I'll mention it. She's only been there once before. Probably just wanted to see what everyone's raving about."

Jack stuck out his hand. "Thanks, and I'll get those jewels back."

"I'm counting on it."

Jack pulled away from the driveway, leaving Ben on the front porch with his arms folded. To hell with Bobbie Jo. She needed to keep her nose out of his business and her hands out of his g-string.

Vivica stood with Chanel outside the new Galaxy Casino as they watched the glass elevators speed up and down the side of the building.

Chanel sighed. "Looks like something out of Star Wars, doesn't it? That's what I love about Vegas. You can visit Venetians, Romans, Egyptians, pirates, knights, and now robots all in the same crazy city."

Vivica laughed. "Sounds like our club."

They stepped onto a people-mover, and the doors whisked open, depositing them inside the interior of the casino, replete with stars glittering against a black ceiling. Like a tack to a magnet, Chanel's head swiveled toward the cacophonous clanging of the slot machines. "What time and where do you want to meet?"

Vivica shook her head. "Are you sure I can't entice you to try your luck the blackjack tables tonight?"

"Nope. Give me the quarter poker machines any time."

Rolling her eyes, Vivica said, "Okay. Let's meet in a few hours at the Sky Bar. Then maybe we can see a show."

Vivica barely finished her words before Chanel heeded the siren's song of the slots. Unceremoniously abandoned, Vivica circled the blackjack tables once, and then settled on a hundred dollar table with a few players. She sat on the end and slid several bills across the green felt in exchange for some chips.

She didn't understand Chanel's attraction for the slots or the allure of the roulette wheel, both of which were based on pure chance. She preferred to take destiny by the throat with both hands rather than leaving it to Lady Luck.

With the first few hands, her pile of chips grew. A man perched on the stool next to her, and his fresh clean scent sliced through the cigarette smoke at the table. "Having any luck?"

She jerked her head to the side. Jack's boyish grin greeted her, his regular jeans and t-shirt replaced by a black silk shirt tucked into a pair of black wool slacks. "I didn't recognize you with your clothes on."

The woman at the other end of the table giggled and the dealer lifted one brow. Jack's grin got wider. He tossed several hundreds at the dealer, who slid small, neat stacks of chips in front of him.

She tapped one of his stacks with her fingernail. "Those represent a lot of hard work, or a lot of hard... something."

"I'm feeling lucky tonight. How about you?"

She scratched the top of her card, and the dealer flipped up an eight of clubs to give her twenty-one. "I believe in making my own luck."

"I do too."

After the dealer slipped two cards to each gambler, Jack swept his cards over. "Blackjack. I guess that proves us wrong. Sometimes luck finds you first."

She felt comfortable sitting next to Jack. His presence took the edge off her usual wariness when alone in a crowd. His witticisms made her laugh, and his conversation put her at ease. She couldn't remember when she'd enjoyed a night out so much.

They played several more hands, and the cards kept turning in their favor. As she reached for another few chips for her bet, Jack's warm hand covered hers. "Let's see if we can extend this lucky streak. Do you want to join me for a drink in the Sky Bar?"

Well, she could actually think of several reasons why she shouldn't have a drink with Jack, but none of them made much sense when he squeezed her hand in his, sending vibrations clear down to her toes.

She glanced at her watch. "I'm meeting Chanel there in about forty minutes anyway. Why not?"

After tipping the dealer and cashing in their winnings, Jack guided her to a bank of elevators.

He studied her reflection in the mirrored doors of the elevator. She wore her silver-blond hair swept up, revealing the graceful curve of her neck. One strap of her blue velvet dress hung off her shoulder, and he nudged it back into place. She shivered beneath his touch.

The doors whooshed open, and they stepped aside for two couples stumbling through the doors. Spying three people heading for the open doors of the elevator, Jack grabbed Vivica's hand and pulled her into the car. He jabbed the button for the top floor several times as the doors whisked shut on three disappointed faces.

Vivica's brows collided over her nose. "Why'd you do that?"

"To do this." Jack punched the red stop button and the elevator halted mid-way to its destination.

Vivica lurched toward the panel. "Are you nuts? We'll have the entire casino coming to our rescue."

Placing his body between her and the elevator buttons, he captured her hands. "Way too many elevators for them to notice one off-line, at least for a while. Besides, didn't you just say you believed in making your own luck?"

"I don't consider being trapped in an elevator with you lucky."

"Sure you do. I just took the logical decision-making out of your hands." And out of his.

"Jack, what happened last night when you auditioned—"

"Was amazing."

"Maybe for you."

Did she resent that he got off and she didn't? "You wouldn't let me return the favor, but now I'm claiming my rights."

Her mouth made a valiant effort at pursing, but it trembled too much to get the job done. He put a stop to that by running his tongue along the seam of her lips, tasting her juicy lip gloss. She opened her mouth to protest, and he slipped his tongue inside.

His deep kiss stifled any more objections she might have as she entwined her arms around his neck. Gripping her waist, he dropped to his knees in front of her. She backed up against the glass wall of the elevator and planted her hands on his shoulders. "Jack."

"Shhh." His hands skimmed up her long legs, resting on the backs of her thighs. He pulled her closer and buried his face in the soft velvet of her dress. Then he gripped the hem and inched it up while her fingers dug into his back.

He sprinkled kisses on the insides of her thighs, as velvety smooth as her dress. She whimpered while reaching back to grab the metal handrail. Shoving her dress up further, he cupped her bottom, guiding the V of her lacy, black panties toward his mouth. He teased his tongue along the waistband before yanking them down with his teeth. They got caught on her heels, and he disentangled them and shoved them into his pocket.

"Jack, we can't do this."

"Sure we can."

"People will see us."

He lifted a shoulder. "We're too high for anyone to figure out what we're up to. Besides, I'm an exhibitionist by trade. Let 'em watch."

He gathered her dress around her waist with one hand, while the fingers of his other hand traced her cleft. He spread her damp lips open, and she gasped and banged her head against the glass.

Was that a no? He froze. He wanted to tread lightly with her, reassure her. She sighed and rolled her pelvis forward. "Don't stop."

Definitely not a no. He flicked his tongue along her creamy folds, and she rocked toward him, throwing one leg over his shoulder. He let her set the pace, which grew faster and more furious, as her clit hardened beneath his lips. She pressed against him for a moment before her sweet juice gushed over his mouth and she cried out in a crescendo of ecstasy.

Before she could come to her senses, before he came to his, he stood up and spun her around to face the glass wall of the elevator.

Vivica knew what he intended to do but didn't have an ounce of will or desire to stop him. Instead, she facilitated his plan by hiking up her dress and bending forward, gripping the handrail.

He unzipped his pants, and his cock nudged her bottom. She spread her legs as his blunt tip plowed against her opening. He slipped in easily and wrapped one arm around her waist, keeping the two of them joined together.

As he rode her from behind, she glimpsed her wild-eyed reflection in the fogged-up glass. Beyond her reflection, the lights of the Vegas Strip twinkled and winked, and people milled about searching for a good time, searching for the elusive Lady Luck. Did those people see her and Jack?

Did they know what they were doing?

She didn't care. His gaze met hers in the glass, and in that moment, only the two of them existed. He closed his eyes and groaned, nearly lifting her off her feet with the power of his orgasm.

He shot into her again and again, and she clenched around him, encouraging every drop of his warm effusion. Before he pulled out, he kissed the back of her neck.

She turned in his arms and whispered, "Remember, what happens in Vegas...."

"Is one helluva good time." He kissed her again, depressed the stop button, and zipped his pants.

She glanced at him sharply as she yanked her dress over her hips and thighs. What did he mean by that? Did he plan to use this against her?

The elevator doors whispered open on the top floor of the casino in front of the Sky Bar. A gaggle of people waited to get in the elevator. Jack gave her a push from behind. "You go have that drink with Chanel. I think I'll try my luck somewhere else tonight."

With a sinking heart, she jockeyed through the crowd, her thighs sticky with Jack's fluid. Behind her, the doors closed on the heavy scent of sex and her black panties in Jack's pocket.

# *Chapter 5*

The following night, he tried to catch Vivica's eye for about the hundredth time. Did she regret their little ride in the elevator as much as he did? Okay, so his body didn't regret a thing, but his brain had been calling him an idiot ever since.

He couldn't stop himself. When she shut him down after his audition, she shut herself down too. He wanted to pleasure her, to give her the same thrill he experienced. They fit together like pieces of a puzzle, not only physically but on a deeper level. He wanted to make everything right for her.

He'd tracked her down. He knew she and Chanel spent their nights off together, and Chanel had been only too happy to give him their destination for the evening. And he did please her. She couldn't deny it. But she could avoid him.

When the couples started dancing, she'd retreated to her inner sanctum and hadn't returned. So much for the perfect puzzle. Jack slammed out the backdoor of the club and spotted Derek leaning against a black convertible.

Sex in the elevator with Vivica last night made him a traitor in the parking lot tonight. He shoved his hands in his pockets and joined Derek.

Derek tapped a pack of cigarettes against the palm of his hand. "Smoke?"

"No, thanks."

Derek stuck a cigarette between his lips and cupped his hand over the end to light it. He inhaled deeply and blew out a smoke ring. "Looks like you raked it in again tonight."

"I did okay, but it's never enough."

"Seems the ladies can't get enough of you either. You should talk to a few of the straight guys about controlling your erection. Me, I don't have that problem around the women, but the straight guys have a few tricks. Although your permanent hard-on just might be your big selling point.

And I do mean big."

Great. The guy had him out here to proposition him. He crossed his arms over his chest. "I told you, I'm not interested in any of that shit. Do you really have a plan to make more money, or were you just blowing smoke up my ass?"

Derek smiled and took a drag from his cigarette. "In my dreams. No, I really have a plan. A few of us, gay and straight, have a scam going."

Jack tamed the eagerness in his voice. "What kind of scam?"

"We encourage some of the wealthy women who frequent the club, pay special attention to them, and slip them our phone numbers."

Bingo. "Then what? You date them and they become your sugar mamas?"

Derek flicked some ash to the ground. "It starts out that way, but we have our eyes on a bigger prize."

"Marriage?"

Derek snorted. "Way too obvious, and most of their families would never allow them to marry a Lollipop Boy. They'd be all over us."

Jack hunched his shoulders and continued to play dumb. "What then?"

"We get our hands on their money, jewels, artwork. They're usually too embarrassed to go to the police, and we walk away."

Jack's stomach turned. "How do you get rid of the stuff?"

"We have a local fence. He puts it out on the market, takes a cut, and we earn a nice profit."

"Sounds good. How do I get started?"

"Zero in on a regular, watch her spending habits, study her clothing and jewelry, and then give her your all."

"How do you know who has money and who's faking it?"

Derek tossed his cigarette to the ground and flattened it. "Vivica keeps a computer database on all her customers."

God, no. Jack's pulse quickened. "Is Vivica involved?"

Derek put a finger to his lips and slid into his car.

What the hell did that mean? He either just confirmed her involvement or warned him to keep her in the dark. What did it matter? He'd let the cops sort out whom they wanted to arrest. Ben had hired him to get his mother's jewels back, not crack the entire ring or its ringleader.

He had to get to this local fence before he broke up and sold Mrs. Crawford's jewels. He'd rope in one of his friends to pose as a rich woman looking for some hard candy at the Lollipop Lounge.

Then he'd find the jewels and shut down this whole operation, and if Vivica controlled it, she'd have to come down with the rest.

And to hell with this attraction between them.

Maybe Jack didn't need to be a dancer. He seemed to make plenty of money as a waiter, always got the first tip rip of the evening and always had the liveliest section.

He had a steady stream of regulars vying for his station every night, and he catered to a few special ladies. What the guys did on their off hours didn't concern her, but the thought of Jack hooking up with the women he served carved a hollow hole in her heart. How had she allowed him to get so close so fast?

Ever since the night they made love—had sex in the elevator, he'd avoided her, and she appreciated it. She hadn't come this far to fall under the spell of a male stripper. Besides, Buck still hadn't delivered his report.

She didn't reward Jack with the promotion because she had to somehow regain control of the balance of power. Her decision didn't make much sense from a business standpoint since she knew the women would go wild for him on stage, but she had to show him she had a handle on everything. On him.

Yeah, right. She had a handle on him during that elevator rendezvous all right.

Chanel floated up next to her and whispered in her ear. "Why don't you just go for it?"

"Go for what?"

"Oh, come on. You can't fool me, girl. Your eyes follow him everywhere."

"He is an eyeful."

Chanel swept her arm across the room. "So are all these other guys. Face it, he saved you from Charlie Champagne, and forever earned a spot in your heart."

Chanel's words rang with truth, too much truth. Giving Jack access to her heart also gave him the power to bruise it. She shrugged and gestured toward Jack. "His interests lie elsewhere."

Jack flirted with his latest conquest, an attractive middle-aged woman, glittering with diamonds. She hooked a finger in the band around his hip and pulled him forward to fold a bill around the elastic. House rules didn't allow the Lollipops to touch the women, but Jack caressed his benefactress with his smoldering gaze.

A stab of jealousy lanced Vivica's belly, and she almost doubled over. Maybe she could give up control to a man like Jack. He wouldn't use her, would he?

The show over, the men swarmed into the club for the dancing, and Vivica retreated to her office. Several minutes later, someone tapped on the door.

At her invitation, Jack entered the room, a light sheen of sweat glistening on his oiled body. "I thought I told you to lock this door. That guy's back."

Her heart jumped. "What guy?"

"The one in your office my first week."

She pushed out of her chair and gripped the edge of her desk. "Is he coming up here?"

Jack closed the door behind him and locked it. "I don't think so. He came in with the other men, and he's downstairs dancing and drinking like everyone else."

What did Charlie want? She wouldn't allow him to ruin her. She'd get a restraining order. She'd give security orders to keep him out. She swayed and felt strong arms catch her. Jack's warm body pressed against hers, and she leaned into him, soaking up his heat.

He guided her to the sofa, and then poured her a club soda. "Drink this. You almost fainted."

Did she? She closed her eyes and rolled the cool glass over her face.

"Who is this man to you, Vivica? Why does he have the power to reduce a strong woman like you to jelly?"

She inhaled, and Jack's masculine scent comforted her. She blew out the breath and opened her eyes. Could she trust him enough to tell him? The guy had already saved her once. He deserved the truth.

"I met Charlie Champagne when I first arrived in Vegas as a scared seventeen year-old runaway."

His dark brows shot up as he clenched his long hair into a ponytail. "What were you running away from?"

"Neglect, disinterest, insincerity."

"Your parents?"

"Foster parents. Just the last in a long line. My mom died when I was three, and I guess my dad just didn't want to be a single parent."

"I'm sorry."

His words reverberated with understanding, as if he knew the pain that still sliced her heart. Tears pricked her eyes, but this time she let them well up. "Charlie met me at the bus station. He took me in, fed me, and cared about me, or so I thought."

Jack's jaw formed a hard line. "What did he do, force you to turn tricks?"

She gasped. How did he know? "He tried. The clothes he bought me got more and more suggestive. He got me a fake I.D. and took me to bars with him. He introduced me to his friends and encouraged them to buy me drinks."

A low sound rumbled in Jack's throat.

She gulped the club soda. "I acted like an idiot, but I never got so much attention in my life."

"You were seventeen. You were lonely. He took advantage of you."

She rarely told people her story because she couldn't bear to read the judgment in their eyes. But Jack's eyes held only kindness.

"One night he told me to go with one of the men from the bar because he had a special present for me. My greediness blotted out my common sense. I went with him, and he took me up to a room in the hotel. When he started unfastening his slacks, I realized Charlie set me up—a real light bulb moment."

He touched her knee. "Don't be so hard on yourself."

His strong fingers tingled against her flesh, and she wanted to throw herself against him to block out the ugliness of her past. "I pretended to go along with it until the man got completely undressed. Then I ran out of the room."

"Did Charlie follow you?"

A sob escaped her lips, and Jack put an arm around her shoulders. "He had all my stuff at his apartment, so I went back to collect it. He caught me and started to hit me."

He traced a finger along her throat. "Did he hurt you?"

The gentleness of his voice and touch caused her tears to spill over, leaving hot trails on her cheeks. "He punched me a few times, but I kicked him in the crotch before running out."

He grinned. "That's my girl."

Despite the agony of dredging up the story, a smile quivered on her lips. She brushed the back of her hand across her face to reclaim her composure. "I don't know why I'm telling you all this. It happened so long ago."

He leaned over and plucked a tissue from a box on the coffee table and dabbed her wet cheeks. "It still affects you, nothing wrong with that."

His manner unraveled her, and she had to weave those threads back together. Had to stand on her own. She grabbed the crumpled tissue and blew her nose. "I don't need your sympathy."

Gripping her shoulders, he turned her toward him. "You don't have it. You have my admiration. You accomplished a lot from that rocky start in Vegas."

Did he realize her dream grew from her desire to punish all men for the sins of Charlie and his friends? Would he admire her then?

His hold on her shoulders turned into a caress, and her tension seeped into his fingers. "Jack, I...."

His lips closed over hers, cutting off her words. His tongue probed her deeper and deeper until she met it with her own. He pulled her close, her breasts exposed by her low-cut dress and pressed against his bare chest. She wanted this, wanted it from the moment he swaggered into her office for the interview. She wanted more than sex in an elevator.

He swung her legs up on the couch, straddling his body, and lowered her to a reclining position. He hesitated, waiting for her protest, but her lips parted in a silent moan instead. He kissed her eyelids, her nose, and her chin before teasing his tongue down her throat and cleavage.

He cupped one of her creamy breasts and lifted it from the silky material of her dress. Her rosy nipple peaked in anticipation, and he swirled his tongue around it before sealing his mouth over her breast.

She arched her back and raised her hips to make contact, and oh, he wanted that contact. He pushed her dress up and pressed his face against her warm, moist panties, breathing deeply of her musky feminine scent.

Her nails raked his hair, digging into his scalp. He glanced up. "Do you want me to stop?"

Her head thrashed from side to side as a breath hissed between her teeth. He'd take that as a no.

He slipped a hand beneath her and cradled her smooth, rounded derrière, lifting her toward his mouth. His tongue toyed with the waistband of her snowy white panties before he nipped it between his teeth and tugged them down.

His fingers danced through the soft, blond curls that dusted her mound, and she gasped. "Oh, Jack."

"More?" He wanted to take this nice and slow. He wanted more than a quickie in an elevator. Maybe some day they'd actually make love on a bed, but for now this would do.

She rotated her pelvis forward in answer, so he grabbed the side of her panties and ripped them off. Not quite as fluid as a tip rip, but much more satisfying.

Her swollen lips pouted inches from his mouth, but he had to see more of her. He cupped her bottom with one hand, tilting her forward and nudging open her glistening petals with his other hand. She squirmed and whimpered under his intimate gaze but didn't struggle to escape.

With his fingers still spreading her asunder, he ran his tongue up one side of her lips and down the other. Her hips bucked. He nestled his lips among her creamy folds, kissing and lapping at her sweetness.

Her clit hardened and trembled, and he took it gently between his lips. He sucked on it while his fingers dipped into her heated core. She groaned and moved against him, one hand combing through his hair, while the other gripped the arm of the sofa above her head.

She tightened around his fingers as her hips undulated in a sensuous dance. Then her body froze, she screamed, and raised her pelvis off the sofa. He continued feasting as she wet his face, her spasms gripping his fingers.

Thank God for Velcro. He ripped his g-string from his throbbing cock and drove into her silky sheath. She wrapped her legs around his hips as he rode her.

Just before he exploded, her warmth engulfed him, and she cried out again and again. He thrust into her, wanting to give her everything he had, everything he was.

His sweat dampened her silk dress as he collapsed on top of her. Her hands skimmed down his back, clenching his buttocks. He rolled to her side, throwing one leg over her hip.

A smile tugged at her lush lips. "I've wanted that again ever since the night in the elevator."

He kissed her ear. "You did a good job of hiding that fact."

"You're still my employee."

Smoothing her dress over her thighs, he said, "I know. You don't toy with the Lollipop Boys."

Her eyes searched his face. "You're different, Jack."

She had no idea how different. How could he explain that he came here under false pretenses, that he still considered her a suspect? "I am what I am, Vivica, an actor hoping to make a few extra bucks working it for the ladies."

Had he just compromised his case? He squelched the wave of uneasiness that threatened to spoil the moment. Right now, feeling Vivica's soft body mold against his, he didn't care. He kissed her, and as if to seal the kiss, he ran his thumb across her lips.

She caught his thumb in her mouth and while she sucked on it, he felt the pressure further down. He moved against the smooth material of her dress.

She disentangled herself and rolled off the sofa, leaving a chill in her wake. "That was stupid."

Stretching out, he lifted his thumb. "I'll recover."

She slipped into her heels and pushed her hair back. "I mean all of it."

He knew she'd regret it, but didn't count on that regret kicking in so fast. Grinning, he folded his hands behind his head. "I'm not going to sue you, if that's what you're worried about."

"I—" A sharp rap at the office door interrupted her.

"Viv, are you in there?"

She folded her arms across her mid-section and almost doubled over.

Jack scrambled from the sofa and took a step toward the door, but Vivica grabbed his arm. She shook her head and whispered, "No."

Jack shook her off. He'd take care of Charlie Champagne once and for all. He took another step, but she spun in front of him, blocking his access to the door. She swept one hand the length of his body, calling attention to his nakedness.

Damn. He couldn't go after Charlie buck naked. Couldn't give the guy that kind of advantage. He scanned the floor for the only piece of clothing he wore in here and spotted it under the sofa. He scooped it up and as his fingers struggled with the twisted material, Charlie banged on the door again and jiggled the handle.

"If you're in there, open up. We have business to discuss."

Jack's fingers froze. Business? A little fencing business?

Vivica ripped the g-string from his hand and tossed it behind her desk. He opened his mouth to protest, but she put a finger to her lips.

She seemed desperate to keep him from opening that door. Did she want to keep her business with Charlie a secret?

A loud voice boomed outside the office. "Hey, you. Didn't we throw you out of here before? Get lost before we toss you out again."

A slight scuffle ensued before Charlie barked, "Okay, man. I'm leaving.

Just keep your hands off the suit."

With the sound of each retreating footstep, Vivica's frame drooped. She sank on the sofa, but Jack didn't plan to go there again. Maybe Charlie terrified her because she owed him money. Maybe she refused to give him his cut of the take.

Jack crouched behind her desk to retrieve his g-string, and then stuffed himself back inside.

Before he got in even deeper with Vivica, he had to discover the truth.

# Chapter 6

Warm water pounded Vivica's back, and she rolled her shoulders. She must've been insane to confide in Jack last night. She leaned against the tile and sighed. Bring on the insanity.

If he'd been fully dressed, she would've flung open that office door herself and let him have a go at Charlie.

She shoved off the tile and snorted. She rarely saw Jack fully dressed. Why did he waste his time flaunting his male charms around the club? Didn't he have more self-respect than that?

She couldn't allow herself to fall for a man who strutted around allowing women to stuff his g-string, stroke his pecs, and pinch his buttocks, all for money.

Of course, the Lollipop Lounge made that possible for him and all the other Lollipop Boys. She provided entertainment and excitement to all the women who enjoyed the show, enjoyed turning the tables and treating men like sex objects. Nothing wrong with that, especially when the men got off on the attention.

She just didn't want to get involved with one of those sex objects. Or, at least, she wanted her own private sex object with no sharing. Like last night.

She finished showering and slipped into a pair of cut-off denim shorts and a t-shirt. While she brushed her hair out in front of the mirror, her intercom buzzed. The brush froze mid-stroke. Did Charlie know where she lived? She prowled toward the intercom and punched the button. "Yeah?"

Buck's gravelly voice scratched across the speaker. "It's me, Viv."

She let him up and waited by the door. He ambled down the hallway, the inevitable toothpick clenched between his teeth. He enveloped her in a bear hug, smelling of the peppermint candies he stashed in his pocket since giving up tobacco.

She eyed his gaunt frame. "Have you eaten yet?"

His weathered face cracked into a smile. "You're worse than Elsa ever was."

His wife, Elsa, who'd finally succumbed to cancer two years ago, had been like a mother to her, her first, long-overdue mother. Her nose tingled with tears, as she twisted the gold band with the single diamond on her finger–Elsa's wedding band. "She made me promise that I'd take care of you."

Winking, he said, "She made me promise the same for you." He placed his battered briefcase on her coffee table. "I have some interesting news for you."

Her heart skittered in her chest. She should've waited for Buck's news before jumping head-first into Jack's arms. "Already?"

"Already? This took me longer than I expected."

"Why?"

"Sit down. Anything going on at the club I should know about?"

Other than her foolish obsession for a Lollipop Boy? "No. Everything's running smoothly."

She had no intention of telling Buck about Charlie. Buck would kill him.

He pulled a crumpled manila envelope out of his briefcase. She held out her hand, but he clutched the envelope to his chest.

"What is it, Buck? Is Jack Savage a criminal?" He'd already stolen her heart. How much worse could it get?

He puffed out his cheeks and exhaled. "He's not even Jack Savage."

She gripped her hands in her lap. Maybe Jack worked for Charlie and they'd acted out a fight for her benefit. Why didn't she think of that before? "Who is he?"

"Jack Slater, a former cop from L.A. turned high-priced, exclusive P.I."

Her jaw dropped, and she felt light-headed. "A P.I.?"

"Private investigator to the rich and discreet."

"You mean he's working undercover at my club?" Her giddy relief almost made her laugh out loud. He wasn't a stripper.

"I'm afraid so."

Her elation sank like a brick in a bathtub. "Why are you afraid?"

"He must think you're involved in whatever he's investigating, or he would've approached you on the up-and-up. No need for deceit if he thought he could get your cooperation."

She dropped her head to stare at her white knuckles. That's why he

MIA VARANO 49

seduced her. He wanted information. She swallowed the bitter disappointment that threatened to gag her. He used her. Just like all the rest.

"Vivica? Are you okay? As long as you don't have anything to hide, you're fine. I'd sure like to know what he's after. Maybe I'll ask him."

"No!" She jumped from the sofa. Jack humiliated her, took advantage of her. He had to be punished.

Buck's shaggy gray eyebrows shot up. "What's the problem?"

She flung out her hands as if to push away the memory of Jack's heated kisses. "How do we know he's not working undercover for some nefarious reason? Or person?"

He shook his head. "Not his style. From what I can tell, he's strictly legit. Except...."

She snatched at the word. "Except?"

He tossed the manila envelope onto the coffee table. "He's a former cop for a reason."

She pounced on the envelope and fumbled through its contents with shaking hands. Jack's picture floated to the table, and she stared into the familiar dark eyes, his clean-shaven, sculpted features set off by close-cropped hair.

She turned the picture over and flattened out a sheet of paper from his police personnel record. She read aloud, "Terminated for conduct unbecoming a police officer. What does that mean?"

Buck scratched his stubble. "Seems a witness in a drug case, an eighteen year-old girl, accused Jack of seducing her to get her to change her story. The accusation destroyed the case and Jack's career. To avoid criminal charges against Jack and a big, embarrassing lawsuit, the department settled with the girl and fired Jack."

She crumpled the paper in her fist. "And I'm supposed to sit back and let this scumbag infiltrate my club, investigate me? I'm going to fire him tonight."

Buck raised a brow at her. "I don't think that's a good move."

"Sure it is. No wonder he's so good at his job. He's had lots of practice using his body to get what he wants." She turned her back on Buck and marched to the kitchen so he couldn't see the tears burning her eyes.

"Viv, he's there because something's not right at the club. Someone's paying him big bucks to get in there and snoop around. I say we join forces with him, find out what he suspects."

She couldn't let on to Jack that she knew his identity, knew that he scammed her. She needed revenge first. "No, Buck. My innocence will be more convincing when he discovers it for himself. Besides, I don't trust the man, not with a background like that."

Buck ran a hand over his face. "I don't know."

"You don't know? He had sex with a witness to get her to change her story. What more do you need to know?"

He held up the envelope containing Jack's life and shook it at her. "I read the report of the incident, and something doesn't ring true to me. He retained an attorney to fight it, and the investigation is ongoing. Witnesses lie all the time."

She shrugged. "I don't really care about Jack Slater's past. It's his future that concerns me."

And she held his immediate future in her hands.

"I can't believe you strut around that club in a thong. I've worn thongs before, and they're damned uncomfortable."

Jack tilted his head at Elizabeth Garwood, her graceful neck curving above regal shoulders, and then glanced at her husband. "Bruce, did you know Liz used to wear a thong?"

"Hell yes. I bought them for her. Frankly I'd be concerned about Liz venturing into that hotbed of male sexuality and stuffing my hard-earned cash into your underwear if she weren't old enough to be your—"

"Bruce!" Liz shot up in her chair and glared at him.

"Older sister," he finished with a chuckle.

"I really appreciate your help, Liz. It's working. The guys at the club all know you're hot for me, and as soon as I steal your diamonds, I can get close to that fence."

Bruce choked, his coffee spraying Liz's white tennis dress. Scowling, Liz grabbed a napkin. "All cubic zirconium, darling."

Bruce mopped his face. "That part doesn't concern me. It's the part about your being hot for Jack. What exactly do you two do at that club?"

Jack winked at Liz. "The usual. She gropes me and stuffs money in my crotch."

Bruce's booming laughter caused all four gardeners to glance up from their work on the Garwood's vast lawn.

Liz rose, stood behind Bruce, and massaged his shoulders. "Jack ain't got nothing on you, darling. No, really, Jack I'd do anything for you after you located my daughter."

"How is Emily?"

Bruce beamed and patted his wife's hand. "She's expecting another baby and invited Liz to Seattle for the occasion."

Liz leaned over and kissed Bruce's cheek. Bruce had displayed incredible tolerance and love when Liz presented him with the fact that she gave birth as a teenager to a little girl and gave her up for adoption. When Jack located Liz's daughter, Emily, Bruce took her in as one of his own.

That showed real love, not the fake stuff his ex-wife had for him, the kind that crumbled under the first sign of hardship. She dumped him even before the department fired him.

Bruce cleared his throat. "Do you think the owner is involved, or is this a free-lance operation?"

Liz smirked. "He's hoping she's not involved."

Of course, he hoped Vivica didn't have a hand in the scam, but how did Liz know that?

Bruce's gazed bounced between the two of them. "Why?"

"When Jack and Vivica Steele come anywhere near each other in that club, the air sizzles with an electric current so strong it could curl even your hair." She rubbed her husband's bald pate.

Was it that obvious? Jack jerked his head back and forth. "That's just the atmosphere of the club. The men are hot, and the women are hot for them. The air's so thick with sexual overtures you could bottle it and sell it as axle grease."

Liz laughed. "Or petroleum jelly. Come on, Jack. Even when you're bumping and grinding, your eyes follow her, and she's no more discreet than you. Whenever the women fondle your assets, which is quite often, by the way, Vivica looks ready to claw their eyes out. Not your typical reaction for a club owner hoping to bring in the customers."

Bruce rubbed his hands together. "The plot thickens. What are you going to do if she's involved, Jack?"

If she encouraged the Lollipop Boys to dupe vulnerable women, he'd hang her out to dry. He lifted one shoulder.

"If she's involved, the cops will see that she goes down with the rest."

That night, Jack ground his teeth as he yanked his jeans over the indecently small g-string. He might as well be naked for the amount of coverage this thing afforded him. What next, something see-through? Better not give Vivica any ideas. He knew he had her to thank for his over-exposure. Every night when he reported to work, a small g-string hung on the edge of his locker, and each night it seemed to get smaller and smaller.

What did he ever do to her, except light a fire under that icicle she called a heart? Well, that and investigate her club.

He slipped his watch over his hand and latched it. He hoped he didn't miss Derek in the parking lot. Vivica kept him late again cleaning up the club.

Sean, the night guard, stuck his head into the locker room. "You all done in there, Jack?"

Jack slammed the locker door shut. "I'm done, going out the back."

Sean waddled into the room, his arms crossed over his big belly. "I'll lock up behind you."

Vivica didn't take any chances. She always had Sean do a sweep of the club before locking up at night. She didn't want anyone left behind after closing time. Afraid of what they might discover?

Jack stepped outside, and Sean bolted the door behind him. A glowing end of a cigarette signaled Derek's presence on the dark side of the parking lot away from the Strip. Jack jogged toward him.

Derek grinned. "The boss sure has you earning your pittance."

Jack hunched his shoulders. "Maybe she'll lay off once she gets her cut from my score."

"You score yet?"

Still no confirmation of Vivica's involvement. "I'm close. That lovely lady sporting all the diamonds is my number one fan. I hung out by her pool the other day, and she invited me to house sit and watch her dog this weekend. I'll have her jewels as my payment when I leave."

Derek nodded as he took a long drag from his cigarette. "You work fast. Give me the sign when you have the ice, and I'll take you to our contact."

"You got it."

Derek peeled out of the parking lot, choking the night air with exhaust fumes.

He'd find out where this fence stashed the spoils, recover Sadie Crawford's jewelry, and call in the cops. And if it turned out Vivica didn't have a hand in the scam? He'd find out why she pushed him away and turned his life into a living hell.

If that elegant, silver-haired broad rubbed Jack's ass one more time, she'd—she'd what? The guy was a fraud anyway. He must really be getting off on this assignment, a dream come true.

She'd wrestled with the reason behind his charade all week. Drugs? Not in this club. She made sure of that even to the point of having her security guards randomly search the lockers. Prostitution? She gave the guys strict orders to take all extracurricular games off-site. Besides, a P.I. wouldn't be interested in that type of illegal activity.

Had to be something of a private nature, but then why leave her out of the loop? She might've been able to help him. All bets were off now.

If she could only shake off her attraction to him, sweat it out like a raging fever. One problem—this attraction was more than just physical. He'd cracked her shell, and now he had to pay.

She took immense pleasure in treating him like a slab of prime beefcake. She had him working extra tables and helping the busboys clean up at closing time. When he had a tip rip, she instructed the announcer in the booth to darken the room and shine a spotlight on Jack. She told Chanel to give Jack the skimpiest of g-strings.

Didn't matter. Nothing worked. He remained unshakable. Someone must be paying him a lot of money for this gig. His greed obviously knew no bounds. She wished he'd finish his investigation and get out of her life.

The disappointment she felt in him almost outweighed her anger at being duped. When he first started working, she sensed something special in him and wondered why he didn't do something better with his life than strip for wild and crazy women. Now she realized he did something worse. He used women to get what he wanted, and to hell with the consequences.

God, she had whacked-out radar when it came to men.

Jack weaved through the crowd toward her, balancing his tray of empties with one hand, his leather pouch barely concealing his family jewels. He dropped the tray on the bar and folded his arms. "I thought your license didn't allow nudity."

"It doesn't."

"I'm getting close enough."

"You could make a little more room in that pouch if you learned to control yourself better."

"I could control myself better if I could stop thinking about that night in your office."

That one got her. The witty comeback died on her luscious lips. "We made a mistake." Her eyes widened, and she lodged the tip of her tongue at the corner of her mouth.

"Didn't feel like a mistake to me." Okay, but this did feel like a mistake. He didn't have any business getting in any deeper with her until he could separate the bad guys from the good guys. Bad or good, this woman had him by the balls, in more ways than one.

"Your adoring fans await you."

"I'm interested in only one adoring fan."

In the low light, he detected a faint pink tide washing over her cheeks. She shook her head, and then smacked his ass with the palm of her hand. "Go take care of business, beefcake."

He let a slow smile play over his lips as he took inventory of her heaving bosom, glittering eyes, and hands digging into her hips. Yeah, she wanted him. He turned his back on her and threaded his way back to his tables and Liz's raised eyebrows.

As he dipped to deliver her drink, she whispered in his ear, "Quite a show you two put on."

His eyes followed Vivica as she traipsed up the stairs to her office. "It may be the last one. Tonight's the night."

✷⟫(☾)⟪✷

Jack slid into the front seat of Derek's convertible and pounded the dashboard. "Let's go."

Derek started the engine and glanced at Jack. "Good thing the boss didn't have you on clean-up duty tonight."

Jack wondered about that. Did she know he had a meeting with the fence tonight? Is that why she excused him from bussing the tables? So far, Derek had kept mum about Vivica's participation.

Jack would leave that investigation to the cops. Once he recovered Sadie's jewels, he'd collect his money from Ben and then blow this town for the wide, open spaces of Idaho and get to work on his ranch.

And Vivica? If she came out of this thing clean, would she ever consider giving up her club for some fresh air? She could understand those lost kids even better than he could. She'd been there herself. Was he nuts?

"We're here."

Jack's stomach sank as Derek wheeled into the parking lot of a run-down motel in downtown Vegas. The fence wouldn't keep priceless loot in a dump like this.

Derek pulled into a parking slot in front of a corner room where a light burned behind some crooked shades. Jack clutched the duffel bag of fake gems to his chest as he got out of the car.

Derek rapped out a code on the door, and it inched open on a chain, an eyeball peering out of the crack. The door swung open, and Jack stepped across the threshold onto the threadbare carpet and looked straight into the face of Charlie Champagne.

# Chapter 7

Scowling, Charlie looked him up and down, and then turned to Derek. "What the hell's he doing here?"

Derek dropped to the edge of the sagging mattress and shook a cigarette out of its package. "I told you, he scored a load of diamonds off some rich broad."

Charlie spat out, "Idiot. This guy beat the shit out of me in Vivica's office."

Jack stepped back and held up his hands. "Hey, no offense, man, just trying to protect a lady."

Charlie's icy blue eyes narrowed. "Don't believe a word she says, and she's no lady. She worked for me when she first came out to Vegas. I had her on the streets first and then sold her up in the hotel rooms on the Strip. One of my hottest girls."

Jack's gut clenched and a muscle twitched in his jaw. Was he telling the truth? Lots of hookers feared their pimps, but Vivica's story sounded real enough to him. He shrugged. "I can believe that, but don't hold it against me. My first week on the job, I wanted to impress the boss."

"Okay, but I'm the boss here." He gestured to the bag. "Whaddya got?"

Jack released a measured breath and dropped the bag on the floor. He crouched beside it and unzipped the top compartment to reveal a tangle of diamond necklaces, bracelets, earrings, and even a tiara.

Charlie whistled and knelt beside him. He ran his hands through the jewelry and laughed. "Whatever you had to put out is worth this pay-off."

Jack sat back on his heels. "What next? Do you wait a while before putting it out on the market?"

"Yeah, we do, but none of our ladies have called in the police yet. Too embarrassed. That's the beauty of the scheme."

"How long do you wait?"

"About six months. Don't be so impatient. Keep working at the club, enjoy yourself, maybe zero in on another victim ripe for the picking."

Six months? That meant they still had Sadie's jewels. "You don't expect me to hold onto this stuff, do you?"

"No. We have a place for it. When the time is right, we send it on to another guy who breaks up the pieces and cuts the diamonds. Then we sell it all. You get your cut then."

"And I'm supposed to trust you?"

Charlie grinned. "What are you going to do, call the cops? You can keep a couple of pieces for insurance if you want."

"Where's the rest of the stuff? Can I take a few pieces from someone else's stash? I'd rather not have my own mark's stuff on me." Jack fingered the fake jewels in the bag and held his breath.

"Can't do that, Jack."

"Why?"

"All the other stuff's at the Lollipop Lounge."

A vice squeezed Jack's chest, and he bent further over the bag to hide his face. "It's at the Lollipop Lounge?"

"In Vivica's office."

Jack gripped a necklace so hard, the fake gems dug into his flesh. "She keeps the spoils in her office?"

Charlie straightened up and peered down at him. "That's right, Jack. You see, that argument you broke up between me and Viv concerned business. This business. She's taking too long to get the stuff out, and the boys are getting restless. They want their cut, and they want it now. Viv has a hard time giving up control. Perhaps you noticed that."

Jack relaxed his jaw muscles and pushed up from the floor to face Charlie. "Yeah, I noticed."

"I'll stash these with Vivica." Charlie hoisted the bag over his shoulder and kicked Derek's foot hanging off the end of the bed. "Get going."

Jack waited while Derek rolled from the bed and fumbled for his car keys, and then asked Charlie, "Why don't we just deal directly with Vivica if she's keeping the stuff at the Lollipop Lounge?"

"She wants to keep her hands clean. Only you and Derek know she's in on it. I told you just to clarify things between us."

Still didn't seem right, but he didn't want to arouse Charlie's suspicions. He stuck out his hand. "No hard feelings, man?"

Charlie gripped his hand. "Not if you can bring in loot like this."

As he and Derek walked back to the car, Jack wiped his hand on his jeans. Slimy bastard.

He didn't know whether or not to believe Charlie about Vivica's involvement in the scam, but he did know one thing. If Vivica had Sadie Crawford's jewels in her office, he'd use any means necessary to find them and get them back.

Maybe it was time to come clean with her. Lay all his cards on the table and give her a chance to defend herself. He'd confess his identity, tell her about his meeting with Charlie, and they'd talk it out. Maybe Charlie was coercing her? If so, he wanted to protect her. Hell, he'd felt protective of her since the moment he walked into her office.

"I tell you, Viv, it stinks. Something's not right with that whole scenario."

Pinpricks of hope dashed up her spine. She wanted to believe Buck. She wanted to believe that Jack Slater hadn't used that witness to secure evidence in the drug case. But did it really matter? He'd used her in a similar manner, hadn't he?

The other night when he told her he couldn't stop thinking about what they did in her office, his warm voice sent trembles of longing down to her toes. If only she could trust him. She thought she could before she learned about his rocky past.

The sex felt different with him than with anyone she'd ever slept with before. For the first time in her life, she made love with someone. At least that's what she thought. She didn't have a clue what he thought, but his tender touch and whispered endearments made her feel safe and loved. Maybe he hadn't lied about the acting experience on his resume.

When Buck revealed Jack's true identity, she just figured he got close to her to solve his case, and that called for revenge. As much as she wanted to punish and humiliate him though, it just didn't work. The barely there g-strings only garnered him more attention from the hot and feverish clientele. Although watching other women maul his body turned her on, it also ignited a flare of jealousy in her chest that she couldn't snuff out. In short, she suffered more than he did.

Buck dropped his feet from her desk. "I think his department wrongly accused him. I think they set him up, and I have one of my friends in L.A. looking into it."

"Whatever. His former crimes don't concern me. Soon enough he'll wrap up his investigation here, and he won't find anything on me. Then he'll be on his merry way. Who knows? Maybe this is just a divorce case—some guy hoping to get the goods on his wife while she's out carousing with her girlfriends and sticking her hand down some guy's g-string."

"He doesn't work those kinds of cases."

"I don't care."

Buck drew his brows together. "I think you should care. What if it's something that's going to bring down the club?"

"I run a clean place, Buck."

"I know that, but you don't know what those guys do on their own time. They could bring the club some bad press. I say we come clean with Slater."

She pounded the desk and jumped up. "We have nothing to come clean about. Let him do the scrubbing. He came here under false pretenses."

"Okay, but now that we know who he is, let's tell him. Let's join forces. It just might save the club."

"No."

The lines criss-crossing Buck's face deepened. "What happened, Viv? Did this guy get to you? Have you fallen for him?"

Her laughter crackled through the air. "Don't be ridiculous."

She never could fool Buck. He swept his baseball cap from her desk and tugged it over his forehead. Then he hugged her and kissed the top of her head. "It's all right. I'll do whatever I can for you if the club comes under fire."

She pressed her face against his rough denim jacket, the peppermint wrappers crinkling under her cheek. She knew she could count on Buck, but she had to handle this her own way.

She watched him amble down the hallway. Her hand clutched the handle of the door as Jack bounded up the stairs just as Buck reached the top of the staircase. Jack flattened himself against the wall to make room for Buck, and Buck nodded in acknowledgement.

Jack's brows drew into a V over his nose. He jerked his thumb over his shoulder. "Who's that?"

"Just another Lollipop looking for a job."

"Very funny. He looked familiar."

She pursed her lips. Probably recognized him as a fellow cop. Buck told her cops shared mutual radar sometimes. Well, she didn't owe Jack any explanations. She squared her shoulders across the space of the door. "What are you doing up here? You're too early for your shift."

For once the man had clothes on, but the faded jeans that sat low on his waist and hugged his thighs did nothing to temper her desire for him. Even if he did have "rat" written all over him.

Pushing his way into the room, he drove her back and closed the door behind them. "I have something to tell you, Vivica."

He licked his lips, pulled in a deep breath and reached for his back pocket. As he yanked his wallet free from his tight jeans, it flipped onto the floor, landing beneath the sofa. "Oops."

Her eyes narrowed as she watched him grope for the wallet on his knees. He acted nervous. Usually he had the grace of a jungle cat.

He stumbled to his feet, clutching his wallet in his hand, his other hand bunched into a fist at his side. The skin on his face paled beneath its usual bronze hue, and a muscle in his jaw twitched. Look like someone just sucker punched him in the gut.

"What's wrong?"

"Nothing. I missed lunch, low blood sugar. Got dizzy when I bent over."

"Would you like some water?" She'd never seen Jack so rattled.

"No." He shoved his wallet back in his pocket.

His eyes searched hers, almost pleading. What did he want from her? "What is it, Jack? Why are you here?"

A knock on the door made him twitch, and he stuffed his hands into his pockets.

Her daytime security guard called out, "Your accountant's here for your appointment, Viv."

She called back, "Send him up in a few minutes." She turned back to Jack. "Well?"

He swept his hands across his face. "I want to ask you a favor."

She sucked in her breath. Was this it? Was he going to confess his true identity and ask for her help? "What favor?"

"I think I did a pretty good job at my audition, and I pull in more money than anyone on the floor. I'd like another opportunity to audition for the stage."

Her cheeks burned at the memory of his last audition, and she shook her head.

"Before you say no, I already checked with Chanel, and she's willing to give me another chance."

Why did he want an audition now? He must want another crack at her, another chance to break her down. God, she wouldn't mind seeing him up on that stage just one more time. "All right. If Chanel's says it's a go, it's okay with me, but no guarantees."

"I understand. We already set it up for tonight, after the club closes."

"Fine. Meet me at the stage." She stepped around him and swung the door open. He straddled the threshold, leaning against the doorjamb. She lifted her brows. She didn't want him in her office again. She seemed to lose all reason when confined in a small space with him.

He folded his arms across his chest. "I saw my so-called 'outfit' for the evening."

She wrinkled her nose. What had she told Chanel? Find something outrageous for Jack to wear. "Chanel puts them out. I have no idea what she chose for you."

He leaned toward her, his warm breath caressing her earlobe. "It's mesh, like fishnet."

She gulped. "It's not transparent, is it?"

"Close to it. It has a thin layer of material covering the holes, but it's pretty flimsy. You can definitely see flesh beneath the white."

She couldn't wait to see him in it. "C'mon, Jack, it'll earn you lots of money tonight since all the women will want to get close enough to determine if it's see-through. And that's what you're here for, right? To earn lots of money?"

His thick dark lashes fell over his eyes briefly. "You're right. No time to be modest when money's at stake. What are scruples and morality in the face of cold, hard cash, right?"

Her lips peeled back in a smile. "Now you're talking like a true Lollipop Boy. Go out there and wow 'em, and then wow me at your audition."

She slammed the door in his face before he could respond.

Standing at his locker, Jack fingered the diamond bracelet he found beneath the sofa in Vivica's office. Did Charlie tell the truth for once in his miserable life? Were the rest of the diamonds stashed there?

He tried calling Ben to check if the bracelet matched the description of anything Rock stole from his mother, but Ben hadn't returned his calls. He knew the bracelet didn't belong to Vivica. He'd never seen her wear any jewelry except a small gold band with a single diamond on her right hand. She didn't even have pierced ears.

He'd intended to confess all to her until he found that bracelet. It changed everything, deepened his doubts about her. He'd have to get the truth from her another way, so he set up an audition. He'd get her alone, vulnerable. Then he'd get to the bottom of this mess.

He started his shift, dreading the first hundred dollar tip.

Damn Vivica and her games. Did she even know he was the one who delivered all those diamonds? Her comments earlier hinted she did. So why did she have it in for him? Her attraction to him pissed her off for some reason. Maybe she just didn't want to get too close to one of her flunkies.

Charlie's claims along with Derek's hints and Bobbie Jo's suspicions had already fueled his doubts about Vivica, despite his gut feelings. But finding that bracelet almost sealed the deal. Almost. He could taste victory. Why was it bittersweet?

He worked just one section tonight, but the women packed the tables. He tried to keep a low profile, but Vivica noticed and told him to pick up the pace if he wanted that audition. And he wanted it. He wanted to get her alone in the club tonight.

So he catered to the ladies and played along with their outrageous demands, and sooner than he wished, he got a hundred. He jumped to the table, and the hot spotlight that swung in his direction caused beads of sweat to form on his brow. The generous tipper yanked and ripped at his Velcro trousers until she held them bunched in her fists over her head.

Word must've spread fast because women all over the club stood up to get a better look. Feeling naked in the mesh g-string, Jack undulated his hips and thought about multiplication tables.

Before jumping off the table, he kneeled before the woman waving the Ben Franklin. Her eyes, level with his crotch, widened. "Is that see-through?"

He pumped his hips. "See for yourself, darling."

She fingered the webbed material before shoving the bill right into the small oblong that protected his essentials. Maybe he should just let the money gather in there all night to cover everything else he had stuffed inside.

At what just might be his last gig at the Lollipop Lounge, Jack earned more in tips than he ever had before. After Chanel ushered the last of the guests out of the club, he stuffed handfuls of cash into his locker while exchanging jokes with the other guys.

He took a long time sorting through the costumes and waited until the last employee, including the busboys, exited the back door.

Then he stepped into the shower and lathered the sweat and oil from his body. Over the spray of the shower, he heard Sean yell out, "Anyone still here?"

Jack grabbed a towel from the rack and wrapped it around his waist. "I'm here, Sean. I have an audition with Vivica."

The soles of Sean's shoes squelched as he crossed the locker room floor to the back door. "I'll lock up here and let you out the front when you're finished."

Jack spun the lock on his locker, reached in, and grabbed two hundreds. He folded the two bills between his fingers and held them out to Sean. "It's a very private audition. We'll let ourselves out."

Sean swallowed and licked his lips as his gaze shifted between Jack's eyes and the outstretched money. "Well…."

"Remember the last time I auditioned for her? She dismissed you that night as well."

"Yeah, but she didn't say anything about tonight."

"Come on, man. Vivica deserves some fun."

Grinning, Sean lifted his shoulders and held out his hand. "You got that right. She works too hard."

Jack slapped the money in his hand, and after Sean left through the backdoor, Jack drew the deadbolt.

Out of habit, he slathered a generous amount of oil on his body. Then he smoothed out the phony cop uniform he pulled out earlier and dressed quickly. Might as well play the part. He replaced the fake handcuffs with the real ones he smuggled into his locker, dropped the diamond bracelet into the pocket of his shirt, and then padded into the club barefoot.

He lowered the room lights and flicked a switch, bathing the stage in red and blue flashing lights. He queued up an old disco song, cranking up the bass so that it thumped through the club. Then he leaned against the pole on the stage and waited.

Showtime.

The floor reverberated with a pounding bass. Did they start the party without her?

Vivica logged off her computer and checked her appearance in the mirror while slipping on her heels. Jack's plans remained a mystery, but his performance tonight in that fishnet pouch only whetted her appetite for more.

Maybe she should admit that she knew his true identity and had been stringing him along the whole time. She might save some face.

She swept down the staircase, her footsteps slowing at the bottom as she peered into the dark club. He should've waited for her to set the stage. He just couldn't help trying to take control of matters.

Red and blue lights splashed the stage, playing over Jack's form as he lounged against the dancer's pole. She covered her smile with her hand. A cop's uniform. How appropriate. Was he ready to reveal himself?

Her eyes darted around the perimeter of the stage, and she yelled out over the music, "Where's Chanel?"

He shrugged off the pole and prowled to the edge of the stage. "Another hot date."

Her heart thumped along with the music. Did he send Chanel away? "And Sean?"

"Since you let him go last time, I told him he could leave." He wedged his hands on his hips, the hardware on his belt shining in the flashing lights.

How dare he? She stalked to the booth and stopped the music, and then marched to the end of the stage. "Do my security guards take orders from you now?"

She didn't blame Sean, since she had dismissed him the last time Jack auditioned. Jack had a commanding attitude and presence. Born to be obeyed.

His white teeth gleamed against his olive skin. "I am the law."

She folded her arms across her chest as a ripple of desire wove its way to her nipples. "Whatever. Let's get this show started." She turned toward the booth to start the music.

"Ma'am, I'm afraid I have to question you about reports of lewd conduct at your club." He hooked his thumbs in his belt loops and stood with legs apart.

Heat scorched her cheeks, and that now-familiar tingle of anticipation and desire crept up her inner thighs. She sauntered back toward the stage. "Oh really? What kind of lewd conduct?"

His eyes brimmed with a challenge. "It's a delicate subject. You need to come up here so we can speak privately."

Might as well end this thing with a bang. Before she could climb the steps, he reached over, grabbed her around the waist, and hoisted her up to the stage. She landed in front of him, her heart skittering in her chest.

With his hands resting on her hips, he pulled her forward. "I think I may just have to pat you down. Looks like you're packing some dangerous weapons."

She should just push him away, tell him to go to hell. She moistened her lips, but the words lodged in her throat.

With his hand pressed against the small of her back, he nudged her toward the pole. He spun her around and pushed her up against the cool metal. Her knees trembled, and she leaned against the pole for support.

He captured her wrists in one hand and raised her arms above her head. Pinning her hands to the pole, he leaned in and sealed his lips over hers.

She closed her eyes and parted her lips, inviting his tongue into her wet mouth. She heard the tinkle of metal on metal and a felt a cold clasp around her wrists, which contrasted sharply with the warm kiss.

As Jack pulled away, her eyelids flew open. His eyes glittered, and she flinched at their hardness.

She tried to reach for him, but the metal bracelets around her wrists clanged against the pole. She slid her hands down the pole until they rested on top of her head. Her fingers scrambled to identify what secured her wrists to the pole. She tracked along the hard edges of a pair of handcuffs.

The toy ones the dancers used should break easily enough. She yanked her wrists against her restraints, but they held tight. "Very funny, Jack. Our patrons won't like being handcuffed for real."

His chest rose as he drew in a breath, straining against the tight-fitting blue shirt. "You won't like it either."

"These games don't turn me on." Okay, technically they did, but only if she scripted them out in advance. She rattled the handcuffs again.

"I thought you liked games, Vivica. You've been playing with me since the moment I stepped into your office."

This didn't make sense. If he wanted to reveal his true purpose behind landing a job here, why did he cuff her to the dance pole? Unless he didn't trust her. "You seemed to be, uh, up for the games."

His jaw hardened and a dangerous light flared in his dark eyes. He had this same look when he attacked Charlie, and a puff of apprehension touched the back of her neck. She beat the handcuffs against the pole. "Let me go."

His lip curled, abolishing all signs of the boyish grin he bestowed on his customers. "Not until you tell me where the jewels are."

# Chapter 8

Her full lips parted while her breasts rose and fell rapidly beneath her black halter dress. She hadn't expected that, hadn't even seen it coming.

He came close to abandoning his scheme when he'd felt her warm mouth close around his tongue. Her light floral scent almost hypnotized him, but he had a duty to perform for Sadie Crawford and those countless kids waiting for a second chance.

She choked out, "What jewels?"

"Sadie Crawford's for starters."

Her glassy eyes grew wide as she snapped to attention against the pole. "Sadie Crawford?"

"I see you're familiar with the name."

"She's a regular. At least she used to be a regular, a real firecracker."

"Until Rock, or whatever his name is, relieved her of her jewels."

Vivica's slim body sagged against the chrome rod behind her as she gripped it to keep from sliding to the floor. "That's what you're investigating?"

He narrowed his eyes. She caught on fast. "That's right. I'm a P.I., and I've got you dead to rights. Now tell me where you're hiding the goods. I know you have them stashed at the club."

This time her grasp on the pole failed, and she slid to the floor, her black dress pooling around her long legs. "Stashed in the club?"

He couldn't browbeat her while she huddled in a heap on the floor like a lost little girl. He grabbed her arm and yanked her to her feet. His fingers bit into her soft skin. "Tell me now, and I'll see that the cops go easy on you."

"The cops?" Her lips trembled, and he hardened his heart against her feminine appeal.

"Stop repeating everything I say, and tell me where you're hiding them, or I'll tear this place apart." He shook her and her head bumped against the pole. Immediately, he reached out to sooth the spot with his fingers. Damn.

He couldn't go through with this. Why didn't she just tell him?

Tears welled in her eyes and she shook her head. "I don't know what you're talking about. I don't have any jewels."

If those tears spilled over, he might as well pack it in. He dropped his hands from her shoulders and retrieved the bracelet from his pocket. "Really?"

Her gaze followed the bracelet swinging from his fingers, the flash of the diamonds reflecting back to her eyes. "Where'd you get that?"

"I found it underneath the sofa in your office. Funny place to keep an expensive piece of jewelry."

"I don't know where that came from. I don't know anything about Sadie Crawford's jewels."

"You're lying. I heard it from two different sources."

She sniffed. "Who told you?"

"Sadie Crawford's daughter-in-law, Bobbie Jo Crawford."

Vivica gasped. "Bobbie Jo is married to Sadie's son?"

"Too bad you didn't know that before you had Rock go after Sadie."

One tear rolled down her cheek, but her body no longer shook and she drew her shoulders back. "I didn't know because she used a different name than Crawford, and before Rock insinuated himself with Sadie, he did the old bump and grind for Bobbie Jo almost every weekend."

Jack froze. Bobbie Jo knew Rock?

He recalled the avaricious light in Bobbie Jo's eyes when she asked Ben about his mother's jewels. Had she used Rock to get them for herself and get a little extra-marital action? Had Bobbie Jo set up her mother-in-law?

Not just her mother-in-law. "Why would Bobbie Jo want to set you up?"

"I don't know, maybe just to throw suspicion off of her. Who hired you?"

"Sadie's son and Bobbie Jo's husband, Ben."

"Bobbie Jo must've freaked when her husband told her he hired a P.I. to recover Sadie's jewels. She probably wanted to throw you off track by implicating me. You said you heard about my involvement from two different sources. Who else told you?"

He said slowly, "Charlie Champagne."

Her lips tightened, and her eyes narrowed, shooting daggers. "You believed Charlie?"

"Coupled with Bobbie Jo's suspicions and Derek's hints, it made sense. Even then, I wanted to give you the benefit of the doubt. I almost told you everything until I found this beneath your sofa."

Her mouth formed an O. "Charlie must have planted it that night he came into my office. It seemed odd that he collapsed on the sofa while he was threatening me. He must've shoved it between the cushions, and it fell onto the floor. Do you believe me or do you believe Charlie?"

"Without this planted evidence, I would've never taken Charlie's word over yours. That's why I wanted to come clean with you. Look, Vivica, I had my doubts, but you didn't always make it easy for me to believe in the best of you. You always pushed me away."

"So you seduced me to get closer and find out the truth?"

Her words punched him in the gut. Is that what she thought? Did he blame her?

"I believe you, Vivica."

Her lips softened and trembled, and he reached out to comfort her, reassure her... until the click next to his ear made him freeze.

Vivica screamed as Jack spun around to face Charlie, who gripped a gun in front of him with two hands. Charlie sneered. "How touching. I should've known you were trouble. I told Derek to recruit a new hire because he told me the long-time Lollipops had too much loyalty to Vivica to agree to scam the customers. Too bad that new hire turned out to be you."

Vivica struggled against the handcuffs that imprisoned her. "How many of my customers did you rip off?"

Charlie laughed. "That's the joke. None."

Jack stepped in front of her, blocking her from the aim of Charlie's gun. "What about Sadie Crawford?"

Charlie inched to his right and lifted his shoulders. "I wish I could take credit for that and get my hands on even half of those jewels, but Rock cooked up that scheme with Bobbie Jo Crawford."

Jack swore. "Does Bobbie Jo have the jewels?"

Charlie answered, "I have no idea. I don't even know the woman."

Vivica shook her head. "Wait a minute. Then what's you're involvement?"

"I didn't start this for money but revenge. I planted Derek at your club and told him to scope things out, see if he could discover anything dirty on you. Rock told him about a hot, young, rich wife who had her eyes on her mother-in-law's jewels."

A growl sounded from Jack's throat, and Vivica's hands, slick with sweat, grabbed onto the pole above her head as Charlie steadied the gun on Jack. *Please don't do anything stupid, Jack.*

Charlie continued. "Rock's plan gave me the idea to start a rumor that the Lollipop Boys scammed the clientele on Vivica's orders. I figured I might as well make some money myself, so I instructed Derek to find another taker. Too bad his stupidity led him to a P.I. working undercover."

Jack shifted toward Charlie, who took one step back and swung the gun toward Vivica. "You make one more move, and I'll shoot her."

Her stomach clenched with the old fear, but this time something boiled at the edges of that fear. Rage. "Did you tell Bobbie Jo to implicate me?"

"Like I told you, I don't even know the woman, and I sure as hell didn't know her husband hired a P.I. to infiltrate the club. She probably threw your name out there to shift suspicion from herself, and it worked. Jack believed me when I told him all the jewels went to you."

Tears stung her eyes, but she blinked them back. Did he think so little of her?

Jack snorted. "Not quite, Charlie. You wouldn't be here now if you thought I swallowed the story hook, line, and sinker."

A dark cloud scudded across Charlie's face. "When Derek called to tell me you planned to stay behind tonight, I figured something was up. I hid out so I could hear your conversation. Didn't turn out exactly as I planned, but I always have a plan B."

Vivica licked her lips and laughed, and Charlie's brows shot up. "What's so funny, sweet cheeks?"

She gathered up all her strands of courage. "You are, Charlie. All these years and all your time and energy spent on getting even with one little seventeen year-old girl who slipped out of your slimy grasp. You're pathetic."

His eyes blazed. "Who's pathetic now? You're the one handcuffed to a pole, courtesy of your white knight here. When Derek's referral turned out to be none other than your savior, I had my doubts, but knowing you, I figured I could convince him of your guilt. Of course the fact that he's the one who found the bracelet I planted was just icing on the cake. I knew I could count on your playing it close to the vest, not trusting him, pushing him away. You're damaged goods, baby. I see the way you treat the men here. You can't give up control. You can't trust any of them, and all courtesy of me."

He waved the gun toward Jack, who stood erect with his hands fisted at his sides. "Here's another one you can't trust. Poor, unlovable Vivica

Steele."

She gripped the pole harder with damp hands to keep from sliding down. She wouldn't give him the satisfaction of collapsing into a heap. Instead, she stoked the fire of her anger to burn through the self-pity threatening to overcome her.

Jack helped with the fire. "Shut up, Champagne. Vivica trusted me enough to tell me all about you."

"Ah, but you obviously didn't return that trust."

"That's my problem, not hers, but as soon as she revealed the connection between Bobbie Jo and Rock, I believed her, even after finding that planted evidence. I never considered you a credible source."

Vivica stood up straighter, the pole lining up against her spine. Jack spoke the truth. She hadn't needed to do much to convince him of her innocence. She saw it in his eyes, heard it in his voice before Charlie intruded on the scene.

Charlie grinned. "Doesn't do you much good now, does it, Viv?"

Wrong, Charlie. It gave her strength and banished her fear. She cleared her throat and tossed her head back. "What now, Charlie? Your plan failed. Jack's going to the cops with a very different story than the one you planned."

"Maybe, but before he gets to the cops, I'll be long gone. And so will you."

"You're going to give Jack a murder to report as well as receiving stolen goods and false imprisonment? I'm sure you've broken a few more laws carrying out this charade of yours."

Charlie chuckled, a sound drained of all mirth. "Who mentioned murder? I'm just taking you with me for some unfinished business. If I can't bring the club down, I'll bring you down. You're not seventeen anymore, but I think plenty of men would pay good money for a prime piece of ass like you."

Jack stirred, and she laughed, a slightly high-pitched, hysterical sound. "That's ridiculous. There's nothing you could do to me that would make me turn tricks for you."

"I'm not planning to do anything to you, but Derek's stationed outside Buck O'Hannigan's house right now awaiting my call. If you don't cooperate, he has his orders."

Cold fingers of dread gripped the back of her neck and she screamed, "No!"

Jack reached out for her, but Charlie swung his gun in his direction. "Don't let chivalry be the end of you, Jack. I'm not a murderer, but if pushed

I can give a good impression of one."

Charlie's cold eyes roamed up and down her body, and she cringed in revulsion. He grinned at her response.

"Don't be so upset, sweet cheeks. It's for one night only. I'll hook up Jack to the pole in your place when we leave, so he can't interfere, and you'll come with me and be my lady for the evening—just one evening—just so I can show you what you missed by running out on me."

Jack ground out through clenched teeth, "Don't do it, Vivica."

Charlie clicked his tongue. "It won't kill her, Jack, but it may kill you. If you don't come with me, Viv, I'll shoot Jack first, and then I'll put a call in to Derek and have him do a number on Buck. You decide."

She already decided she at least would make a show of going with him to protect Buck. Now she had to protect Jack too. "I'll do what you say."

"Good girl. Jack, unhook her. Any funny business and I'll shoot both of you."

Jack took a step toward Vivica and stopped. "I don't have the key on me. I left it in my locker."

Charlie waved the gun. "Take that belt off and slide it over here."

Jack unhooked his belt with the fake cuffs, pepper spray, and plastic billy club and shoved it across the stage toward Charlie.

Charlie pointed the gun at Jack with one hand while he pulled the instruments off the belt with the other. He held up a small key. "What do you know? Before you unlock her, take off the rest of that outfit. I want to make sure you're not hiding anything."

Jack ripped off the slacks and shirt and dropped them in a heap.

Charlie eyed Jack's crotch. "She had you wearing that? She either had it in for you or had the hots for you." He tossed the key back to Jack. "Unlock the cuffs."

Jack drew next to her, beads of sweat clustering on his brow. He leaned in to unlock the cuffs and brushed her ear with his lips. "Do what I say."

She swallowed and dipped her head. The click released the handcuffs, and she pulled her hands free. Jack dropped the cuffs in her outstretched hands and took her place against the pole.

Charlie waved the gun at him. "Not yet. Vivica's going to need that pole before we leave. Stand by the edge of the stage, Jack, and put your hands behind your back. Vivica, hook him up."

Jack moved away from the pole, and rested his hands against the small of his back. Her heart jumped when she saw him rubbing his hands and wrists against his back, still slick with body oil. Could he do this? Did she want him to risk it? She snapped the cuffs around his oily wrists and said a silent prayer.

"Turn around."

Jack turned to show Charlie the cuffs and pulled against them to show how tightly she hooked him up. Charlie nodded. "Sit down."

Jack sank awkwardly to the floor with his arms pinned behind him, and Vivica's heart ached to see him so helpless. But Jack Slater wasn't a man to stay helpless for long.

Charlie turned his icy gaze on her, and the chill seeped into her flesh. He gestured toward the Plexiglas booth with his gun. "Put some music on and give us a show. It'll warm you up for what you have to do next."

She waited for the bitter bile of fear to rise from her gut, but a hard core of anger had replaced it. With Jack close by, she didn't fear Charlie.

She strode to the booth and queued up a sexy Prince song. Under Charlie's amused gaze, she marched back and stood in the center of the stage with her back toward Charlie and Jack. She'd give the most pathetic striptease of her life.

As she glanced over her shoulder, she caught Jack's eye. He mouthed, "Go for it."

She scowled. What did that mean? He had sex on his mind at a time like this? Her scowl stayed in place as she took in Charlie waiting expectantly, his mouth slightly slack. Charlie had sex on his mind too.

Her gaze darted back to Jack as the first notes of the song thumped through the club. She got it! Jack wanted her to put on a show to end all shows to distract Charlie.

She spun around, grabbed the pole behind her and slithered down its length with her knees spread to the sides, her dress falling between her legs. Charlie's eyes widened, and his Adam's apple bobbed.

She slid back up, arching her back, thrusting her pelvis forward. With her knees trembling, she lunged off the pole and strutted to the side of the stage while her hands traced her curves.

She reached behind her neck and untied the knot of her halter dress. She held the two ends of silky material above her shoulders as she teased the cloth across her breasts, giving Charlie and Jack a peek-a-boo glimpse of her bare breasts.

Charlie, eyes glittering under heavy lids, dipped the gun toward the floor. She dared not steal a peek at Jack, didn't want to draw Charlie's attention to him. She just hoped he was enjoying the show… for different reasons.

Jack would've been enjoying the show a lot more if he didn't have to work so hard to slip his hands out of the cuffs. The metal bit into the heels of his hands. He just needed to get the ring of the cuff over the rise at the base of his thumb.

Vivica turned her back on them again and dropped the strips of cloth that formed the top of her dress. She reached around and dragged the zipper of her dress down from her hips. Her creamy white derrière peeked from the folds of black material. Jack's hands stopped struggling with the cuffs. Did she have panties on?

He got his answer as she dropped the dress to the floor, revealing a lacy, black strip running up the center of her buttocks and clinging to her gently curving hips.

To his right, Charlie sucked in air like a drowning man, and Jack was right there with him, but he had to get free to save Vivica from what Charlie had in store for her. She'd obviously do anything to protect her friend, Buck. Was he a boyfriend she kept hidden away? The thought gnawed at him, but he couldn't let jealousy stop him from rescuing the woman he loved.

Teetering on her high heels, Vivica swayed her almost bare backside from side to side before kicking her dress to the back of the stage. She grabbed the pole, leaned back and swung around until she faced them, clothed only in her tiny thong.

Reaching up, she grabbed the pole and hooked one leg around it. She climbed the pole, almost to the top, and then twisted slowly down, her body wrapping around it like a sweet ribbon of caramel. When she got to the bottom, her legs opened wide on either side of the pole.

Charlie's gun almost pointed to the floor as his eyes followed Vivica's every move.

With a final jerk, Jack pulled one cuff from his left hand.

Still on the floor, Vivica raised her spread legs and entwined them around the pole. She pumped her hips in a simulated sex act, the silver rod impaling her over and over. Jack had to release his pent-up testosterone somehow.

He eased forward, his eyes trained on the gun now dangling from Charlie's slack fingers. He didn't know what Vivica just did, but Charlie's eyes bugged out of his head, and he leaned forward, putting himself just enough off-balance for Jack to make his move.

As Vivica unraveled her legs from the pole and slid into a sideways split, she detected movement from Jack's corner of the stage. Was he free?

She'd have to go all the way to give him the chance he needed. She hoisted herself up from the floor and hooked her thumbs under the elastic of her thong, peeling it from her body as her hips undulated. Charlie inched in for a closer look.

Charlie choked as Jack crashed into his side, yelling, "Get down."

She dropped to the stage as a loud crack echoed through the club and a bullet whizzed over her head. Jack slammed Charlie's wrist to the floor. The gun skittered across the stage and the two men rolled toward it, grunting and throwing punches.

She lunged toward the gun and grabbed it before it plunged over the edge of the stage. She leveled it at the grappling bodies and shouted over the music. "I have the gun."

The men froze, and then Jack landed one last punch against the side of Charlie's head before hoisting himself up.

He'd lost his g-string in the struggle, the handcuffs dangled from his right wrist, and blood trickled from his lip and nose, his best performance yet.

As he took the gun from her trembling hand and pointed it at Charlie's prone form, sirens wailed outside the club and someone pounded on the front doors. "Open up."

Vivica's eyes met Jack's. His brows quirked in amusement as his gaze took in her nakedness, save her black high heels. Her eyes took a similar journey, trailing down his nude body.

Before either of them could move, the glass on the club doors shattered and several cops stumbled across the entrance, guns drawn, mouths agape.

Buck pushed through the throng of officers, and his shaggy brows disappeared beneath his hat. "I thought you were in trouble, Viv."

# Chapter 9

The following morning, Jack sat at Vivica's dining room table with Vivica and Buck O'Hannigan, retired LVPD homicide detective. Finding out this hardened old cop claimed Vivica's affections banished the jealousy he felt at her protectiveness toward him.

Dark circles shadowed Vivica's brilliant blue eyes, and a tiny frown slivered between her brows. He longed to smooth it away.

She curled her hands around the steaming cup of coffee. "I still don't understand how you knew I was in trouble, Buck."

He patted her arm. "Old instincts die hard. When I saw that guy stationed outside my house, in a convertible, no less, I figured he had his eye on me for some reason. With Jack investigating your club, I figured that reason had something to do with you. When I called you at home after closing time and you didn't answer, I assumed the worst."

She grabbed Buck's gnarled hand. "I'm glad you did."

He shrugged. "You and Jack had things covered. Well, sort of."

Jack laughed as Vivica's cheeks bloomed pink roses. He tilted his head. "Why didn't you two tell me you knew my identity?"

Vivica sipped her coffee as her blush deepened. "Buck wanted to, but I thought if I proclaimed my innocence instead of allowing you to discover it yourself, I'd look guilty."

Buck coughed. "You have to begin any relationship with trust." His faded blue eyes shifted to Jack. "She thought you used her and she wanted to punish you. Vivica thinks by punishing every man she meets, she's getting revenge on her father and Charlie."

A tight fist squeezed Jack's heart. "I didn't use you, Vivica."

Buck slapped his palm against the table and pushed up from his chair. "I'll let you two work things out on your own." He dropped a kiss on the top of Vivica's head. "You get back to bed and call me later, and give Jack a break. I have it from a reliable source that Jack's department set him up to keep him quiet about department irregularities."

Buck ambled toward the front door and gave them a wink before slipping out.

Vivica dropped her lashes, which formed a velvet crescent against her smooth skin. A sigh rattled in her chest.

He repeated softly, "I never used you. I cursed myself nightly for my attraction to you, but I couldn't stay away."

"Why didn't you just tell me?"

"At the beginning I suspected you. Bobbie Jo made sure of that, and then just when I'd decided to tell you everything, I discovered that diamond bracelet in your office. As soon as you told me about the connection between Bobbi Jo and Rock, I knew you were innocent."

She lifted her eyes to his face and covered her mouth. "Bobbie Jo. What are you going to tell Ben Crawford?"

"I already told him this morning. It didn't come as much of a shock since he had his own suspicions. My guess is that he's already wrung a tearful confession from his wife."

"What's next for you, Jack? More investigations? More undercover work?"

"I'm done."

"You're going back to L.A., back to your job?"

"No. Although it looks like my name might be cleared, I'm not going back. I'm going to buy a ranch in Idaho and turn it into a bootcamp for troubled youth, try a little tough love."

Her hand jerked, and her coffee sloshed over the edge of her cup. "Really? That's a great idea. So many kids need help these days."

A shimmer of tears brightened her eyes, and he gave voice to the crazy thought that had been bouncing around in his head for weeks. "Why don't you come with me?"

She blinked and licked her lips. "Come with you?"

He hunched over the table, warming to the idea. "You'd be great with the kids, Vivica. There'd be no phoniness about you. They'd trust you."

She sawed at her lower lip. "I'd love to help kids, really help them. Are you offering me a job?"

God, she still couldn't believe someone wanted her, really wanted her to belong? He'd have to change that. He had a lot of hard work ahead of him, and not just with those kids. He kneeled beside her chair and pried her hands from her coffee mug. Then he brought them to his lips and kissed every finger. "I'm offering you a job as my life partner, that is, if you want the position."

Nodding, she caressed the side of his face. That was all the answer he needed. He pulled her down for a long kiss, and Vivica Steele, hard-as-nails man-eater, melted against him.

She pulled away and brushed his hair from his brow. "Is this a position that requires an audition?"

Encircling her waist with his hands, he pulled her up with him. "As a matter of fact, it does, and I have just the Lollipop you need to make it a success."

## *About the Author:*

*Mia Varano has hordes of virile men and strong but luscious women in her head, all clamoring to escape and realize their destinies. It makes for some interesting headaches until she sets them free to fulfill their fantasies and those of her readers. In addition to highly sensual, and somewhat kinky, erotic romance, Mia writes nail-biting romantic suspense as Carol Ericson. If you just can't get enough, please visit Mia's website at* www.miavarano.com.

# Shadow Wolf

## by Rae Monet

## *To My Reader:*

*Shadow Wolf* is a continuation of The Solarian Wolf Warrior Series and weaves the eradication of the wolves into the story-as do all my Wolf Warrior books. Each Wolf Warrior book stands on its own, so if you want to further explore this world please come and visit me at RaeMonet.com. *Shadow Wolf* is the sixth book in the series and will introduce you to half-breed Lupine Dia Nahiutras and Wolf Warrior First Class, Roark D'Reincolt. They will take you into a futuristic world riddled with war and betrayal. The pair must overcome many obstacles to discover their true path in life. I hope you enjoy Roark and Dia's story. I know I loved writing it for you. Of course, always close to my heart are the wolves; please visit my adopted wolf Wana, who lives at WolfMountain.com. And I love to hear reader feedback at Rae@RaeMonet.com.

# *Prologue*

The year 2643
Lupine Settlement Beta, Planet Alagon

"Unless you want a blast to the temple, I suggest you state your purpose." Rhiannon Nahiutras shoved her blaster against Zarik Rallan's shaved head and wondered what the most feared assassin on Alagon was doing in her apartment.

"Now Dia, is that any way to greet a fellow co-worker?" he drawled.

She wasn't fooled by his casual manner. If Zarik wanted her dead, she'd already be twitching on the ground of her one-room hole. Which meant he had another reason for invading her space.

With a flip of her thumb, Dia switched the blaster to kill. The high-pitched squeal warned Zarik in a way she knew he would understand.

"You're not any co-worker of mine, Zarik. Why are you here? Talk now or lose your head, and I'd prefer not to mess-up my floor."

"Relax." Zarik set down the knickknack he was handling and lifted his hands in the air. "I'm here to offer you a job. If you kill me, you're robbing yourself of some easy money. From what I can see of this slum, you could certainly use it."

At least she had a place. Besides, she'd seen much worse on the streets of this Lupine Beta settlement, so she chose to ignore his baiting.

"I do all right," she lied. Business was slow. She had been on a downward slope lately. Work for bounty hunters was hard to come by since the war. Her food replicator was on the fritz, the vid screen only worked half the time, and her expandable sleep compartment was so frayed and worn she expected it to crap out any day.

Dia switched off her blaster and holstered it. She made her way around Zarik and took a seat in front to study him. He wasn't an attractive man. The scars of war wore heavily on him, crisscrossing on his face to create a macabre and frightening visage, one he used to his advantage when the occasion demanded. But his commanding presence set her on edge.

"Spill. Who are you working for now?" she asked.

"The only establishment paying a frack."

Dia sucked in a breath. "The Dange Alliance." It wasn't a question, only a statement left hanging in the air like she'd murmured a nasty word. "So how's the Lupine/Dange war these days? The Dange master race coming out on top? Oops, I forgot, since they poisoned the water and altered the Lupine's DNA pattern so they can't shift into the creatures who can kick the Dange's asses anymore... they should be doing okay, shouldn't they?" She traced a pattern on the chair. "Not that it matters to me... being a half-breed and all with no shifting ability."

By her glib remarks, Dia made sure her indifference to the bloody conflict wasn't lost on Zarik. She was just a gal trying to make a living, not a solider on either side of this bloody war.

"See, that's the thing. I'm in need of a registered tracker with certain skills to sniff out—how should I put this?" He raised a finger to his chin, then stared pointedly at her with those eerie black eyes. "Delicately."

She shook her head. "Oh frack, Zarik, when has insulting anyone ever bothered you?"

He chuckled and sat down across from her. Extending his legs, he crossed his ankles and leaned back, spreading his arms along the back of her best and only lounger. His size made the thing look tiny. She wasn't taken in one millisec by his casual demeanor.

"Zarik, you're a true blood killer, through and through. You'd just as soon wipe me off the planet as talk to me, so you must need something—bad. I'm registered as a third rate tracker and hunter, so coming to my level isn't your usual mode of operation." There was only one thing that made her different from the other trackers on this planet. She raised both eyebrows. "You need the wolf side of my nature?"

"True, Dia, so very true. Let's say your Lupine heritage will come in handy for this mission. I need someone who can easily sniff out a wolf, but not any wolf. This wolf is special, they call it a Shadow wolf. It has a unique DNA pattern. With your Lupine blood, you should be able to sense this breed easily."

He threw her a pulse scanner. She caught it and flipped on the display to get an idea of what he was talking about.

"Never seen this kind of wolf before. It's not Lupine." She studied the photo and DNA profile.

"Precisely. This mission would require you to travel to Earth, where this wolf is said to reside."

Dia suppressed the shudder curling down her spine at what the Alliance would do to the wolf once she delivered it. Despite the fact she was half Lupine and half Dange, she didn't stand with the Dange Alliance at all. They played dirty in a war already filthy. Not that the Lupine were much better, but in her mind, they did fight with dignity.

"Why would they care about this wolf? There are barely any Lupines left with the ability to shift. Thought the Alliance was calling the war in their favor?"

"Yes, well. Let's just say they don't want anything to impede their ability to keep the Lupine down and this wolf could be the key. Other than that, details aren't what they are paying you for. It's to retrieve the wolf and bring it back to the Alliance. Are you in?"

Dia set the scanner down and pondered his offer for about five microns. "What's the pay?"

Zarik smiled and nodded, as if she'd already accepted the job. Dia wasn't stupid. She needed a good-paying job. She didn't swear allegiance to any faction of this war except the almighty credit. Dange or Lupine had never done anything for her, except to leave her orphaned as an infant on a dirty Lupine street.

"Two hundred thousand credits deposited now to be held in your account. If you don't deliver the wolf, the credits will be withdrawn."

Dia nearly choked. Two hundred thousand credits would keep her in necessities, and then some, for years. Maybe she could even get off this godforsaken planet. She couldn't turn down the offer.

"I'm in."

Zarik rose and she followed him.

"Very good." He handed her an e-chip. "Instructions are here. Single user ship is awaiting you at D. Alliance bay five. It has a tracker, so don't even think about stealing it."

Zarik leaned forward and ran a finger down her cheek to her pulse. She tried not to squirm under his touch, but he was making her feel dirty, so she inched away.

"So pretty. Don't screw this up or the next time you see me, it will be at the end of my blaster and I won't hesitate... like you did." He tapped her temple, then gave her a quirk of his lips—which she supposed was a smile—but it looked more like a smirk.

Dia grabbed the chip and slid it into the pocket of her battle fatigues. She tipped her head to Zarik. "Of course."

"Good hunting, Dia." And with his departing remark he left as stealthily as he arrived.

Dia shivered, hugged herself, rubbing her hands up and down her arms. Why did she think there was more going on here than Zarik was revealing? There was a part of her—her Lupine nature—wanting to rebel. But experience told her going against the Alliance would only get her thrown into one of the local dead body burning pits.

She shrugged and went to load up. Wasn't her problem. She finally had a paying job, and she wasn't going to screw it up with Lupine emotions she had no business feeling. Lupine emotions brought weakness. Weakness got you killed. *Keep focused, Dia.*

# Chapter 1

Planet Earth
Scottish Highlands, Solarian Guard Outpost, Entrance to the Solarian Realm

"What do you say, girl?"

Roark D'Reincolt wiped the drops of sweat off his brow and the back of his neck. Wacipi, his midnight-black wolf, gave a full body shake and plopped down beside him. His gaze strayed to the waterfall they guarded. Behind the crashing power lay the entrance to the secret Solarian Realm where his people had lived in peace and safety since the thirteenth century.

"I definitely regret taking guard duty this week. Next time one of my Wolf Warriors is sick, remind me to tell him or her to man-up."

Wacipi produced a whine, her way of agreeing with him.

"It's got to be a hundred and ten degrees out here."

His wolf made an audible huff and set her muzzle between her front legs. He set his hand on her head. Wacipi, his unusual, petite wolf, was the whole to his half. Shunned by her pack because of her small size, she gradually struggled for a place of honor among her mates. She was a fighter, just like him. As with all Wolf Warriors, he had a strong telepathic connection with his wolf, and he could feel her displeasure.

Roark scanned the green forest for threats, taking in the lush oaks and overhanging foliage. The smell of Scottish heather blanketed the area while mist from the waterfall encircled the woodland around him. He sucked in a soothing breath and tried to enjoy the peace his home always brought him, but was only weighed down again by the oppressive heat. The roar of the falls called to him. A refreshing dip wouldn't take long, and if Wacipi and he didn't cool off, it was likely they would pass out from heat stroke. The area was clear. He didn't sense any danger.

"Should we take a few to cool ourselves off?"

Wacipi gave a resounding ruff and followed him toward the water. Strip-

ping down to his loin cloth, Roark set aside his sword and rifle at the water's
edge. He stepped into the river, instantly relieved by the chill.

Like a cub, Wacipi danced around him, barking and splashing. Roark
laughed and dove until he was completely submerged in the refreshing water,
then broke the surface to float and relax.

Suddenly, he felt stillness around him. The birds ceased their chatter,
and an eerie quiet enveloped the area as if something magical was coming.
Roark paused, his Wolf Warrior senses stirring in anticipation. Wacipi swam
toward the shore with a growl.

Roark rotated in the water to face the unknown danger. Caution made
him swim ever so slowly toward his weapons until his feet touched the bottom. He moved, step by step, out of the water until he was within an arms
length of his sword. Only another foot and he would be armed.

As he reached the water's edge, his threat walked from the mist. Appearing like a wood nymph, she was a mystical creature, mesmerizing him
with her appearance. Her creamy skin was surrounded by long crimson hair
curling around her face and cascading down her shoulders. Her light green
eyes were so startling, he blinked from their brilliance. Her lush curves
overflowed from the barest of jade-colored gossamer cloth, crisscrossing
over her breasts, around her back, and flowing to her hips. She wore hiking
boots and had a back pack slung over her shoulder in complete contrast to
her bare outfit, which seemed more in line with a woman wanting specific
attention from her lovers.

Roark's heart pressed against his chest, *thump, thump, thump,* in rhythm
with his rapidly accelerating pulse. His cooled body heated back up, so
quick and so hot, he could feel the sweat trickle down the side of his face.
The hairs on the back of his neck stood at attention, along with other parts
of his body. He reached down and tried to adjust himself to conceal his
raging erection. He couldn't figure out what it was about her, but she was
having an immediate and powerful sexual effect on him.

"I come in friendship." She held up her hands in the universal sign of
surrender and gave a pointed stare at his growling wolf.

Roark relaxed a bit, his tense muscles easing as he confirmed this beautiful woman was likely no threat.

"I'm in need of a good cooling off myself. I'm gathering a special plant
for my settlement." She held up a botanist's capturing device.

Roark gave a mental command to Wacipi. *Stand down.* The wolf quirked
her head in clear curiosity and sat back on her haunches, undoubtedly to
watch the drama unfold. His wolf was attuned to him as no other. She obvi-

ously sensed Roark's attraction to this woman.

"Would you mind if I joined you? It's so hot. I've been working all day trying to find this one specific plant specimen. It's been impossible. I'm so frustrated."

Dropping her backpack and device, she stepped closer, her small body easing down to sit on the mossy bank in front of him. She was tiny, maybe only five feet tall. He wasn't sure how she carried the large pack she had slung down.

As she edged closer, he could smell her unique flowery fragrance. His nostrils flared as he tried to take in more of her scent. Although he was fairly sure she wasn't there to harm him, he was still a soldier, and by nature suspicious. He needed to quit mooning over the woman and get back to business. Not saying anything, Roark stepped onto the bank, and slowly began picking up his weapons. She didn't try to stop him, confirming her limited risk.

"I'm Dia." She held out her petite hand like a queen might ask her subject to kiss her fingers. Roark almost felt the need to bow.

"Roark D'Reincolt." He clasped her fingers in his. He felt it then, a burning centered in their touched palms, radiating out, sending a tingle all the way down his spine to his toes as if he had been electrocuted. *What the hell was that?* He eased his grip from hers. "What settlement?"

"The one down the rise." She waved her fingers in the air, "Over there."

Dia flipped her hair over her shoulder, displaying her pert breasts under her gauzy top. The fabric was as close to transparent as cloth could get, and Roark was extremely grateful for that fact.

Roark sat down to study her. Up close she was even more beautiful. The classic lines of her face reminded him of royalty—a straight, pert nose, chiseled cheekbones, full lips and a rosy hue to her light sun-kissed skin.

She smiled, a single dimple appearing in her cheek as she reached down to unlace her boots. Out of courtesy, Roark set aside his weapons, brushed her hands aside and went about finishing the task for her.

"What's the name of that settlement?" he asked.

"Braemere, Laird Leone's settlement. I'm Kailey's cousin from London."

Roark let out a slow sigh of relief. He was aware of the settlement. It would be hard to fake knowledge of the Laird's family name and his sister, Kailey. Last time Roark was in their town, Kailey had spoken about her cousin the botanist visiting from London.

"Yes. I know it."

"Where do you come from?" She tilted her head to the side as she awaited his answer, and her red hair shifted, caressing her shoulder. Roark gritted his teeth in sexual frustration and tried to stay on task.

"I'm only here for a visit. Camping. Enjoying the outdoors." Roark slid her boot and sock off her delicate foot, keeping vague about where he came from. If she knew Laird Leone's family, then she would piece together he wasn't from around the area. He held her ankle for a moment. The contrast of his large hand to her small foot was substantial. There was a part of him craving to caress the tiny arch. He wondered if the rest of her body would look as delicate as her foot. Her skin was so soft. He shook his head and removed the other boot.

"I love to camp. How long have you been here?"

"A while." Roark moved her boots aside to take off her socks, and against his better judgment he began to massage her foot. Her sweet fragrance was drawing him in, closer, closer, and he wanted to lean over and sip from her lips to see if she tasted as good as she smelled. Need became his number one companion.

"Oh, that's delicious." She moaned and arched her back, pushing her taunt nipples hard against the front of her shirt. Roark heard a low guttural sound come deep from his throat.

"Would you mind if I joined you?" she asked.

Roark blinked several times at her request. He'd lost track of the conversation while he thought about lining one of those pink nipples with his tongue, taking the pertness slowly into his mouth, tugging on it with his teeth—not too hard—just enough to make her arch like that again.

"I mean, do you mind if I camp here with you for a few days? I still have several plant species I have to acquire before I can return. These woods do have wild animals. I wouldn't mind having a camp-mate for a couple days. It's blind luck I came across you."

Something protective reared up in Roark. He didn't want her camping out here alone either. The woods *were* dangerous. Roark set her foot down, sat back and made a quick decision.

"I'd be honored to have you join me."

"Thank you." She rose, untied her top and began unwrapping the cloth around her body until she stood totally naked before him. As he tried to swallow, all the moisture sucked out of his mouth and he ended up gulping for breath. He had fantasized about it seconds earlier, and now the dream had come alive.

Her body was a work of art, all curves and soft lines, and her breasts were as he imagined, full nipples standing at attention, teasing him. She turned, showing him her lovely sloping back, arching into a perfectly formed ass. He was having a difficult time not reaching down and stroking his hardness so he could relieve the tension he felt forming there.

"You don't mind if I take a swim, do you?" She watched him from over her shoulder, her knowing smile and the twinkle in her eyes telling him she knew exactly how she was affecting him.

"Not at all."

*What is this woman up to?*

"Drop your suit and join me." As she walked toward the water, her parting remark before a splash had him standing.

Roark gave Wacipi a mental command to guard the perimeter and his wolf went loping off. Roark reached for his loincloth. Who was he to deny the lady?

# Chapter 2

Yes, she had him just where she wanted.

She wanted to sail a fist up in victory as she watched Roark drop his shorts and dive into the water. She surely had him by the cock, and what a wonderful specimen that organ was, like the man it adorned! *Holy Frack*. If she had known earth males where so well-endowed and fracking beautiful she would have scheduled a trip much sooner.

Dia tried to control her scrambled thoughts, but the hard lines of his body stood out, begging for her attention. He was a sensual masterpiece of a human male, every muscle sculpted, every exposed body part honed to perfection, every fluid movement gracefully masculine. *Gods*. And his *voice*. It was deep and sexy with a slight accent that sent her pussy clenching and her body shivering in excitement. She thanked the Gods English was a universal language for both their planets, or snagging him would have been a lot harder.

Wouldn't you know she'd finally found the animal who had lit her scanner up like a pulsing Alagonian white gem, and *this man* had to accompany the wolf. This totally stunning man, with the chiseled features and rock hard body. This totally distracting man, with a unique scent of male, sweat, and something she couldn't identify drawing her from as far as ten feet away.

He was not to be taken lightly. She had been studying him for three days. Warrior breed through and through—this fact couldn't be disregarded. On her planet he would have been assigned as one of the top Dange soldiers.

She needed to gain this man's trust for what she had in mind. Stealing his wolf would be no easy task. She'd seen the affection between the two hunters and Roark wouldn't let his wolf go without a fight.

A fight Dia couldn't afford to initiate.

There was no doubt in her mind he would prove to be more than a match for her in battle. She had watched him practice. She could see his expertise in the way he moved and held his weapon, as his eyes continually scanned and his body arched in perfect symmetry to his sword. He would fight until the death. Dia wouldn't be getting the drop on Roark unless she used the oldest technique a woman could engage—her body.

There had been tell-tale signs of his interest, such as the way his eyes had lit when she sauntered up in her handmade, bare outfit. His nostrils had flared in his arousal, his body hardening and his breath quickening.

She allowed him to trail her through the water, beckoning him on with a smile and casting him a look over her shoulder in what she hoped was a blatant invitation. She turned until she was swimming backwards, watching, waiting. As far as she could tell, her technique was working. He swam closer as she floated, then stroked away from him. He looked like a predator now, pursuing his chosen prey, chasing as she ran. Her heart tripped a fast beat. He wasn't the only one affected by this game. The closer he came, the slower she swam until he was within arm's length. She dropped her legs beneath the crystalline surface. Treading water, she was fair game for the warrior. He did not disappoint her. His arms reached out, captured her waist and pulled her close.

"The water's deep here. Let me hold you up." His voice caressed her, causing a spike of awareness to tingle down her spine. His hands slid around her back to cup her ass against his hardness, settling his erection into the V of her legs. Her nipples peaked and her breath puffed out in an aroused sigh.

If it wasn't for the water, she was sure he'd smell her interest creaming between her legs. She spread her legs and wrapped her feet around his ass, bringing them together in a position made for only one thing. Being this close to him was creating erotic sensations she had never felt before. A primitive craving to couple began to take hold of her. She told herself *this* was for the cause. Over and over, *the mission, the mission.* Even as she chanted it in her mind, her body was taking a different course.

*Take him. Make him yours.*

"You're very alluring," he said quietly as he balanced them above the water, slowly swimming them in a gentle circle. The friction of their bodies wasn't helping her concentrate on anything except what it would be like to have him slip that extraordinary, long, hard cock inside her. Being in his arms was giving her an otherworldly feeling, as if her brain was no longer in charge of her body's cravings. Her mind was shutting down as her body turned on.

"I could say the same for you." Her voice came out in a breathy groan she didn't even recognize.

"Are you mated?" His question temporarily shocked her out of the sensual haze he was weaving. *Mated?* Like she would ever tie herself to any man. *No way.* She liked her life *solo.* She'd learned early on in the streets of Alagon that men were not to be trusted. They only wanted one thing, and it certainly wasn't to care for their woman.

"No. No man in my life."

"Why?" His gaze narrowed as if he was trying to stare into the depths of her soul.

"Busy. Being a botanist takes most my time." She was proud of the way she pronounced the strange earth occupation. What an odd job, studying plants.

"That's a shame." He didn't sound like her un-mated status bothered him at all.

"Well you know how work can sometimes take everything you have."

"Yes, I'm aware."

All these questions were beginning to divert her from her purpose. Seduction wasn't going to happen with all this idle chatter in the way. She needed to engage a more aggressive method. *The mission. Remember the mission. Distract him enough to slip him the drug. He'll sleep for hours, long enough for you to snatch his wolf and get the hell out of here.*

"Wha—"

Winding her arms around his neck so he held her entire weight, she tilted her head, dipped forward and literally attached her lips to his. It started with a gentle nibble, one, two, three, then exploded into a hurried mating of lips and tongues. Soft, his lips were so soft and *masterful*. He quickly took over her awkward kisses with his own open-mouthed attack. Their bodies propelled toward the shore. She wasn't exactly sure how, but she didn't care. She felt herself spinning until her back hit the solid ground. Roark was maneuvering her onto the mossy bank, his body falling on top of her as his mouth traveled from her lips to her neck and lower, down her body.

"What is it about you?"

She couldn't answer Roark's guttural question. Her body screamed to couple with his.

As his mouth latched onto her nipple, she sucked in a strained breath and arched up. *What's happening to me?* A simple seduction plan to distract her prey was quickly flaming out of control. It had been so long since she felt this type of desire, if ever. She slid her hands into his wet hair and clutched his head to her breast. A fire burned in the pit of her stomach so hot she couldn't breathe, couldn't think, couldn't do anything but feel. Enjoy. Savor. *Give.* Give him *everything* he wants.

Roark lifted and carried her like she was nothing. The veins in his arms bulged as he laid her inside his tent-like structure, onto the softness of his bedding. His kisses burned. His tongue singed his way down her body. He devoured her like a starving man.

She wasn't complaining.

His wet hair fell, cascading over his shoulders and dropping onto her stomach, leaving a cold trail on her heated skin. A temporary relief before she started to burn again. His outdoorsy male scent drew her in. She felt the need to lay him back on the blanket and feast. She could still taste him on her tongue, sweet man, sexy human, a mixture of flavors she wanted to bottle. She ran her tongue over her lips to savor. He was making primitive noises, a cross between a growl and a groan, telling her he was as out of control as her. It was nice to know she could make such a strong man needy. She touched his shoulder and ran her hand down the sculpted arch of his upper arm. He was hard strength, such a contrast to her womanly curves.

As he moved closer to her clit, her core body temperature heated to the point of explosion. She was wet in arousal. Lifting her legs over his shoulder, he dipped in his tongue, opening her to him fully. He lapped her labia, slowly at first, then with more vigor. Her back bowed. *What is he doing?* She had never felt such pleasure.

"Ahhhhh. Roark." She didn't know what she was pleading for, but she needed more, *had to have more.*

Suddenly, a white light exploded behind the back of her eyes, sending her breath out in a huge explosion of air followed by a scream. Roark dropped her legs down and crawled up her body. The masculine tilting of his lips told her he enjoyed her scream of satisfaction. He kissed her, a sweet coupling. She could taste herself on his lips, an arousing mixture of his flavor and hers. His tongue danced with hers as he eased himself into her body. He stopped.

"So tight." The words growled out of his mouth as if he was forcing them.

"Don't." She slapped her hands on his ass. "Gods, don't stop."

This was *it, this* was what all those Alagon woman had meant when they talked about the bliss in coupling. Dia had never felt it before, had never cared much for the whole sweaty act, but this was different. She was full, complete, as if this was the only man in the world for her.

"Dia. Look at me." Roark's nearly iridescent blue eyes made contact with hers as he lifted her hands above her head and linked their palms. "Am I hurting you?"

"Noooo," she groaned out as he thrust a tiny bit forward. She clenched her pussy.

"Hold on," he whispered on the tail end of a moan. Then he thrust full forward, so deep she wasn't sure where they both ended. He was seated fully in her, thrusting in and out. She moved her hips to meet him almost instinctually, wanting to be closer, closer. *So good.* Something else was happening, too. She could sense him, not just his cock buried to the hilt, but it seemed like she could almost feel his mind brushing against hers, sharing their emotions, linking them more than physically. It seemed impossible; nonetheless, she couldn't mistake the gentle awareness of another person there with her.

"Roark," she yelled as she arched into him, her second orgasm taking her over. He was panting, sweat rolling down the side of his face as he forcefully rocked their bodies together in a sensual dance. Her mind filled with their shared ecstasy. He roared and made a final thrust forward. She could feel his essence spilling inside her, filling her.

As Roark's body eased onto hers, a feeling of utter completeness settled upon her. She wrapped her arms around him, sliding one hand into his hair, playing with the light mass. He panted against her neck and gave what she assumed was a satisfied groan. If she didn't know any better, she'd say the man was purring like an Alagonian street feline.

"Thank you," he murmured against her neck. She stroked his hair.

"No. Thank you." She smiled and felt like giggling in joy. She had never giggled in her life. She stopped herself at once.

"We'll take that slower next time."

Dia wanted to squeak out a protest, but she was too tied up in knots to argue. There wouldn't be a *next time* for them. This was a one time occurrence, bordering on insanity. An animalistic attraction they had both acted on. Dia had a job, and this distraction was just that—a distraction. A fantastic episode between two strangers, but she couldn't let it go beyond that. Roark sighed and rolled onto his back, taking her with him, draping her body over his. She smoothed back the hair over his brow. His breathing was steady. He appeared ready for a good nap.

"Rest for a few. We'll worry about next time after you recover."

He nodded and caressed her cheek. "That was incredible. You are incredible."

She grinned and gently kissed him. He responded by sliding his hand down her back and cupping her ass.

"Rest," she said softly against his lips.

"Okay," he said as he closed his eyes. "Just a few minutes to recover.

Don't go anywhere." He tightened his hold on her.

"I won't. Don't worry. I'll be right here when you wake." She ran her fingers to his temple and lightly massaged. He let out a puff of air. She could see his body relaxing, until his breathing evened. He was asleep.

Gently, Dia disengaged herself from him and eased out of the tent. Grabbing her backpack, she quickly dressed in her uniform, and loaded two hypos.

Dia stood and walked toward Roark, taking a minute to study him. The hard ridges of his stomach muscles flexed as he took air in and out, a lock of blond hair had fallen onto his cheek, and a light shadow graced the line of his squared jaw. Even in sleep, he was still a compelling man. His face was calm now, but she had watched him for nearly three days and had seen the warrior-like intensity he could exhibit. But when he was just being a man, he was incredible. In one lovemaking session, he had taken her somewhere she had never been before, a place where she'd felt accepted and wanted. Would she ever touch that place again? She doubted it. She couldn't afford to feel this way about him. *Job.* He was a job. She'd played enough. It was time to get serious.

*He won't feel a thing.* She gently applied the hypo to his neck, directly at the vein running to his brain. The minute she touched the device to his artery, his eyes popped open. Leave it to Roark to always be on the alert. It had to be the soldier in him. But it was too late.

"Dia."

Before he could even register what she was doing, Dia touched the plunger and administered the shot. His eyes immediately rolled back in his head. With his size, she hoped she had given herself enough time. She only had so much of the drug, and she hadn't expected to use it on more than the wolf. She laid a therma register to his skin and checked his vitals.

*Sleeping.* Good. *Stats normal.*

In case he did wake early, Dia dug a pair of force cuffs from her bag. She assessed the pole running down the middle of the tent, shaking it back and forth. It stood solid, and she guessed must have been driven into the ground a good four feet. Lifting his arm to the pole, she attached the cuff to his wrist and the other to the pole. Now she felt a little more secure in her position.

Exiting the tent she eased into a crouch and lifted her hand to the wolf slumbering next to Roark's encampment. The wolf's ears perked up as she tilted her head to the side and regarded Dia.

"You trust me now, don't you girl? I've proven myself to your master."

The wolf yawned, all her deadly, pointed teeth momentarily showing before her mouth closed. She allowed Dia to approach. *She really is a beautiful wolf.* Dia ran her hand down the smooth pelt, soothing her with calm, cooing noises. Too bad she had to kidnap her. Ever so slowly, she flipped the hypo in her other hand up to the wolf's hind quarters and pressed. The wolf struggled for a milli-second, as if fighting the drug, then eased back on the dirt and dropped into sleep. Dia knew the effects of the medicine were instantaneous, especially when applied directly under the skin with a hypo device.

She stroked the wolf's dark head in apology. There was a part of her that sympathized with the wolf's plight. But Dia had a job to do and the money from this one would get her off Alagon for good. Besides, she certainly didn't want to get on Zarik's hit list, and that's where she would end up if she didn't get this assignment done right.

Despite the wolf's small stature, she grunted as she hefted the animal's body over her shoulder, thankful she was in top condition. Before starting the hike to her ship, she took a final glance at the slumbering man and shook her head as regret swamped her. *Too bad.* Too bad she couldn't stay.

# Chapter 3

Roark jolted awake, his breath an exhalation of confusion. What was going on? He studied the length of his naked body. He jerked his arm, only to find it numb and secured to the stabilizing bar of his bio-dome. He gave himself a minute to get his bearings. All he could remember was making crazy, passionate love to the magical creature strolling out of the forest. Next thing he knew, she was stabbing him with a hypo and after that, everything went black.

*Fucking bitch!*

Using his mind sense, Roark gave a silent command for Wacipi, only to come up empty. What the *hell?* Where was his wolf? He made another mental push, and still, *nothing.* He'd never been out of telepathic link with his wolf before. And what in the hell had possessed him to stand down from guard duty when greeted by a sexy expression thrown out at him over the shoulder of a naked woman? Where was his well-maintained control? It was as if an alien had seized control of his body and taken over his brain. The only thought in his head, after she'd dropped her clothes and stepped into the water, was making her *his.*

His heart pounding, he reached over and ran his finger along the bottom of the stabilizing ballast.

"De-activating this beam without proper breakdown protocol will collapse the structure," a mechanical voice warned him.

*Damn computer.* He knew what would happen if he broke the center beam out of build order. He touched the trigger again.

"Stand clear. This beam will collapse in five seconds, four, three, two." The device emitted a warning beep, then slid up inside itself. The cloth walls fell down around him, enclosing him in a sea of treated neoprene. He growled out a roar and removed his cuffed hand over the top of the now small, two foot tube. Pushing the material of the tent aside, he climbed his way out.

Dia's pack was gone as well as any traces of her and Wacipi. *I have to use the Astro mind link.* Using the technique he was contemplating was rare and painful for both he and Wacipi, but clearly, this situation called for drastic measures. Roark raised his hand to his head and projected himself into Wacipi's body.

He could feel a presence. He wasn't sure if it was Wacipi or not, but he could definitely sense another being. The familiar rush of the green forest raced by him. Human feet running, the boots seemed familiar, the same hiking boots of—

"Dia," he snarled.

The boots skittered to a halt for a nano-second, then kept moving. He rotated his vision in a circle, trying to catch a landmark so he could home in on her location. There, *Burke's Peak*. He knew where she was now, he recognized the jutting, cragged rock above the tree range about ten kilometers south of him. He shifted his line of sight forward and followed the path Dia was taking. *A space ship.* Not a normal ship, like one he'd never seen before.

*She's not from this planet.*

He should have known she'd cast some sort of spell on him, probably a mind control device. He'd heard of them on other planets. It explained the connection he'd felt to her and his resulting insane actions.

He zeroed back out and saw the entire image of her running with Wacipi thrown over her shoulder. She placed a hand to her head as she rushed along. *She can feel me. How strange. Has to be another one of her tricks.* Maybe whatever she injected in him was connecting them. No matter, he had her now.

"I know exactly where you are, *Mo Daor*. I'm coming for you and my wolf, if it's the last thing I do," he whispered, the traditional Gaelic slipping into his speech.

She pivoted toward his voice, her expression wary, almost frightened, and shook her head. She continued.

Roark was galvanized into action, donning his clothes and boots and gathering his weapons. He touched a few buttons on his wrist COMM unit. With a high pitched whine, his hover cycle floated down from the tree top above him and glided to a stop. By now, Roark was smart enough to hide his mode of transportation. Looters where common in these woods, so parking the cycle above ground was a good alternative to having it stolen right out from under him. And better, Dia wouldn't realize he had a means to catch up with her.

He swung his leg over the cycle. As he headed south, he activated his

COMM.

"Jared."

"Go for, Jared." His trusted second's voice floated over the unit.

"I need you to take over guard position three by the water fall. I have something I need to take care of."

"Roger that. Be right there. What are you doing, Roark?"

"I'll explain later. Just get here fast."

"I'll be there within five minutes."

"Thanks, Jared."

As Roark set the control on his hover to high-speed and steered the cycle toward his target, he had one thought in mind: *revenge*.

Leaving his cycle in what he considered a safe place, Roark set off on foot. He was close, *really close*. Then he spotted Dia no more than twenty yards ahead of him.

Everything was going as planned until a shuttle's afterburners lit up the calm, Scottish sky. The foreign craft made a swift landing in the clearing in front of him, kicking up dirt and debris as it settled. He watched as a patrol of a dozen uniformed individuals poured out.

Apparently, this group seemed to have the same purpose as him—getting their hands on one beautiful and diabolical woman—because they promptly engaged the fleeing Dia. She began returning the combatants' fire as she scrambled, using the trees for cover.

This wasn't Roark's war, but obviously, if he had a chance to save his wolf, he was going to need to rescue the woman first. Shouldering his rapid-fire laser rifle, he circled around from the opposite side of the enemy and methodically picked off the men, one by one, until he made his way to Dia.

When he came upon her, she was holding her stomach while she hid behind a huge oak tree, still returning fire, taking out as many men as he. Dia was just as accurate with a blaster as she was at seducing a man. He grudgingly admired her determination to continue to fight even injured. Positioning himself in front of the tree next to hers. Roark pointed his rifle point-blank.

"Don't move."

She froze. "Roark."

He enjoyed the tremor in her voice.

"Hello, Dia. You left me in a less than desirable position." He held up his wrist. "I'd like to get rid of these. You're the only one with the proper code."

He studied the woman who had betrayed him. Clutching her abdomen, she let out what had to be an expletive, winced and fell back against the ground.

"I see I'm not the only enemy you've made lately," he snarled as he held his wrist to her. "I should leave you here."

She lifted her head and bared her teeth like a cornered wolf, but unlocked the restraints. But Dia still had a grain of spirit left.

"Leave, then. I didn't ask for your help anyway. Fracking men, not worth a single credit…." Her voice trailed off as her head dropped back and her eyes fluttered closed. The rosy color began to fade from her face. Her chest rose and fell in agitated movements.

Checking first to ensure they had taken out the enemy, Roark knelt to inspect her wound. He peeled back her limp hand. The hole was the size of a lemon. And she was losing too much blood. *Not good.*

His gaze touched on the foliage around them as he assessed their situation. The soldier in him was back and alert to the fact they were in a very precarious situation. Shouldering Wacipi and balancing the weight so he could take them both, Roark lifted Dia into his arms. She didn't even struggle. He shouldn't care about her sudden complicity, but for some warped reason, he did.

When a laser blast hit the tree next to his head, he gritted his teeth and ducked down. Between him and Dia, he had hoped they had taken all the shooters out, but obviously not. Rushing forward with his load, he made his way toward what he assumed was Dia's ship.

She groaned as he weaved up the ship's open entrance ramp. Dia must have been close to making it when the other shuttle landed, which would explain why the hatch was up. He turned and slammed his hand onto what he hoped was the closing device. As soon as the door hissed down, he could hear the muted sound of another laser blast, then subsequent hits on the outside of the hull. He prayed Dia had some sort of force field in place, or they might be dead before he even finished this rescue mission. Placing Dia down on the floor, he jumped into the pilot's seat and tried to power up.

"System is locked by order of the Captain," the computer said. "Unauthorized access is denied."

"Shit." Roark propelled out of the seat and slid down next to Dia. Her coloring was worsening, her breathing shallow.

"Dia. Dia." He set his hands on her shoulders and squeezed.

She moaned and tossed her head from side to side, but didn't respond.

Roark bit down on his lip as he lifted her neck. *Come on, Dia! Come on, I need you to unlock the controls.*

"I hear you. Stop yelling." She raised a hand to her head. "Authorization code Rhiannon Nahiutras, computer unlock controls."

"Authorization code confirmed. Controls unlocked. Welcome back, Captain."

*Yell at her.* What the hell was she talking about? The strange happenings began to tumble into place—his insane attraction, the crazy, uncontrolled, lovemaking, and his stupid need to save her. It wasn't the unconscious Wacipi he had projected into, it was *her*. They were mated. They were a mated pair and making love to her had solidified their bond. Once a Solarian pair intimately bonded, they could hear each other's thoughts. To test his conclusion, he closed his eyes and projected.

*Dia, can you hear me?*

Her eyes snapped open and the green gaze glared daggers at him. "Yes, Roark. I can hear…." Her voice ceased and her eyes closed.

*Oh great. Just great. Wouldn't you know I'd bond with this crazy woman.*

He couldn't afford to sit around and ponder what had happened between them. He needed to get Dia and Wacipi to safety.

Sliding back into the Pilot's seat, he powered up and thanked God Jared talked him into getting his deep space pilot's license. He was grateful the other ship wasn't airborne yet. He wasn't sure he could handle an in-air battle right now.

"Weapon inventory," Roark demanded as he studied the controls. He could do this. Dia's ship controls didn't look that much different then the Solarian fleet shuttles.

"Ship's weapon inventory is full. Two ballistic laser-guided missiles. Three on-board atomic sub B bombs—."

"As soon as I clear the tree line, launch a ballistic missile at the adjacent ship."

"Missile launch order confirmed. Take note, a ballistic missile will not penetrate a model T-51 fighter shields."

"Disable their shields then."

"To disable the shields—"

"I don't care what you have to do. Destroy that ship," Roark yelled as he set his hands on the controls and slowly lifted the bird into the air. The noise in the bay ratcheted up ten-fold as the turbo engines came on line. The stick trembled under his hands. He shifted to the right and maneuvered the ship up and to the side, banking until she was skimming the tree tops. A huge explosion lit up the sky and the blow-by pushed their ship forward. Roark cursed and fought with the controls to straighten their aeronautical axis.

"What the hell was that?"

"Your instructions were to destroy the adjacent ship. I complied with your orders. In order to destroy the T-51 fighter, I was required—"

"Never mind. Cease explanation."

"Complying."

Rolling his eyes at the computer, Roark maneuvered the ship toward the Realm of Solaria. There was only one place he could take Dia. The one place forbidden to outsiders. But she couldn't survive without medical attention and the Realm was the closest station to find a healer. He hit his wrist COMM.

"Stanway, here."

"Stanway. I need you to uncloak the landing site. I'm setting down a ship."

"What kind of ship?" He could hear the shock and question in Stanway's voice.

"Ship, identify yourself."

"I am a Class II, P53, long range, single user, Alagonian vector travel cruiser. I have two rear turbo engines—"

"Ship, cease explanation." Roarck activated his wrist COMM. "It's a P53, Class II Alagonian cruiser. I'll explain later what's going on. Call the medic to stand by. I have one severely injured. Stomach wound. Large blood loss. Also, the vet, please."

"Understood, Commander D'Reincolt."

Roark signed off and concentrated on landing the ship. It had been a while since he piloted a rig like this one. The ten minute ride and landing went without incident.

Wacipi was beginning to stir as he reached down and lifted Dia into his arms. *Hold on girl. Let me take care of Dia, I'll be right back for you.* Wacipi shook her head and laid her muzzle down with a muffled whine.

He carefully lifted Dia. "Computer, open rear hatch."

"Complying."

The door slid open, he simultaneously activated his COMM device.

"Jared here."

"Jared, have a troupe pick up my turbo cycle. Use the finding beacon. Also check for survivors on the ship I just destroyed about fifty yards from the cycle. If you find any, take them into custody.

"What ship?" Roark gnashed his teeth as he passed Dia into the arms of the Realm medic. Did *everyone* need to question him?

"I can't explain right now. Do as I ask. I'll be there to join you as soon as I can."

"Yes, sir."

He returned to the ship and lifted Wacipi into his arms. She let out a subdued ruff. *Hang in there, Wacipi. I'll take care of you.* He cradled her close. She set her muzzle on his arm and gave a lick.

He handed her over to his very capable Realm vet, Shara. "I think she's been drugged. A heavy sedative. It would have been something foreign from the planet Alagon. The same drug was used on me and I'm fine."

"Come with me Roark. Let me get a blood sample and we can do a once over with the medic to ensure you're okay, too." Shara laid her hand on his arm.

"I'll give you the blood sample, but then I have to get back into the field. I've left a mess out there."

Once done giving blood, Roark prepared to leave but was forestalled.

The Solarian Clan Leader was striding toward him with a definite, fast-paced clip, obviously wanting answers.

"Son, what's happening? Are you okay? Who is this strange woman? Do I have to remind you bringing outsiders to the Realm without my permission is strictly forbidden?"

Roark ran a hand over the back of his neck and tried to rub the tightening muscles knotted there. How could he explain what had happened? *Well, father, I was seduced by a beautiful woman while on the most important Realm guard duty. I was too busy fucking her to wonder what was happening around me. I fell asleep after the best sex of my life, then the woman drugged me, tied me up, and stole my wolf. And on my way to rescue Wacipi, I had to blow up a foreign shuttle, so it's possible I started an intergalactic incident. Oh, and we're mated.*

Roark dropped his arms and spayed them wide. "It's complicated, father."

"Well, uncomplicate it for me."

"I'll explain everything later. Right now, I have to go join the troop I ordered into the field. Trust me, father, I will tell you everything that's going on. Just not right now."

His father laid a hand on his shoulder and made eye contact with him. His stern expression wasn't lost on Roark. "I do trust you son, or I would have never made you the Commander of our Solarian Wolf Warrior Security Force. The most important question right now is, are you all right?

Roark softened under his father's concern. "I'm fine. I need to go."

His father lifted his hand. "Go protect our Realm, as you were born to do."

Roark stepped back, gave a single salute, and strode after the medic.

# Chapter 4

Dia moaned, tried to shift, and sucked in a sharp breath when the pain hit her like a laser blast through a failed force field. Opening her eyes, she took in her surroundings and assessed every corner of the room. She was in a wooden structure, possibly a small house. The furnishings were simple, a wooden bench, weaved baskets, a knitted blanket draped over a rocker. A crackling of lumber in the fireplace warmed the room and a beautiful painting of a waterfall rested above the hearth. She spied a high tech mechanism sitting on the table and a digital display beeping on the wall. It was cozy, an odd mixture of old charm and modern technology.

Then she remembered making love with Roark and drugging him. Stealing his wolf and encountering the Lupine soldiers at her ship. Getting struck by a laser blast to the stomach….

Dia tried to move, only to pull in a hissed wheeze at the ache in her abdomen. Didn't take her long to realize her hands and feet were tied to the bed.

"You are awake, I see." Roark's voice rolled over her. She strained against the leather bindings. He came over and sat on the edge of the bed.

*He looked so good.* Better than she remembered. His dusty blond hair was tied back with a leather thong to show the clean lines of his gorgeous face. He was encased head to toe in fitted leather, various weapons strapped to his body, with shiny black boots to complete the outfit. Badges littered his chest and an insignia was embroidered on his upper right arm. Dia always had a weakness for a strong man in uniform.

Just the sight of him sent her heart into a brisk pattern of thumps. Her face flushed with heat as she remembered what it felt like to have him buried deep inside her, the ridges of his hard muscles under her fingertips, the satisfying weight of his body on hers.

He leaned over and began to untie her. As his scent wafted over her, her nipples peaked and pressed against the sheet. *Oh Gods.* She mentally pinched herself. Right now, she had to stop any further musings of sex with this man again.

*Where am I?*

He answered her silent question. "You are at the Realm of Solaria. My home. We are a secret society formed in the thirteenth century to protect the wolves."

"Why am I bound?" She tugged against the restraints and flinched.

"You are bound for your own protection. You caught a fever and began thrashing. You re-opened your wound twice. I can tell there are nightmares in your past, *Mo Daor.*" He finished unstrapping her.

"How long?"

When she was free, she rubbed her wrist and studied his stern expression. His eyes were such an incredible shade of bright blue. She remembered those eyes locking with hers as he entered her. She rubbed the back of her hand over her forehead, trying to wipe out the visions of them making love.

"Three days."

Dia puffed out a sigh, laid back against the pillows and squeezed her eyes shut. No wonder she felt so weak. "What will happen to me now?" She opened one eye and peered at him.

"Make no mistake, Alagonian Captain, Rhiannon Nahiutras. You are my prisoner. You will not leave here without my knowledge." He pointed to a bracelet attached to her ankle. "Directional locator. Set to alert me when you even think of going outside the established perimeter of the Realm. If you attempt to remove it, I will also be notified."

Her eyes widened at his words. "You know who I am?"

"Once you released controls, your ship was very forthcoming. And irritating. She says you cheat at Diamondo."

Dia hid her smile. She had programmed the personality of her ship to match her own. Space travel could get boring. The only one she had to talk to was her ship.

"What happened to the Lupines?" She lifted herself up further on the pillows. The movement caused shooting pain. She gnashed her teeth and groaned. Roark immediately leaned over and adjusted the pillows behind her, then carefully set her up higher. He was a vexing combination of formidable guard yet gentle lover.

"I assume the Lupines were the ones attacking you?"

She nodded.

"I destroyed them and their ship. There were no survivors from the battle. The destruction site has been sanitized. Your ship's computer removed all records of their flight and communicated a delayed distress signal to their home world from a spoofed location in deep space. I believe their people will think a mechanical failure lost the ship in space."

"You are very thorough."

"The Solarians have lived in this cloaked Realm since 1281, when the original Solarian Leader hid his people here to protect them and the wolves from the eradication order of King Edward. I'm not about to reveal our location now. You're lucky our leader has agreed to allow you medical treatment. I had to do a lot of convincing."

Dia ran a hand across her heated brow. She was safe *for now.* "Just out of curiosity, what did you tell your leader?" She tilted her head and watched him. How could she have ever thought of leaving such a magnificent man drugged and tied up? Her mission seemed so unimportant now.

"I told him the truth." His abrupt reply told her she needed to tread carefully.

"And that would be…?" She raised her hands splaying out her fingers.

"That we are a mated pair."

Her mouth dropped open.

*We're a mated pair, Mo Daor. You and I.*

She raised her hand to her head when she heard his voice inside it. She remembered now hearing him there before and feeling him tracking her.

*When we made love, a chemical reaction in our brains mated us in every way. We now have the ability to communicate telepathically as all mated pairs do. I don't know why we ended up mated. Usually this only occurs between Solarian Wolf Warriors. I'm not happy about it either.*

She was staring at his mouth and it wasn't moving, yet she was still hearing him. A throbbing in her temple made her stifle a moan. Roark leaned forward and gently massaged the area.

"I don't understand."

*I know you don't, Dia. Give it some time. You're tired. Get some rest.*

"Roark." She captured his hand in hers. She couldn't explain why, but she felt the need to unburden everything. "I need to tell you why I'm here, my mission. My ship has a tracker, they could send someone after me. I have to explain."

Roark stroked her wrist with his thumb and nodded.

"Is your wolf okay?" she asked.

"Yes, Wacipi is fine."

For some reason, Dia couldn't release her grip on Roark's hand. She had never felt like this before, this all-encompassing need to connect with another person, but it was there, flaring as hot as the logs crackling in the fireplace. She needed Roark.

"Gods." She dropped her head.

"Take it slow, *Mo Daor.*" He tenderly caressed her thumb with his.

"I'm from another planet, Alagon."

"Yes, your ship's computer filled me in on your home world and your medical and personal history."

*Dang computer, I should have programmed it for privacy.* Now Roark had an advantage over her. She sighed. *I guess it doesn't really matter anymore.*

"There's a governing body, The Dange Alliance. The planet has been in the throes of a civil war over land rights between the indigenous Lupine tribes and the invading Dange Alliance all my life. The Lupine had a unique shifting ability which swung the war in their favor. In their shifting form, the Lupines were invincible soldiers."

She studied hers and Roark's married palms. His hand was so large, it dwarfed her smaller one. The difference between their sizes was startling. He made her feel delicate, feminine. It had been a long time since she had felt like a woman.

"Go on, *Mo Daor.*"

"The Dange developed a biological weapon. They introduced it into our community water supply to attack pure Lupine DNA. The weapon was designed to alter the Lupine's DNA pattern, basically rendering their shifting ability inactive. I wasn't affected by the drug because I'm a half-breed and can't shift. I was hired by the Dange to retrieve a wolf with a certain DNA structure. Your wolf, Wacipi carried the pattern I was looking for. That's why I tricked you, why I stole your wolf."

Roark disengaged their hands and paced to the window.

"Do you have any idea what the Dange wanted to do with Wacipi?"

Dia had very little regrets in her life, but right now, she felt totally beneath Roark. She could tell his people were strong and righteous, and here she was, a lowly bounty hunter from the slums of Alagon, trying to explain her greedy actions. What must he think of her.

"I didn't ask. They offered me enough credits to get me off of Alagon. You don't understand how horrible it is there."

"Why did the Lupines attack you?"

"I don't know. I imagine it was to retrieve the wolf. As much as the Dange want the wolf, I'm sure the Lupines want her even more. They have been desperately trying to develop an anti-serum to rejuvenate their shape-shifting abilities. Without it, they're dying. Although I didn't ask, I suspect the Dange have a spy in the Lupine tribe, someone who clued them into the Lupines' intelligence about the wolf. It's likely the Lupines have known where the Shadow wolf was located even longer than the Danges."

He strode from the window, eased down and raised her chin with his finger.

"It was just a job, Roark. I'm sorry." She blinked back tears. What was wrong with her? Why was this man affecting her so much? Her emotions were jumbled so much her head throbbed with the perplexity of sorting them out. She'd never apologized to anyone in her life, but this time, she meant it.

He gently wiped the wet drops from her cheeks. "I understand, Dia. But until we can sort through this mess, you must remain here as my prisoner. I can't allow you to jeopardize any of my people."

"I wouldn't—"

"Dia," he insisted. "My people are my priority. If it wasn't for the fact we were mated, you would have been executed by now."

Her heart pounded.

"Do you understand?"

She gave a shaky nod. She did understand. She realized she was a threat to his people, to their very being, the core of their existence here. She felt honored he had allowed her to join them.

"I don't want to hurt you, Roark, or your people. I won't dispute your right to keep me as a prisoner. Now this mating deal, not so sure about that."

He kissed her, a rough, wild claiming sending tingles to her toes. Gentle Roark was gone, replaced by the masterful man she craved. She buried her hand in his hair and returned his kiss. She could hear him in her head and feel his annoyance at her cavalier dismissal of their mating. *You are mine. Say it. Say you are mine.* His mental chanting was like a constant shout, pecking away at her doubt.

"Yours, yours," she murmured between kisses.

"Speak with your mind," he growled as he trailed his lips down to her jaw.

*Yours.*

He slowly released her lips and sat back. His voice hardened, as well as his expression. "You will have to earn back my trust as well as my people's. Do not publicly dispute my claim. It will only bring problems you're not prepared to deal with. Do not betray me again, Dia."

She raised her finger to her mouth and ran it along her wet, bottom lip. Despite his harsh speech, his gaze followed her movement, his blue eyes turning almost black.

"I understand. I won't let you down." Dia had never been gifted with someone's trust before. The feelings he invoked were beyond confusing. How could he trust her after what she had done?

Roark smoothed her hair from her face. "Rest now."

Roark walked away from his slumbering mate and headed to the security compound. What in the hell had gotten himself into? Could he trust this woman after everything that had already occurred? He wanted to. *God, I want to.*

Only time would tell.

"What can you tell me about Solarian bond-mates?" Dia threw another green bean into the strainer. She couldn't believe she was actually handling real agriculture. On her planet, food grown from the ground had ceased to exist centuries before her birth. Replicators were the norm, and they certainly didn't produce the wonderful Solarian meals with garden-fresh vegetables. The people made a big deal out of eating the evening "fare", as they called it, together. Long wooden benches and tables ran the length of the dining hall in their automatic, temperature-controlled building.

The hall was where everyone met, laughed, shared their lives. The first night Roark had taken her there she'd been stunned nearly speechless at the friendly reception she'd received. She'd been accepted at the table, given a plate piled high with food, and shared in exchanging what Roark called "war stories" but it was really the Solarian male soldiers grandstanding for their mates.

"Roark has not explained this to you?" Allie asked while she too split the end off of each bean and threw it into the strainer next to hers. Allie was Roark's younger sister and a remarkable woman. She'd taken Dia into her home, no questions asked ,and shown her the Realm and the village where most of the residents where housed. They had everything they could ever want here, and the fact it was cloaked from the outside world helped them maintain their old traditions as they kept up with current technology.

"Well," Dia raised her shoulder in a shrug. "We haven't had much time to talk." She nodded her head toward her stomach.

"Yes, your injury has kept you occupied."

"Angus is a wonderful healer. He had me sealed up and back into action within three days. Amazing."

"Yes, Angus is a great healer," she sighed as she peeled another bean with a dreamy countenance on her face. Dia suspected Allie had a little crush on Angus, but wouldn't admit it.

"The bond-mate?"

"Oh. Yes. Well, there was a tale long ago that said two warriors of the wolf would bond together and save Solaria from certain destruction. Once united in an intimate fashion—" Allie paused and blushed.

"Yeah, got it."

Allie cleared her throat. "Anyway, once they were united it was said they would be bond-mates in every way, a mated pair for life. They could use their mind sense with each other, similar to the psychic connection Wolf Warriors have with their wolf protectors. When close to each other, they would even have an increased physical strength, an unstoppable pair. Most of the Solarians expected this tale to be a silly myth until Serena D'Reincolt, the daughter of the Solarian Clan leader, and an Englishman named Lord Roan Aston met in the year thirteen eleven. The two forged an unbreakable bond with their love and became known as the first mated pair of Solaria. All the legend of their powers came to pass. After them, more generations of mated pairs found each other. It's an instinctual bond and it can't be broken. And once you're—"

"Yes, I get it, intimate."

"Then they become inseparable, bonded in every way," Allie finished with a winsome sigh. "I wish I could capture my mate."

"So not everyone will have a mate?"

"No, mostly the Wolf Warriors are the ones who seem to have the ability to make the connection, but some of us non-warriors have been blessed with finding our true bond-mate."

"So you know pretty much from the beginning that you'll be mated if you meet this other person?"

"Well, most do. Sometimes it takes a while, a certain age, the journey through puberty completed, a few have to be coaxed along until they realize they're true mates."

"So it's not always immediate, just most the time. Have you ever experienced it, this bond-mate?"

Angus came shuffling over. The man wore the Solarians' standard baggy leather breeches and a loose-fitting beige tunic. Books were piled high in his arms. His green eyes were covered by a rounded pair of spectacles, and he rushed as if he were late.

"Dia, how are you feeling? Is your wound bothering you?"

He set down the books and stepped forward as if he was going to pull up her shirt in the middle of the dining hall and examine her. She held up a hand. He stopped.

"Angus, I'm fine. It feels great. That balm you gave me has taken away all the pain. It's nearly healed. You're incredible."

"Oh, okay." He ran a hand through his hair, messing it up in an attractive way. "You'll be sure and come to me if there are any changes in your condition?"

"Of course." Dia inclined her head.

"Angus, the annual fall dance is this weekend. You will be going, of course?" Allie said. For the first time since he approached, Angus angled his head toward Allie. His face reddened.

"Yes. Yes. Of course. Yes. Well, I must be off." He picked up the pile of books and turned. One of the books went flying. He stumbled, reached over and plucked it up off the floor, and rushed off.

Allie turned and faced her. She shot up an eye-brow. "See what I mean about coaxed?" She lifted the side of her mouth in a half-smile as she threw her final bean into the strainer.

Dia laughed. There was a merry twinkle in Allie's eyes.

"So D'Reincolt," Dia said. "That's also Roark's surname. I assume your family was related to Serena?"

Allie gave a positive nod. "Roark D'Reincolt is a true warrior. Born into leadership as the eldest son. Our family has led the Solarian Clan for as long as the sacred scrolls can document. You've met our father, the current leader."

"Oh yes, a formidable man." Dia was grateful he didn't order her execution. Didn't hurt that she'd sweet-talked Roark's father into liking her.

Allie smiled. "Yes, he is. One day, Roark will assume his role."

"That's a lot of responsibility, the entire clan." Dia sucked in a long pull of air and whistled it out. She was beginning to understand why Roark was so protective with his people.

A panting Wacipi came loping up. If Dia didn't know any better, she'd say the wolf was smiling.

"Hello, girl." She ran her hand over the wolf's pelt. "Where's Roark?"

"She wants you to come to the practice field," Allie commented.

Dia rubbed behind Wacipi's ear. The wolf shoved her head into Dia's leg, her way of asking for more petting. "Can everyone communicate with the wolves?"

"No, only a Wolf Warrior can communicate telepathically with the wolf who's chosen them."

"Then how do you know what she wants?"

Allie smiled and winked. "I'm guessing."

"You said the wolf who's chosen them. What does that mean?" She'd been curious about the relationship Roark had with Wacipi.

"It's instinctual, the bond between a Wolf Warrior and their wolf protector. The warriors are actually chosen at a very young age, around six. The wolves adopt them in a way, and if they both agree to the union, the wolf opens its mind to the Wolf Warrior. It's very similar to the psychic communication bond mates have, but the wolf doesn't actually talk back. They sort of feel and obey. The trust between the two goes without question. Wacipi was considered the runt of the pack, but that didn't stop her from adopting Roark."

"That's amazing." Dia sighed and tickled Wacipi under the chin. The wolf sneezed and produced a *ruff* noise. What she wouldn't give to have that type of relationship with another. Dia wasn't sure that sort of commitment was in her makeup.

"Shall we go watch the warriors at practice?" Allie stood and brushed her hands together.

Dia slapped Wacipi in the hindquarters. Thinking about watching Roark half-clothed and sweaty gave her rush of heat radiating to the tip of her toes. "Yes, why don't we?"

Dia followed Allie and Wacipi to the practice field, waving at fellow Solarians trekking in and out of the village. It was so beautiful in the Realm. Lush foliage, towering oaks, and jutting rock formations covered in green moss and purple heather enclosed the valley. She pulled in a deep breath and enjoyed the clean and fresh air, so different from the smoky pollution spreading across Alagon from the constant warring. She was amazed at how content she was, but she didn't dare trust the feeling. In Alagon, whenever she felt this happy, without fail, bad news was always lurking around the corner, waiting to set her back. She wondered how long it would take before it showed up.

# Chapter 5

Roark's gaze raked over Dia, noting how her nipples pushed against the soft leather of her top, the way her body moved in synchronization to her sword, the red flush spreading across her skin from her exertions. Her appearance set his body aflame.

In the fortnight since she'd been at the Realm, Roark had gotten to know the guarded Dia of Alagon. Abandoned as an infant to the streets of the harsh planet, a half-breed Lupine/Dange, he could see why she shielded her heart against outsiders. She was used to relying on one person: herself.

Trust wasn't something she gave easily.

He was beginning to understand what had brought her to him, how she had used him to get what she wanted, then promptly left. It wasn't easy getting through the hard shell she had woven around her heart, but he had, slowly, and his people paved the way for him with their kindness and acceptance. He could tell by the frequent smiles gracing her expression these days.

She was outfitted in traditional Wolf Warrior gear, suede beeches and a soft leather halter-top covered with a hand-made vest. Crafted for Solarian Warriors and fashioned after the leather armor of old, the outfit allowed her freedom of movement without restriction.

Roark watched as Dia executed a complicated fighting move and bested her opponent. Her female partner laughed and bowed, and then they grasped wrists in a traditional warrior handshake, indicating the end of the practice session.

For him, these past two weeks had been an exercise in self-denial. He wanted to be sure before he moved forward in his relationship with Dia. Sure he could trust her again.

"I see you've fully recovered." He nodded toward an obviously surprised Dia then shifted his gaze to her fighting partner. "Nora. How's Jared?"

Nora smiled and embraced Roark. "He's sorely pissed to be on guard duty station three for the rest of the month. Keeps complaining about the heat, but I know, deep down, he is honored to be stationed in one of the highest position a Warrior First Class can be placed."

Roark laughed. "Yes, he's an honorable warrior. I didn't want to interrupt." His stare strayed to Dia. She was practically glowing. He fisted his hand. He didn't know how much longer he could take not touching her.

"No, we were just finishing. I have to go grab Toby from school." She turned toward Dia. "You'll come by tonight. Tell Toby a story?"

Dia inclined her head. "I will. Who could resist a five year old with such a cute face?"

"He loves you, Dia."

For a moment Dia's controlled façade faltered as if she didn't know what to say. "I enjoy him as well, Nora."

Nora gave Dia a quick hug and trotted off through the trees.

"It's hard for you, isn't it?"

She pulled her scabbard off the ground and sheathed her sword. "What?"

"Family?"

"I love these weapons." She ran her hand over the leather scabbard. "Primitive, yet effective. Why do you still use them when there are blasters and much more sophisticated weapons?"

"Certainly laser blasters and rifles have their place, as you saw during the battles with your Lupine adversaries. However, technology can be flawed. People grow lazy and overconfident with a blaster." Roark drew his weapon from his back and nodded to her. "But a sword can never be underestimated."

She quirked up a single brow and pulled her sword again. It was a smaller version of his, made for her size, but it was still deadly effective.

"We use swords to remind ourselves of the lessons of old. To hone our battle skills, senses, and balance. Anyone can pick-up a blaster and kill another. But to fight with swords takes cunning and bravery. Honor. Integrity. Skills every Wolf Warrior must master."

He gestured her forward with an upward flick of his weapon.

"Where is Wacipi?" She eyed the area.

"I have given her leave to run with her pack-mates. Sometimes wolves need to function as a pack. They crave the social structure the pack allows them."

"Sure, makes sense." She shrugged her shoulders up and down. In mock battle, she had already bested a good many of his younger Wolf Warriors.

"Why have you changed the subject? Have my people not made you feel welcomed?" he asked as he circled her. They were alone, practicing on the shore of the river. A quiet, serene setting Dia seemed to prefer. He didn't blame her. A perfect environment for him to take control of the seduction this time, not her.

She dropped the line of her sword down to look him in the eyes. "Roark, your people are wonderful. I've never felt like I belong anywhere as I do here."

"Then what's the problem?"

They engaged each other, Dia parrying left, her sword clanging against his as he put her through a complicated practice pattern. She executed it flawlessly.

"Very good." He gave a single nod. "Again."

"There isn't a problem." Dia panted out as she struggled to match his moves.

"Yet you're still uncomfortable letting anyone close to you." It wasn't a question, it was a statement based upon his observations and it needed to be said. She faltered, creating an opening. Roark's sword fell toward her shoulder. He pulled it up before it struck.

"Yes, Roark. I'm still uncomfortable letting anyone close to me." She laid her sword down and held her arms in the air. "There, I said it. Do you want me to yell it? Do you want to hear me scream it from the hills? I don't like to get close to people; they always disappoint me." She dropped her hands to her knees and bent over, panting. Her gaze lifted to his. "Feel better?"

He sheathed his sword, unhooked it from his back and laid it on the ground next to hers. Ever so slowly, he gathered her into his arms. He could tell by her rigid back and unyielding expression, his job was not done.

"I don't feel better. I want you to be happy. My people have accepted you into the Realm. This is no easy feat. Enjoy their good graces, enjoy belonging somewhere. Enjoy being with me," he finished as he trailed his mouth from her forehead toward her lips.

*Be with me, Mo Daor.* It had been a while since he'd spoken to her with his mind sense. *Too long.*

He'd been waiting until Dia was comfortable before he attempted to push her, but now he was getting desperate. A bond-mate without intimacy was like a half who could never form a whole. His soul missed her—that was how connected they'd become in one night of lovemaking. Their fates were intertwined. Dia was his bond mate as sure as a Solarian male could be mated.

*Let me show you what pleasure can be again, Mo Daor. Be with me.*

*Be mine.*

"What is *Mo Daor*?" she puffed out against his lips.

*A term of endearment in my native language, the Gaelic. It means you are my most cherished, Dia.*

"Oh, Roark." She melted against him, a systemic breakdown of all her barriers. Roark could sense it in her mind, feel it in her body, and see it in the heat of her eyes.

*Yes, Yes. I'm yours. Yours, Roark.*

Her returning mind-sense pleased him. She had only communicated with him like this once. It was a relief to again feel the brushing of her mind with his.

"Dia," he moaned and claimed her lips in a kiss so deep, so all-encompassing, he forgot everything but her, the feel of her wet lips under his, the brush of her body against him, the touch of her fingers sifting into his hair, the flowery scent of her.

How had he ever survived without this woman?

His tongue mating with hers, he tried to tamp down on the desperation he felt. She made a sweet noise and wrapped her arms tightly around him.

Roark walked her three steps to a sprawling oak and placed her back against the tree. He grabbed her ass, lifting her off the ground.

"Wrap your legs around me."

She complied. Her heat came in contact with his hardness.

"Feel what you do to me, Dia."

She moaned against his lips.

Taking a deep breath, he gazed down into the face of the woman he loved.

*Can you feel my need? Can you sense it?* He pressed his forehead against hers.

"Yes."

"Tell me what you feel toward me." Roark gently rocked his cock against her.

She groaned as he laved her neck, working his mouth down to her breasts. "Remember me touching your nipples, squeezing them, how good that felt?"

"Yes, Roark. Gods, yes."

*Tell me that you want me, Mo Daor.*

His tongue touched her hardened nipple through the cloth. Her head dropped back against the tree.

"God, Roark, you know I want you. I want you more than anything I've ever wanted."

Roark stopped his onslaught and released her long enough to shed their clothing. They became a tangle of hands and fingers in their impatience to unclothe.

"Roark, someone will come," she protested as she helped him shed her vest.

"No one will come, Dia, except maybe you." He eased her down onto the soft, mossy ground on top of their clothing.

"Are you cold?" He asked as he took his time to lap at each erect nipple.

"No, hot. Really hot." The flush on her face told him his seduction was working. He fingered the flush down her chest to the curls between her legs.

"It is my intention to make you even hotter," he said as he swirled his finger around her clit. Using the wetness, he eased one digit inside. She arched against his hand. He leaned over and worshipped her with tongue and mouth until she was crying out, arching, her body and mind losing control. This was the way he wanted her—under him, mindless, seeking the release only he could give her.

"Roark." Her mouth fell open with long groan as she came into his hand.

*That's it, Mo Daor, ride it out. Feel the pleasure. Fly.*

He worked her with his finger and mouth until she came back to earth with him, her body settling. He rolled over, draping Dia on top of him.

*Touch me. Please.*

He sucked in a breath when her mouth connected with his nipple, lining his areola with her tongue. She sucked the peak in.

*Are you as sensitive here as I am?*

Roark's hands fell to her hair as his lower body thrust up, instinctively seeking to bury itself deep inside his mate.

*Anywhere you touch brings me pleasure.*

She licked her way down his chest to his stomach. He tensed against her hands as she trailed her fingers to follow her tongue. His erection was hard and veined against his stomach, standing straight and straining toward her mouth. She slowly ran her tongue down him, then back up. He already felt like he was going to explode by simply watching her perform the act of tasting his cock.

"God, Dia."

*Do you feel pleasure here?* She asked as she worked around his head them took him full into her mouth. She sucked hard, slid down and up. She raised her head and watched him, poised to take him into her mouth again.

"I can't hear you."

He hardened his jaw and growled. She smiled. She ran her tongue over him and watched him stare at her. His nostrils flared as he moved himself against her teasing tongue, following her.

"Yes," he hissed as she pulled him in and out. She placed her hands on him and went to work on his hardness, sucking, licking, her hands pumping while working together with her mouth. He arched into her.

"Dia, stop." At his command she lifted her head. He leaned forward and tugged her up his body. He rolled her onto her back and settled between her legs.

"I want to be inside you when I come," he said as he ran his hands down her sides and back up to her breasts. Softly kneading her, he slid in gently. He sucked in air and then gave up breathing in response to heated sensations pounding at him.

He was only feeling now, edging into her inch by inch until he was fully seated. He buried his face against her neck and took in her scent, pausing to bring himself under control. She caressed his hair a gentle stroke. *Don't stop, Roark.*

"I won't," he said softly against her mouth, then he took charge and moved inside of her, his lips nibbling on hers. *Such pleasure.* It was like this before with her. An almost animalistic bliss seized hold of him and drove him to take her any way he could, hard and fast. His heart was pounding so rapidly he could feel the pulsing in his cock. He thrust forward, faster and faster, pushing toward the ultimate release. He needed her to come with him, wanted her to take what he was feeling and make it her own. He opened his mind fully to make them one.

"Roark," she cried out as she climbed close to her release. He married their palms as they moved together in unison. Their bodies gleamed with sweat, and the breath he was holding puffed out and fanned her neck. He leaned forward and licked her there, tasting salt as she clutched at his hands. He stayed with her until he felt her so close, a whisper away.

"Come with me, *Mo Daor.*" His voice was rough.

"Yes." She arched against him, her body clenching, her heat milking him. He went with her and she took every drop of cum he had to offer. His body strained against hers. His back arched him closer, then the veins in his neck pumped in unison with his pounding heart as he emptied himself.

She released his hand and ran her fingers up his chest, then slid them into his hair.

Cupping the back of his head, she brought his lips to hers. Lifting her lips, she panted against his cheek.

"That was…." Then she smiled. He adored that cute tilt of her mouth, that sexy dimple. She was such a serious woman, her smile was a gift.

"Out of this world?" he finished.

He hardened inside of her. She tilted up an eyebrow. "Was it now?"

"I don't know. You tell me." With a tilt of his hips he started to move again. She bowed into him and he ground his teeth.

"I'll tell you when we're finished." She released the sentence as a whimper.

His heart began speeding up, tapping against his chest. He couldn't believe she could arouse him again so soon, but she did. She ran her hands down his body and cupped his ass as he plunged into her.

"You do that, you tell me when we're finished… tomorrow." Sweat dripped down his cheek and onto her collarbone.

She smiled and leaned forward to slowly kiss him. "Can we find a softer place to finish this?"

"We can. Soon. My bed," he ground out as he thrust into her tight channel. "Can't. Stop." He was talking like a caveman, but couldn't help it. All thoughts were rapidly leaving his head and migrating to a much needier location.

"Take your time, Soldier," she laughed as she wrapped her legs around his ass.

He *was* going to take his time. He was going to take all night.

# *Chapter 6*

"Sir?" Roark jerked awake when his remote COMM activated.

"Go ahead, Jared." Roark slowly extracted himself from Dia's embrace and climbed out of bed. She moaned and rolled over. She had certainly let down her guard during the evening, weaving a sensual spell around him so tight he never wanted to leave the heat of her body. He *had* managed to get them back to his bed, sometime between the second and third time he'd taken her. The woman pushed his honed control right off the planet.

"We've got activity on the south ridge. A ship, certainly not anything from around here. I'm assuming it's another group searching for Dia."

"Acknowledged. I'll grab a troop of warriors and meet you at the lookout. Post a replacement for yourself at the waterfall and meet us there."

"Roger, Jared out."

"I'm going with you." Dia sat up and pushed her mass of dark red hair back from her face. Her look was sexy as hell. Her eyes were half-closed in sleepiness, a red mark from his suckling stood out prominently on her neck, and the sheet riding low on her chest gave him a view of her luscious breasts underneath. Oh, he remembered taking his time exploring those breasts, sucking those peaks into his mouth, kneading the soft flesh. But he had Wolf Warrior business to attend to. He leaned hard against the wooden kitchen table and clutched the edge to keep from reaching for her.

He inclined his head. "If you'd like."

"I'd like." She tossed the sheet aside, causing his breath to hitch. She pointed at him when he growled.

"Stay right where you are until I can get dressed. I don't trust you."

He shrugged a shoulder as she pulled on her pants. "Now you're just hurting my feelings."

She threw on a shirt and ambled over to him. Positioning herself between his legs, she leaned forward and kissed him on the cheek. Her scent washed over him. The combined musk of the evening activities didn't help him focus on anything but her body under his. His cock immediately hardened.

"Ah, I'm sorry, but see how it misbehaves." She angled her eyes to his erection and raised both brows. "Now get dressed."

He gave her a mock snarl and reached for his clothes. "You'll pay for that remark."

They both took a few minutes to strap on their weapons, swords, and a blaster Roark had lent to Dia.

Roark crooked a finger at her and pointed to the chair. "Sit."

Once she was seated, he reached into the cabinet under the sink and produced a release sweeper. He picked up her ankle and swung the apparatus over her foot. The ankle bracelet bleeped, then tumbled onto the floor.

"I don't think we need this anymore, do you?"

Dia brushed her hand over his cheek. "No, we don't." *Thank you.* He could sense she wanted to say more, but they needed to get moving.

*You're welcome, Mo Daor.*

He ran his thumb down the curve of her neck, fingering his visible mark with pride. *Anytime.* "Now let's go see who's invaded my territory."

⁂

They'd stationed themselves on the south ridge above the foreign ship. Lowering the vid glasses, Dia swiped at the sweat beading her brow and tried to ease the sudden, rapid pounding of her heart.

"It's Zarik Rallan. He's the bounty hunter who hired me for the Dange job. He's very dangerous. Don't let any of your warriors near him. He kills with deadly accuracy." She handed him the vid glasses. He raised them up.

"We'll keep a watch on him. He can't find us. I'm not worried."

Dia tried to keep her mouth from falling open at Roark's casual attitude toward the most feared hunter on her planet.

"You should be, Roark." She grabbed his arm and jerked him toward her. "He's a killer."

Roark tucked her hair behind her ear. He was trying to ease her worries. She could sense his intentions as if he had them written on his forehead. They'd formed a strong bond in the last two weeks that had only been solidified further by a night of lovemaking.

"*Mo Daor.* We are also killers when the need arises. Our people have been protecting the Realm since the thirteenth century. We are more than able to master the task." He gave her one of those gentle smiles she loved so much. Matter of fact, she loved everything about this man. It didn't take her long to fall so deep for him she couldn't see the light of day. It was downright frightening to be this close to another individual.

"How?" She wanted details. She wouldn't be satisfied until she was sure.

He puffed out a breath of air that sounded like a growl and looped his arm around her shoulders as he led her back to his turbo cycle. "We have cloaking device shielding the Realm, so you can't see it, even from the air. We have high resolution motion sensors established around our perimeter, including digital vid interface. And just in case the technology fails, we have lookouts stationed at thirteen strategic locations, each equipped with a high-tech COMM device and plenty of weapons, including long-range sniper rifles. He won't find us. If you'd like, I can give you a tour of the security center when we return to the village and you can see how it all works. Would that make you feel better?"

"Please don't underestimate this man," she warned as she leaned into Roark's body. She couldn't seem to help herself. His strength drew her in. He was everything she'd ever desired in a man. And his people had offered her more than she dreamed of in life—a family, a sense of belonging, a oneness with a society that had always been out of her grasp until now.

"I won't. Don't worry." He turned her into his arms and ran his hand down her back, settling it on her ass. She suppressed a shiver. The man could manipulate her body in ways that went way beyond their telepathic connection. Even his simple touch sent a zing of excitement shooting down her spine. Leaning down, he whispered in her ear, "Let's go back to my place. I have other plans for the day."

She took in a calming breath, trying to reclaim her wits. "You always seem to have plans for me." She grabbed his hand when it started sliding up her side toward her breast.

*Yes, I do.*

When he was in her head like that, she couldn't feel anything but him.

With little resistance, she allowed him to lead her off the lookout and back toward the Realm of Solaria. She learned very quickly she didn't have a lot of power to deny Roark. As they headed down the hill, he instructed his warriors through his wrist COMM to maintain surveillance on the unwanted visitor and to report to him every hour.

Dia pressed her finger to her temple as she followed Roark. He had no idea how dangerous Zarik was, and she had no intention of leaving the man on his own so close to the Realm. She vowed to ensure Zarik didn't drag

the Solarians into his fight between the Lupines and Dange. She had plans
of her own, and she was sure Roark wouldn't be happy about them.

Dia secured the force cuffs to Roark's wrist and then to the top of the
bed post. The bed was solid carved wood. This time, it would take Roark
a while to get out of the cuffs. Enough time to give her the opportunity
she needed to get Zarik off the planet. He moaned and stretched his im-
mobilized wrist.

Dia froze.

Then he snorted and went back to snoring. She blew out a breath. Drawing Wacipi outside, she pointed at her. "Protect him, girl. Don't move from
this spot." Wacipi gave a single ruff and sat down at the front door. Good,
at least one person was cooperating with her today.

Dia quickly strapped on her own gear over her Alagon uniform. Leaving the sword on the outside table, she stroked her hand down the leather
scabbard. She couldn't let Zarik know she had been with the Solarians.
Her purpose was clear: get Zarik out of the area by any means necessary.
As she started the walk out of the Realm, she briefly wondered if she'd
ever see the Solarians again.

It didn't take her long to find him. She established surveillance and
waited until he came out of his ship before she made her move. He was
standing there, taking in the vast green forest as he obviously contemplated
his next move.

"Zarik," she raised her hand in greeting. He turned, blaster up. When
he saw it was her, he restored the weapon to the holster at his waist. She
heaved a silent sigh.

"Dia, this is a pleasant surprise. I was hoping you'd get my communication. Where's your ship? I couldn't pick it up." Dia smiled and stopped
in front of him. *Gods, he is big.* She dropped her head back and made eye
contact with the deadly bounty hunter.

She swung her arm in the general direction behind her. "It's below the
north ridge. I have it cloaked. Had an encounter with the Lupines a couple
of weeks ago. They took out my long-range communications. Good to see
you." She clasped her hand in his and gritted her teeth as she tried to keep
from trembling. "Why are you here?" She pushed her hair back from her

face. He seemed to be lapping up her innocent act like a hungry wolf.

"When I couldn't get in touch, I decided I better come myself and assess the situation." He turned toward his ship and waved Dia after him. "Come on in." She hesitated. She didn't want to be in an enclosed space with him. Better to take a stand in the open. She didn't follow. He stopped and turned around.

"Sorry, no time to socialize. I was actually going to head back to Alagon myself. I've been on this planet for nearly three weeks and haven't found hide nor hair of this Wolf. Apparently, there was this huge eradication of the species in the thirteenth century by King Edward. The last wolf was seen in the late 1600's and then no more." She raised her hands up, palms out. "They're extinct. Gone. Not one wolf in this entire country. Obviously, the source who gave the Dange this information was wrong. Must have missed the eradication time period."

"Hmm. That's a shame." Zarik tilted his head to the side as he studied her with a deadly intensity he'd mastered so well. She tried not to shuffle her feet from side to side. She needed to convince him he was wasting his time on this planet. Zarik hated to waste his time.

"Might as well head back to Alagon. This mission is over."

"Really?" Zarik took a step back and glared at Dia. "Not totally over, Dia. I have one more element to this mission you weren't privy to. I guess if you can't find the wolf, then I'll move onto the second half." In a blink, he drew his blaster from his side holster.

"What the frack?" She fumbled for her weapon.

Zarik sent a blast next to her foot. "Don't touch it, Dia."

She raised her hand from her gun as she stared at Zarik. She could see her own death reflected in his eyes.

He reached forward, ripped her blaster from her holster and tossed it on the ground. He stepped back.

"See, the second part of this mission, after you retrieved the wolf, was to kill you, Dia. Since there's no wolf, I don't see why I need to wait. I have a fair amount of credits coming for the job. Raise them up." He jabbed his gun at her. She slowly raised her hands in the air. If she was going to defend herself, arms up was a better position.

She ran options around in her head. She was in real deep frack now, so she did the only thing left to her. She cried out for Roark with her mind sense.

Roark jerked awake and was immediately taken aback by the fact his arm was positioned above his head and didn't seem to be moving.

"What the hell?" He jerked his wrist, only to have it rebound back. *Not again.*

"Dia," he screamed as he tried to rip the force cuff off. His struggles only caused the cuff to tighten. Glancing at his wrist, he could see she had removed his COMM unit. He was going to kill her this time. Fury seethed out his skin like steam from boiling water. He was absolutely going to murder her. This wasn't even funny.

*Wacipi. I need you in here.* With a distinct scratching noise and rapid barks, his wolf came barreling through the door as if the fires of hell were on her heels.

*Wake the village. I need to be released. Now!*

Giving a bark, Wacipi raced off. He'd have a discussion with his wolf later. Suddenly, he heard a yell from Dia in his mind.

*Roark. I'm in trouble.*

His anger abated as fear ripped through his chest.

*Hold on, Mo Daor, hold on.*

Dia heard Roark's answer in her mind. He knew she was in danger. If she could only stall Zarik long enough for Roark to get to her.

"Now, Zarik. Seems like a waste of good female flesh to just go and kill me." She cocked her hip and dropped her chin. The oldest trick in the planets had certainly worked to seduce Roark. Could it work on Zarik? She concealed a shudder of revulsion.

Zarik's blaster wavered. "What did you have in mind, Dia?" I'm open to your proposal." The sneer Zarik gave her, along with his gaze cruising over her body in a blatantly sexual way, made her want to vomit. She was in serious frack, but at least she had his attention.

"Well, I'm sure we can arrange a little trade," she offered, despite the fact her gut was churning.

Zarik circled the wrist holding the gun. "Do continue."

She was playing him hard now. She'd heard of Zarik's famous need for the hunt. On Alagon, he'd paid dearly for the privilege of tracking live prey. He was also notorious for a sexual appetite rivaling the best paid companion.

"You like a good hunt, don't you Zarik?" By the way his eyes lit up at her question, she assumed she had hit his hot spot. "You give me a five minute start." She gestured to the forest behind her. "And if you can catch me, I'm willingly all yours." She reinforced her offer by unzipping her uniform and caressing the swell of her breasts pressing their way out the front. "If you can't catch me, you're out of luck. You tell the Dange you fulfilled your contract, and I'll stay off Alagon for the rest of my life."

"What's to keep me from taking 'all mine' anyway?" He arched up his forehead.

"Never heard you were into rape before, Zarik. Thought you enjoyed your partners willing." She dropped her arms and picked at her fingernail, her pulse throbbing so hard she could feel it at the base of her throat. "Certainly not much of a challenge that way, is it? How long has it been since you had a good challenge?"

"I like your style, Dia. Have I ever told you that before?" He stroked the end of his blaster over her cleavage. "I would like to have a little sample of what lies beneath that uniform. And a willing taste is even sweeter."

"So it is." She lifted her lips in a smile and lowered her eyes.

"If I happen to kill you on the hunt, so be it."

Dia slid a hand down her throat. "So be it."

Zarik gave a decidedly curt nod and sheathed his blaster. "You've got five minutes, Dia. I suggest—"

Dia didn't even wait to hear the rest of his suggestion. She took off running as fast as she could, hoping she could make enough gain in five minutes to save her life, or at least to give Roark enough time to get to her.

Five minutes should be plenty of time for her to make some head way. Dia mentally swore as she hugged the back of the huge oak and prayed Zarik would pass by without noticing her. *Why did he have to be such a good tracker?* Now she wished she hadn't left her sword on that table outside Roark's house.

Just thinking about Roark made her mouth dry and her palms sweat. She might not live to see him again, touch him, love him. Sure, she'd tried to keep her emotions out of their relationship. But she'd failed miserably. If she had to guess, she'd say she'd fallen in love with him the first time she'd laid eyes on him, outlined by the crashing waterfall behind him, tall, muscular, his sword strapped to his back, dusty blond hair falling into his face. A true warrior through and through. Her soul mate. What if she never had a chance to tell him how much she loved him? Regret left a bitter taste in her mouth.

"Come on, Dia. I can smell your fear. You don't think you're fooling me, do you?" Zarik sang out as he neared her hiding place. She picked up a log.

She held her breath as he took another step. If fear had a scent, then yes, she was fracked good. As he walked around the side, she eased near the back of the tree and came at him from the rear. Using the log, she drove the wood into his skull as she kicked him behind the knee. He faltered, stumbled and fell.

Hand to hand might be the only way to take him. She kicked out and struck him in the temple. He rolled, and came up with his blaster in hand.

He shot, and she dove.

The blast hit the tree, sending bark flying. A piece embedded in her flesh. She could feel the heat of her own blood running down her arm. Several more blasts followed and she took off running. She crashed through the trees, Zarik behind her. She could hear the stomp of his boots and the rhythm of his breath as he ran. *Too close*, he was too close.

"Very good, Dia. But you can't outrun me."

Branches cut at her face as she stumbled on. Another blast singed her side. She cried out and veered left. The foliage opened up into a clearing, leaving her wide open for an attack. She ran toward the opposite tree line, but she could feel Zarik right on her heels. Panting, Dia tried a zig-zag pattern, but Zarik's next blast hit her in the calf, taking her down to the dirt with an "oomph" temporarily knocking the breath out of her. Blood running down the side of his face, Zarik stood over her, weapon raised.

"It's over." Zarik waved his blaster. "Get up."

Placing her hands on the dirt, Dia tried to push into a standing position, but the ache in her leg radiated pain to her toes. She could tell the nerves were shot. Her leg was going numb and not obeying her orders to lock. That couldn't be good. Setting her jaw, she tried again, only to slip back down to the dirt.

"Well," Zarik raised his gun and pointed it at her head. "Willingness seems to be off the table, Dia, much to my disappointment. Guess I'll just dispose of you now."

Darting her gaze, left, right and left again, Dia searched for an escape.

"Don't bother. No one's going to save you now, Dia."

All of a sudden, the surrounding trees came alive. A dozen men seem to melt into the clearing, snarling wolf protectors at their sides. They were so at one with the background, it was almost as if they had already been there, waiting and watching. They formed a circle around Dia and Zarik. Simultaneously, they drew swords, sending a ripple of sound through the forest. *Holy frack*, if she didn't know they were on her side, she'd be frightened.

"I don't think that's true. I think Dia has several Wolf Warriors at her assistance."

"What the frack?" Zarik whirled, taking in the troop of fierce warriors encircling him. While he was distracted, Dia scooted back on her elbows, trying to inch as far away from Zarik as she could get. Zarik started to laugh, a low pitched cackle that made the hairs on Dia neck stand on end.

"You have intruded on our territory." Roark stepped forward, his sword poised in front of him in a battle-ready position. Wacipi stood by his side, all her razor-sharp teeth exposed, the black hair on her back standing straight-up.

"Do you all expect to cut me down with those swords?" Zarik raised his blaster and swung it in a circle. "I could take every single one of you out right now with one press of this button."

Dia had to agree with Zarik. She wondered how the frack these warriors expected to best Zarik with technology on his side. Why hadn't they brought their own laser rifles?

"I invite you to try," Roark said as he assumed a fighting stance.

Zarik shifted his gaze back to Dia. "Is this your rescue squad?" He shook his head as a smug grin crossed his face. "Maybe you better think about keeping company with a more advanced group of warriors." At the drop of his statement he pivoted, blaster in hand, and began to shoot a steady stream of heated laser toward the warriors.

Everything happened so fast, Dia barely got out a warning yell before the Solarians and wolves sprinted into what appeared to be a choreographed dance. Roark crouched and dove at the same time. The blast fell over his shoulder, ineffectively hitting the ground, while the other warriors scrambled in separate directions with lightening speed. None of them were hit with the laser.

Roark jumped off the ground in a move so graceful her mouth fell open. His sword in hand, he did a somersault, a dip, then came up from underneath Zarik and drove his sword directly into Zarik's heart. Dia had never seen anyone move so fast.

Zarik screamed, dropped his blaster and clutched his chest. He swayed, and finally, his knees buckled as he dropped to the ground. "Frack," was his final statement before he collapsed, face first into the multi-colored leaves covering the forest floor. He didn't move. Wacipi sniffed him and barked, as if to say, *he's done, all in a day's work.*

Panting, Roark stood over Zarik, bloody sword in hand. "Never underestimate your opponent, or a good sword." He nodded to the warriors around him. "My thanks. Sorry your assistance was not needed. I can take it from here." They all sheathed their swords and blended back into the foliage.

Dia shook her head as she clutched at her leg. She could feel the world beginning to spin. Had she just imagine Roark and his warriors saved her in a matter of seconds? Maybe it hadn't really happened. Roark *was* the only one standing before her now, and his image was blurring in and out.

Roark leaned down and eased Dia into his arms. "This is becoming a habit with you, *Mo Daor.* I have a shuttle beyond the trees. I'll have you back to the Realm and under the care of Angus in no time." Dia hung onto his neck as he carried her inside the small shuttle and laid her across the seats. He broke out a first aid pack and injected her with something.

"Ouch," Dia whimpered as he pulled back the auto injector.

"This will slow the bleeding, and take away the pain until Angus can fully seal your wound. Better?"

Dia nodded. The fog was lifting, clearing her head. "Someone needs to take care of Zarik. No one can see him or his ship," she groaned as he began to tightly wrap her leg.

"Jared has been assigned to clean up your friend's mess."

"He wasn't my friend."

Roark's brow furrowed as he worked on her leg. "I don't know what in the hell you were thinking."

She could see he was keeping a fine rein on a temper about to bubble over. She ran her hand over his brow, trying to soothe the anger she sensed.

*I was thinking I would dissuade him from coming any further into your Realm.* She spoke with her mind sense now, wanting to connect with him on the deepest level they could.

*You'd do good to remember the Solarians can protect their own. We work as a team, Mo Daor, not on our own. That fact aside, mated pairs do not separate, even in battle.*

His blue gaze trailed up from her leg to lock with hers. She could see his fury now, and something else, something she couldn't name. Concern, worry, and a deeper emotion she hoped to hold onto—love.

*I'm not used to relying on others.*

*Get used to it! We are a bonded pair, Mo Daor. We do not separate. You do not tie me up with force cuffs and go out on your own. We do not part like that.*

His mental tirade ceased when Dia pressed a finger to her head. His words were strong and angry; they pounded at her brain like a knife. She felt his hand on her face. His fingers replaced hers on her temple as he circled the area with his thumb.

"I'm sorry." His touch helped sooth the pain in her head. "I love you, Mo Daor. More than I can say, more than words will communicate. You are my life now, the other part of me missing all these years. I want you to feel you belong with us. I want you to stay and be my mate in all senses of the word. Tell me you want the same." He stroked her hair back from her face and gently kissed her cheek.

Dia's head was swirling at the implications of what he was saying.

*You love me?* She felt weak with emotions.

*Yes. I love you.* He answered in kind, his lips claiming hers in a soft kiss.

"Stay with me," he said as he slid his lips from her mouth to her neck.

Dia clutched her hands in his hair and raised his face up.

"Are you sure? You've seen what trouble I can bring to your people. Are you sure you want me to stay?

"I can protect you, *Mo Daor*. You're mine now. I'm sure. The question is, are you sure?"

Dia wrapped her arms around Roark.

"I'm sure, Roark. I love you with everything I have. I'm sure. How did I ever live without you?" Tears leaked out of her eyes and ran down her cheeks. She had never cried as much as she had these past two weeks. She prided herself on always being strong and in control. This man had broken down every barrier she had erected, and it felt good.

"Don't cry, *Mo Daor*. Don't be sad. This is good. We should celebrate." He dabbed the wetness from her cheek.

She shook her head and let out a relieved laugh. "I don't think these are sad tears."

He smiled back, that sexy grin that sent her heart rapping against her chest.

"Can we talk about this tying you up thing? I kind of like you, under me, all helpless and at my mercy," she said and watched his eyes go dark blue.

He chuckled and kissed her deeply. She was panting and achingly aroused when they came up for air, ready to fall back into bed with him for another all-night lovemaking session.

"I'll leave some room for negotiation there, with certain parameters."

"With certain parameters," she agreed.

"Let's get you home," Roark said as he laid her back against the seat.

"Home," she murmured as she closed her eyes. She was finally home, and with the man she loved.

## *About the Author:*

*Rae Monet is a multi-published, award winning, sensual romance author and speaker. She is former Air Force, FBI agent and now is a licensed Private Investigator as well has having a Bachelor and Masters Degrees in business. Rae loves to write strong female characters, lots of action, and hot romance. Please come explore her other books on her website* www. RaeMonet.com.

# Bad to the Bone

❧◌◍◎◌❧

## by Natasha Moore

## *To My Reader:*

I was a good girl, I admit it. Maybe that's why I love stories where a good girl throws caution to the wind and hooks up with the kind of guy her mother always warned her about. I hope you enjoy Annie and Luke's story.

# Chapter 1

"Whoa, look at these two. Anyone recognize them?"

Luke Kendall glanced up from the pitcher of beer he held. He was getting ready to pour a second round. Or was it the third? Even though Sean sat right beside him and Dave, his voice was loud enough to carry across the entire bar. All the guys in the area whipped their heads around to scope out the newcomers.

Hot. Both of them.

Luke remembered the shorter one. Lacey Brooks appeared about the same as he remembered with her long blonde hair, big blue eyes and turned-up nose. Same curvaceous body poured into a shimmering gold dress. He'd had his hands on that body a time or two. The memory made him smile.

But it was the tall, shapely brunette beside her that made Luke catch his breath. He set down the pitcher before he spilled beer all over the table. Who was she? Did he know her?

Wild chestnut curls spilled over her shoulders. Wide, dark eyes sparkled beneath long lashes. Lush red lips moved slightly. He wished he could hear what she was saying to Lacey. What did her voice sound like? How would her lips taste?

He found himself standing as the two women turned toward their table. Sean and Dave glanced curiously at him and then stood up too.

"Good evening, ladies," Luke said, using the smooth practiced tone that never failed to charm women. He caught the eye of the sexy brunette and her warm gaze washed over him. Hot gaze, was more like it. She seemed a little familiar, but he couldn't place her.

"Hey, Luke," Lacey said. Her voice was as cold as a Buffalo blizzard. Damn, was she still holding a grudge after all these years? "I didn't think you'd come all the way across the country for our reunion."

"Are you kidding? Couldn't pass up a chance for beer and wings at Bernie's," he replied lightly, his eyes still focused on the brunette. "Would you like to join us?"

"No, I think we'll—"

"We'd love to," the brunette cut in. Her voice was a husky mix of sin and seduction. She slowly rounded the table and lowered herself into the empty seat next to Luke. Lacey frowned but sat down beside her.

Luke and his two closest friends from school sat down as well. The three of them used to hang around the local garage, shooting the breeze and learning about cars. Who'd have ever thought back then that he'd open his own little garage and build it into a successful business?

His stomach clenched as he thought about Vanessa. He had to remind himself that his business was still successful. The jobs were still coming in. He had plenty of work to do.

If he could afford to pay the mortgage and his employees.

Luke drained the rest of his beer. He wasn't going to worry about it this weekend. He was going to chill, catch up with his friends, and have a good time. Sunday would be soon enough to get back to the real world.

He and Sean and Dave had been talking non-stop all evening, catching up on their lives, but now that the women sat down, there was an awkward silence at the table. Luke poured them all a glass from the pitcher of beer.

Then the brunette spoke up.

"Luke Kendall, right? I don't think we ever had any classes together, but you stopped and helped me once when my car broke down on the way to school."

Luke frowned. Who the hell? He remembered a beat-up Chevy with a cracked distributor cap on one of the coldest mornings of the year. But that had been—No way. He took a closer look. "Annie Shane?"

The laugh was low and lazy, but he saw a flicker of what might have been uncertainty in her eyes. "So you do remember me."

He lifted an eyebrow. The Annie Shane he remembered had worn dumpy clothes and been a hall monitor. He let his eyes travel over her, noting the swell of her breasts spilling out of that skimpy top. The long length of leg bared by the short skirt. "You've changed."

"So have you." She took his hand and spread his palm on top of hers. "No grease under your fingernails."

Sean and Dave burst out laughing. Luke would have joined in, but he couldn't make a sound. He could barely catch his breath. Her hand felt so smooth against his calloused fingers. His palm itched with the need to touch her everywhere. Her heated gaze caught his and he felt his engine rev.

Suddenly, she dropped his hand and glanced away. "I'm starving," she said. "How about some of those wings?"

"Sure, I'll go order them." Luke stood up. He needed to back away for a minute before he spontaneously combusted. He wasn't sure what Annie's game was, but if she was offering, he wouldn't turn her down. This was looking to be one hell of a way to wipe the worries out of his mind. "How do you like them?"

She grinned. "Hot."

Of course.

Annie's legs were shaking as Lacey dragged her to the ladies room while Luke ordered the wings. Lacey practically pushed Annie through the door before turning on her.

"What do you think you're doing?" Lacey leaned back against the sink in the tiny room and crossed her arms in front of her.

Annie could barely think about anything but Luke's dark eyes raking over her body. She'd never had a man gaze at her like that before. As if he were burning the clothes right off her body. "I told you I was changing my image. I'm a bad girl now. How am I doing?"

Lacey let out a string of curses that practically turned the air blue. "Clark Brown is an asshole. Don't let what he said push you into doing something you're not ready for."

Annie looked away from Lacey and felt her cheeks heat up. It was weeks ago, why couldn't she get over it?

"He told me I was boring, Lace. Plain and boring. Like it was my fault he fell asleep during sex. I should have been the one falling asleep!"

"Sweetie, don't let one lousy guy make you do something crazy."

"He's not the first. Just the only one to say it out loud. I am boring." She took a deep breath. "Past tense. Was boring. Not going to be any more." She straightened the tight shirt that stretched across her breasts and adjusted the deep V that exposed more cleavage than she'd ever shown in her life.

Lacey frowned. "Maybe I shouldn't have loaned you that outfit."

Annie thought about Luke's hot gaze on her and itched to get back to the table. "Let's go back out."

Lacey grabbed Annie's hand. "Look, you put your life on hold while you took care of your mom. No one deserves getting out and enjoying themselves more than you do. But you're just getting back into the dating scene. You need to start by getting your feet wet. Not jumping into the deep end with Luke Kendall."

"Oh, God, he's so hot." Annie could think of a few things she'd like to jump into with Luke. Then she clasped her hand over her mouth, as if she'd actually said the words out loud. What had gotten into her? The minute she walked in the bar, she'd been drawn to Luke, and it had to be more than his rugged good looks. Maybe it was because of the charming bad boy vibes he put out. Maybe he was exactly what this newly discovered bad girl needed.

"He's way out of your league," Lacey went on. "He'll eat you up for dinner and be on to someone new by dessert."

"Is that experience talking?"

Lacey grimaced. "Yeah, I was the flavor of the week during spring break our senior year."

"Ten years is a long time," Annie said. "Maybe he's changed." She gasped softly. "Or maybe he's married."

Lacey shook her head. "Dave told me he's still Mr. Non-Commitment."

"Good." Annie turned to the mirror and fluffed up her already wild hair. "He's just what I need."

"What are you talking about?"

"Come on, Lace. I'm not looking for Mr. Right. I'm certainly not looking for a commitment. You're right, I'm ready for some fun in my life. And Luke Kendall is perfect for what I have in mind. Don't worry. I know what I'm doing."

Lacey shook her head. "I hope so."

Annie led the way back to the table where Luke and his friends were sitting. The tangy scent of wings made her mouth water. So did the sight of the guy at the table waiting for her. Luke's blonde hair curled over his collar and shone in the shadows of the bar. She'd like to think his dark brown eyes lit up when he saw her, but she couldn't give herself that much of an ego boost.

But she did feel incredible tonight. Sexy and strong. Powerful. She'd never felt that way about herself before. It may have started with Clark and the borrowed clothes and the wild hair, but Annie knew it was more about attitude. And she was changing her attitude for good.

Make that for *bad*.

Luke stood again as she reached the table. He held out the chair for her, and brushed his hands against her shoulders when he helped push her in. Shivers of awareness ran through her. Or were they shivers of nervousness? Was he as bad as Lacey made him out to be?

"Man, Luke, you're giving us guys a bad name," Sean said with a whine in his voice. "My wife gave up on me helping her with her chair years ago."

"Yeah, and my wife would tell me she's more than capable of getting into a chair by herself," Dave added.

"Of course she is," Annie said with a smile. "But that doesn't mean she wouldn't appreciate your showing a little consideration now and then. Try it, you might be pleasantly surprised."

"You really think so?" Dave asked.

Lacey rolled her eyes, then turned her attention to Luke. Her smile had an evil slant to it. "So, Luke, do you have a wife and kids back in— California, is it?"

"Yes, I live in California. No wife and no kids."

"You mean you haven't found a woman you'd like to settle down with?" Lacey asked. Annie kicked her under the table, but she barely flinched. "Or aren't you the settling down type?"

"Settle down with one woman?" Luke started to laugh, but must have thought better of it when Lacey glared at him. "No. I haven't been lucky enough to find a woman to settle down with. No offense to you married guys, but I don't think it's going to happen for me."

Their wings arrived and after the baskets were passed out, Luke slid a sidelong glance at Annie. "How about you? Are you married?"

"Nope. Not looking to either." She picked up a chicken wing. The tangy scent of the hot sauce went straight to her already stimulated brain.

"A woman who doesn't want to get married?" Sean exclaimed. "I didn't think they existed."

"Sure we do. I agree with Luke a hundred percent," Annie said. "Life's too short to settle for only one man. There are too many out there I haven't sampled yet."

Lacey started coughing and Annie patted her on the back. "Wicked hot sauce, huh?"

Soon Annie's fingers were coated with sauce from the wings. She'd started to lick off the sauce when she thought she heard a strangled sound next to her. Her index finger was still in her mouth when she glanced over to Luke. His eyes darkened as he stared at her. His mouth hung slightly open.

She slowly slid the finger out of her mouth, meeting his gaze as he watched her suck off the rest of the sauce. He looked as if he were aching to devour her. Her heart pounded at the sight of such naked hunger.

She tore her gaze away and grabbed a napkin to wipe what was left of the sauce off her fingers. As she concentrated on the napkin, she suddenly found herself fighting a smile. Wow, she did that to him.

The bar was filling up with people. Annie recognized quite a few of them, but she had no interest in making the rounds of the other tables. She wanted to stay by Luke. To hear him talk and feel his smooth voice pour over her like hot fudge. She ached to touch him too. But the good girl deep inside her stopped her from reaching out and putting her hand on his strong arm. Or better yet, on his muscular thigh.

Oh, God, already she wanted to do more than simply touch him. She wanted to taste him. Tempt him. Tangle with him.

Nerves tickled her stomach. Was she actually thinking about seducing a man she'd only met a couple hours ago? The heat from his eyes threatened to melt all the makeup Lacey had put on her face, so she didn't think he'd take much persuading. But was she ready for a one night stand?

A slow song played on the juke box. The need to touch Luke overrode the sensible side of her. She was a bad girl now. She could go after what she wanted. Bad girls didn't have to wait for the guy to make the first move.

She put her hand on his shoulder. The heat, the strength of him seemed to vibrate beneath her hand. He turned from whatever he and Sean were talking about.

Annie leaned close to him so she wouldn't have to shout over the din of the conversations all around them. "I love this song. Will you dance with me?"

A quick grin spread across his face. The wolfish gleam in his eye simply made him all the more appealing. "I'd be happy to." He stood and pulled her chair out. "Excuse us."

She rose and he put his hand on the small of her back as they made their way through the crowd to the tiny dance floor in the corner of the barroom. When they reached the polished wood, Luke slid his arm around her waist and curled her into his embrace.

She slid her arms around his neck and brazenly pressed up against the hard length of him. Whoa. Tremors of desire swept through her like a wildfire.

"Annie. Annie," he murmured. His voice was rough now, his breath warm against her cheek. "What are you doing?"

She rubbed her breasts lightly against his chest. "It should be obvious what I'm doing."

He stepped back slightly and frowned at her. "Annie, what happened to the nice girl..."

She leaned forward and brushed her lips against his. Tingles buzzed through her, the kind she'd never experienced with any of the good guys she'd dated. "I'm not a nice girl."

He groaned, but pulled her tightly against him once more. "Annie..."

She rubbed her cheek along his and then whispered in his ear. "I'm bad, Luke. Bad through and through."

He chuckled, but the sound was a little shaky. "I see. You're a bad girl now." He captured her lips with his then, quick and hard. Almost bruising. She started to pull away, but he plunged his hands through her hair, cupping her head with his hands and holding her there. His lips brushed against hers when he spoke again, his tone mocking. "Yeah, I can see you're bad. Bad to the bone."

Annie tried not to tremble. It was easier than she thought to ignore the little voice screaming at her to run away fast, before she got in over her head.

She slid her hands along either side of his face and stared at his lips. "Does a nice girl kiss like this?" she murmured, just before she crushed her lips to his.

# Chapter 2

Luke was surprised as hell when Annie urgently pressed her lips to his, but he couldn't help but go with the flow. He opened his mouth to her insistent tongue. She slid her tongue along his lips and they tingled in response. Then she plunged into his mouth and he drank her deeply, memorizing her taste. She moaned and he swallowed the sound.

His heart rammed against his ribs. His cock strained against his fly. He almost slid his hand up to cup her breast, but then he remembered they were in the middle of the crowded dance floor at Bernie's.

It wasn't as if he'd never had women throw themselves at him. Most of the women he hooked up with at car shows came onto him first. Since he spent a lot of time on the road, he recognized the fact that there was something about the attraction of a short time fling that seemed to appeal to a lot of women.

There certainly had never been a woman who wanted to stick around and get to know him. Not even his mother.

He still couldn't read Annie. One moment she seemed so sure of herself, the next he thought he saw uncertainty in her eyes. Her body trembled beneath his fingers. Was it bad girl desire? Or good girl nerves?

He rubbed her back lightly with his hands. The thick blood sloshing through his veins caused a roar that nearly drowned out the sound of the music. He swayed slightly from side to side, so it would appear as if they were still dancing.

But as she moved her mouth over his, nibbling his bottom lip, sucking on his tongue, all his blood deserted his brain for parts farther south. He couldn't think anymore, couldn't wonder about the woman in his arms, or why he thought he should be protecting her from herself. He could only feel her wet lips sliding against his lips. Her soft body rubbing against his body. He could only react to the buzz of desire thrumming through his system and want more.

He buried his hands in her thick hair and answered her kiss with enthusiasm. Her body fit so well against his. Her soft breasts pressed into his chest, the hard nipples burning through his shirt. Her hips wriggled against his, pressing up against his already hard and aching cock  Oh,.God, he didn't know how much more of this he could take.

Suddenly, someone bumped into him, knocking them apart. Through a haze of passion, he saw Dave laughing at him, swinging his hips on the dance floor beside them. When had Dave come up here with a former football cheerleader? When had the music changed to a fast song?

"Come on, you guys," Dave called out, "why don't you get a room?"

Annie's face turned an attractive shade of red, nearly matching that tiny strip of skirt she wore. She might claim not to be a nice girl anymore, but Luke was foolishly pleased she could still be embarrassed.

"Got a room already," Luke said lightly. At least he hoped his voice sounded light. He grinned at Dave, trying to act as if his body wasn't so aroused he was ready to explode at any minute. Simply walking back to the table without limping would be a feat. He threw an arm around Annie's shoulder. "Come on. I'm ready for another beer, how about you?"

He gave her credit for the lopsided grin that spread across her face. She had to have been as aroused and aching as he was. She looked up at him and her sparkling eyes seemed to hold a promise.

Of the night to come?

He threaded his fingers through hers and led the way back to the table. Lacey and Sean were still sitting there with several other old classmates. Luke sipped beer and exchanged stories, all the while acutely aware of the woman sitting beside him.

As the evening wore on, half a dozen different conversations droned on around him. People came and went. Some he recognized, some he didn't. But the only face that was clear was Annie's. She wasn't even touching him, but he could feel her there. He could smell her soft scent even over the smell of wings, popcorn, and beer. She was all he could think about.

He planned on taking her up on that earlier promise. He'd peel that tiny skirt off her luscious body. He'd strip that poor excuse for a blouse from her body and explore what lay beneath. His mouth would enjoy every square inch of her skin before the night was over. He would bury himself deep inside her soft body and he'd make sure she came apart in his arms.

He enjoyed sex. He wasn't going to apologize for it.

He enjoyed women. He wasn't going to apologize for that either.

Annie's hand trailed up his thigh and his muscles twitched in response. He raised his eyes from the glass of beer he'd been contemplating and met her come-on gaze. She took a sip of beer, her eyes never leaving his. Then she ran her tongue slowly along her upper lip, washing off the foam and leaving her lip wet and shiny.

"So, I hear you still work on cars," Lacey called out from across the table. Luke reluctantly tore his gaze away from Annie's and buried the desire to kiss those wet lips.

"I restore classic cars," he told her, still feeling the sweet burst of accomplishment that went along with it. Nothing Vanessa had done could take that away from him.

"Sweet," a skinny guy standing nearby said. Luke thought he recognized him from homeroom. He wore a suit and tie, unlike most of the guys here in casual clothes. Probably a lawyer. "I'm into classic cars myself," the guy went on. "I bought a sixty-nine Camaro that needs some major interior work. I sent it out to Classic Car Restorations of Southern California. They're supposed to be the best. You ever heard of them?"

Wow, what a rush. Luke wished his old man was still around so he could rub it in his face. Oh well, a high school reunion was the next best thing.

"The best, huh?" Luke said, feeling a silly grin spread across his face. He stood up and shook the guy's hand. "That's my place. It's nice to hear we have a good reputation here in the east."

"Oh, man, yeah. Everyone I talked to said that was the place to go. And it's your place? Sweet. Is it a big operation?"

"We've grown a lot in the past few years," Luke said. "Started with only me and a one bay garage about seven years ago. Got a whole crew working for me now." He pushed away the dark worries of making payroll and contemplating lay-offs.

"So do you still get to work on the cars yourself?" Annie asked, looking up at him.

How could she know he missed working on the cars? Missed getting his hands dirty and turning something broken into something beautiful?

He sat back down beside her. "Not as much as I'd like to. I mostly handle the business end of it now. And travel around the country to car shows. Meeting old friends. Drumming up new business." And once all his troubles got straightened out he was going back to being a hands-on kind of guy.

That was a promise to himself.

Annie's eyes grew wide. "You get to travel all over the country?"

"Is that a hint of envy I hear in your voice?"

"Well, yeah. I haven't exactly traveled anywhere."

"Why not?"

She shrugged. "Too busy working."

"Don't you get vacations?"

A shadow fell over her eyes. "Yeah, but traveling hasn't been practical lately."

He could tell there was a story here. And not a happy one.

"Don't pick on her," Lacey called out.

Pick on her? "What–?"

Annie placed the tips of her fingers on his lips. He barely resisted the urge to take them into his mouth. "Ssh, it's okay," she said. "Don't let her get to you. She's got a thing against men right now."

"I—I—no, I don't," Lacey sputtered.

Annie stared her down until Lacey blushed and looked away.

Then Annie leaned over until her lips were brushing his ear. Shivers of awareness ran through his already aroused body. "Would you like to go somewhere quieter?"

He nodded and leaned over to whisper in her ear. "I'm staying at a hotel a couple blocks from here. We could go to the lounge for a drink."

"Or we could just go to your room."

Well, that was straight and to the point. His hard-on strained against his pants. "Yeah, if you're sure that's what you want..."

She jumped to her feet. "Hey, see you tomorrow night, guys."

"Where are you going?" Lacey asked with a frown.

Annie leaned over and kissed her cheek. "I'll call you tomorrow."

She glanced at Luke, raised her eyebrows and grinned. When she grabbed his hand, he let her pull him toward the door. As soon as they were out onto the sidewalk, she leaned back against the side of the building and sighed. "Wow, the quiet sounds wonderful, doesn't it? It was getting so noisy in there."

"And crowded," Luke agreed. He faced her and put his hands against the wall on either side of her head. A streetlight shone overhead, so he could see her clearly. But did he really see her at all?

He tried to search for answers in her face. Her eyes were greener than he thought they'd been in the shadows of the bar. Her skin was smoother, softer, even more lovely. He couldn't resist brushing one finger along her cheek. "Is this really what you want to do?"

She appeared to be searching his face too, but with the light at his back, he must have been mostly in the shadows. She wouldn't try too hard. No one did.

She nodded and gently brushed her lips against his. "You said you had a room?"

Annie tried to keep her hands off him until they got to the room. She really tried. But after they crossed the quiet hotel lobby and got on the elevator, she couldn't resist stepping into his arms as soon as the doors slid shut.

She inhaled his musky scent and soaked up the warmth of his body next to hers. "Mmm. I wish I'd been a bad girl in high school."

He laughed. "Oh, yeah?"

"You know, I always thought of you as like that guy in the movie, *Grease*, working on his car." She felt a little foolish admitting it to him, but once the words were out of her mouth, she figured she might as well go on. "You remember? He sang about the car being 'Greased Lightning' and how it was a chick magnet."

"Wait a minute." Luke stepped back and stared at her. "You thought about me back in high school?"

Annie rolled her eyes and began unbuttoning his shirt as she went on. Her hands hardly shook at all. "He made out with the bad girl in the back of the car. I always wanted to do that."

"You never made out in the back of a car?"

Oh, great, now he'd know how inexperienced she really was. She started to rain kisses down his chest as she released each button, like she'd seen some actress do in a movie. She'd never admit that everything she knew about sex came from the movies or guys like Clark.

The elevator opened and they stepped into the hall. She curled her arm around his and tried to sound blasé. "Yeah, I know, hard to believe from a bad girl like me, huh? The opportunity just never came up."

"Well, um, maybe we can take care of that sometime."

"I don't own a car," she said. She looked around at all the doorways lining the empty hallway. She could hardly believe she was walking down a dim hotel hallway with a man to his room. "Do you have a car here?"

"Yeah. It's out in the parking lot."

"Well, that wouldn't work, would it? There's all those big security lights. Maybe we could drive out to a dark road somewhere, huh? What do you think?"

"To have sex?" Luke stopped halfway down the hall and slid his key card in the lock. He turned back to look at her and the gleam in his eye heated her even more. "How about a bed?"

He opened the door and motioned her in. She stepped into his hotel room and tried to ignore the pounding of her heart. A king-sized bed dominated the small space. "Well, it's a bit conventional, but I guess it'll have to do."

She heard him close the door. She felt him standing behind her. The heat from his body seared her skin and they weren't even touching. She wished he'd take the first step. Say something, or reach out to her. But she knew this was her night, her idea, her step to take. She closed her eyes for a moment and took a deep breath. Was she ready to do this or not?

# Chapter 3

She turned and stepped into his arms.

His mouth was hot as it captured hers. Hot and wet and hungry. His hands were everywhere, one moment caressing her back, the next tangling in her hair. Then he lowered his hands and cupped her bottom, pulling her harder against him. His rigid arousal pressed into her.

She broke off the kiss so she could look at him. His dark blonde hair framed a face that was just rugged enough not to be pretty. Long lashes lined those chocolate brown eyes. The sly smile on his face was obviously in reaction to her appreciative attention.

"Oh, you are too beautiful," she said on a sigh. With shaky hands, she tugged the shirttails of his deep blue shirt out of the waistband of his slacks and then fumbled with the rest of the buttons. His bare skin was hot as she slid the shirt over his shoulders and down his arms. It fell and crumpled silently on the carpet.

"Mmm," she murmured, then rained open-mouthed kisses along his smooth, muscled chest. She slid one hand down across his flat, rippled abdomen. Wonderful. There was nothing soft on this body.

Not that she was comparing him in any way to Clark.

"My turn," he said, the words coming out half laughter, half groan. In an obviously practiced move, he grabbed her blouse and stripped it up and over her head. She knew the flimsy black lace bra didn't leave much to the imagination and had to resist the urge to cover herself.

"Talk about beautiful," he said, that charming tone back in his voice. "Come here."

He grasped her waist, his hands hot on her bare skin. She followed him as he backed up to the bed. When he sat down on the end of the bed, he drew her in between his open legs. She shivered as she realized her breasts were even with his mouth. He fastened his gaze on hers and slowly licked his lips. Her knees nearly buckled. He slid an arm around her and tugged her close. Then he took one lace covered breast into his mouth.

Shocks of desire zapped through her body and Annie dropped her head back. Luke sucked deeply, drawing her nipple into his mouth. Her knees weakened and she grabbed his shoulders to steady herself. There was a throbbing between her legs greater than she'd ever experienced before and her panties grew damp.

"You're very good at that," she said with a gasp. He could keep doing that for the rest of her life as far as she was concerned.

He released her nipple and she almost whined with disappointment. "Is that from one expert to another?"

His eyes sparkled, but he was breathing as heavily as she was. "Of course. I just wanted to give you my expert opinion."

"Glad I measure up."

She could hardly believe it when she actually reached down and cupped his erection through his khakis. "I'd say you measure up just fine."

He growled and grabbed her waist. He pulled her, laughing, onto the bed with him. She rolled onto her back, her head falling back onto the lumpy pillow. Luke straddled her, his thighs on either side of her hips. His thick shaft was heavy against her stomach. The throbbing between her legs grew stronger.

He reached out and traced her nipples through her bra. "We have to get rid of this thing."

"Oh, yeah." Annie couldn't get rid of it fast enough. She twisted the clasp and released her breasts from the lacy fabric. She slipped the straps off her shoulders and tossed the bra away with a flick of her wrist.

Luke's hands latched on her breasts. He squeezed their fullness and then rolled her sensitive nipples between his fingers. She moaned in delight and arched up against him.

"You like that, huh?" She could hear the humor in his voice. He leaned over until his mouth was poised over one tight beaded tip. "How do you like this?"

He took a nipple with his teeth and gently teased the pebbled peak. An electric charge seemed to run from her nipple to her clit and the pulsing power increased with each twist of his teeth.

"Oh, Luke," she cried. She raised her hips, pressing against his hard arousal. She was gripped by a primitive urge to rub her lace-covered mound along the length of his zipper.

Lacey's skirt was up around her waist and the stupid pantyhose were twisted. Everything was in the way. Frantically, she struggled to peel the stockings off without interrupting the exquisite torture Luke was performing on her nipples.

But he sensed her struggles and released his grip. He helped her get rid of the stockings and the skirt, but didn't strip the red panties from her bottom. Instead, he reached down and cupped her mound with his hand. He ran a finger along the damp panties, tickling her sensitive flesh, teasing her with the light pressure.

"You like this too, don't you?"

"Yes," she gasped. "Yes, I like it all." She reached out and unbuckled his pants. "I think it's time for these to come off."

Luke grinned and stood up. "You are so right." As he stepped out of the pants, she stared at the black boxers he wore. Or rather, the obvious erection beneath the black boxers. Luke noticed her staring at him and slowly slid his boxers down his hips. When his rigid penis sprang free, Annie sighed, loudly and deeply.

"As you can tell," Luke said, climbing back onto the bed, "I'm really ready for this. I hate to tell you, but you've got me so hot, the first time might be kind of quick."

The first time? "Oh, yeah?"

Wow, *she* got him so hot? No one had ever told her that before. But she couldn't forget he thought she did this all the time. She took his shaft, hot and smooth, into her hand. "Glad I haven't lost my touch."

He moaned and rolled on top of her. When he ran his tongue along her neck and down to her nipples, the delightful pulses of need started again. But while she thought he might linger there, he continued downward.

"Open for me, Annie," he said in that charming, seductive tone he did so well. He dropped down off the edge of the bed and knelt on the floor. Then he grabbed her ankles and pulled her down to meet him.

Blood thrummed through her veins. Desire throbbed through her body.

She knew what he was going to do. Had heard of it. Read about it. Wondered about it. But none of the guys she dated had ever even hinted at being interested in oral sex.

He stroked her thighs, and after just the tiniest hesitation, she bent her knees and opened herself to him.

He grasped her thighs and pulled her into position. The first long lick from that velvet tongue had her nearly going through the ceiling. Who knew it could feel like this? Why had she never felt anything like this before?

Sensations spiraled quickly, beginning at the very core of her, touching every part of her. Wild currents of excitement built within her, growing stronger with each stroke of Luke's tongue. Oh, God, she never knew. Never imagined it would feel like this!

She grabbed onto his head, curling her fingers into his silky hair. Her hips began to move in a frantic rhythm, rubbing herself harder against his amazing tongue.

When she shattered into a million pieces, laughter burst from her mouth. And yet she wasn't surprised to taste her salty tears. Incredible waves of sensation pulsed through her, making her body move in ways it never had before. Luke's tongue continued to stroke her gently as the waves crested and receded, and she pulled herself back together again.

"Oh my. Oh my. Oh my," she said as she pulled him up next to her on the bed. She wrapped her arms around him. "I've never—" She stopped. She'd almost admitted she'd never had an orgasm before. "I've never come that quickly before. You must have a magic tongue."

He chuckled. "I told you I wouldn't last too long this time, either. I wanted to make sure you got taken care of first."

Who had ever said he was a bad guy? He reached over the edge of the bed and she heard him rummaging through a bag. A moment later he came up with a condom. She was fascinated by the pleasure that washed over his face as he closed his eyes and rolled the condom over his rigid penis.

He caught her eying him and smiled. "Do you want something?"

She nodded.

"Tell me what you want."

Oh, God. Did he want her to say the words out loud? Annie felt her muscles clench with the desire to have him deep within in her. "I want you."

He raised his eyebrow and remained still, kneeling beside her on the bed, his erection standing at proud attention. "How do you want me?"

The words rushed out of her. "I want you inside me, Luke. I want to feel you deep inside. I think I'll go crazy if you don't get over here right now." Probably not what a bad girl would say, but no other words would come.

He laughed softly and straddled her hips. "I sure don't want you going crazy." He stared down at her for a moment, the intensity in his expression making her shiver. Then he whispered, "Open for me, Annie."

She spread for him, slick and wet and ready. He entered her slowly, inch by rigid inch. So slowly, she decided he wanted to drive her crazy after all. "More, Luke, more," she whimpered. "I need it all." She wrapped her legs around him and pulled him deep within her.

At first, he kept his strokes slow, pulling almost completely out before burying himself deep within her once again. And again. He obviously was trying to draw out the pleasure a little longer. But he didn't have any more luck than she did at delaying the inevitable. Soon he picked up speed, plunging into her, the slap of skin almost as loud as the moan escaping her mouth. He cried out her name as he came, thrusting into her over and over with a frantic need she could finally understand.

Then he collapsed on top of her and she wrapped her arms around him. Oh, this felt way too good. No wonder bad girls were bad.

Once his breathing returned to normal, Luke groaned and pushed himself off of her. He placed a quick kiss on her nose and got up. "Be right back," he said and headed for the bathroom.

Annie didn't know nearly enough about being a bad girl yet, but she knew bad girls wouldn't hang around. She wanted to lay there and bask in the satisfying fatigue of well-used muscles, but she reluctantly got up off the bed and gathered her scattered clothing together. When she put her bra back on, the lace was still damp from Luke's mouth. Her panties were wet and twisted and it took a few frazzled seconds before she could step into them. Lacey's skirt and top didn't look all that great, either. She put them on the bed and tried to smooth out the wrinkles. Now where were those pantyhose?

"Where are you going?"

She glanced up from where she sat on the floor, struggling with her twisted pantyhose. Luke looked magnificent standing there, even with a frown on his face. Annie indulged for a brief moment to really study him naked for the first time. Tanned muscles, washboard abs, penis standing at attention again. She wanted to reach out and touch him, but she knew she would get distracted. "I can't stay. I have to work in the morning."

"Oh." Did she hear disappointment in that one word? She thought there were shadows in his eyes for a moment, but just as quickly they were gone. "Well, you're going to the dinner/dance tomorrow night, aren't you?"

"Sure."

"Will you go with me?"

What would a bad girl say? She looked up into those deep brown eyes and didn't give a damn what a bad girl would say.

"I'd like that." Yeah, but did she have to sound so breathless when she said it?

"Can I pick you up?"

She shook her head, feeling a little headstrong at the desire Luke displayed. "I'll meet you there."

He helped her to her feet, then swept a wayward strand of hair away from her face. "Are you sure you don't want to stay for a second round?"

She let him gather her back into his arms. His musky scent filled her senses. His warmth seeped into her bones. Without the heels on, her head rested comfortably on his shoulder. What did he just say? "Um, second round?"

He stroked her back, starting at her shoulders and caressing her all the way down to her bottom. "We tried hard and fast. We could slow it down a little now and enjoy it more."

Boy, it was tempting. Her body nearly melted beneath those hands. "I... I enjoyed it just fine."

He pressed his hard arousal into her stomach. "We could enjoy it longer."

She couldn't stay. If she did, she'd never leave. "I really have to get up early tomorrow."

He sighed. "Well, then maybe tomorrow night we could try to make it last more than thirty seconds?"

She kissed him deeply, then pulled away before she changed her mind about leaving. At least she had tomorrow night to look forward to. "Great idea."

"Let me walk you to your car."

She shook her head and curled her fingers into fists before she touched all that gorgeous male flesh. "No car. I, um, I rode with Lacey. I'll have the desk call a cab."

"I'll drive you home."

She started to decline, but saw the stubborn look on his face. He wasn't going to let her go out by herself at night. And actually, she appreciated his concern.

"Okay."

They were both quiet while they finished dressing, but she felt his eyes on her the whole time. When they were ready, he grabbed his keys off the dresser. "Thanks for the warm welcome back to town."

She grinned and walked in front of him to the door of his hotel room. She threw a glance over her shoulder. "My pleasure."

Annie wasn't sure what was going to happen after this weekend. She was just starting to get the hang of this bad girl thing, but of one thing she was positive. After one night with Luke Kendall, she was never going to have sex with an uptight good guy again.

It would be bad boys all the way.

# *Chapter 4*

Ray's Service Station looked nearly the same as it had the last time Luke was in the neighborhood. The white paint might have been a little more faded now on the doors of the two service bays. The gas prices posted on the tall sign were certainly higher than they'd been in the past. But as Luke walked through the door and up to the counter, the years rolled away. Ray Benson looked up and smiled at him with the same toothy grin he'd always had.

"Hey, son, how's your day going?" Ray wiped his hand on his grease-stained overalls, then held it out to him.

Luke shook the hand of the man he always wished had been his father. "Couldn't be better, sir."

He looked around and knew things had been better for Ray. Both service bays were empty. No one had pulled up to the gas pumps in the few minutes he'd been here. Independent service stations, like other small businesses, had a hard time competing with the huge conglomerates.

"I hear things are going well for you out in California."

"I'm keeping busy," Luke replied, though the knot in his stomach sunk a little lower. There was no way he was going to tell Ray that he lost all his money to a dishonest, discarded ex-lover.

"From what I hear you got a waiting list a mile long."

Luke shrugged. It was the only thing keeping him going. "Not quite a mile."

"You always did know your way around an automobile. I'm real proud of you."

Damn, he was choking up. "You taught me everything I needed to know to get started."

Ray nodded. "What brings you back to Buffalo?"

"Don't suppose you'd believe me if I said I wanted to see your ugly face again?"

"Hell, boy, I could e-mail you a picture."

Luke laughed at the image of the old man in front of a computer. He shook his head. "Not the same." He leaned against the counter. "Class reunion's this weekend. Catching up with Sean and Dave." He grinned at Ray. "And I thought you might like to take a look at my latest project."

Ray's eyes lit up. He peered over Luke's shoulder, trying to see out the grimy windows behind him. "Where is it?"

"Come on out and see."

Luke followed Ray outside. When they rounded the building, Ray whistled at the Corvette convertible Luke had spent the past year restoring. "She's a beauty. Fifty-seven, right?"

"On the nose."

"Did you drive her out here from California?"

"Sure did. Hit one car show on the way out. I'll stop at another one on the way back."

"On the road a lot, aren't you?"

"Yeah." Luke sighed. If he couldn't be honest with Ray, who could he be honest with? "I used to love it, but I have to admit it's getting a little old. I'd rather spend more time getting dirty in the shop instead of on the road playing nice and drumming up business."

Ray nodded. "Still no one back home waiting for you?"

"You know me. I'm not the kind of guy a woman wants to stick around with."

"Don't be foolish," Ray said sharply. He stared at Luke with those bright eyes that never missed a thing. "Did you ever think you might be pushing those women away before you can get too close?"

"What?"

Ray put his hand on his shoulder. "Son, just 'cause your mama left you doesn't mean every woman's going to do the same thing. If you give a good woman half a chance, you might find someone special to settle down with."

Settle down? Not ready to think about it, Luke lifted the hood so Ray could take a look at the engine.

"V8?" Ray asked.

"Yep, fuel injected."

For the next few minutes, they went over the entire car, every feature, every detail. Luke hadn't realized how much it meant to him for Ray to see what he had done.

"Why don't you take her for a spin?" Luke asked when he saw the old man was dying to get behind the wheel.

"Don't have any help coming in 'til noon."

Luke tossed him the keys. "Go on. I can pump gas if someone pulls in while you're gone."

Ray took off with a gleam in his eye. The wheels squealed as he took the corner and Luke winced and laughed at the same time. He'd almost spent more time here at the station than at home. He hated to think what his life would have been like if Ray hadn't taken him under his wing. Ray showed him that a man didn't have to be angry all the time.

Luke grabbed a cola from the machine next to the door and sat down on the bench in front. A woman with long dark curly hair walked down the sidewalk. She didn't look anything like Annie, but that was all it took to put her back in his mind. As if she hadn't been in his mind ever since she walked out his door last night

He still didn't know how to read Annie. She was trying so hard to convince him she wasn't the good girl he remembered, and in some ways she wasn't. His body stirred as he thought of the ways. But there was something else about her.

Something sweet.

He had the feeling she wasn't as bad as she pretended to be. But if she wanted to play the bad girl for the weekend, he wasn't going to complain. Only next time he got her into his bed, she wasn't running away so quickly.

The dragon lady was in rare form today. Myra Montgomery kept throwing more and more reports on Annie's desk, telling her she needed the results immediately. The way she was going, Myra was going to give herself a stroke.

Annie didn't usually work on Saturdays, but with the IRS auditing one of their biggest clients, she'd agreed to put in some time this morning. Myra had recently been promoted to manager and she obviously was feeling the pressure. The problem was she took it out on everyone else. Annie used to like her job, but lately she'd been considering looking for a new one. She just didn't know where. Myra screeched into the telephone. Right now working at a fast food restaurant didn't sound all that bad.

To top it off, Annie's mind wasn't even on the upcoming audit that had her boss in such a state of anxiety. She couldn't stop thinking about Luke. About last night. About tonight. The feel of his hands on her body.

The things his mouth could do to her.

The numbers in front of her blurred as she tingled with the memories. Her nipples puckered with nothing more than the thought of his fingers playing with them. Would he tease them into tight little buds again tonight? Would he slowly build her body into a frenzy again, stroking and licking and sucking until she came apart in his arms? Her sex clenched with the mere thought of another night with Luke.

She kept glancing at the clock, but the hands were moving way too slowly. When she'd agreed to work Saturday, how could she have known she'd meet up with Luke just at the time when she was ready to finally spread her wings?

She didn't regret spending the last few years taking care of her mother during her slow, doomed fight with cancer. Almost a year after the funeral, she'd finally stopped reaching for the phone to call her mom to chat. Annie never knew her dad and even as a child she understood how hard it was for her mom to work and raise a daughter all by herself. So Annie had been the good girl and never caused any trouble. And turned into the boring woman Clark accused her of being.

No more.

She was going to have some excitement tonight. A thrill ran through her. She imagined the look on Luke's face when he saw her walk into the banquet room in that little purple dress. Better yet, she imagined him peeling it off of her, little by little, his lips following his fingers as he slowly bared her skin. Then she'd strip off his tie and drape it over her bare shoulders, letting her nipples peek out from beneath the soft silk. She'd slowly unbutton his shirt and then rip it out of the waistband of his trousers. The belt would come next. And then the zipper.

Whew. Annie picked up a tax statement and began to fan herself. When had it gotten so warm in here?

Myra burst out of her office, tearing Annie away from her daydreams. "Bad news. We're going to have to work all evening on these reports. The CEO wants them on his desk in the morning."

Annie jumped to her feet. "But I have plans for tonight."

"You'll have to cancel then," Myra said, glaring at her. "There's nothing that could be more important than this."

"Yes, there is." She thought about Luke's mouth. His hands. His zipper. "I have plans." She took a deep breath. Had the air always smelled so stale in here? "I can't work tonight."

"You'll work tonight if you want a job," Myra replied, her voice as cold as the blood that must have flowed through her veins.

"Well, I don't want *this* job," Annie heard herself saying. The good girl, the responsible one who did the right thing and worried about how to pay the bills, screamed silently in protest. The bad girl, the one who thought about Luke and a life of excitement, grabbed her purse from the bottom drawer of the desk and lifted her chin. "I quit."

# Chapter 5

"I can't believe you did it!" Lacey exclaimed as they climbed out of her car in the restaurant parking lot. "How could you quit your job when you don't have another one lined up."

"Actually, it was pretty easy." Annie tugged down the short purple skirt and tried not to stumble in the stiletto heels she borrowed from Lacey. Acting out of character seemed to be the new norm for her lately.

Or maybe she'd actually changed her character. Things would work out somehow. She wasn't going to worry about it tonight.

"What are you going to do now?" Lacey asked.

"Now? I'm going to go inside, get a good stiff drink, and find Luke Kendall."

"Luke Kendall certainly isn't going to support you."

Annie stared at her. "I can't believe you said that. Support me? I don't need anyone to support me. All I need is someone to have good time with this weekend." And that's as far ahead as she was going to look right now.

They reached the door to the restaurant. Once inside, they followed the signs down a hallway toward the banquet room. A flood of people milled around the registration table. She recognized quite a few of them from high school. Excitement buzzed through her. She wasn't in the least apprehensive as she had been only yesterday. Maybe it was the outfit she'd armored herself with. Maybe it was knowing that her life was never going to be the same again.

Luke must have been waiting for her, because the moment she and Lacey left the registration table with their name tags, he appeared beside her. He stepped up to her and brushed his arm against hers.

"Hi, beautiful." His voice was soft and smooth.

He smelled wonderful. Some mixture of spice and musk and Luke. She took in the loose black jacket, tight black slacks, bright white shirt and colorful tie. Somehow she knew he'd be wearing a sexy tie. He looked so sharp, and knowing the muscular package beneath, made him appear even sexier to her.

She turned into his arms, surprising herself by feeling strangely shy, suddenly awkward and unsure of herself. "Hi there." Her voice was soft, tentative even, but if he noticed any change in her, he didn't comment. He simply ran his hands along her back.

"Did you wear that dress to drive me crazy?"

She grinned. His light-hearted words somehow put her at ease. She pressed her hip up against his. "Is it working?"

He groaned. "What do you think?"

"Then, yes, I did."

Lacey sighed loudly. "Can't you at least play hard to get?"

If Lacey only knew how easy Annie had been to get. Bad girls didn't bother with that. She winked at Luke, but answered Lacey. "Nope."

Lacey shook her head. "I'm going to get a drink."

Annie nodded, but didn't turn away from Luke's gaze, even though she could hear the whine in Lacey's voice. "Okay, Lace. I'll see you in there."

Luke cleared his throat and stepped slightly away from her, his hands resting on her waist. A few people wandered around them, but Annie barely registered their presence. She was overwhelmed by the solid weight of his hands on her hips, the heat from his skin seeping into her body.

"I suppose we should go in and get a seat," he said. Did he sound as reluctant as she felt? After looking forward to this reunion for weeks, now she could care less.

She nodded in response to his words, shocking herself for even considering grabbing his hand and high-tailing it for his hotel room right now. "Um, yeah. We did come here to see our old classmates, right?"

He smiled, a come-on grin that had her knees trembling. "Right."

"And we have already paid for the dinners."

"Yes, we have."

He took her hand and the slide of his fingers against hers reminded her of the slide of their bodies in his bed last night. Oh, she wanted to go back there right now. But, of course, they headed toward the entrance to the banquet room.

"Or there's my favorite reason for going in there," he said lightly.

"What's that?"

"Seeing the envy on the faces of every guy in the room when you walk in with me."

She stopped and stared at him. "Wow. You do that good."

He frowned. "Do what?"

"Spread those lines like honey."

"Sweetheart, that's no line. You're a knockout."

She hadn't been fishing for a compliment, but a rush of pleasure swept through her all the same. A bad girl was probably used to hearing those kind of words from the mouths of bad boys, but Annie Shane wasn't. She let herself smile and then reached out to smooth his tie. "I think you may drop a few jaws in there yourself, handsome."

"Oh, I bet you say that to all the guys."

She laughed out loud at the thought. "You know, there's probably quite a few of our classmates in there who will be shocked to see the two of us together."

"The hall monitor and the detention regular?"

She tucked her hand under his arm. "Exactly."

"Then let's go in and raise a few eyebrows."

Luke didn't really care what anyone else thought of him. He'd learned to let all the comments about white trash and his drunken old man roll off his back years ago. He'd only come to town to see Sean and Dave.

Running into Annie was an extra bonus. An unexpected pleasure. He rested his hand lightly on the small of her back. Her slinky dress dipped so far down, he could almost touch her soft skin. But he decided to wait until they were alone. If he started touching her now, he wouldn't be able to stop.

They wound their way through rows of round tables covered with long white tablecloths and decorated with streamers and confetti in the red and gold school colors. A few classmates stopped them to say hello. A few more stared as they walked past. Luke wasn't interested in any of them, but Annie seemed to get a kick out of their surprise at seeing the two of them together. Or maybe their surprise at how much she'd changed.

"Whoever planned this should be shot."

At the sound of Annie's outrage, Luke pulled his attention from the way her hair softly curled around her jaw. "What?"

She pointed to the wall in front of them. Large black and white year-book pictures of everyone in the class covered the entire wall. A lot of people were checking out the pictures, pointing and laughing and commenting. Luke led her over to where his picture was, a portrait of a cocky gear head who couldn't wait to get out of school

"You didn't like your senior picture?" Luke asked, searching the wall for hers.

"No." She pulled at his hand. "Let's go find a table."

Luke didn't push it. He'd already caught a glimpse of the young Annie, her hair pulled back in a frizzy ponytail, a serious expression on her face. Sure, she'd changed. But her basic beauty had been there all along.

Luke caught sight of his friends. Sean and Dave brought their wives with them tonight. Luke had met them each at their weddings, but hadn't seen them since. Sean's wife, Ginny, was a tiny blonde with a ready laugh. Dave's wife, Heather, was a tall redhead with a face full of freckles. Luke and Annie joined them at their table and they were soon swapping stories of their high school days.

"So the guys tell me you were very different back in high school." Ginny looked at Annie in that purple piece of sin she was wearing.

"Guilty as charged," Annie replied. "I was a regular goody-two-shoes back then if you can believe it."

"And we're so glad she's changed," Luke said. He leaned over and kissed her neck. She didn't smell soft tonight. She'd put on some kind of pungent perfume that tickled his nostrils and made his blood pulse just a little bit faster. "Hey, I'm ready for a drink, how about you?"

Annie nodded. "Surprise me. Bring me something wet and wild."

She was surprising him every minute. Luke lifted his eyebrows and grinned. "Babe, that'll have to wait for later." Laughter rang out around the table. He kissed her on the nose and then got up to get the drinks.

Luke had just given his order to the bartender when he heard his name called.

"Luke, old buddy!"

He looked up to see Bob Kulig approach him. Buddy? When had they ever been buddies?

Luke shook his hand. "Hey, Bob. How are you? Looks like life's treating you good."

Bob looked fit and tan. Gold chains sparkled beneath the open neck of his bright blue shirt. "Hear you work on cars out in California."

"Classic cars. I specialize in restorations."

"Yeah? Well, what do you know, we're in the same business."

"You restore cars too?"

"Nah. Sell them." He laughed loudly and nudged Luke with his elbow.

"Hey, was that your wife you walked in with?"

Luke shook his head and wished for the bartender to hurry it up. "Never been married."

"Yeah? Me, I'm divorced. I'll tell you what, that's a looker you have there," he said with a smarmy smile.

So Bob didn't even recognize Annie. Good. Luke wasn't going to enlighten him, either.

Luke may have looked forward to the reaction of other guys seeing him with Annie, but he didn't like the thought of creeps like Bob gawking at her. He tried to shake off the unexpected emotion. He had no business feeling jealous.

Jealous?

No way. He didn't get jealous.

"So, is she, like, your steady girl?" Bob asked.

"No. Just a date for tonight."

"Yeah? What's her name?" Bob winked at Luke. "Give me her number. I specialize in one night stands. I'll have to give her a call."

Luke froze. No way in hell. The bartender finally came with the drinks and saved him from growling an obscenity. "See you around," Luke called over his shoulder as he headed back to Annie.

Dinner conversation was light and fun. Sean and Dave seemed happy and their wives did too. Luke was in awe of anyone who actually made marriage work. He couldn't imagine any relationship that lasted years. His parent's marriage had barely made it to five. He couldn't seem to make any relationship with a woman last longer than a few weeks, a few months at the most.

Annie drove him crazy sitting beside him in that made-for-sin dress, brushing up against him every chance she had. He had a perfect view of her cleavage and felt no remorse at checking it out every chance he got.

When they danced after dinner, her body fit against his as if they were made for each other. While the thought should have made him uneasy, Luke realized he kind of liked the idea. He didn't want to think too closely about what that meant.

When the band took a break, they all headed back for the table. Luke noticed that Dave held the chair out for his wife and couldn't help but grin at the surprised smile Heather flashed her husband. The guys started telling stories about hanging around Ray's service station, learning to change oil, change tires, and change their opinions about a lot of things in their lives.

"Sounds like Ray set a few restless kids on the right path," Annie said.

"You got that right," Dave said.

"Remind me to stop in and thank him some day soon," Heather said, curling her arm into Dave's.

"I stopped by to see Ray today," Luke said. "Is his business always that slow?"

Sean nodded. "It's not good lately. Most people hit the big stations with the cheaper gas and the convenience stores attached."

"I think he's going to retire soon," Dave said. "He's been talking about moving south to the warmer weather."

"Hey, he could go out to the west coast and see you," Sean said.

"He'd be welcome any time," Luke said. When Ray retired, a big part of his past would be gone. What would happen to the building that was so much a part of his history? A crazy thought burrowed itself into the corner of his brain. Something to think about another time.

"So, Annie," Ginny said, "what did you do today while Luke was doing the guy thing?"

"I had to put in some overtime," she said, making a face that told everyone what she thought about that.

"That sucks," Ginny replied.

"Poor Annie," Luke said. He turned to smile at her and when she smiled back, she simply took his breath away. Then he slid his hand onto her lap beneath the tablecloth, caressing her thigh because he couldn't wait to touch her again. Her bare leg was soft and warm. She shifted her leg closer to him, a blatant invitation. "So how was work today?"

She slid her hand along his leg underneath the table cloth. Her long fingers danced across his thigh. "I quit."

He stared at her. Did he hear her right? She didn't seem upset. In fact, she slid that tantalizing hand farther up his thigh, squeezing his flesh, teasing him with her proximity to his groin. "What? What happened?" The others at the table joined in with their questions.

"My new boss has been riding me for months. She told me I had to work tonight or else." Annie laughed, actually laughed. She kept on surprising him. "So I quit. It was the easiest decision I ever made."

He leaned into her and put his arm around her. "Are you going to be okay?"

"I've got a lot of money saved up. I'll be fine until I find something else." She slid her chair even closer to his, so that their thighs were touching, his arm still around her, their bodies pressed together. He had to read that as encouragement for his other hand still resting on her thigh. She leaned over and kissed him on the cheek. "Thanks for the concern." Then her tongue darted out and flicked along his skin before she straightened.

Luke slid his hand farther up her thigh, sneaking it under the edge of her skirt. Annie slid a quick glance his way, but didn't say a word when his finger caught the edge of her panties. He leaned over to whisper, "Open for me."

Her eyes widened and scanned the people sitting at the table with them, but she slowly spread her legs.

"So what are you going to do now, Annie?" Heather asked.

Luke scraped his finger along the satin covered space between her legs. A tiny cry escaped her lips, so soft he didn't think anyone else heard it.

"What am I going to do now?" Annie repeated, her voice breathless. He loved making her breathless, just like she did to him.

"Yeah, are you going to look for a new job right away?" Heather asked. "Are you going to take a vacation? I think I'd like to take a long vacation."

"I haven't... um... haven't really thought about it yet." Annie's cheeks looked flushed, but she seemed to recover quickly because she moved the hand that had been resting on his thigh and slid it right up to his crotch. He supposed it was only fair. She smiled at Heather. "I think I'd like to travel a little before I look for another job."

"Travel where?" Luke asked. He strummed his fingers along the silky wet satin of her panties and caught the soft gasp that escaped her wide, wonderful mouth.

She sighed and settled a little lower into her chair, pushing her pussy into his hand. "Anywhere."

The words came out of his mouth before he thought about them. "I'm going to a car show in Pennsylvania next weekend, a little town outside Pittsburgh. Want to come with me?"

Her eyes grew wide. Her smile even wider. "Seriously?"

He'd never taken a woman with him to a show before. The scary part was that he *was* serious. "Absolutely."

Her hand closed over his cock. It was his turn to gasp.

"You okay?" Dave asked.

Annie squeezed his cock, stroking it with her hand beneath the cover of the tablecloth, her face innocent, her lips turned up.

"Fine. I'm fine." He nodded to Dave, careful to keep his expression as blank as possible. He hadn't been this hot in ages. Well, at least since he was on the dance floor with Annie last night. How far could they take it? How far would Annie go here at the table tonight?

The songs from the past were still blasting around them. Sean and Ginny, along with a number of their other classmates, were burning up the dance floor. Dave and Heather turned their attention to the dancers.

Luke took the opportunity to lean over and whisper in Annie's ear. "You are a very bad girl." Her eyes lit up at his words and he found himself wanting to do anything to keep the sparkle there. He caught the edge of her panties and slid a finger underneath. The scent of her arousal mingled with that spicy scent she wore and the combination nearly drove him over the edge. His finger slid in her slippery juices, dipping deep into her hot center.

"And you're a bad boy," Annie whispered back hoarsely. Her body was awash with sensations, her nerve endings afire. She was so aroused she wouldn't be surprised if a single flick of his finger on her clit was all it would take to make her come right here at the table.

Who'd ever believe she'd be going at it under the table in a public place, surrounded by people she knew? She barely resisted the urge to moan out loud as he worked his nimble finger in and out of her. Maybe a bad girl wouldn't mind if the people at her table knew she was getting finger fucked under the tablecloth, but Annie did. Didn't she?

Looking around she could see that no one knew what they were doing. No one was paying any attention to them. The bad girl whispered in her ear, telling her to go for it. Who knew when she'd get another chance like this.

She slid a glance at Luke. He was looking at her boldly, a sly grin on his face. Was he wondering if she was going to go through with the game? Or did he think she'd chicken out?

The music pulsing around them was loud enough that she didn't think anyone heard the rasp of Luke's zipper as she slowly lowered it. Luke raised his eyebrows, but otherwise didn't betray her actions. His penis sprang into her hand, neatly escaping the silky boxer shorts she felt beneath his trousers. Annie spent a few moments exploring the hard length of him with her hand beneath the long, white table cloth. She marveled at the smooth skin, the long ridges, the velvety soft head. Oh, how she'd love to feast her eyes on it.

Or simply feast on it.

Whoa. Where did that thought come from? Heather and Dave were turned away from them, still watching the people on the dance floor. Was that Sean and Ginny leading everyone in the Macarena? Annie resisted looking at Luke. Instead, she kept her eyes on the dancers bouncing to the music blasting through the speakers. She was afraid he might see the naked desire on her face.

Just then, Luke drew his finger along her slick folds, circling her clit, coming closer and closer with each turn. Almost touching it. Almost, but not quite. She turned to look at him, not caring if he saw the need on her face. With each flick of his finger, the buzz grew stronger, the need grew deeper. She tried not to move, but there was no way she could stop pulsing against his hand, angling her hips so his finger would touch that one spot. The one spot that would satisfy the craving gnawing at her. The one spot that would relieve the pressure building within her.

Her breathing was coming in short gasps now. Her face felt flushed. If he pressed just… there… she'd burst into a million pieces. If he touched her right… there…

And then his finger swept across her throbbing clit and she came apart in his hand. Her body rocked as the spasms of release swept through her. She grabbed a large white napkin off the table to smother the cries of passion she couldn't quite keep inside her, and hopefully cover the way her body shook.

Heather turned around. "Are you okay?"

Annie coughed noisily and nodded. "Just got a tickle."

Luke laughed out loud. She tossed the napkin at him and it landed in his lap. She loved the sound of his laughter. Hers was a bit shaky when she joined in.

Dave looked back at the two of them laughing and probably thought they were reacting to the group waving their arms on the dance floor. "Want to go up there?" he asked them.

Annie shook her head, her hand still firmly on Luke's cock, his fingers still hooked on her panties. Dave shrugged and pulled Heather to her feet and they joined the others on the dance floor.

How much time would they have at an empty table? She looked at him then and licked her lips slow and long. She lightly squeezed his erection, smoothing the skin up as she drew her hand slowly from the base to the tip. Must be he couldn't resist that throaty groan that escaped his mouth. He'd given her so much pleasure, she wanted to give him some back.

If only she could…

Annie glanced quickly around them. No one was looking at her. Did she dare? It was now or never. She winked at Luke and, heart pounding, quickly slid out of her chair and under the table.

"Annie?"

It was dark under the table. The long table cloth touched the floor everywhere except where it draped across Luke's lap. She knelt in front of his legs and ran her hands over the hard muscles in his legs, along his calves, and over his thighs. She gently pressed his legs apart so she could fit in between them and reach the cock bobbing before her.

She took him in her hands first, learning the majestic curve, the pulsing veins, the velvet softness, the throbbing hardness of him. He seemed to come alive in her hands, pulsing, growing longer, harder, stretching toward her, asking for more.

Tentatively, she swept her tongue up the full length of him, tasting for the first time the slightly salty skin. Then, chalking up another first, she opened her mouth and took him fully inside. It took a moment to learn the size, the space, he took in her mouth. To learn the way he touched the back of her throat when she took him in as far as she could. The way her tongue would glide over the soft skin. The way her mouth would suck, without her even thinking about it, riding him up and down, his shaft getting wetter and slicker with each probing thrust.

Soon she was getting into it like a pro, at least she hoped she was. She rocked on her knees, using her whole body to move him in and out of her mouth. There was something primal about the act, something that satisfied a previously unknown need in her, even as she pleasured Luke. She was going to have to insist on oral sex a lot more from now on.

"Where's Annie?"

Annie froze when she heard Lacey's voice.

"Well, actually she's under the table giving me a blow job right now," Luke said. Annie's gasp would have been heard over the deafening music if her mouth hadn't been full.

"Yeah, right." Lacey laughed loudly. She sounded like she'd had a little too much to drink. "When she gets back from the bathroom you wanna tell her I left with Bob Kulig? You can give her a ride home, can't you?"

"Sure. No problem." Annie began moving again beneath the table, taking him in so deep he hit the back of her throat. She didn't want Luke to be able to sound so nonchalant. She was giving him a blow job, dammit.

"Don't hurt her," Lacey said, her voice suddenly fierce. "She's not as tough as she pretends to be."

"Believe me, I don't want to hurt her."

"See that you don't."

Annie heard Lacey's heels stomp away. Why did she have to use the word pretend? Did Luke know she'd exaggerated her sexual experience? Or even worse, could he tell? Was she so laughably inept... so obviously inexperienced... The thought made her back away from him, for the first time noticing the crumbs under her knees, the song winding down in the background.

A hand snaked under the tablecloth and cupped her head. "It's okay," Luke said softly. "She's gone." He guided her back between his legs, back to the cock still standing at attention. Wanting her attention.

She must not have been doing too bad a job if he wanted her to continue. She must be at least adequate if he still hoped for release.

The brazen bad girl fought for control from the doubting good girl. Of course, she was good. She knew what she was doing. He hadn't complained yet and it didn't look like he was going to. In fact, as she licked the length of him, and then sucked him deep inside, she swore she heard a moan of pleasure come from above. Man, she'd love to see his face right now.

Annie turned her concentration to the task at hand. She knew there wasn't much time before Luke's friends and their wives would be returning to the table. They could be on their way back right now, for all she knew. She wanted to bring him pleasure, wanted to prove to Luke and to herself, that she wasn't inept.

She doubled her efforts, stroking him with one hand while her mouth took him deep one moment, almost released him the next. His hand clenched, still tangled in her hair, still guiding her up and down. Suddenly she felt him tense, felt his thighs tighten, knew he was about to come.

She hadn't thought about this part when she crawled under the table. What did she do now? Did she pull away and grab the napkin half hanging off his lap to take care of... what needed to be taken care of? Or did she suck it up and suck it down? She knew what a bad girl would do. She wasn't going to run away from this experience either.

So when he came in her mouth, she drank him in. Sucked him dry. Milked him of all he had.

When he was done, she sat back and nearly laughed out loud. How many clichés were there for what she had just done? Whatever it was called, it was not at all the unappealing experience she thought it would be. Warm. Creamy. Salty. Earthy and primal. In fact, it was so erotic she wanted to do it again.

Later. When she could see his face when he came.

But soon. When had she become so greedy?

She heard voices coming back to the table. Oh, no! How the hell was she going to get out from under the table now? What was she going to do?

"Hey, Luke." It was Sean, his voice a little breathless. "Where's Annie?"

She did the only thing she could do. She grabbed the corner of Luke's napkin and whipped it off his lap. Then she stuck her head out from under the table, waving the white cloth before crawling back into her chair.

"I found my napkin!"

# Chapter 6

"So how about going to Miller's Valley with me?" Luke asked later that night, as they lay sprawled in his hotel bed after another energetic bout of sex. Annie had never been so relaxed in her whole life, not even after she and Lacey had finished a whole carton of Ben and Jerry and vegged on the couch all night watching movies.

Annie stilled the hand that had been stroking his shoulder. What should she say? This thing with Luke was only supposed to be for the weekend. The plan was to practice on him and then go on to other bad boys. She was already in danger of becoming too attached to him.

Bad girls, she was certain, never got attached.

He rolled over on his side to look at her. "Have you ever been to a classic car show before?"

Oh good, small talk. She could put off the heavy thinking. "Never. What goes on at a car show?"

"Local car enthusiasts bring out their cars to show them off, sometimes win prizes, hang out with other classic car buffs. I go to network with owners and garages. A lot of local shops do general restorations and we hope they'll send the cars to us for the custom work."

The dim light on the nightstand sent rays of gold shooting through his blonde hair. His face was in the shadows, but she was close enough to admire the lean planes of his face, the warm brown of his eyes. She struggled to regain the thread of conversation. "So you get cars from all over the country? Don't they cost a lot to ship, like Steve did, across the country?"

"Steve?"

"Yeah, you talked to him at the reunion. Remember?"

"The Camaro. Right. Usually if they can afford our prices, they can afford to ship the cars to us," he said with a grin. Then he was quiet for a moment. "I have toyed with the idea of opening an east coast branch. We get a lot of work from this end of the country."

She silenced the little thrill that ran through her at the thought that he might want to manage the east coast store himself. But why would he want to move back to the snow belt when he could live in sunny southern California?

And not that she wanted him to. That sure would put a cramp in her plan to play the field.

She forced her voice to be light when she said, "Ooh, branching out. That means you're doing well, doesn't it. I'm glad for you, Luke."

He rolled onto his back and stared at the ceiling. "Yeah."

He was quiet again. Too quiet. She wished she knew what he was thinking, but she didn't have the right to ask. So she did the only thing she could think of, the one thing she'd discovered she was pretty damn good at. She rose up on her knees and began to rain kisses over his body. She started with his strong forehead, brushing a lock of hair away from his eyes as she went. Then she swept her lips gently across his brows and over his eyelids. He had such long, thick lashes she was almost jealous.

She drew her tongue along the curve of his ear, then softly blew over the damp skin. His ears were small and strong looking, masculine in a way she'd never noticed about ears before. She played with his earlobe, teasing the flesh between her teeth, murmuring nothing at all, but finding the sounds flowing from her lips as she loved his perfect ear.

After a moment, Luke growled playfully and rolled over, gathering her in his arms. "You drive me crazy. Why do you drive me so crazy?"

The words may have been playful, but the expression on his face was intense, serious, as if he yearned to have the answer to an unanswerable question. She didn't know what she did to him any more than she knew what he was doing to her. For he was making her crazy too.

This wasn't the way it was supposed to be.

She had to get her mind off her problems as much as she needed to get Luke's mind off his questions. So she rose up, and in a pretty darn graceful move, straddled his body at the waist. She grabbed his wrists and, without any resistance on his part, drew his arms up over his head. Luke took advantage of her position and captured with his mouth one of the nipples dangling in front of him. She'd been planning to go back to kissing him, but, hey, she was always open to a little change in plans.

Oh, God, that was good. He sucked hard at her breast, causing prickles that fanned out to every part of her body. She kept a hold on his wrists, stretching over his body, but by holding his hands above his head, hers were effectively trapped there as well. But, who cared? She didn't want to move from her position above Luke's face. He abandoned the one nipple and was now giving the other equal time. She gasped as he rolled the nipple between his teeth, almost to the point of pain. As distractions went, it was one of the best.

Then without warning, Luke flipped her over onto her back. So much for pinning him down. He had her arms stretched above her head now, his lips even with hers. He brushed his soft lips across hers, sending a buzz that tickled her lips. Oh, yeah, he was good.

"So how about this weekend?" he asked, his lips still brushing hers. The man was so stubborn, obviously not about to be distracted by lips and wrists and nipples.

She sighed. "When are you leaving?"

"Friday."

"What are you doing until then?"

He frowned as if he realized she wasn't answering his question. "I have some business stuff to take care of. Going to hang around with Sean and Dave some. And I was hoping to spend some more time with you."

"You were?" Okay, that sounded sufficiently sappy, but she couldn't stop the stupid grin from spreading across her face.

"Yeah, if that's all right with you."

"Sure." The bad girl had taken a hike. Annie didn't even know what a bad girl would say in a situation like this, but she figured a few more days of awesome sex sounded too good to pass up.

He grinned, and that coaxing tone was back in his voice. "You've said a couple times now that you wanted to travel."

Like she needed to be reminded. She wasn't able to return the smile. "Yeah, I did."

His face suddenly grew serious. "I don't like those shadows in your eyes. Why haven't you traveled, Annie, if that's what you want to do?"

She supposed it didn't hurt to tell him. It was no secret. Maybe then he'd realize how much she needed time to spread her wings, and not fall for someone she was seriously close to falling for. "Well, first I went to college. And then got settled in my job. And just about the time I built up some vacation time, my mom got sick. It was long, dragged out, horrible. I took care of her until she died." She was pleased she could finally talk about it without crying.

He gathered her into a warm embrace. "Oh, sweetheart, I'm sorry."

Her mouth was buried in his shoulder. "Yeah."

He rained soft, soothing kisses across her face. "So would your mom want you to take the opportunity to travel now? To see, maybe… southern

Pennsylvania?"

Annie smiled. She couldn't help it. Her heart felt somehow lighter now that she'd shared that with Luke. "Yeah, she would."

"Then you have to come with me to the car show."

Before Annie could answer, Luke's cell phone rang. Who would be calling him after midnight? He didn't blow it off, like she thought he might since she was naked in his arms. He placed a quick kiss on the tip of her nose and rolled away. One glance at the caller ID and he flipped open the phone, jumped out of bed, and crossed to the other side of the room.

"Vanessa, where the hell are you?"

Annie sat up in bed and watched him pace the short distance back and forth in front of the window. Who was Vanessa? An old girlfriend? A current girlfriend? And why did he look so upset?

"What? Why should I apologize? You're the one who—"

Luke snatched the phone away from his ear and stared at it for a moment, like he could get some answers from looking at the screen. Annie could hear a female voice screaming, but couldn't make out any words. Then he put the phone back to his ear. "Look, it's not too late. We can still make this right." He glanced over his shoulder at Annie and then lowered his voice. He had the nerve to turn his back on her, but she could still hear his next words. "Just tell me where you are."

That was all Annie needed to hear. She untangled herself from the sheets and climbed out of bed. If he wanted to go find Vanessa, whoever the hell she was, Annie wasn't going to stop him. This was the way it should be anyway. She didn't need to go spending a whole week with him, falling deeper under his spell. Lucky for her she saw his true colors. Lacey was right. He wasn't a one woman man.

And that was the way she wanted it, dammit. She would always be grateful he showed her what a bad boy could do. He showed her how good a bad girl she could be. But she wasn't going to stick around and listen to him try to sweet talk an old girlfriend back into his bed.

Annie gathered up her clothes and ran into the bathroom.

Luke turned around when he heard the bathroom door slam shut. Vanessa kept screeching in his ear, saying over and over that it was his fault she had to take all the money. She sounded frantic. She had to know the police were looking for her. She couldn't think he wouldn't have reported a theft like that.

He heard water running in the bathroom. Shit. Annie was probably washing up. She'd want to go home now and he'd have lost his chance with her. He had to convince her to stay. To go with him this weekend.

"Luke, are you listening to me?"

"Yeah, but what you're saying doesn't make any sense."

"You're not listening to me. You never did."

"Look, if you return the money I'll drop the charges. I'll tell them it was a mistake. Just put the money back."

"Not until I talk to you face to face."

The bathroom door opened and Annie stepped out. Yeah, she was going home all right. She'd put her dress back on, that purple piece of sin that had his palms itching to take back off. Her shoes were in her hand.

"Okay," he said into the phone, "tell me where you are and I'll come to you."

Annie stared at him. Shit. He was going to have some heavy explaining to do.

"Tonight?" Vanessa asked in a sarcastic voice. "You'd drop everything and come to me right now?"

Was she in Buffalo? How did she know where he was? "Where are you, Vanessa?"

"You got a girl with you, don't you? You always have a girl. Is she in your bed? Does she know how you like it? I know how you like it, Luke."

His biggest mistake was going to bed with his bookkeeper. No, the biggest mistake was going to be letting Annie walk out his door. She'd turned away from him and was reaching for the door knob.

"Annie, wait!"

"I knew you had someone with you," Vanessa said, the pout evident in her voice. He pictured her platinum blonde hair, her big tits and the long red claws she tried to sink into him. He really didn't need this right now.

He leapt over the bed and stopped Annie at the door. "Don't go."

She turned around when he touched her shoulder. She didn't look pissed off. More like resigned. "Hey, you're obviously busy. I had a good time this weekend. I'm really glad we ran into each other."

Boy, that was a brush-off if he'd ever heard one. He grabbed her hand. "Don't go. Spend the week with me. Go with me to the car show."

"Luke, I…"

He'd never felt so desperate before. He knew if he let Annie walk out that door he'd regret it for the rest of his life. He gently cupped her jaw with his hand and leaned in to kiss her.

She pulled back before his lips touched hers. She stared pointedly at the phone he'd forgotten he still clutched in his other hand.

"Shit." He lifted the phone to his ear. "Vanessa?"

Silence. He checked the screen. Great, now she'd hung up. Did he call her back, try to charm her location out of her? Or did he try to charm Annie into staying a part of his life?

Since when did he ever want a woman to be a part of his life?

He threw the cell phone down on the bed. It bounced off the mattress and landed on the floor. He stared at it, his mind a complete blank.

"Girlfriend?"

"She used to work for me," Luke said, frantically trying to decide how much to tell her. He sure didn't want to admit that he'd screwed his book-keeper, and when he went on to the next lover, she got pissed and robbed him blind. "She's been missing for a while. I was worried about her."

Annie nodded slowly. "So where is she?"

"She wouldn't tell me."

She dropped her shoes to the floor. "Then why did she call you?"

"Good question."

She held onto his shoulder as she stepped into the heels. "Luke, listen. Like I said, I've had a ball this weekend. But I'm not looking for anything serious. There's no point in continuing this… this… affair any longer."

Now why did he get a knot in his stomach when she said she wasn't looking for serious? Since when was he?

Was he?

He didn't want to think about that too closely at the moment, so he grinned and said, "Great sex isn't an important point?"

She blushed a pretty shade of pink. "Well, I have to admit the sex is more than adequate."

He brushed his lips over her neck. She still smelled so damn good. "Oh? More than adequate? That's in your expert opinion, I take it?"

She cleared her throat, but she didn't step away. "Of course."

He slid his hand up to her breast and cupped it passionately. "Why throw away a few more days of awesome sex?" He scraped his thumb nail across one distended nipple and smiled at her tiny gasp. "And if you come to the show with me, we can stretch it out for a full week. If we're both not looking to get serious, what harm is there in enjoying ourselves?"

"You make it so hard to say no."

"Then don't say no." He pulled her into his arms and brushed his lips across hers. "Say yes, you'll stay with me tonight." He swept his tongue across her tasty lips, leaving them wet and shiny. "Say yes, you'll be with me this week." He cupped her ass and pulled her up against his raging arousal. "Say yes, you'll come with me next weekend and see me work."

She nodded, but the expression on her face was so pained, he could have been forcing her to cut off her right arm. He stroked her back, gently, slowly. He scattered light kisses across her face, until she relaxed against him. He didn't want her regretting her decision. He wanted her enjoying it as much as he was.

He captured her lips with his and heat built around them. He could almost see the sparks flying in the air, the smoke rising from where their bodies met, touched, rubbed.

"I'm melting," she murmured, lifting that heavy mass of curls off the back of her neck.

Without a word, he grabbed the clingy dress and peeled it off of her. He tossed it over his shoulder, not caring where it ended up. Then he stepped back and smiled. "I like the look of you in nothing but those fuck-me heels."

She turned that pleasing shade of pink all over, but the look on her face was anything but innocent. The naked hunger on her face was unmistakable. She licked her lips and took a couple sultry steps in his direction. He was hard again, although how he could be when she'd milked him dry less than an hour ago was a mystery that might never be solved. He was aching and needy, as if he hadn't had sex in months instead of minutes. The longer he stood there looking at her, the more his cock throbbed with the need for release.

"You keep looking at me like that, I'm going to come just standing here," Annie said, the cry in her voice betraying her need.

"Bend over the bed," he said, his voice suddenly more like a croak than the smooth tone he liked to use. He ran his hands down her sides until he grabbed her waist and turned her to face away from him. "Babe, I'm hurting so bad I can taste it."

He bent her over the bed so that her gorgeous ass was facing him, her legs long and lean in those stiletto heels. He ran his hands over her smooth white cheeks, then he leaned forward, rubbing his cock along the cleft between. The pale globes shone in the dim light. What a perfect ass. He rubbed the cheeks briskly. The supple flesh felt so good beneath his hands. When he lightly slapped her ass, he was as surprised as she was.

And he was more than surprised when she leaned back on her heels, lifted her butt toward him, and silently asked for more.

Her flesh was so firm beneath his hands, the skin turned pink after only a few playful spanks. The sharp sound of his hand against her skin seemed to echo off the walls, but then her soft moans of delight rose and mingled with the slaps. "Oh, yes, Luke. I've never... Oh yes. Oh yes."

She continued to surprise him.

After a moment, Luke gave her a break. He leaned over her, covering her back with his body. Burying his face in her soft hair. Rubbing his cock on her sensitive ass. He reached in front of her to finger her nipples and when he rolled them with his fingers, she pushed her ass up to pulse against him.

She lifted her head to look at him and smile. He placed a kiss on her cheek and then pushed her head down on the mattress again, grabbing a handful of her dark, curly hair as he did. He stood back up, again rubbing his aching cock over her pink cheeks. Then he slapped them again, this time with his rock hard cock. It bounced off the firm flesh and slapped down again. And again.

A squirt of pre-cum leaked from the head of his penis and he rubbed the warm cream into the cleft of her ass with his cock. Oh, God, that was so good. He didn't know how much longer he'd be able to last, and he wanted to make sure Annie was satisfied too.

He reached down and slid his finger along her slippery folds. She was wet and ready for him, primed and open and eager. He plunged his finger deep into her, delving into her moist heat. He drew it slowly back out and then, just before he was clear of her body, he thrust it in again, this time adding another finger into her cream. She whimpered and pushed her body against him. She wanted more. He understood the concept, but right now he was intent on getting her hotter. Needier. Hungrier.

He started to play with her folds again, his fingers soaked with her juices, slippery with her cream. He drew his fingers up and down, in and out, drawing close to, but never quite reaching the spot she wanted him to touch. She writhed beneath him, her head on the mattress, her ass wriggling against his crotch. She was panting now, her breaths coming in quick puffs, her moans not quite muffled by the bedspread.

When he finally found the little nub of her clit, she nearly jumped off the bed. He kept hold of her hair and held her head down onto the mattress so she could bury her screams of release into the bedding. She continued to buck for a long time, rubbing her clit against his finger, rubbing her ass against his cock. Panting. Gasping. Crying.

Finally he couldn't stand it any longer. He tore open one of the condom packets strewn on the top of the bed and quickly rolled it on. She was still convulsing when he plunged into her from behind, one hand squeezing a butt cheek, the other once again tangled in her hair. He rode her for what seemed like forever, but then again it seemed like only a few seconds. When his climax rocked him, he pulled her head up by the hair and crushed his mouth to hers, burying his tongue deep into her mouth, claiming her every way he could.

While the thought scared him, confused him, mystified him, deep down he knew he'd taken Annie as his. Not just for the week, but for always.

After Annie had fallen asleep on the bed next to him, Luke carefully crawled out from under the sheet and found the cell phone where it lay on the floor. But while he dialed over and over again through the night and the next day, Vanessa never answered.

# *Chapter 7*

"You're spending another night with Luke Kendall?" Lacey had shown up at Annie's door, dressed in party clothes, begging her to go out to a bar with her.

"Lacey, it's only Monday. It's only been three nights. And yes, I told you, I'm planning to see him as much as possible this week. Then he'll be gone and I'll probably never see him again." The thought made her want to cry and that pissed her off. She didn't want to care about him that much.

"At least until the next reunion," Lacey said wryly.

Ten long years until she saw him again? Annie didn't even want to think about it. And she didn't want to admit to Lacey that she was in danger of falling hard for this bad boy. It wasn't just the awesome sex, although that was a big part of it. He had a soft, caring side. They both liked beer and hot wings. Dancing cheek to cheek. Wry humor.

She just wasn't strong enough to walk away from him. Not yet. So she kept her voice light when she lied, "I'm sure I'll have forgotten all about him by the next reunion."

"So what are you doing tonight with Mr. Forgettable?"

Mr. Unforgettable was more like it. They had fun yesterday at a picnic at Sean and Ginny's house before spending the night at her apartment. And enjoying another bout of amazing sex. But she hadn't heard from him since he left her bed before breakfast. "He hasn't called me yet."

"So go out with me 'til he calls. He has your cell number, right? Don't tell me you're just going to sit by the phone waiting for him to call."

"Of course not." A bad girl would never sit by the phone. That was pathetic. There was no reason she shouldn't start checking out the other bad boys around town. Luke would be gone soon enough and she might as well get a head start on the rest of her life as a bad girl. "What should I wear?"

"Nothing you have in your closet," Lacey said. "Tomorrow you and I are going shopping. Come on up to my place and I'll fix you up."

After dressing in another of Lacey's short skirts and clingy tops, Annie let herself be taken to a new dance club in town. Monday night was a slow night, Lacey told her. She said didn't want to throw Annie into the deep end on her first night out on the town.

The music was loud, the flashing lights bright, the drinks watered down. As she and Lacey sat at the bar, Annie scanned the place for likely bad boys. But how to tell? She supposed long hair and tattoos and piercings would be a good indication, but that wasn't all she could go on. Look at Luke. He wasn't a rough looking bad boy. He was a charmer. He dressed well, with no adornments of any kind on his body. Not that he needed any.

"How do you know a bad boy when you see him?"

Lacey took a sip of her white wine. "Are you looking for one, or trying to avoid one?"

Annie stared at Lacey for a moment before she realized she'd asked the question out loud. "Looking for one."

Lacey nearly spilled her glass of wine as she slammed it down onto the bar. "Are you crazy?"

"No, I'm being smart. Before I went out with Luke, all I'd ever dated were boring good guys. Remember Clark? Never again."

"Yeah, well, the bad guys aren't all that great either. Remember Bob Kulig?"

"That slimy jock who thought he was God's gift to women? Oh, my God, is that who you went home with after the reunion?"

"Yeah. I took him back to my place. What a jerk! He talked about himself all evening and then was out the door before the sheets cooled down."

"But you did heat up the sheets, right?"

Lacey sighed and grinned. "Oh, yeah."

"Well, that's not so bad then. We're not looking for guys who want to stick around, right? We're looking for guys to enjoy at the moment."

"You know, Annie, I'm worried about you."

Annie took a tentative sip of the Martini she'd ordered. "Why? I don't want to go back to my old boring life, that's all. I want to have fun. Experience new things. Have awesome sex. Is that too much to ask?" She probably wouldn't experience another Martini, though.

"I'm just afraid you're going to get hurt."

"Don't worry about me, Lace." Annie glanced up and saw the bartender eyeing her. Had he heard her comment about wanting fun and sex? Hmm, he wasn't bad looking. Dark hair, silky mustache, broad shoulders. But his eyes were kind of squinty and a weird shade of light green. Not warm and open and brown like melted chocolate.

And then there was that guy at the end of the bar. He was cute, but a little too young and nice looking. But then, Luke was nice looking. He was hot. Sexy. Damn, was she always going to compare other guys to Luke Kendall?

Were they always going to come up short?

Her cell phone started chirping. She glanced at the caller ID and her heart sang. Pretty sad for a bad girl. She flipped it open. "Hey."

"Hey yourself. Did you have a good day."

Just the sound of his voice had her mooning like a teenager. "Yeah. It's crazy. I feel like I'm on vacation." She'd never tell him she spent the day cleaning the apartment. And waiting for him to call.

"I thought about you all day." His voice oozed like warm caramel.

"You did?" She had to stop sounding like a love struck good girl. "So where were you all day?"

Oh, no, that didn't sound good. That sounded like she was checking up on him. A bad girl would never do that.

But Luke just chuckled. If he got the idea from her words that she thought about him too, he was right. "Talking with an old friend. I'll tell you about it sometime soon." He paused for a moment. The promise of sometime soon with Luke shot right to her heart. "Right now I just want to see you. I want to touch you. Taste that little spot on your neck, right behind your ear. It's so sweet."

A long tingle ran up her neck. She closed her eyes. "Mmm. I can almost feel your lips there."

"I'm going to taste you everywhere. That ticklish place under your breast. The sole of your foot. That wet, hot place between your legs."

She was on fire. Her breasts swelled in anticipation. Her foot itched with longing. Her pussy seeped with need. "Oh, Luke," she sighed.

"Oh my God. Gag me!" Lacey cried. "Do I have to be here for this?"

Annie's eyes flew open. She'd forgotten she was sitting at the bar with Lacey. What was wrong with her?

"Who's that?" Luke asked. "Where are you?"

"Having a drink with Lacey."

"I'll be right over. Where are you?"

What would a bad girl do? A bad girl wouldn't melt over some pretty words. A bad girl wouldn't jump when a guy finally gets around to calling. "Um. How about if I meet you after we're done? Girl talk, you know."

"Oh. Sure. Give me a ring when you're done."

"Okay." She closed the phone and looked at Lacey's frown. Well, this was going to be fun. Hmm, how long before she could call him back? "Sorry about that. He's just a sweet-talking guy."

"Oh, God, now you're quoting song titles."

"I like him, Lace. He's brought out a side in me I never knew I had." Like who knew she'd get turned on getting spanked? That had always sounded a little too kinky for her. But look at her—kinky Annie. "I'll always be grateful for that, no matter what happens next."

"So are you going to get hurt when Luke leaves for California?"

She had to be honest about this. "Yeah. But at least I'm going into it with my eyes wide open. I know what I'm getting into." But she never dreamed she'd get so attached to him.

She had to look forward to the future. To all the other bad boys out there waiting for her. Luke was only the first. She had to stop thinking about him every minute. She needed to look ahead to all those other bad boys.

The bartender winked at her. She flipped open her phone and called Luke.

The rest of the week flew by. Luke kept trying Vanessa's cell, but she never answered. He left a bunch of messages. Some charming. Some threatening. She never called him back, so he figured he blew his only chance to get his money back. His talks with Ray were fruitful though, and his visits with Sean and Dave – as well as his nights with Annie – told him he was on the right track.

So he'd start from scratch. He'd done it before. He could do it again.

He woke up early this morning with the sunshine streaming in Annie's bedroom window. She looked like an angel sprawled across three-quarters of the double bed. Her face was nearly hidden beneath a mass of dark curls. He loved to tangle his fingers in those wild curls, feel them wrap around his hands, tug at his skin.

Gently, so as not to wake her, he smoothed Annie's hair away from her face. Her skin was smooth as satin, her cheeks a soft blush. The sunshine threw lush shadows beneath her lashes and highlights along her jaw. The more he stared at her, the more he noticed. The smattering of freckles across her nose that she must have been hiding beneath her make-up. The way the end of her nose turned up just the slightest bit. The little pout her lips made while she slept.

What would it be like to wake up beside her every morning? The idea wasn't as frightening as he thought it would be. Would he continue to discover new things about Annie as each day went by? He had no doubt she would continue to surprise him.

He found himself looking forward to it.

That is, if she'd want to stick around with him.

The bubble of joy that had been rising around him fell flat. What made him think Annie was going to be different than any of the other women he'd taken to bed? Yeah, he was good for a few nights of fun and sex, but not to spend any amount of time with. Certainly not good enough to spend the rest of her life with.

Annie began to stir beside him. Now wasn't the time to be worried about the rest of his life. The weekend came first. He was looking forward to taking her with him today. It had been a long time since he'd had company driving to a car show. Jake used to go with him, until Luke made him manager. Then Jake was needed at the shop and Luke never got around to asking any of the other guys to go with him. Luke stared out the window as he remembered those early days, the excitement of every job that came through the door. The satisfaction of using his hands to restore a thing of beauty. He still had the satisfaction, but when had he lost the joy? When had it become just a job?

When he turned back to Annie, she was lying there looking at him. She smiled up at him. "Good morning. Have you been awake long?"

He leaned over and kissed her lightly. Then not so lightly. "Not long. Just thinking about what we need to get ready this morning before we can leave."

She pushed herself up to her knees. "I can be ready in a couple minutes. Honest."

He shook his head. "We've got all day to get there. There's no rush."

"There is for me. I can't wait to get on the road." Her eyes lit up. "On the road. I love the sound of that."

He laughed. She'd brought back the joy he thought he'd lost. Everything was new again when he was with Annie. "Okay. I'll jump in the shower. Pack lightly, remember. Hmm, can a woman do that? Pack lightly?"

She grabbed a pillow and swatted him playfully. "Don't worry about me"

"Okay. Get your packing done and we can be on our way."

"Can we stop for breakfast?"

"A woman after my own heart." He said the words lightly, but he meant them with his whole heart. So when Annie shot him an uneasy look, he once again lost a little bit of the joy.

She so was in over her head.

Annie watched Luke step out of his boxers and walk naked into her bathroom. She wanted to follow him into the tiny shower and steam things up. But she wouldn't be able to think clearly if she did that. Somehow, when she was with Luke her thoughts got all muddled.

She could fall into an easy routine with Luke with no trouble at all. Falling asleep on his shoulder was a simple pleasure. It would be too easy to get used to waking up beside him. She didn't want him to think she was after his heart, but the truth was, he'd already won hers.

Damn. What was she going to do now?

She started pulling clothes out of her drawers. It didn't matter how she felt about him anyway. He'd be leaving after this weekend. His life was in California. And he had plenty of other women.

She grabbed a tank top and shorts to pull on. A couple more to throw in her overnight bag. When she reached for her underwear she paused. A couple of panties wouldn't take up much room, but did she really need to pack a bra? Did she need to wear a bra? She bet bad girls didn't wear bras.

Annie pulled the black tank top over her head and stepped into a pair of khaki shorts. A pair of sandals and a clip to hold her hair up. What else did she need? She turned to look in the full-length mirror that hung on the back of the closet door. Anyone could tell she wasn't wearing a bra. Her breasts bounced when she moved. Her nipples stood out against the ribbed cotton of the top.

A lot of women went braless. It wasn't that big a deal. In fact, once she got used to the idea, she thought it looked kind of sexy. It certainly was comfortable. That cinched it. No bras for this weekend.

But maybe a little makeup. And a bottle of perfume. And that wrap skirt with the fringe she bought when she went shopping with Lacey.

She heard the shower turn off. A nervous tickle ran through her stomach. She looked back in the mirror and saw Luke come up behind her. His eyes met hers in the mirror. His hair was wet and tousled. His chest was bare and he had one of her pink towels wrapped around his hips. He put his hands on her shoulders and bent down to place a soft kiss on her neck.

"You smell good," she said, when she wanted to say so much more.

"That should be my line," he murmured, his lips brushing her ear. "You smell good. You look good. I want to eat you up."

Annie turned into his arms and shimmied her hips against his. "Ooh, that sounds good. But if you do that, we'll never get on the road."

Luke groaned and stepped away. "You're right. We have a long ride ahead of us."

She ran her finger along the edge of the damp towel with the suspicious bulge. "I'll take a rain check, though."

He winked and a thrilling shiver ran through her. "Later?"

"Sure."

"We'd better get going then." He didn't move.

"Hey," she said with a laugh, "I'm the one who's dressed."

Luke reached out and grabbed the hem of her tank top before she had time to react. He pulled it up and over her head. How did her arms get stretched out over her head that fast? She didn't even remember doing it.

"There. We're almost even now," he said with a laugh.

She grabbed the towel and snatched it away from his body. He lunged for it and she ran, laughing, away from him. Toward the bed. They fell laughing onto the mattress.

They skipped breakfast.

# Chapter 8

Annie loved Luke's little Corvette convertible. It was turquoise with white scooped out sections—Luke called them coves—on the side. The interior was mostly a creamy white, soft and bright. They sat close together and low to the ground in the classic two-seater. She'd clipped her hair back, but the wind had teased some strands free and they danced around her face as they drove.

The Corvette took the corners of the narrow, winding Pennsylvania roads with grace and speed. Although she'd never cared much about driving, she'd love to get behind the wheel of this car. It had to be a blast.

"Can I drive?" she asked, after they stopped at a little diner for lunch.

He stopped walking in the middle of the parking lot and stared at her as if she'd grown a second head. "Um, can you drive a standard transmission?"

She rolled her eyes. "Of course."

He narrowed his eyes. "You don't even have a car."

She propped her hands on her hips. "That doesn't mean I can't drive one."

"How long since you've driven a car?"

She had to think for a minute. "I drove Lacey's car last winter when she was sick."

"Last winter?" He looked like she was asking if she could shave his beard with a hacksaw, but she hadn't had a whole lot of practice with the blade. "This car's transmission is a little tricky. Maybe later, when there's not so much traffic."

"Aw, Luke. Come on."

But he was already in the driver's seat, key in the ignition, foot on the gas. The car was obviously his baby and he wasn't about to turn her over to Annie or anyone else without a fight.

Annie dropped into the passenger seat and resisted the urge to slam the car door. She may have lost the battle, but she'd win the war eventually.

Driving this little Corvette was now on the list of experiences she wanted to have before they finished this trip.

They took off down the road with Luke behind the wheel but Annie just couldn't drop it. "You know, just because someone hasn't had a lot of experience, that doesn't mean they can't do a good job."

"This old car is temperamental," Luke said. "Let's get down to the show. Maybe you can drive part of the way back."

That sounded a bit patronizing. Annie stretched out her hand and placed it next to Luke's on the steering wheel. "I just want to touch it," she said, lowering her voice to something she hoped sounded seductive. She ran her hand along the hot, smooth surface of the steering wheel, brushing against Luke's hand as she did. "I just want to feel all that power beneath me. I want to know what it's like to be in control of this power, this grace and beauty. Is that so hard to understand?"

Luke cleared his throat. "No, but why the sudden urge to drive? When we get back to Buffalo, you can buy yourself a car to drive."

"It wouldn't be the same with another car." Annie turned in her seat so that she was facing Luke. "I like the looks of this one." She caressed the soft seat beside his thigh. "The feel of it. The smell of it. The sound of it. Another car wouldn't be the same."

She moved her hand a little farther and ran it up Luke's leg. The muscles twitched beneath her palm. "I like the feel of this." She leaned over and rubbed her lips along his neck. "Mmm, I really like the smell." She ran her tongue along his ear lobe. "And you know I like the looks. How could I settle for anything else?"

She froze with her lips still on his neck when she realized what she'd said. How could she be so stupid? "Um, I was talking about the car, of course."

He glanced her way and then quickly shifted his gaze back to the highway. "Of course. What else would you be talking about?"

"Nothing." Time to get this conversation back on the bad girl track. "But you do smell almost as good as this car."

"Oh really?"

"Uh huh. And you feel almost as good too." She ran her hand along his thigh and palmed his crotch.

"Oh, God, Annie. Be careful. I'm driving."

She grinned. "You could always let me drive."

"No way."

She started to caress his crotch, feeling him grow beneath her hand, feeling the heat rolling off his body. The sun beat down on them from a clear afternoon sky, adding to the heat, and sweat rolled down the middle of her back. "Ooh, you like that. I can tell."

He groaned. "Of course, I like it. But I'd rather we do this when I can concentrate."

"That's right. This little car is tricky to drive, isn't it? It takes all your concentration, doesn't it? Well, I'll help you." She flipped open the button at the top of his shorts and ran her fingernail up and down the zipper.

"Annie…"

The bad girl inside her was like a devil on her shoulder. The bad girl was telling her to whip that bad boy out and give him a thrill right here in this little car while they were speeding down the road. She'd never had an experience like that. She bet Luke never had either.

But she couldn't do it.

"I know. Everyone could look down on us and see what I was doing. Even that minivan full of kids passing us right now." She stroked his crotch, thrilling in the feel of his hard erection.

He cleared his throat. "Not to mention the fact that I'd probably crash the car and injure us both."

"And how would we explain that to the police and the ambulance crew?

Luke laughed. "I can see it now. 'No, Officer. I don't know how my shorts got unzipped.'"

Annie joined in. "And, 'No sir, I can't imagine how my head got jammed underneath the steering wheel.'"

Luke suddenly stopped laughing and stared at her for a second before he turned his eyes back to the road. "I have an idea."

He slowed down as they continued to drive down through thick forests, the heavy trees broken occasionally by a group of houses or a small town.

"Are you looking for something?" Annie asked after a few minutes.

"Hold on a second. It's around here somewhere."

Annie was surprised when Luke pulled off the curvy Pennsylvania highway and turned down an even more secluded road. A canopy of trees covered the narrow road. In some places, low hanging branches nearly brushed the tops of their heads. "Where are we going?"

"You'll see. I was traveling through here a few years ago with my buddy, Jake. He grew up around here and knew this cool place… I think this is the right road." They rounded a curve and a moment later they came up on a large clearing with a pond in the middle.

"It's beautiful," Annie cried.

"Yeah, I guess Jake used to fish out here." Luke pulled off the road and turned to face her, his expression full of heat. "And make out too."

Her heart fluttered. "I can see where this would be a perfect little lover's lane. Doesn't look like many cars drive through here."

Luke reached out and pulled the clip out of her hair. "I'm sorry I can't fulfill your fantasy to the letter, but I think we can get pretty damn close."

The blood was pounding in Annie's head, but she was sure she heard him correctly. Not fulfill her fantasy? Was he nuts? This whole week had been one huge fantasy. "What are you talking about?"

"Sex in the back seat of a car. You told me that our first night, remember? I don't have a back seat."

"Front seat works for me."

Insatiable. That was a word Annie never thought would apply to her. She couldn't get enough of sex with Luke. Would it always be this way? Well, of course, it wouldn't because he wouldn't always be with her. Someday, in the very near future, she would have to do without Luke, without sex with Luke. What would she do then? Just like driving another car just wouldn't be the same, neither would being with any of the other bad boys out there.

And now he wanted to fulfill a fantasy she'd forgotten she even mentioned. But he remembered, the shit. He was supposed to be a bad boy. He wasn't supposed to make her fall for him.

It wasn't fair. She wasn't supposed to fall in love with the first bad boy she found.

But he was nuzzling her throat with those talented lips, that clever tongue. How could she resist? Why would she want to? She leaned into him, rubbing her cheek against his soft hair. Any reason she might have to resist had flown from her mind – along with any inhibitions she might have had about having sex in broad daylight in the middle of a clearing by a public road. There was nothing she wanted more.

The sun beat down on them again. There were no trees for shade. But the sun didn't make her half as hot as the look on Luke's face. If Annie had ever doubted that Luke was attracted to her, those doubts fell away in that instant. He made her feel like the most desirable woman in the world.

Definitely not boring.

She had to thank him for that.

Annie leaned forward and brushed her lips against his, gently, more a tease than a kiss. More an invitation than a demand. She gently brushed his hair off his forehead and smoothed her hand over his face. "You're a special guy, Luke Kendall."

"Nah. I'm just a guy."

"Well, I know what I'm talking about, so don't argue."

"Okay. You're the expert." He lifted his hand to her cheek and cupped her face. "How about if I just kiss you?"

"I'd like that."

If she drowned in his hot kisses, she would die a happy woman. His wet lips slid back and forth along hers, just hard enough to start a buzzing that began with her lips and traveled along her skin, across the arms that circled his neck, the breasts that yearned for his touch, the legs that longed to wrap around him, the hot center that ached to surround him. His tongue followed the lips, tracing a sensuous path across her mouth.

The sun shone brightly above them, heating her even more. She opened her mouth to him and he dipped his tongue inside, as if he were testing her, tasting her. She cupped his face with her hands and moved her mouth under him, drinking him in, taking him in. Mingling their tastes, their moans, their very breaths.

When they finally broke apart, they were both breathing hard, panting and smiling and touching each other's faces. "Wow," Annie gasped. "If you could take that kiss and bottle it, you'd make a fortune."

He shook his head. "It would only work on you."

"Wow," she said again. "You are a charmer."

"It's the truth, Annie."

There was a seriousness to his tone that scared her. The very idea that it might be true was more than she wanted to think about at the moment.

"Whoa, it's hot!" She stripped her tank top off. What tiny breeze there was rippled along her bare breasts, perking her already erect nipples.

"You're beautiful."

She stretched her arms up above her head, lifting her heavy hair off her neck and jutting her breasts out under the shining sun. Another new experience, to be bare-breasted out in the open air with the sun warming her skin and the breeze cooling her. What if she'd gone her whole life never knowing what this felt like?

The clean scent of the forest wrapped around her. She was surrounded by nature. The soil and the grass, the trees and the pond. Birds were singing somewhere in the branches, serenading their secluded tryst.

Luke reached out and cupped her breasts in his hands, skimming his thumbs over the sensitive nipples. She dropped her head back and sucked in her breath as waves like sunbeams washed over her skin and seeped deep within her. Her hair tickled her bare back. His fingers tickled her ribs.

She laughed, but it had nothing to do with her hair or his fingers. It had everything to do with her being here, in the middle of the woods, naked from the waist up, in a classic Corvette with Luke Kendall. A week ago she never would have even considered being part of a scene like this. And yet here she was.

"You like that, huh?" Luke lifted his eyebrow and grinned.

"Oh, yeah." She liked everything about it.

"Let's see what else you like." He put his hands on her waist and pulled her closer. She dodged the stick shift as she wriggled over to straddle his lap. Her pussy felt so good rubbing against his zipper. He sucked her nipple like a drowning man. The sexual charges running through her body were so intense that she could almost ignore the steering wheel digging into her back.

Okay, so sex in a car wasn't quite as romantic as it sounded.

Luke leaned into her when he turned his attention to her other breast. She couldn't stop from crying out, both from the hard steering wheel digging into her and then from the loss of his mouth on her breast.

He pulled her close again, at least relieving one of the problems. "Are you okay?"

"There's not as much room in this car as 'Greased Lightning'."

"Are you criticizing my car?"

Ooh, touchy. "No, I'm just stating a fact. I love this car, Luke. I'm just not sure we can have sex in it."

"Of course, we can. Let's try something else here." He opened the driver's door and they climbed out of the car. "Take off your shorts and sit back down in the seat."

"Okay." She was going to shimmy quickly out of her shorts and panties, but when she saw the hunger in Luke's eyes, she slowed it way down. The snap popped open, but she took her time lowering the zipper, drawing it down slowly, watching Luke's eyes greedily follow its progress. Then she slipped her fingers into the waistband and, using a whole lot of hip action, gradually drew the shorts over her hips and down her legs, until they pooled at her feet.

But Luke wasn't looking down at her feet. He must have caught sight of her new lacy panties and stopped there. Annie stepped out of the shorts and kicked them away. Then, before she took her panties off, she turned away from him and bent over the side of the car.

Luke moaned out loud. "I think I love you."

She laughed lightly. "You like my new thong?"

"Oh, yeah." The words came out on a groan. He stepped forward and swept his hands over her bare cheeks. "Beautiful. Soft. Beautiful." He hooked his fingers over the top of the thong and dragged it down her legs. After she'd stepped out of it, he brought the red lace to his face and inhaled. "I love the way you smell when you're all hot and aroused." He fingered the satin center. "You're wet too. You're ready for me, aren't you, Annie? You're hot and wet for me, aren't you?"

She simply nodded, because the words wouldn't come. A simple yes didn't seem enough for what she was feeling. She sat down sideways on the hot driver's seat and opened her legs to him. Luke stood beside the car for a moment, still fully clothed, gazing over her naked body. The breeze had picked up a bit and ruffled his hair. What a yummy picture he made.

Heat again. His gaze was as hot as the sun as it swept over her. The anticipation was making her even hotter. He dropped to his knees, finally, and pulled her hips to the edge of the seat. She leaned back and grabbed the steering wheel with one hand and the back of the seat with the other.

One long, wet swipe of his tongue and Annie knew she'd never have a fantasy as good as the real thing. And when the breeze blew on her wet folds it brought a whole new level of eroticism to the act. Who knew she could feel hot and cool at the same time? Who knew being completely naked, open, vulnerable could make her feel so powerful?

"I love the way you taste," Luke said, before he dove in again. "And the way you look right now... Annie, a man can only take so much visual stimulation." He closed his eyes to make her laugh, and she did, the sound raining over him like cooling rain. Then he had to taste her again. Had to show her with actions what he'd never had the words to express. Yeah, he'd blurted out that I love you crap when she turned around and surprised him with that barely there thong. But she didn't take it seriously. And he didn't either.

Or did he?

He concentrated on the task at hand, and soon the sensations wiped any rational thought from his brain. She was so wet, he lapped up her juices like nectar, drinking in her sweetness. Her pink pussy lips were plump and looked so delicious he had to suck on them, and when he did he heard her gasp and wriggle underneath his mouth.

His cock was straining against his zipper, aching with the need to spring free and plunge deep into the hot wetness in front of him. But first, he found her clit and it seemed to swell between his teeth. He sucked on it gently, in a rhythm that matched the throbbing in his cock. Her hips were rocking now, matching the same rhythm, pressing into his mouth, silently begging for more. Begging for harder, faster. More. More.

Her clit turned into a hard little bud the moment before she came. The moment before she cried out and locked her legs around his neck and rocked harder, faster against him.

The moment before the car horn blasted.

Annie fell back across the seat, laughing. "Oh my God. Oh my God. I've heard of fireworks but never horns blowing. Wow!"

Luke sat back on his heels, breathing as hard as she was. She was so full of life and energy. She made him feel alive too. He never even realized he hadn't been living before this. Had he only been biding his time until she came into his life?

How long before she left, like every other woman in his life had done?

She pulled herself back up by grabbing onto the steering wheel, managing to blow the horn again as she did. Her eyes lit up and he pushed his worries out of his mind. That's why he was an enjoy-the-moment kind of guy. It was all he could count on.

Annie climbed out of the car in all her naked glory and held out her hand to help him to his feet. Her hand was still in his as she looked around them. "I have an idea. I know we can't have sex in the back seat of this car. But we can have it on the back of the car."

His heart began to pound. He thought he knew what she was talking about, but he wanted to hear it from her own lips. "What did you have in mind?"

Hand in hand, she led him around to the back of the Corvette. She rubbed her free hand over the finish he'd polished countless times, never imagining her hand caressing it.

She turned to him. "Hot and smooth. Just like you." Her voice was slow and seductive. She let go of his hand and slowly unbuttoned his cotton shirt. As she did, she swayed before him, brushing her nipples against his chest. "I need to borrow this for a moment." She stripped the shirt from his body and spread it out over the hot surface. Then, without another word, she bent over, stretching her body over the car, pressing her breasts into the shirt, and leaving her ass sticking up in the air facing him.

Anticipation had run its course. He couldn't hold back any longer. He let his cock out with a rapid rasp of the zipper and quickly covered it with a condom he'd taken to always carrying with him. His straining rod homed in on Annie immediately. She was still hot and wet and ready for him and he slid into her with one mighty plunge. She arched her back and lifted up onto her toes, pushing against him, driving him even deeper inside her.

He managed a few slow thrusts, pulling nearly out of her welcoming body before slamming back in, burying himself deep and hard. He slapped her ass again, knowing she liked that extra sensation. But then all he could do is hold on for the ride, grasping her flesh while he convulsed around her, driving himself over and over into her willing body.

When the climax had run its course and he could speak again, he almost said the words out loud, the words that he hoped might convince her to stay with him after this weekend. But he knew now, in the heat of the moment, was not the time. She wouldn't take him seriously. She'd think it was the sex talking.

But what he felt for Annie was so much more than sex. He'd have to hope he could find the words this weekend.

And that they wouldn't scare her away.

# Chapter 9

Miller's Valley, Pennsylvania was a small town outside Pittsburgh and had been holding a large classic car show, Luke told her, for at least as long as he'd been in the business. The small town went all out. Annie could tell that as soon as they neared the town limits. Colorful signs lined both sides of the road, advertising the cars, the vendors, the music, the food.

They'd dropped off their stuff in a little motel room a couple miles from town and were now making their way slowly in the bumper to bumper traffic inching toward town.

"Is it always this busy?" Annie asked, craning her neck to look at everything around her.

"Yeah, isn't it great?"

She smiled at his enthusiasm. She put her hand on his thigh, trying not to think of the time when he would be gone and she'd no longer be able to touch him like this. "Yes, it is. Or it will be once we get there."

Before too long they reached the show grounds and found a place to park. Looking around, Annie was impressed with the variety of cars on display.

"Wow, these are beautiful. So many different models and colors. It's a little overwhelming."

Luke introduced her to some of the car owners, and Annie was impressed with the professionalism that Luke showed talking with other classic car enthusiasts. They asked his opinion on restoration and repair problems and he gave what sounded to her like experienced advice. Why should she be surprised? She knew he had a successful business, but until now, she'd only seen the sexy, fun, bad boy side of him. It was difficult to think of him as a boy toy she could walk away from when she saw him like this.

"I like that car," she said as they walked away from some guy with a long, shiny Chevy that looked like it belonged on *Grease*. She gave Luke a mischievous smile and a meaningful glance into the large back seat.

The steamy look on his face heated her more than the sun overhead. He laughed, the sound a little strangled. He put his arm around her waist and pulled her tight. "You would."

A delicious aroma wafted on the breeze. "What's that awesome smell?"

"The fire department holds a chicken barbeque every year."

Her stomach rumbled. "I'm starved. How about you?"

Soon they were loaded down with plates of chicken, baked beans and potato salad and cans of ice cold sodas. Luke led her around the back of the fire hall to a shady spot under a group of large maples. As they settled onto the soft grass, Annie sighed and said, "This is nice."

While they ate, they chatted about the cars they'd looked at, agreeing and disagreeing about the different models. She was nearly done with her chicken when she noticed Luke had hardly eaten any of his dinner. He was just sitting there, watching her eat. Shivers ran over her body as she became aware of the intensity of his gaze. The noise of the crowd seemed to fade away. They could have been the only two people in the town. In the world.

"Mmm, I love this chicken, but, boy, it's messy," Annie said lightly, trying to ease the tension in the air around them. She searched the ground, but couldn't find the white paper napkin she was sure she grabbed on the way out of the fire hall.

"Let me," Luke said. He wiped his hand on his napkin and then circled her wrist with his long fingers. "Remember that first night at Bernie's? The chicken wings? The sauce on your fingers?"

She nodded, her heart pounding.

"Do you know what you did to me when you slid your finger into your mouth? I nearly had a heart attack. I wanted that finger in my mouth. I wanted to taste you so bad, I almost came right then and there." She held her breath as he brought her fingers to his mouth. "Now I get my chance." He slowly sucked her index finger into his mouth.

She gasped as wet heat surrounded her finger. Strong suction drew it deep into his mouth. His tongue swirled around, lapping the sauce off from her skin. Still holding onto her wrist, he drew the finger in and out of his mouth. He made a little moan of enjoyment and her pants of delight joined in.

One by one, he sucked the barbeque sauce off her fingers. The deep suction started at her fingers but seemed to pull down into her center. Her nipples prickled and moisture pooled deep within her. Annie closed her eyes and threw back her head. She'd never known her fingers were so sensitive. Was this what it felt like when she gave him a blow job? His penis had to be so much more sensitive than her fingers, she couldn't imagine the feeling of plunging deep into a warm mouth… a wet body. This was probably the closest she'd ever come.

And she was about ready to come. Just from the sucking sensation, the pulling of his mouth and the licking of his tongue. She'd never felt anything so decadent. Except of course when that mouth and tongue was between her legs.

"Luke Kendall!"

Annie's eyes flew open at the sound of the angry, female voice. Luke pulled her finger out of his mouth and dropped her wrist like he'd been burned.

Or caught.

Luke jumped to his feet and watched the six foot tall redhead stomp over to them, steam practically pouring out her ears. Her short shorts were tight as always, her breasts bouncing with each step she took. Shit. He'd forgotten all about Sheila. They met up at this old stand of maple trees every year for car show weekend. Her fiery passion had been what attracted him to her years ago. It drove him wild in bed. It wasn't such a good quality when she was pissed.

Was there any way he could sweet-talk his way out of this one?

Probably not. Still, he held out his hands in a gesture of surrender and forced himself not to look down at Annie. "Sheila!"

Before he had a chance to brace himself, Sheila hauled off and slapped him across the face so hard his head snapped and he stumbled in the grass. Damn, that hurt! Hand to his stinging cheek he whirled around to see her stomping away from him.

Luke looked down at Annie. Her eyes were wide with surprise, but he noticed she didn't jump up to see if he was okay. Not a good sign.

There was a time, only a week ago, when he would have laughed this off. But he realized he cared what Annie thought of him. And if he had his way, his womanizing days were over.

"Bet that hurts like hell."

She could still make him laugh. He sat back down beside Annie and pushed the rest of his meal aside. "Um, that was Sheila."

She nodded. "When I first saw her, I thought maybe she was Vanessa."

He looked at her sharply. "What do you know about Vanessa?"

"She called you the night of the reunion, remember? You said she was just an employee." She looked down at her plate and picked at the chicken. "But that wasn't the way you talked to her. You talked to her like she was an old girlfriend." She looked back over to him. "Or a current girlfriend."

Luke sighed. Time to be honest and hope she understood. "Vanessa was an old girlfriend. Not really a girlfriend, even. A former lover." He picked up Annie's plate and piled it on top of his, out of the way. Then he moved a little closer to her. "Annie, I'm not going to pretend there haven't been a lot of women in my past. Sheila and Vanessa are only two of them. Can you deal with that?"

"Sure." Annie shrugged, like the thought of him being with those other women didn't make her stomach clench. "No big deal. I've had my share of other guys too."

"So did any of them piss you off so much you slapped them across the face?"

She remembered the night Clark told her she was boring. "No, but I did throw an alarm clock at one."

He lifted his brow at that. "Did you hit him?"

"Missed his head by inches. Smashed the clock to bits."

He laughed out loud and made her smile. "That's my girl. So can we both agree that we've each had a past before we met up again? We can't change the past. Right? So, no apologizing. No explanations. All we can do is move on from here."

That sounded serious. "Move on?"

"Yeah, I've come to a couple decisions this week that I'd like to discuss with you."

That sounded way too serious. "Why do you want to discuss anything with me?"

"Because I've had enough women in my life that I can recognize when I've finally found the one woman I want to spend the rest of my life with." He took her hand and Annie was shaking too hard to pull it away. "I love you, Annie. I'm tired of traveling. I'm tired of going from car show to car show and woman to woman. I want to settle down. I've bought Ray's station and I'm going to turn it into an east coast branch of Classic Car Restorations."

"Uh, wow." That sounded stupid, but so many thoughts were whirling in her head she didn't know which ones to say first. Her first thought was to burst out that she loved him too and she wanted to settle down with him and have his children. But then reality set in. How could she explain?

"Hey, Luke!"

They both looked up as an older man with a long white pony tail strode over to them. Luke rose to his feet and helped Annie up. He introduced the man as Chuck, the owner of a local body shop and used car dealership.

"A customer of mine just bought a sixty-five Mustang and I'm not sure I can do what he wants. Would you mind taking a look at it?"

"Uh, sure." Luke glanced over at Annie. He had to be aware of the fact that she didn't shout out her love for him. He was still holding her hand and squeezed it as if he didn't want to let her go.

"Go ahead," she told him. She was glad for some time alone to think. "I'll clean up here."

He nodded and kissed her, hard and deep and quick. Then he released her hand and walked away with Chuck.

"He's such a fuckin' sweet-talker."

Annie whirled around as a curvaceous blonde walked out from behind the trees. "Excuse me?"

"He's the world's biggest bull-shitter, but I'm sure you've found that out."

Obviously another one of Luke's women. Big brown eyes and a wide red mouth. "So which one are you?" Annie asked, putting on her best bad girl attitude.

"Honey, I'm Vanessa. I was looking for Luke and couldn't help but overhear your conversation."

"Didn't anyone tell you it's rude to eavesdrop?"

Vanessa laughed. "I just wanted to give you a warning. He's never going to settle down. A bad boy like him? No way. He didn't do it for me and he's sure not going to do it for you."

Annie tried for a haughty look on her face and hoped she succeeded. "Good thing for me that I'm not ready to settle down."

"Just remember that." Vanessa looked across the field to where they could see Luke looking at the Mustang. "Excuse me. Confrontation time."

Annie watched Vanessa cross the field, her hips swaying. She'd love to hear what the confrontation was about, but she resisted the urge to follow her across the field. It was none of her business. She didn't need to know anything else about Luke Kendall. Or his women.

She was in way too deep already. She should have broken things off after reunion night like she'd planned. A shiver of fear ran through her.

She had to get the hell out of here.

The interior of the Mustang was in pretty rough shape, but Luke was sure he could fix it up. He was about the climb into the driver's seat when he heard his name called out.

"Hey, Luke. Long time no see."

He'd recognize that high pitched voice anywhere. He nearly hit his head on the door jamb when he quickly straightened up and whirled around.

"Vanessa. What are you doing here?" Her clothes were as tight as ever, but what he used to think was sexy now simply looked tacky. And the heavy make-up only made her look hard.

She stalked over to him, like a panther ready to pounce on her prey. "I told you I wanted to talk to you face to face."

"How did you know where to find me?"

"Who do you think booked your fuckin' shows for the year?" she snapped. Her voice was sharp at first, then it softened as she said, "I've missed you."

He grasped her arm and dragged her away from the guys gawking at them. "You have a funny way of showing it."

"I know. I was pissed off. I didn't think it through. What can I say? It was a stupid bid for attention."

He wished women wouldn't talk in riddles. "Attention? What are you talking about?"

"I just wanted you back, Luke. I thought you'd come after me to find the money."

What kind of twisted logic was that? "Then you should have left me a treasure map, dammit. You know, some clues to follow. The police couldn't find you. How was I supposed to know where you'd gone?"

She sighed. "You never listened to anything I said, did you?"

"Sure I did," he said quickly. But if it didn't have to do with work or sex? Probably not. Luke didn't like what that said about him.

"Do you remember the times I told you about my grandfather's old place? That cabin in the mountains? How I liked to go there if things got too much to handle. How I went there to relax when I got stressed."

Vaguely. "That's where you've been hiding out?"

"That's where I was waiting for you."

"God, Vanessa. I had no idea."

She nodded. "I know. And I finally realized that I had to be stupid to want someone like you. Why would I want someone who doesn't care about my feelings? Who never listens to me? Who only cares about cars and sex. I don't." She tossed him a small book. "Here. I opened a new account. The money's all there. I hope it keeps you warm at night."

Luke stared speechless, the bank book clasped in his hand, as Vanessa turned and walked away.

Annie wasn't beneath the shady maples behind the fire hall when Luke finally made it back. He didn't blame her for not waiting all this time. After he finished with Vanessa, and the Mustang, and calling Jake and the police, he had no idea how much time had passed. All he knew was he had to talk to Annie. Had to get things settled with her. He had to convince her that he was a changed man. He wasn't the same man he'd been with Vanessa. He had to convince Annie to give him a chance even if he had to get down on his knees and beg.

He finally found Annie over on the next block at Chuck's place. They were standing by a late model Chrysler convertible and appeared to be deep in conversation. He dashed across the street, but the closer he got to Annie, the slower his steps became. It was as if a dark cloud passed overhead, although the sky was clear blue. He suddenly had a feeling he didn't want to know what was going on.

When Annie noticed him crossing the lot, she straightened her shoulders, and an almost guilty look crossed her face. In fact, she definitely looked guilty. Guilty and sad.

"Hey," he said as he approached them, hoping he sounded light and easy when his heart suddenly felt heavy and apprehensive.

"Hey, Luke," Chuck said cheerily, obviously unaware of the tension vibrating in the air between Luke and Annie. "The little lady has a good eye for vehicles. Did you teach her that?"

What was Chuck talking about? "No," Luke said warily. "Guess she picked that up on her own."

"I bought a car," Annie said, the words coming out in a rush.

"Really?" His stomach clenched. "What made you decide all of a sudden to buy a car?"

She wouldn't meet his eye and that pissed him off. "Chuck gave me a good deal?"

Rage, pure and simple, flared up inside him. He knew this meant she was leaving him. Would she have even said good-bye? What the hell happened since he left her behind the fire hall? "Come on, Annie, I think I deserve a better explanation than that."

She finally looked at him and he could see tears glittering in her eyes. "Yes, you do." She turned to Chuck. "I'll be back in a little while."

"Take your time."

Luke grabbed her arm and pulled her across the car lot and over to a bench that sat along the sidewalk. So spilling his guts meant nothing to her. She was just another woman who didn't want to spend the time to get to know him. Looks like his old man was right after all. Never trust a woman.

"Do you want to tell me what's going on?" He tried to hold onto his anger, but she looked so miserable, his rage drained away.

"I decided to buy a car. My very first car."

"Earlier today, you said you didn't want to buy a car."

"Well, you're not giving me the Corvette, are you?" she shot back. "I never needed a car before. I could walk to work. I never went anywhere. So why did I need a car?"

"Now you suddenly need one?" Okay, so maybe he was still a little pissed.

She nodded and took his hands in her trembling ones. "Luke, look, this is so hard for me. This has been the best week of my life, this week with you. You made my every fantasy come true." She paused and cleared her throat, and looked out over the show grounds instead of in his eyes. "But you and I are at different places in our lives. You're tired of traveling. I've just begun! You say you've been with enough women to feel ready to settle down. Well, I haven't, Luke." She turned then to look at him and he saw her blink away some more tears.

Right now he didn't give a damn if she cried. "Well. This has been one roller coaster of a day. Answer me this. Do you love me?"

"I don't know. How can I know?"

"When you look at that person and can't imagine not waking up beside them every morning for the rest of your life. When that person makes you laugh and makes you glad that you're alive. And when you're willing to do anything to make that person happy."

Luke squeezed her hands and then let her go. He stood up. "Travel, Annie. Drive your car all over the country. Go screw as many guys as it takes for you to realize that what we have is special. It's the real thing." He shoved his hands in his pockets so he didn't reach out and grab her and beg her to stay. "When you've had enough bouncing from town to town and man to man, maybe you'll realize that love is worth the risk. And you won't be afraid to love me anymore."

He turned then and walked away, leaving her sobbing alone on the wooden bench.

# Chapter 10

"So where are you tonight?" Lacey asked.

Annie stretched out on the hard king-sized motel mattress and closed her eyes against the bright orange bedspread that almost matched the picture of bright orange poppies on the wall. She tucked the cell phone under her chin. "Chicago."

"Cool, tell me something about Chicago."

What was there to say? "It looks pretty much like every other big city I've been through in the past couple of weeks."

"Luke bought Ray's Service Station and the vacant lot next door."

Just the sound of Luke's name was enough to bring back the memories of his hands on her skin, his laughter in her ear. "Lace, you tell me that every time we talk."

"Oh, well, I thought you might have forgotten."

Like she could ever forget him. He truly was Mr. Unforgettable. Her nipples prickled unbearably as she remembered the incredible way his mouth felt when he teased them. She fingered them, pulling, rolling them through her fingers, trying to relieve the ache. But nothing could. Nothing but Luke. Her pussy wept. "I don't want to talk about him."

"Okay."

Whoa, she was hot now. How long had it been since he'd licked, sucked, and fucked her? Too long. She'd have to pull out her new toy after she hung up from Lacey. And afterward she'd still ache. But it was the way it had to be. "You're the one who warned me away from him, remember?"

"I thought you didn't want to talk about him."

"Shut up."

Lacey's tone turned serious. "I think Luke really has changed, Annie."

Whoa, a lot of things had changed. "I never thought I'd hear you say that."

"In fact, I'm pretty damn sure he's in love with you."

Annie shot up in bed, her heart galloping. "You've talked to him?"

"Yeah, we talk now and then. Mostly about you."

Did she want to know he'd been talking about her? Yeah, she did, even if she shouldn't. "I talked to one of his old girlfriends and she told me he'll never settle down."

Lacey snorted. "And you believed her?"

"No, not really."

"Good, cuz he hasn't been dating anyone. I even tried to tempt him, and he didn't bite."

"What?"

Lacey chuckled. "Just looking out for you, sweetie."

"Well, it doesn't matter, because I can't come back to him right now. I'd end up resenting him. He'd end up unhappy."

"What are you talking about?"

Time to put her fears into words. "I'm afraid if I settle down with him, or with anyone, I'll go back to my old life. The boring life that makes guys fall asleep on me. Lace, I couldn't bear to go back to that."

"So what kind of exciting bad girl things have you been doing since you've been on the road?"

"Um." Annie flopped back down onto the bed as the truth smacked her in the face. Nothing. She'd burned a lot of gasoline and ate in a lot of cool diners, but she hadn't met up with one new bad boy and she hadn't even been looking for any. "Well, to tell you the truth, my life is pretty damn boring right now."

"Then what is this all about? What are you really afraid of?"

"What if I'm wrong about loving him? I thought I was going to try out a lot of different guys before I found the one who was right for me. Instead, I met Luke right off the bat. What if I find out down the road that I made a mistake?"

"Sweetie, no one is guaranteed a perfect life. You just have to ask yourself if he's worth the risk."

Luke's last, bitter words came back to haunt her. Was love worth the risk?

Annie jumped off the bed and almost dropped the cell phone. How quick could she be on the road? "Lace, don't tell Luke, but I'm coming home."

The huge sign on the front of the building said, "Classic Car Restorations

Coming Soon." A small sign in the window said, "Bookkeeper Wanted." Annie still didn't know what she was going to say to Luke, but she hoped the words would come to her when she needed them. She didn't see anyone in the office when she walked inside, her heart in her throat. It wasn't really even an office at the moment. The walls had been stripped down to the plaster and the counter was nothing more than studs. Since there was no one to greet her, she wandered through the open door into the two-bay garage. One bay was empty. The other held a turquoise and white Corvette she knew intimately.

And sticking out from underneath was a pair of long blue-jeaned legs.

Good. She had a captive audience. And coward that she was, she was relieved she wouldn't have to look him in the eye when she apologized.

She cleared her throat and then blurted out, "Luke, I need to talk to you."

He started to roll out from under the car.

"No, don't. This will be easier to say if I'm not looking at you. And don't interrupt 'til I'm done, please, or I'm afraid I'll never get it all out.

"I was stupid. I thought I had to have all the answers. I guess I thought finding the perfect man was like finding the perfect pair of shoes. I thought I needed to shop around before I found the perfect fit. But sometimes you find the best pair of shoes right off, and if you shop around for too long, when you go back to get them, they're gone.

"I hope it's not too late for us, Luke. I love you. I do. No doubt about it. I'm ready to settle down, but I hope we can compromise and take trips now and then. It's no fun to travel alone."

She stared at the blue-jean clad legs. "Did you know that Vanessa came and talked to me that day at the car show? She told me not to trust you. That you'd never settle down. Well, what she said scared me. Not because I believed her, but because I knew she was wrong. I knew you better than that. I knew you were being serious with me, when you never had been with all those other women you'd had in your life.

"That's a pretty heavy responsibility, Luke. You were willing to lay everything on the line for me, but... what if I'm not the woman you think I am? Because, you see, I'm not. I'm not a bad girl, Luke. I was only pretending. I'm a boring good girl, and now I've gone and fallen in love with you, but I'm afraid that now you won't love me anymore."

"I still love you."

It was Luke's voice, but it came from behind her. Annie whirled around and saw Luke in a tight black T-shirt and grease-stained jeans, standing in the doorway of the office, a cup of coffee in each hand.

"But…" Annie looked down to the legs peeking out from underneath the Corvette.

"You can come out now, Jake. I've got the coffee."

A tall, lean man rolled out from under the car. He blushed to the roots of his bleached blonde hair when he looked at Annie. "I'm sorry. I tried to warn you."

Annie stood tongue-tied while Luke walked over and gave him one of the coffee cups. "Why don't you take your break now."

"Okay, boss."

Luke fished his cell phone out of his pocket and tossed it to him. "Take a long break."

They both were silent as they watched Jake walk away. When he shut the door behind him, the click echoed around them. The silence stretched out as they turned and stared at each other.

"Um, nice place you have here." Annie cringed inwardly. Well, that sounded lame.

Luke looked around them. "Yeah, we have a lot of work to do before we can open, but it's coming along. I'm excited about it. I brought Jake in to help get things set up. He can't wait to get back out to the west coast, though."

"How about you?"

"I like it here."

"You won't say that when the first snow storm hits."

"I will if you're here to keep me warm." Luke put his cup of coffee down on the cement floor and walked over to her, not stopping until he was so close she could feel his breath on her cheek. "What's all this nonsense about you not really being a bad girl?"

"I'm not. It was all pretend."

He cupped her ass and pulled her up against him. "Oh, so you only pretended to crawl underneath the banquet table and give me a blow job? Funny. It felt damn real to me."

"Um, well…"

He rubbed his hard cock against her, showing her just how real their passion was. "And I suppose you only pretended to bend over my car hood and offer me your ass."

"Um…" She couldn't even think straight. She never could think straight around Luke. All she wanted was that cock buried deep inside her.

"Good girl. Bad girl. Annie, I don't care what you call yourself, as long as you say you're mine."

She laughed, relief flooding through her like a shot of Tequila. Or so she'd heard. That was still on her list of things to try. Along with driving a classic Corvette.

"So, you think you know me?" Luke asked, sounding a little vulnerable.

"Well enough. No, I take that back. It's not enough. I think I could spend the rest of my life getting to know you."

"Did I tell you I love you?"

"Only once today."

"I'll tell you everyday for the rest of my life."

"I love you too." She buried her nose in his neck and breathed in his musky scent. This was where she was supposed to be. She nibbled on his ear a moment, and then whispered, "I see you need a bookkeeper."

Luke released her and stepped back to look her in the eye. "Yeah. She needs to be trustworthy, though. Do you have anyone in mind?"

"I happen to know an out-of-work accountant you can trust."

He chuckled. "If I can trust her with my heart, I guess I can trust her with my money."

"Does that mean I have the job?"

"Yeah."

"Good, because I spent a big chunk of my savings on a car." Annie stroked his chest. She loved the way the cotton clung to his muscles. She couldn't wait to get it off of him. "Hey, Luke, know why I picked the Sebring?"

"Tell me."

"Because it's a convertible and it has a back seat."

Luke started to laugh. Then his eyes suddenly darkened and he grasped her breast as she'd been dying for him to do. "Let's try it out, right now."

She held onto his shoulders and leaned into his hand. "Now?"

He rolled her nipple between his fingers, sending those familiar and all too infrequent sparks flying through her body. "Pull it in this bay here. No one can see in."

She looked around them as he continued his assault on her nipple. No windows. Office door closed. "But what about Jake?"

He reached out and cupped her between her legs. Could he tell how wet she was for him already? "Don't worry. He won't come back until I call him."

"Oh. That's why you gave him your cell?" He nodded, a smug expression on his face. "So you just assumed you were going to get a little action this morning?" She tried to sound outraged, but couldn't pull it off. She was just so damned glad she hadn't lost her chance with Luke.

"A guy can hope."

"Well, you're just lucky I've been dying to try out the backseat." She captured his mouth, putting into the kiss all the passion of that first night on the dance floor, when she thought she had something to prove. "I'll be right back."

As soon as the shiny, silver car, with its top down the way she liked it, was safely behind the closed overhead door, Annie turned to Luke. The passion on her face was enough to burn him up where he stood. "I want to undress you."

A charge ran through his body, like he'd just stuck his cock in an electrical socket. "Be my guest."

But first she rubbed up against him, and he ended up backed against her car. Her soft breasts were a contrast to her hard nipples burning into his chest. Then her hip brushed up against his straining cock and he sucked in his breath. There was that electrical socket again.

"You're killing me, Annie," he moaned. "I've been without you too long."

"Now we don't want to rush things," she said, her voice low and lazy. She ran her wet tongue across his lips and he tasted her sweetness once again. "I think we should take our time. Celebrate our love."

"Honey, I'll celebrate it every day of our lives, but I'm dying here."

She reached down and swept her hand over his erection. Oh God, such sweet agony. "I think you might live a little longer." She tugged his T-shirt out of his jeans then and yanked it over his head. "I love your chest," she said on a sigh. Those busy lips of hers nibbled their way down his neck and straight to his nipple. When she lightly scraped her teeth over the nipple, he gasped and buried his hands in her hair.

"I swear I'm not going to last much longer."

"Sure you will."

He almost growled at the laughter in her voice, but he was too happy to know he was going to hear that voice for the rest of his life.

She made her way down his chest and abs, stopping short of the waist band of his jeans. "Suck it up, big boy. It'll be worth it, trust me."

"I do."

She looked up at him then, her eyes wide, her smile wider. "I love you."

He was going to reply, but she quickly flipped open the button and lowered the zipper, effectively shutting him up as he was overwhelmed by the sensations. His cock, released from its bondage, swelled in relief. Annie drew the jeans and boxers over his hips and down his legs, where they became stuck on his work boots.

"Whoops," she said with a laugh. She dropped down onto her knees and began to untie the laces, then suddenly stopped. "Hmm, seems like I have you captive right now."

Luke moaned, but his cock perked up even more. "Why do you want to torture me before you kill me?

"Oh, babe, this will be such sweet torture," she murmured. Then she took his cock deep into her mouth.

Dark, wet heat engulfed him. Drove him closer to the edge. Backed up against the car door, he grasped onto it and closed his eyes. She moved over him with enthusiasm, taking him practically down her throat in a way he could certainly appreciate. Then she let it slide through her lips until he almost sprang free. When she covered him again with the moist heat of her mouth, he groaned out loud. Her tongue swept over him too, licking his swollen flesh in long strokes that threatened to push him over.

"Annie…" he moaned. "I'm serious. I can't hold on much longer. I promised you sex in the back seat."

She sat back on her heels and looked up at him. "So you did."

What a picture she made, her hair a wild halo around her face, her breasts stretching out her snug white shirt into luscious curves . The only way this view could be better would be if she was naked.

Annie finished untying his boots and he kicked them off. She helped him get rid of the jeans and he climbed into the back seat of the convertible.

"Now I want to watch you undress," he said, sprawling out on the seat.

She raised her brows. "Are you sure you can wait that long? I'd hate to have a dying man on my hands."

"I'll try to hang on for a little longer," he said wryly.

"Okay. You asked for it." She was dressed in a short white shirt with a deep V neck, a brown print skirt with sexy fringe that swayed around her knees, a strappy pair of sandals and not much else. Luke braced himself as she played with a tie at the waistband of her skirt. She loosened the bow, then swung the tie like a stripper would do. The mischievous look on her face told him she knew what the sight was doing to his blood pressure.

One quick pull on the tie and the wrap skirt fell open, exposing long, lean legs… and a shaved pussy.

Oh, shit. Luke could barely breathe. He sat up straight and almost came right then. His mouth was so dry he couldn't utter a sound. She stripped the shirt over her head and sauntered over to him.

"I did this for you," she said, sliding her hand over the newly bare skin, then dipping her finger inside for a long, hot moment. "But, you know, it's amazing how much more sensitive I am now. I can feel the slightest breeze and the brush of my skirt is quite arousing."

Luke groaned. "Annie, grab a condom from my pants pocket and get in here right now."

"Oh, don't worry. I came supplied." She climbed into the back seat with him and sat down between his legs that were stretched across the seat. "This is quite roomy, isn't it?"

He growled and grabbed onto her waist and pulled her over him. She was soft everywhere. "You've teased me long enough, you bad girl."

She laughed and wriggled away from him. "But I have something else to show you."

"I don't know if I can handle anything else."

"Sure you can, you're a big boy."

Then she stretched over the front seat, and opened the glove box. Her ass was in his face, her pretty pussy glistening. He couldn't resist leaning forward and running his tongue along her wet slit. He loved the taste of her cream. He could live on it, day and night, and never tire of it.

She must have found what she was looking for and started to back up, but Luke grasped her hips to keep her in place. "My turn," he growled and slapped her playfully. "I'm so hungry I think I'll eat you up."

She wiggled her butt in response, but didn't make a move. Luke dove in then, lapping up her juices like a fine wine, breathing in her musky scent. His tongue diddled with her luscious lips and explored the newly smoothed skin. He loved the little gasps that escaped Annie's throat. He tried to ignore the throbbing ache in his cock and delved his tongue deep, exploring the tight opening to her vagina. His cock throbbed with the need to take its place.

He sank back down onto the seat, breathing heavily. As Annie turned around, he looked up to see what she'd pulled from the glove compartment.

A condom and… a vibrator shaped like a long, thick bullet?

"I had to keep myself company these last couple weeks," Annie said, a sexy little pout in her voice. She rubbed the vibrator along her cheek. "Would you like to see what I can do with this, Luke?"

"Oh, yeah." He leaned back and watched as Annie stretched out across the seat. She spread her legs and braced one on either side of him. He had died and gone straight to heaven. "So you weren't out screwing other guys while you were gone?" He tried to say it lightly, but the thought had been driving him crazy since she'd been gone.

"Only James here," she said smoothly as she twisted the bottom and a little buzz, like a bumble bee, ran through the air. She slid the vibrator into her vagina, coating it with her cream, and then slid it out where his tongue had recently been playing.

He swallowed. "James?"

She nodded and closed her eyes as she moved the toy through her slippery folds. "James Dean. The ultimate bad boy."

Then there were no words as he watched her pleasure herself. He made note of the places she lingered, like close to the clit, circling and teasing the little bud that soon jutted out as it begged to play along. She made those sweet little gasps in the back of her throat and then slid the vibrator back through her folds to dive into her body again.

"Does this turn you on, Luke?" Her voice was soft and sultry, with a raspy throatiness that betrayed her arousal. "Do you like to watch while I play with myself?

Luke's cock strained, demanding release, and soon. Yeah, he loved watching, but he was ready to join in. When he could see that she was so close to coming he was afraid he was too late, he leaned forward and slid his hands along her legs until he reached her sweet, smooth pussy. "Let me help," he said, and took the toy from her. He turned the base until it was buzzing at the strongest level and then plunged it deep inside her, holding it in as far as it would go.

"Oh," she gasped and spread her legs farther, bending her knees and opening herself to him as wide as she could.

He leaned over and touched his tongue to her clit while the vibrator hummed inside her. She bucked against him and he rubbed her clit with his tongue again, this time a bit harder, a little rougher. Then he took it in his mouth and sucked. That was all it took. She screamed as she came, clenching his shoulders and rocking against him, finally crying, tears streaming down her face.

"Are you okay?" he asked as he eased the vibrator out of her body.

She nodded and silently swiped the tears away. Then she beamed him with a wide smile as if the tears had never happened. "I've never come that hard before. Wow! I thought I'd died for a minute."

Luke switched off the vibrator and sank back against the seat, his cock reminding him that he hadn't been taken care of yet and he wasn't as dead as he thought. Annie took the vibrator from him and turned it back on.

"Um, Annie."

She smiled at the look of desperate arousal on his face. She knew he was hurting. She knew he'd postponed his satisfaction to make sure she got hers. But she knew first hand what part anticipation played in sexual arousal and she was going to make sure that this time he screamed when he came.

She stroked his awesome erection, the skin like velvet to her touch. The veins were bulging and she could tell he was ready to burst. Starting with a low setting, she placed James at the base of his cock, resting it in the nest of hair above his balls.

His hands clenched, but he didn't make a sound. She glanced up to see him staring at her, but whether this was pleasure or torture for him, she couldn't tell. She turned it up, the vibration stronger, and ran it slowly up and down the length of him. This time he gasped and when she looked back up, his eyes were closed.

Annie debated whether to turn the motor up to its highest setting, but decided today probably wasn't the time. There would be plenty of other times when they could play. So she turned James off and tossed it down onto the floor. She grabbed the condom packet she'd dropped there earlier and ripped it open. She would have liked to linger while she smoothed the latex over him, but she knew that wasn't for today either. As gracefully as was possible in the backseat of a Chrysler Sebring, she straddled Luke, and lowered herself onto his shaft,

He cried out when she took him into her body. She cried out when he filled her completely. He grabbed onto her hips and held on tight. He lifted her up and down, controlling how deep the thrusts were. How fast he plunged into her body. When he came, he screamed out her name, digging his fingers into her hips, thrusting into her over and over again.

Annie collapsed on top of him, breathing every bit as heavily as he was. She nuzzled her face into the crook of his neck and kissed his salty skin. Her hips would complain in a moment, but right now she was where she wanted to be. Luke wrapped his arms around her and hugged her close.

"I'm glad you came back," he murmured.

"Me too." Her hips began to cry out, so she kissed him lightly on the lips and then pushed herself back up. She was still sitting on his cock that felt almost as hard as it had a few minutes ago. She threw her arms out. "I love this car!"

Luke laughed up at her. "Just promise me one thing."

"Anything."

"Don't ever stop surprising me."

And what would a bad girl say to that? "Don't worry. There's nothing more exciting than being a bad girl with the man I love."

## *About the Author:*

*Natasha Moore fell in love with the written word as soon as she could read. As she grew up, she discovered with romance and now enjoys the chance to add some extra sizzle to her stories. She lives in New York State with her real life hero who is happy to tell everyone that he's her inspiration. They travel in their RV whenever possible. The great thing about writing is she can take it anywhere. Find out more about Natasha at* www.natashamoore.com *and feel free to drop her at note at* natasha@natashamoore.com.

# War God

by Alexa Aames

## *To My Reader:*

Greek and Roman myths have always been favorites of mine, and Ares, the ultimate bad boy, is so dangerous and sexy that it seemed only right that a modern woman should try to tame him. I hope you enjoy *War God*.

*Chapter 1*

Estella Eaton pushed up from the buttery-soft brown leather chair she'd been sitting in for two hours. She inched around the footrest where her books were resting. She'd been working on her thesis so long that her brain felt like scrambled eggs.

She stretched her long legs and rubbed her hands along the pale blue denim of her jeans as she looked around Nelson's Books. The small independent bookstore had survived despite not serving lattes or giving deep discounts. Sheila, another student in the biochemistry department, had introduced Estella to the bookstore as a popular student hangout, and Estella had loved it immediately. The battered but comfortable chairs, the smell of old books, the turn of the century photos on the walls gave Estella a sense of permanence, of history preserved just for her pleasure.

Estella wandered up the creaky stairs into her favorite part of the shop. Rare books. The old volumes had an intriguingly musty smell. She slipped between the stacks and ran her fingers over the bindings. Her index finger stopped on a book of mythology that she'd looked through a few times before. She pulled it out and leaned back against the shelf behind her.

She flipped yellowed pages, looking at the illustrations. The images of the gods and goddesses were stunning. Clearly, it was good to be adored by artists. She came to the place where a page was missing and glanced at the final paragraphs describing the god of war. There was writing in the margin and a small sketch that someone had drawn. A perfectly-sculpted male torso. She turned the book sideways and whispered the words written in black ink.

*Ball of fire from the hand*
*War of mountain, sky to land*
*Darkest god who none can see*
*In the flesh now, come to me.*

She took a deep breath, her heart pounding in her chest like a woodpecker's beak hammering a piece of wood. She swallowed hard, dragging her pinky over the written words and closed the book. She replaced it on the shelf, walking down to philosophy. Existentialism would be a lot less unsettling than naked pecs inked in unsuspecting margins.

She rubbed down the denim over her outer thighs, aware that the place between her inner thighs was what really wanted rubbing. She sighed. It had been months since she'd had a boyfriend. Lately, it seemed like the smallest thrill triggered pulses of excitement.

Ares, the god of war, leaned against the wall. He was invisible to mortal eyes because he chose to be. His coal gaze followed the swing of the Estella's white-blonde hair. A straight shimmering curtain of it fell across her eyes, and she blew it away with bee-stung lips. He was sure those full lips would be as succulent as the peach color that stained them. He was also sure they would feel like crushed rose petals against the iron stiffness of his cock when he was in her mouth. He groaned softly, releasing himself from his tight calf-skin pants. How he would like to bury himself into her depths, but it wasn't time yet. She needed to be primed.

He took his erection in his hand and stroked it slowly, staring at her ass as she bent over to reach a book on the bottom shelf. The curve of her hips seemed to call to his hands. He imagined his thumbs spreading her cleft open to receive him.

Estella stood and walked toward him. She'd left whatever book she'd been looking at on the shelf. Her hands were empty, and he guessed she was going back downstairs. Back to her work.

He shoved his stiff cock back inside his pants, and moved to stand a few feet in front of the stairwell. He waited with a salacious smirk.

She strode toward him, a golden gazelle advancing unknowingly on a panther. She passed through him, tasting like vanilla. He spun a half turn and took a step back to watch her fall to her knees.

She panted, palms on the floor. Her head hung below her shoulders, leaving her long neck bare. He leaned over, running a long finger over her spine from neck to tailbone. He laid his palm on her ass, cupping her so that his fingers gripped between her legs.

She shuddered and then slid down and away from his hand as she fainted.

"Coward," he whispered.

Estella woke lying in her bed, naked under her sheets. It was strange since she didn't normally sleep in the nude, but the details of getting ready for bed were fuzzy. She blinked at the tops of her breasts.

A cold gust of air ruffled the sheets, exposing and hardening her nipples. She glanced over at the open window and at the dark figure standing next to it. She froze.

He was black-haired and nearly seven-feet-tall. He rubbed his goatee and eyed her body.

She took a tiny gasp of breath into her tight chest and started to lower her arms slowly, planning to pull the sheet up. Her arms stopped midway. Startled, she looked up to find a pale blue satin tie binding her wrists.

When her eyes darted back to the stranger, he was standing next to the bed.

"What do you want?" she asked, her voice bizarre in its calm. *What's wrong with me?*

He caught the sheet in his fist and pulled it off her in a slow surreal moment. The sheet floated to the floor. She lay nervously under his onyx gaze.

"I'll scream."

"No, you won't," he said in a deep voice that poured over her like honey.

The muscles of his chest twitched under the open vest hanging off his massive shoulders. He was so overtly masculine. She'd never seen him before, but a sense of déjà vu coursed through her.

"You summoned me." A hand huge enough to palm a basketball slid over his chest, down to his rippled abs and then to the front of his skin-tight leggings.

"What?" she whispered.

He licked his lips, looking her over again. "You heard me."

Her throat was tight with fear and lust. He shrugged off the vest then unhooked his belt. He let it dangle from his hand, and it flickered over her skin like a serpent's tongue.

"Are you the devil?" she asked.

He threw his head back and laughed a low rumble of thunder. He dropped the belt on the floor, still smiling. "No, but I'm just as feared, and I do better work. Spread your legs, and let me show you."

She stared up at him with wide eyes.

"Go ahead," he encouraged, letting his hand catch her left knee. "This is just a dream anyway."

She stared at him in confusion. Was it a dream? Was he real? His touch burned like no other man's ever had, and there was something otherworldly about him.

"Now, open for me. Unless you'd like to play a game where I pretend to force you. I'm very good at domination," he whispered.

Her heart stopped for an instant. He was so menacingly virile. She wanted him, but she was afraid of him too. She licked her dry lips.

He smiled at her and, in an instant, he gripped the backs of her thighs, pulling her body down so that her arms were stretched taut over her head. She arched, trying to escape.

He held her legs, sliding his hands over to the tops of her thighs as he knelt on the bed. He ran his fingers down to her ankles catching them in his grip.

"Take a moment to enjoy your last seconds of freedom. When I'm done, you'll belong to me."

"Let me go," she rasped, trying unsuccessfully to kick loose.

He gave her a black grin. "I can taste your heart fluttering on my tongue. But that's not what I want to taste. Do you think I'll feel your heartbeat throbbing between your legs when I put my mouth there?"

She gasped, and her breathing grew ragged.

"Are you wet enough to quench my thirst?" he asked as he lifted her left leg and licked the inside of her ankle.

Her legs trembled in his hands. He bit the back of her calf, pulling her bottom off the mattress as he held her leg to his mouth. She was like a wishbone. Her breath caught in her throat as he pushed her right ankle outward several inches. The span of his arms seemed infinite.

Damp heat pooled inside her. She tried to retract her legs, instinctively trying to regain some control.

He looked down as he lowered her left leg a fraction of an inch. Her behind bumped back against the mattress. He pushed her left ankle outward and stared directly down into her sex. It made her want to squirm. It also made her want to feel him make good on his threats.

"I'm going to spread you so far open," he said, studying the space between her legs. "Like a book with a broken spine, all its secrets exposed." He moved his hands up her legs, pushing her thighs apart as he went. Being handled and having her legs spread seemed to trigger some primitive need to couple.

"Blonde and pink and creamy." He licked his lips again. "Is all that cream for me?"

She panted, trying to catch her breath. She felt dizzy, wantonly splayed. Her hips had started to move involuntarily, the scent of her wet sex drifting through the air. She saw his nostrils flare.

*It's not real. I wouldn't feel like this. It's a dream.*

Her breasts swelled like her lower lips. She wanted him to take all of her at once. Her hips gyrated faster.

"Please."

Finally, he lowered his head, his palms pushing up and out on the bottoms of her thighs so that her calves were several feet apart and suspended in the air. Her knees hung back toward her slightly curled body, her pelvis tipped up to his face. His thumbs inched between the cheeks of her bottom, pulling them apart.

She groaned at being spread even further open. *Touch me. Lick me,* she thought with wild desperation.

She screamed when he finally flicked the tip of his tongue over her throbbing clit. Her body shook as he sucked. She shrieked as she orgasmed.

He lapped her juices. His thick tongue grazed her orifices as he moved his mouth back and forth then plunged into her pulsing cleft. His tongue burrowed into her vagina deeper than the cocks of her former lovers ever had.

"How?" she gasped almost incoherently.

She screamed again a few minutes later, toppled into the abyss of multiple orgasms, lost in sensation, her pelvic walls clenching and unclenching like a fist, her pussy and bottom tingling with unbearable intensity.

Her ears popped, and she woke suddenly, sweating and breathless. She inhaled sharply, startled to find that three of own her fingers were inside her vagina. She pulled them free, sitting up. The window was closed. Lights out. She sat, shaking with arousal, alone in the dark and disappointed that he wasn't there.

A minute later, she flung herself back onto the pillows. She rubbed her legs together, like a cricket trying to make music. She closed her eyes and saw his gorgeous face again. She cupped her breasts in her hands, pinching her aching nipples.

She sucked hard on her bottom lip. Her sex tingled and twitched. She reached a hand down, rubbing against her soaked panties, and then snaked her fingers inside the elastic and back between her plump lower lips.

The image of him swam in front of her as she brought herself to orgasm.

Ares stood invisibly at the end of Estella's bed, jerking his cock while he watched her masturbate, dreaming of him. He gritted his teeth against the urge to shove his rigid cock into her boiling body.

Her perfectly round globes of softness shimmied as she gyrated. He wanted to suck those breasts so hard that they would give up drops of milk. Thin sweet nectar. She'd have weeping eyes by the time her body relented. There were certain pleasures that could only be born from pain.

He glanced down at himself. He was hung like an animal. Huge heavy balls, full of the liquid that triggered lust and rage in equal measure. With his free hand, he squeezed his sac. It would take a hard coupling for any mortal woman to accommodate the length of his organ, but then Estella wasn't fully human herself. And they were drawn together by the forces that neither he nor Aphrodite had ever been able to control.

He looked back at Estella's smooth, golden body, gleaming with sweat. *She's mine. She doesn't know it yet, but then she's got a lot of things to learn.*

# Chapter 2

Estella walked down the shadowy hallway of the Cage Science Building to the office she shared with two other graduate students. The cramped quarters were the reason she often lugged her work to Nelson's Books.

The building was air-conditioned, but never truly cool in mid-summer. Sheila Cook sat under the rickety ceiling fan, a pencil peeking out from under her unruly auburn hair.

"Hey, Sheila."

Sheila lifted her head and looked over the top of the rectangular lenses of her glasses.

"Hello, yourself."

Estella dropped her books on her cluttered desk, glancing at her favorite wall poster. It was an orange that was partially peeled, revealing its contents, the components of a human cell. A surreal hybrid that only a geeky molecular biologist and maybe Salvador Dali fans could really appreciate.

"What have you been up to?" Sheila asked suspiciously.

"What?"

"You're glowing."

Estella blushed, remembering her wet dream of the night before. "I've had the flu or something." *Or something is right.* "Yesterday, I got dizzy and fainted at the bookstore."

"God, are you okay?"

"Yeah."

"Well, you don't look sick."

"I feel better today," she said, running a hand through her hair and giving Sheila a bright smile.

Sheila stared hard at her and then shrugged. "So, listen, Doug's got a friend. His name's Art. You're coming on a double date with us tonight."

"What? We were supposed to go to a movie. You and me and Leslie. Girls night out," Estella said.

"Leslie's staying in with her new boyfriend tonight. And since she's ditching us, I don't see why she should be the only one to get lucky."

"What's this Art like?"

"He's nice. Econ major, finishing his dissertation. Very bright."

"What does he look like?"

"Since when does that matter to you?"

Estella blushed again. Despite her constant attraction to construction workers and bodybuilders and other buff but totally inappropriate guys, she tried to place more value on things like intelligence and wit than looks. She was known for accepting dates from all sorts of men that her friends considered lost causes.

"Well, he's okay-looking," Sheila said. "Certainly better-looking than a lot of the ones you've dated in the past."

"Right. Okay," Estella said, dropping into her rolling chair and opening up her notes. A date would do her good. Given the content of her dreams lately, she'd obviously been too long without the company of the opposite sex.

*I shouldn't have napped. Now I'll never make it in time.* Estella haphazardly spritzed herself with vanilla-scented perfume and then dumped the contents of her brown purse into a cream-colored one that matched the floral print sundress she was wearing.

She ran down the stairs and snatched up her keys on the way out the door. The warm air smelled of jasmine, and she inhaled deeply as she hopped in her car.

She peeled out of the drive and zipped down the tree-lined street. Daylight quickly receded, and she turned on her lights. When she got on Highway 40, she laid her foot heavily on the gas pedal. She smeared on some lip gloss, looking up sharply when her tires spun a little erratically on the gravel that edged the road. She yanked the wheel to get back in her lane just as she saw the flashers.

"Damn." She yanked her foot off the accelerator, looking down at the speedometer. Sixty-two miles per hour and falling. The speed limit was fifty. "Damn. Damn. Damn."

The police cruiser was right on her bumper. There was no shoulder to pull off onto. She turned onto a gravel road and stopped the car, turning off her engine and rolling down the window.

She was digging through her purse when she heard the cop clear his throat. She couldn't find her wallet because the contents of her purse were so jumbled.

"Hi," she said with a smile. She turned her head and blinked as the glare of a flashlight blinded her.

"License and registration." His voice was deep.

"Right," she said, squinting into the light. She turned and popped open the glove box, taking out the ownership papers. She handed them to him.

He had big hands. She wanted to see his face and paused, staring out the window. But all she could see was the blinding flashlight.

"Driver's license."

"Yes," she said, looking back down at the purse in her lap. She fumbled through it. She could not find her wallet. She turned on the overhead light and dumped her purse on the passenger seat. It wasn't there.

She turned back to the driver's side window. "I must have left my wallet at home. I was in a hurry and I switched purses and—"

"Have you been drinking?"

"What?" she squeaked. "No, of course not."

"Get out of the car," he said with a rough-edged voice.

Her heart thudded in her chest. "I haven't been drinking. Unless you count lemonade," she said, trying her prettiest smile. "I had some of that."

"Get out of the car," he said, clearly unaffected by her attempt at being charming.

"Okay," she said. Inexplicably, she felt like crying. He was going to give her a couple of tickets that she couldn't afford. Why had she ever agreed to go out?

*Pull yourself together. You'll manage.*

He backed up, and she opened the door, taking a deep breath. She got out of the car, stumbling a bit as her shoe slipped on the gravel.

"New shoes," she said. *Stop! Stop explaining. It makes you look more guilty.*

"Uh huh," he said.

"I'm serious. You can give me a breathalyzer."

He stepped forward, tilting the flashlight down so that it wasn't blinding her.

Her stomach plummeted to the ground when she saw him. He was very tall, very dark, and very, very handsome. He also looked exactly like the stranger from her dream.

"I guess you think because you've got a pretty smile that I'll let you off with a warning," he said, the hard planes of his face pulled into a sardonic smile.

She couldn't speak. She stared into his green-rimmed black eyes.

"How many times have cops given you a warning when they've stopped you before? I bet you've never gotten a ticket in your life."

She continued staring up at him. He smelled like spicy cologne and something so masculine that it took her breath away. The familiarity was palpable, and it wasn't just the way he looked.

"Have you?"

"What? What was the question?"

He smiled. "Not able to concentrate on a simple conversation. Definitely unfit to drive."

"I'm just—I was distracted because you look a lot like someone I know."

She looked around. No other cars had turned down the poorly lit, deserted road. They were very much alone.

"Who?"

"Just a guy," she mumbled. She couldn't exactly tell him about a fantasy guy from her sex dreams. She should have made something up, but she'd never been good at that.

"What's his name?"

"I really haven't been drinking."

"Maybe not, but you were speeding and driving recklessly. And your mind is certainly somewhere else. I'm not convinced I should let you get back behind the wheel."

He opened the back door of the prowler. She stared at it, heart hammering in her chest.

"You're taking me to jail?" She felt light-headed.

"The breathalyzer machine is at the station."

*Oh, no!* "I'm not drunk. I swear."

"Get in," he said, nodding toward the back of the squad car.

She got in, scooting to the center of the bench seat. He sat down next to her and looked her over.

"Where were you headed tonight?" he asked, voice varnish-smooth. Goosebumps sprung up. *Dammit*, she cursed herself. *Stop thinking about how good-looking he is and concentrate on the questions.*

"Out with friends. I woke up late from a nap, so I was hurrying."

"I saw. You almost spun out and lost control of your car."

"I know. I should have been more careful... and I will be if you let me go."

"You don't have your driver's license. We're talking about a lot of tickets."

"About that," she said, touching his arm. "I'm sorry about the speeding, and I do have a license. I just—if you don't give me a bunch of tickets, I'd be really grateful."

He glanced down to where her hand was and arched an eyebrow. She pulled her hand back. She wanted to touch him again, but she knew she shouldn't.

"Let's take a walk," he said. "We'll see how steady you are on your feet." He stood up and waited for her.

"A walk?" she echoed as she slid from the car.

He led her to the edge of the wooded area next to the road. She hesitated.

"Come on."

She looked around. There weren't any houses nearby. The only signs of life were the sounds of the highway, but no one on the road would hear her from the woods. It didn't make sense, but her feet started to move toward him.

"What are we doing?"

"Come and find out, Estella," he said, holding out his hand.

She swallowed hard. She'd never told him her name. He must have gotten it when he'd run her plates. It made her feel even more vulnerable that he knew her name and address and car and she knew nothing of him. She hadn't even bothered to look at his car's number or license plate.

She put her hand in his, warmth closing around her fingers. *This is a bad idea.*

They walked for a minute and stopped. Her hands trembled as he turned to face her. He crooked a finger toward himself. She took a deep breath before taking a tiny step forward. He leaned down from his impossible height and blew his breath against her lips.

"Kiss me," he said in a soft growl. Her hands caught his forearms to steady herself, and she brushed her lips across his. *What the hell are you doing?*

"You can do better than that," he said. Her hands dropped from his arms, and she took a step back. He caught her forearms in his hands, abruptly preventing her retreat. "When you kiss me, I want to taste you."

"I don't put my tongue in a guy's mouth on the first kiss."

"And you think that's a good thing, do you?" he asked, arching an eyebrow. He looked amused. "You don't need to work up to things with me.

We don't have all night."

"What do you think is going to happen out here?"

"I think we'll both get what we want," he said in a husky voice.

She swallowed against a dry throat and licked her lips nervously. "I'm not sure…."

"C'mon, where's your nerve?" he challenged. He leaned close to her, smelling sexy and male, making her head spin. She couldn't believe how much she wanted him. "Should I kiss you? Or are you ready for something other than my tongue to be in your mouth?"

She gasped, and he smiled.

"It's okay. No one's ever going to know." His hands moved. One against her back. The other was on her butt, gripping her possessively. Her body throbbed. He inclined his head so that his firm full lips pressed against hers. He tasted like spiced pears. His tongue explored, then he withdrew from the kiss slowly.

"I love the way you smell," he murmured.

She stood still, feeling somehow far away from her body. When he put pressure with his palms on her shoulders, she melted to her knees.

She could barely see his hands unhook his belt in the darkness and heard rather than saw him unzip his pants. One of his hands slid into her hair. The other maneuvered his erection free. He smelled masculine and musky. She closed her eyes dazedly.

She felt the tip of him against her mouth. Smooth. It slid over her lips, moisturizing them with a drop of him that had already formed. He ran himself across her lips more firmly and they gave way under the pressure so that he grazed himself against her teeth.

She brought her lips together in a pucker, kissing the bit of his flesh that was between her lips and teeth.

He groaned softly and tilted her head back gently by the hair. Her jaw loosened and he slid the thick, bulbous tip inside. He tasted salty and sweet at the same time. She hungered for him, her stomach clenching in anticipation.

Her mouth began to suck. She slid her hands around his body, gripping his muscled buttocks through his pants. She beckoned him forward with her grip.

There was no resistance from him. He fed himself to her, inch by inch. She sucked in earnest, taking him deeper and deeper, but there was always more. She moved her hands, greedily digging into his open trousers to grip his balls. She squeezed as he thrust.

From above, a drop of his sweat struck her cheek like a drop of rain. He was at her mercy now. She would have smiled, but her mouth was too busy.

An eternity later, he shouted her name and poured thick cream down her throat. Normally, she wasn't very elegant at oral sex. But tonight was different. Her rhythm matched his perfectly, and she loved the feel of him gliding back and forth, spilling liquid sex into her.

His hand shook ever so slightly as it dropped from her hair onto her shoulder. He took a step back. Her mouth, now used to being a vortex, released him only reluctantly. There was a popping sound as he pulled free.

He ran his hand over his forehead then wiped the sweat on his trousers. "Here." He held out his hand to her. "Get up now."

She let him pull her to her feet, but she felt like sitting on the ground all night, listening to him move and breathe, his melodious voice sailing on the darkness.

He bent and gently brushed off the front of her dress and then led her back to the deserted road. It wasn't until they were back at the cars that she realized what a strange impulse it was to want to spend the night sitting on the hard ground at the feet of a total stranger.

He opened her car door. The interior light overcame the darkness for a few feet, and she felt herself coming back to reality, aware of the tight throbbing between her legs. Her panties were soaked with her lust for him.

"Go home. You shouldn't be driving without a license," he said, putting her into her car.

"Wait," she said, as he closed the door. She caught his hand with her fingers. "I don't know your name."

He looked down at her, as darkly beautiful as a fallen angel.

"It's safer that way, isn't it?" he asked. He didn't wait for her to answer. He went to his squad car and got in.

"Safer for whom?" she whispered, feeling strangely empty at the prospect of never seeing him again.

# Chapter 3

Athena's waist-length dark braid rode upward as she bent her head to enter Argus' tent. She barely glanced at Cyril, the old healer, at her lover's bedside. Argus' full lips were pale. She strode over to him, dropping to her knees and touching his tousled blonde hair, which was wet with sweat.

"Why haven't you given him the elixir yet?" she demanded, turning her pale gray gaze on the healer.

"I have given it to him, Mistress. Twice."

"The wound is so bad?" She pulled back the golden animal skin blanket to examine Argus' leanly muscled body. The wound near his left nipple looked well-healed and tiny.

"It's not the wound. I believe the dagger must have been dipped in poison."

"What manner of poison can't be cured with Thero's Elixir?"

"None that I know of. It must have been enchanted."

"Who that could create enchanted poison would attack him?" she asked distractedly, glancing around the tent, but not really seeing the surroundings. She leaned forward and rolled Argus carefully onto his side.

"He regains consciousness only fleetingly, Mistress. He asks for you. He knows that he's dying and wishes that you would stay near him."

"He shall not die." She lifted Argus' shoulder-length golden hair and brought her eyes close to the skin on the back of his neck. "Ares," she exhaled slowly. "Have you failed to notice his mark?"

"What?" Cyril gasped, bending to look at the small crescent-shaped burn. "Why would Ares have a hand in this?"

"We'll soon know. Tell my men to ready themselves. We ride to Ares' palace tonight."

"You won't go inside it," Cyril said hopefully.

"I'm sure Ares leave me no choice."

"Mistress Athena, you must not go. He'll trap you there. Surely, you remember what happened to Aphrodite." He began to wring his hands nervously.

"I remember."

"Argus is mortal. He will die one day whether from poison or not."

"I'm not ready for him to die. Besides, if Ares wants to get my attention, killing Argus will only be the first step. It's best to get to the heart of this immediately."

"I fear you going to his palace."

"As you should, but make no mistake… he'll not find me an easy concubine. He may be the most powerful god on Elios, but he is not the smartest. I am." Athena sprung to her feet and whirled to the doorway. Her dark braid swung heavily and struck the canvas with a thwack.

Athena stared up at the palace of Ares, which stood majestically above the jagged black rock of the beach below. It was impressive. She wondered if he'd taken a room that faced the sea so that he could keep a vigil over the foam, awaiting Aphrodite's rebirth on Elios. Since the loss of Aphrodite, nothing soothed his anger. Athena smirked to herself. Aphrodite had not been particularly clever, but, in the end, she'd foiled Ares's attempt to keep her with him forever.

Athena studied the crescent that was carved into the heavy stone face. Aphrodite was said to have chosen the mark for him in the days when they were happy together.

Athena held out her hand to slow her men. The doors swung open, though they were still a mile down the path. She wasn't quite ready. Then she thought about Argus, his organs fermenting in poison. There was no time to delay if she hoped to save his life. And that, she reminded herself, was why she'd come.

She coaxed her horse and signaled for the others to resume their trot. A few minutes later she was being helped from her mount by one of Ares' burly men. He was well-over six feet and swollen with overdeveloped muscles. Her young guards looked him over appraisingly.

Ares's man said, "Beautiful Goddess Athena, welcome to the Palace of Ares. He's been expecting you."

"Well, let us not delay then. Ares knows very little of patience," she responded curtly.

The man nodded, the thick cords of his neck bulging. "I'm Rhodes, captain of the guard. I'll see you to him and then we'll fetch bowls of cream for your kittens," he said, casting a glance at her guards.

She heard Doran, one of her young warriors, growl indignantly.

She smiled. "I see that the war god chooses his men in his own image. Arrogant and over-confident."

They passed a central courtyard where two beefy men stood naked under the water gushing from a fountain, a marble likeness of the goddess of love held a tipped basin from which the water poured.

Blood washed off the men. One had a hole in his shoulder, the other a slash to his side.

"Just back from battle," she observed, looking them over. They were called members of Ares' palace guard, but, as a god, he didn't need guards. His guards, like Athena's own, were warriors. The gods trained and kept personal armies so that they could fight and provide reinforcements for the loyal nations who waged wars. Ares' army was particularly skilled. When he took them into battle, they never lost.

The fountain's courtyard showed evidence that it had once had an elaborate garden, but the mounds of soil were scorched and the flowerbeds empty.

"Was there a fire?" she asked.

"It was *her* garden. He burned it last year," Rhodes said.

Athena smiled. No weapon forged could deal an injury that could make the war god of Elios flinch, but a soft-fleshed goddess with big blue eyes had wounded him deeply. "Now the ground is barren and bloody. Suits his mood, does it?" she asked.

"That's a question better left for him."

Athena's sandals fell softly against the black marble floor as Rhodes opened a great door. She stepped into a large banquet hall. There were warriors eating, some conversing as they did so, while others watched a group of dancing women wearing diaphanous veils.

Even in a huge room, Ares was difficult to miss. He leaned against a stone column, nearly seven feet tall and dressed in black leather. She knew the exact moment that he spotted her. He didn't acknowledge her with his eyes, but there was a slight change in his posture, a straightening. She picked up her pace, and her young guards fell in step with her.

"Leave your men to eat with mine," Ares commanded when she was standing in front of him.

"We stay with our mistress," Doran said defiantly.

Ares laughed. "You can tell them, Athena, that they won't need you to protect them. My men won't hurt them while we're gone."

Athena fought to keep the smile from her face. Her men were loyal. She wouldn't let them see that Ares's sarcasm entertained her at their expense.

"It's been a long journey. Eat to keep up your strength," she instructed them and fell into step behind Ares who was already striding away.

"I didn't expect you to wear burgundy." He led her into a small room with a round table and a few chairs. "I thought you might have remembered that I like it."

He poured wine the same color as her dress into a glass.

"Do you?" She feigned ignorance.

He smiled. They both knew that she'd remembered. He held out the glass. "Will you have a drink with me?"

"Why wouldn't I?" she asked, taking it from him. She would not bring up Argus yet. She drank the dry wine. It was very strong. Not surprising.

"You look beautiful." He eyed the satin that was pulled taut across her full breasts. "I hadn't planned to seduce you, but you tempt me sorely with those ribbons."

Even a look was dangerous. Ares was as famous for insatiable lust as he was for bloodletting. She felt her nipples harden and saw his eyes flicker to them.

"What did you have planned?" she asked casually. She generally preferred golden-haired boys with long lean lines, but Ares's body promised the ride of a lifetime.

She glanced over his chest and stomach before settling on his groin. She brought her gaze slowly back to his amused black eyes. She reminded herself that she hadn't come to see to her own pleasure. She'd made the journey to save Argus' life because she was in love with him. Ares who had poisoned him to lure her there was not to be trusted or desired. He was to be despised.

"It took you longer to arrive than I expected," he said, taking a step forward.

She could feel the heat from his body. "Why were you expecting me at all?"

"Because I poisoned your lover."

Athena's breath caught in surprise. He'd ended the game so quickly.

"Care to explain why you did?" she asked, planting her fists on her hips.

"So that I could offer you the antidote in trade."

"In trade for what?"

"At the moment, I'd very much like to say your body." His eyes caressed her form.

"But?" she demanded.

"I've found her."

"Who?" she asked.

"The woman who got her essence."

"What are you talking about?"

"When Aphrodite fled, she removed her essence and cast it to the universe. I've been hunting for it ever since, but mortal women live short lives. I usually find it too late."

Athena scoffed. "Aphrodite couldn't cast her essence away. It's not something that can be sliced from the soul like a bit of skin can be sliced from the body."

Ares just ignored this. "She's on Earth."

"Aphrodite?"

"No, the woman I want. It's taken me years to rediscover what I lost. I'm going to bring her here."

"Impossible. Mortals can't travel between worlds the way we can."

"I know. That's why you have to devise another way."

"In exchange for Argus's life? He'll be long dead before I can form a plan."

"I'll give you the cure for him today in exchange for your promise that you'll put your mind to this problem."

"Ares," she said, shaking her head. "You ask me to do the impossible."

"Wisdom, thy name is Athena," he said dryly. "Isn't cleverness your great boast? I lay the challenge at your feet. Prove that your mind is superior to all others."

"You must want this woman very badly."

"I do."

She stared at him, finding it hard to believe that the narcissistic god of war was asking for help to claim some mortal woman whose beauty would decay in the blink of an eye. *The woman must truly have some part of Aphrodite.* Athena wondered if, for once, Ares would get more than he bargained for.

She said curtly, "Give me the cure for Argus. I'll put my mind to use for you."

# Chapter 4

"Your hands are shaking," Sheila accused.

Estella sat on the couch in her living room, bundled in a quilt.

"I've had three cups of coffee."

"Why?" Sheila demanded.

"I don't want to go to sleep," Estella said softly.

"Why on earth not?"

Estella bit her lip nervously. *Because I'm dreaming of him all the time, and I wake up less rested than when I went to bed.* "I just don't want to."

"That's not a reason." Sheila sank into the overstuffed cushions of the couch. She pulled a fluffy stuffed bunny from under her butt and tossed it on the coffee table. "Stuffed animals, Stel? C'mon, hon, what's going on? Two days ago, you get a migraine and can't come to dinner. The day before that you faint. What gives? You don't get sick, honey. You need to see a doctor."

"I'm okay. It was just a virus, and I'm over it."

"Yeah, right. You look like you're over it. What's that?" Sheila said, hopping up and walking over to the magazine bin to pull out a huge book with a shiny cover sticking out. She held it up and examined it. "*Mythology of the Greeks and Romans.* Fifty-six dollars? It wasn't even on sale! Last month you couldn't afford your water bill."

"I paid it. I was just a little late."

"Still."

"It's an old book."

"It looks brand new," Sheila said suspiciously. "I've never seen it before."

*That's because I'm lying.* "It was in a box." Estella averted her eyes.

"Well, I'm glad you're well enough to be climbing in the attic and unpacking boxes because we're going to The Domino Club."

"Oh, I don't think so."

"Leslie's new boyfriend's band is playing at The Domino Club. If you're not dying, she expects you to be there. Are you just going to blow her off?"

"No," Estella said with a sigh. She got up from the couch and tossed the blanket down. She shivered. "I want Doug to protect me tonight."

"From all the guys who will try to pick you up? Estella, you're the only woman I know who views her good looks as an albatross."

"I'm just kind of jittery. I don't think I could handle a bunch of horny guys."

"Righto. Doug and I will be on it," Sheila said. "But wear something sexy. Leslie suggested your red dress."

"Why do I have to dress sexy?"

"The lead singer's a babe. Les thought you might like him."

The band was loud. The crowd was surly. And Estella was doing her best to avoid notice. She'd worn a clingy black tank dress with a short skirt as a compromise since Sheila had been acting like the wardrobe police. To feel less exposed though she'd wrapped herself in a big lavender scarf that covered her arms and the dress's scoop neck.

Their friend Leslie was supremely stylish in retro Gucci, but her dark eye makeup had run after all the wild gyrations, a.k.a. dancing, she'd done. Now she looked slightly raccoonish. Still, Estella envied her wild abandon.

"Estella, baby, I need a favor," Leslie said.

"What?" Estella asked, raising her voice above the noise.

"The hot new king of the bouncers won't let us up into the VIP section because we're with the band, and they're barred from up there because Neal, the bass player, got drunk and smashed some things. Anyway, he—the king bouncer—has been eyeing you like you're a tasty treat. If you flirt with him a little, maybe he'll let us in."

"What do you mean? Just go up there and talk to him? I can't do that." She craned her neck, trying to get a look at the man in question.

"Stel, you can do it for us," Leslie encouraged, pushing her toward the stairs.

"But—"

"Let that scarf slip down a little."

She looked at Sheila for help, but Sheila was nodding like she thought it was the best idea since ice.

"There you go now," Leslie said, pushing Estella up the first step.

Estella tried to turn back, but Leslie and Sheila were blocking her path. She gave them an exaggerated grimace and spun around. She took a deep breath, wrapping her scarf around herself even tighter.

She could feel herself flushing. She watched her feet and practiced her smiles as she climbed slowly. Hopefully the guy liked dumb blondes, and she could just stay mute most of the time, nodding and grinning at whatever he said.

She got to the top and paused, still staring down at her black toe-thong sandals.

"Well, hello," a deep male voice said.

She looked up. *Him.* Her smile evaporated, and she started to fall backward, but he caught her.

"Easy there," he said, pulling her in and holding the entire weight of her body with one of his arms.

It was the cop, but his hair was long. *A wig?* His hair hung just above those massive shoulders, and it was thick and slightly wavy.

*This is no coincidence.* Without thinking, she reached up and grabbed a handful of his hair and yanked. It didn't give.

A nearby waitress clucked her tongue and said, "What the hell are you doing?"

"She was checking to see if my hair's real. Now that she's satisfied her curiosity, I'm sure she'll stop pulling it," he said with an amused grin that she recognized.

His hair slipped through her fingers as she let go.

"I don't understand," Estella heard herself say.

"What don't you understand, princess?" he asked, unhooking the velvet rope with his free hand and pulling her onto his side of it.

"I know you. We just met. Your hair was short."

"How could that be?" He secured the rope again.

"Are you a police officer?" she asked.

"Hardly," he said with a laugh.

"Do you have a brother? A twin?" Was she going crazy? No, it was the same guy. Her body tingled at the memory of his hard cock gliding along the roof of her mouth.

"No. One of a kind... like you," he said.

"Hey, Stel."

She turned to find Leslie and Sheila standing on the stairs.

"Here you are," Sheila said, eyes roving over the bouncer/cop/dream-lover like she was starving and he was a t-bone.

"If you stay up here with me, your friends can come up in twenty minutes."

Leslie and Sheila beamed.

"Why twenty minutes?" Estella demanded, looking up at his face. "Why not right now?" She didn't want to be alone with him.

"There's a private party going on."

"But you're letting me up."

"You must be special," he said in the voice that made her heart speed up.

"But—"

"It's cool," Leslie said with a nod.

"Yeah, totally fine. You stay here and hang out with him," Sheila said with a big grin. "We'll be back in a while."

Her friends plodded back down the steps in their chunky shoes.

"Perry," the guy called into the darkness of the VIP room.

Another man, shorter than her giant bouncer but wearing a similar white tuxedo shirt and black pants, appeared. "Yeah?" Perry asked.

"Watch the rope. No one comes up," he said, gently pulling Estella into the darkness. "C'mon, princess."

"My name's Estella."

"That suits you," he said, his voice caressing her.

"What's… what's your name?"

He smiled, making her blood warm. "Aristotle. You can call me Ari." He pulled back a heavy black curtain and led her past it.

"It's dark up here." She squinted as her eyes adjusted. There were barely-dressed men and women dancing in cages while cozy couples necked or drank and talked on the plush couches.

"This is a party?" she asked skeptically.

"Don't they look like they're having fun?" he murmured.

"Where are we going?" she asked.

"I work here. I know the best spots."

"Maybe I should go back downstairs to wait with my friends."

He ignored her suggestion. "Would you like something to drink? Wine?"

"I don't drink." *Though maybe I should start, to get through the next twenty minutes.*

"Come and enjoy the view with me," he said, pulling her along.

Her hesitating feet shuffled across the hard floor. He stopped at another dark curtain. Her fingers brushed it. Velvet.

He pulled the curtain back, revealing a bay window overlooking the street below and skyscrapers with twinkling lights in the distance.

"Pretty," she said.

"Go in," he said, as if the space were a room rather than four feet of floor and six feet of glass panes.

She didn't move until she felt his palm on her lower back, fingers gently indenting the flesh of her butt. She stepped forward sharply, not wanting anyone behind them to see where he'd put his hand.

"It's one-way glass. We can see out. No one can see in," he said.

She looked back and then noticed that there were ties at each end of the curtain. He knotted them around silver hooks on the wall on either side.

*Why is he doing that? So no one can pull the curtain back unexpectedly?*

He nudged her close to the window by stepping forward. His big body was right behind hers now. The music changed to Fiona Apple. The sensuous sounds were muffled by the curtain.

"What are we doing here?" she whispered.

His arms snaked around her. "Standing." He pulled her back against him, his body heating the whole length of hers.

"Why?"

"No reason." He slid a hand up under the lavender scarf and brazenly cupped her breast.

She gasped in surprise.

He bent his head so that his mouth was near her ear. "Do you believe in fate?"

"I don't know," she said.

His left hand rubbed down the front of her until he caught the bottom edge of her dress with his fingers.

"I believe in fate," he said softly. "Some things are written in the heavens. Some attractions exist even before lovers meet. Sometimes even before they're born."

"I don't know about that," she said, swallowing slowly. Funny that her throat was dry when other places were getting so wet. *I should not be falling for his crazy lines.*

He kissed her shoulder where it was bare and then sucked on the side of her neck. Her head lolled to the other side, providing more exposed skin as her hair fell away.

"I don't know you," she said weakly as he sucked.

"Sure you do." He was slowly dragging her dress up her thighs.

She dropped her arms, laying her hands over the fabric to stop its upward progression.

"Careful, you'll rip it," he said, though he was the one pulling the fabric.

His right hand left her chest and joined his left. He put his hands over hers and then pulled both her hands and her dress up, exposing her legs and panties.

"What are you doing?" she asked in a sharp whisper.

"Getting you ready."

Heat and dizziness captured her. "For what?"

"To be pleasured, princess." His left arm came around her waist so that she couldn't push her dress down. The right hand dug between her tense thighs and rubbed against her curls through the satin of her underwear.

"Wait a minute." She clutched his right wrist and pulled.

His arm didn't budge. His hand cupped her tighter, pressing the satin between her lips. He stroked her twitching clit, causing her breath to catch and her legs to buckle. His strong left arm caught her body as she sagged for a couple seconds.

She straightened back up.

"Who are you?" she asked desperately. This was crazy. Three giant men in a week, taking her over, forcing her to sexual submission with an attitude of possession.

"I'm the one who wants you more than all the others."

He caught the straps of the tank dress and stretched them, pulling them down over her shoulders.

"What are you doing?"

"We covered that." He pulled the fabric down over her left elbow and neatly eased her arm out of the armhole. He repeated the maneuver on the other side and then unwound the scarf from her.

Cool air nipped at her bare breasts. He caught her wrists in front of her and in a blur of speed, tethered them together.

"You don't mind being tied, do you?" he whispered.

"I—" No, she didn't exactly mind, but she could never admit that out loud.

"You never know when you'll become someone's prisoner. It's best to learn to be captured gracefully. That way, you won't panic."

"I'm not—no one's going to take me prisoner. I don't know where you're from, but this is a free country." She trailed off as he put her arms in the air, nudging her forward until her fists were resting against the glass.

"Keep your hands there."

"No. Why?" She started to slide her arms down.

He pressed her suddenly and firmly forward so that her arms were trapped between the window and her body. His body pressed against hers.

"Be good, princess. I'm not equipped to punish you here, but that day will come if you make me angry enough."

"Let me go," she said frantically.

"Not a chance of that."

"I'll scream. You'll end up in jail."

He chuckled. "You're always threatening to scream. I don't think you will."

She was stunned. She'd only threatened to scream in her dream. No one had been there.

Behind her, in a quick movement, he dragged her panties down to her ankles.

"Hey," she ground out, trying to keep her legs together and to keep him from doing what he was most certainly planning.

He pulled her right foot up by the ankle, unlooping the underwear from it. He set her foot back down and then got her other ankle in his hand. She was like a horse getting shoed. He was the master. She could buck all she wanted, but she was going to lose in the end.

Her bare backside twitched as he stood up. He cupped her buttocks, gripping one cheek firmly in each his hands.

"Put your arms back up," he said in a soft growl.

She couldn't move. She was torn between wanting to scream for help and wanting to do exactly what he told her to do so that she could get some relief from the terrible tension that was building in her body.

"Estella, disobeying me is not in your best interest."

"I just need a minute to think," she whispered.

"No, you don't." He pulled her cheeks in opposite directions.

She felt the stretch acutely from back to front. She suddenly wanted to lie facedown, ass in the air, knees apart, so that he could bury his cock in her pussy from behind.

She bit her lip and whimpered at the impulse. *Where is all this heat coming from?* she wondered helplessly as she put her arms back up. Her elbows rested on the glass and her hands hung back toward her head.

He pressed her so that her breasts were squashed against the cold glass. Her breath came out in pants, fogging the window close to her lips.

His hands released her butt and moved to either side of her. Right hand on her belly. Left hand on her lower back.

"You are my demigoddess, Estella. You must understand that things between us will never follow an ordinary course. I will make you naked and touch you wherever I want, as often as I like." His right hand, to illustrate his point, snaked down to her curls. Her cleft was shamefully damp as his fingers probed it.

"Dew covers the rose petals." He pushed a long finger into her. "I look forward to the day when I will bury myself inside you. It won't be tonight. Too many people around. I suspect I'll come very loudly the first time with you."

He stroked her inside, making her whimper. His left hand traveled from her back to her buttocks and down so that if her legs gave way she'd be sitting on his hand. Then a couple of fingers from the left hand joined the one inside her from the right.

Her forehead banged against the glass as she brought it forward sharply.

"Careful. If you knock yourself out, you never know where you'll wake up."

"I can't do this," she said, feeling overwhelmed. She wanted to moan and scream and flail. He was making her feel so hot and so good. It was incredibly unfair to take her behind a curtain in a club full of people and do this to her.

Her breasts rubbed lewdly against the glass as she bobbed. His hands held her and resisted whenever she started to slip off them.

"Please," she cried. "I can't."

"You will."

"No. Not that—I can't keep quiet," she said with a shudder.

"Turn your head, princess. Look at me."

She did and saw him through damp lashes as flames leapt up from her pussy.

She groaned very softly. His mouth descended on hers, and he swallowed her moans as she came in a series of wracking spasms.

Afterward her legs felt so weak. She no longer cared if she collapsed inelegantly to the ground, so she let her knees buckle.

She didn't fall. He held her up, still kissing her. His tongue teased hers, tasting her mouth.

She moved her arms bringing them over his head. They caught on his shoulders.

He straightened up, sliding his hands free, so that she dangled from where the scarf joined her wrists. She hung in a languid stretch for a couple of moments and then he hooked his left arm behind her knees and cradled her in the air, his right arm against her back.

She felt a tear slide over her cheek and down to where their lips were joined. She wasn't crying from sadness. It was the crushing rush of emotions, too intense to handle.

He drew his lips back and licked the tear. "I've given you nothing to weep about." The words were whispered against her lips, and she almost felt them rather than heard them.

She felt so strange. So rapt. It no longer mattered to her that her dress was a tube of material around her waist so that every private part of her was available in the open air. She didn't care about anything except how much she wanted him and how overwhelming that was.

She wasn't sure if he was the same person—bouncer, cop, and dream-lover all in one—or if the cop and bouncer were doppelgangers and she'd somehow anticipated and foreseen them in the dream.

*Anticipated and foreseen?*

Like fate had whispered to her subconscious that he was coming? It strained the imagination to conceive of something like that.

"Ari," a voice from beyond the curtain said softly. "Her friends are at the rope again."

He broke from the kiss. "Make them wait on the stairs." His voice was gravelly with a splash of ice water in it.

Estella pulled her arms over his head again, clutching them to her chest. "Untie me. Let me down."

"Kiss me again first," he said.

"No, they're coming."

"No one's coming."

She turned her head away from his mouth.

"Kiss me again, Estella, or I'll pull the curtain back and we can put on a show for the whole room."

He sounded serious, which would make him utterly crazy.

"I've done everything you've told me to do. Now you need to put me down so I can fix my dress."

"Woman, you try my patience."

"Put me down now," she said firmly. "I'll kiss you again, once, after you untie me and I fix my dress."

He smiled. "If I didn't think you'd faint, I'd prove that you can never really defy me except when I let you."

He set her down, and she looked up at his handsome face as he unknotted the scarf and slid it loose.

She took a step back, feeling his eyes on her as she readjusted her clothes.

"I need my underwear," she said.

He retrieved them from his pocket and put them to his face, inhaling their scent. She blushed, shaking her head at him as he licked his lips. He held them out to her.

"The next time we meet, you won't be wearing any."

"I always wear underwear."

"You can put them on if you want. But you'll suffer the consequences."

"I'm not coming back to this club," she said. "My friend's boyfriend is in the band. We just came to hear him play."

"I never said we'd be meeting in a club next time."

"Then where?"

"You'll know."

"How?" she asked, grabbing the end of her scarf and tugging on it.

"Because I'll make sure of it." He let the scarf slip from his hand. She looked it over. Even in the dim light she could tell that it was terribly wrinkled.

"I can't use this as a shawl. It looks like it's been wadded up in the laundry for a week," she complained.

"Tie it around your waist."

"And leave my shoulders bare?" she asked skeptically. "I don't like to show too much skin. It invites trouble."

"I'm the biggest trouble in this place tonight. And since my lust for you will be unaffected by your bare shoulders, you can expose them at will."

"I'm not worried about you, but there are other guys that are less interesting to me than you are."

He laughed. "Interesting? Your choice of words amuses me, princess."

"Can you stop calling me 'princess'?"

He shrugged. She rolled her eyes, and tried to shove him aside. It was like pushing a concrete wall. "Get out of my way."

"You promised me a kiss after your hands were free and your dress was fixed."

*Damn.* She'd forgotten. "Well, I changed my mind."

"Pity I haven't changed mine," he said smoothly. He folded his arms across his chest.

There was no way she could get past him.

"If I don't feel like kissing you, I don't have to. It's a woman's prerogative to change her mind."

"You tell me not to call you princess, then you act like one."

*Jerk!* "Can you get out of my way?"

"I can, but I'm not going to. You'll never break a promise to me, Estella, because I'll never let you."

His words were so serious, like they'd been lovers for years and he had some right to tell her what he would and would not tolerate in her behavior. She tried to muster up some righteous indignation and a little fury, but it just wouldn't come. She found him so attractive, even with his arrogance, even when he said vaguely menacing things, that she couldn't stop the lust that bubbled up inside her. *I need to get away from him. I can't control how he makes me feel, but I can control what I do about it.*

"Look, my friends are waiting."

"I know. That's your fault. You're preventing your rendezvous with them. "

"I am not."

"Kiss me, and I'd let you pass."

"You think just because you're big you can bully people?"

He laughed. "It's not the only reason, but it's certainly one of them."

Her jaw went slack with shock. He was completely unbelievable. Who admitted to being a bully? There was definitely something off about him.

"My patience wanes. Kiss me." He bent his head so that she could reach his mouth.

She was tempted to punch him right in the nose, but didn't. Still, it was surely a bad omen that violence sprang to mind as she contemplated him. The guy led her emotions in all sorts of crazy directions.

She put her hand on his shoulder and pressed her lips to his. She heard him inhale deeply as she kissed him. He opened his mouth and sucked on her tongue, making her whole body shudder.

She drew back, covering her mouth for a moment. "You are sin made flesh," she said.

"Indeed. As are you." He ran a fingertip over her cheek.

An instant later, he'd unhooked the tie and flung the curtain back. She stepped past him quickly, but he caught her arm before she could make any real progress in separating herself from him.

"Not too fast. My erection isn't anxious to make sudden moves that don't involve sex."

"You don't have to come with me. You can let me go. I'll find my friends by myself." *And get the heck out of here.*

"After that orgasm I gave you, I'd have expected you to be a little more grateful and a little more courteous."

"That whole scene was your idea, not mine," she said as they walked.

"And it was just awful for you," he said. "Knowing you don't appreciate it, I'll be sure to be take less care with your body next time."

"Stop threatening me," she snapped and pursed her lips. Now that they were back in the room with other people and her naked butt was covered up, she was feeling braver.

He laughed. "Stop behaving badly, and I'll stop treating you that way," he said, waving his hand toward himself as some sort of signal to one of the bouncers a few feet away.

"Of all the arrogant—"

Her friends burst through the curtain leading into the room. They rushed over to her.

"Are you okay?" they asked in unison, clutching her and pulling her toward them.

"Doug's down there threatening the manager," Sheila said, looking Ari over suspiciously. "We thought    we didn't know if you were okay."

She felt Ari stroke her arm with his thumb.

"She was perfectly safe. I took good care of her. Didn't I, princess?" he asked, eyes like smoldering coals.

"I'm okay."

"Good. Good," Sheila said, clearly somewhat shaken. "Well, c'mon. I've had enough of this place."

"Yeah." Leslie glanced around the room. "There's nothing special up here. Let's take off."

"We're going," Estella announced, looking at Ari's face for signs of protest.

"Did I give you back your underwear? Oh, yes, I did."

All three women let out shocked gasps.

"Remember what I said about not wearing them the next time I see you." He released her arm and turned his back on their explosion of furious words. He strode away.

Leslie and Sheila each grabbed an arm and hauled her toward the stairs, cursing him the entire time. They all hurried down the stairwell.

It wasn't until they were outside the club that the tirade ebbed.

"Lying bastard. He was lying, right?" Leslie asked.

"Of course he was lying," Sheila snapped indignantly. "Estella wouldn't have sex with some bouncer in the middle of a club!"

Estella felt like hugging Sheila, who was such a good friend, defending her even though she didn't deserve it. And there was no excuse for Ari saying that in front of them. The next time she saw him, she was going to run the other way. But, with her luck, he'd probably catch her.

*And you want to be caught.*

*No, I don't.*

*Yes, you do.*

Ares materialized in the parking lot, but remained invisible. He had played at being flippant in front of Estella, but he was serious now. He wanted to be sure that no one accosted her on her way home. As he trailed after the women, he heard Estella's friends call him a Barbarian, and he was so insulted he almost appeared to inform them that he was no Barbarian. He was a Greek and a god. Then he realized that they were using the term broadly, to describe his manner, not his ethnicity. He saw Estella frown and nod her head as they advised her of how lucky she was to have gotten away from him.

He scowled at their exaggerated outrage. He'd teased her and mocked her, but only gently. He certainly hadn't injured her. Their fury was so out of proportion to his offenses. Was she bloody? Had he broken her bones? Of course not. And yet she said nothing to contradict their scathing assessment of his behavior. *After what transpired behind that curtain, why doesn't she defend me?*

*Because she's not Aphrodite. We have no history, and, even if I feel the old connection between us, she does not. She's mortal and easily shocked, and wary of men because she's not a goddess. If a mortal man attacked her, she* **would** *be defenseless.*

*Defenseless.* Aphrodite had never been that. They'd had bitter fights and passionate reconciliations, and their affair had been a battle they'd both enjoyed until he'd been too distracted by other concerns and she'd left him.

Estella was his chance to recapture what had been lost, and once he had her on Elios, she wouldn't be able to leave him. Until then he must tread carefully. Mortals had fragile sensibilities, and he did not want her to turn away from him. She was important to him. She was the first woman he'd wanted in ages.

# Chapter 5

Sitting inside her palace of periwinkle stone, Athena ran a hand over the folds of her white gown and then picked up an olive and ate it. The great cat Kemo padded across the rug toward her. She ran a hand over his sleek white fur, and he yawned, revealing a jaw span as big as a child's head. The cat's lavender eyes met her gray ones. She fed him several olives, and he purred until a knock on the door interrupted them.

"Yes?" she said.

The door swung open and Argus stood in the doorway. He wore a robe as he had during his convalescence, but he no longer looked ill.

"Come in, my darling," she said.

He strode into the room, frowning, causing her to raise an eyebrow.

"What troubles you, Argus?"

"I've heard you entered into a pact with Ares."

"I did. It saved your life."

"You should have let me die if a pact with him was my only salvation."

Narrowing her eyes, she said, "You question my judgment? Tread carefully, Argus."

"Knowing that you went there to save me, I could not bear for him to retaliate against you if you can't keep your promise. I'd rather have died than see you in his hands."

She smiled at him. His handsome face was lined with worry despite his relatively young age.

"I've wounded Ares on the battlefield. True, he is more powerful now, but we are not so unevenly matched."

"I beg you not to underestimate him."

"Never, but I know his nature. He is bloodlust. I am strategy. The balance between us is easily maintained. And, in any event, he is not interested in me. He is preoccupied with a mortal woman. But let us not speak of Ares, when you are looking so fit again." She slid her chair back and stood up in front of him. His gaze traveled over her.

"They called Aphrodite goddess of love and beauty, but I saw her. Her beauty was nothing compared to yours," he said.

Athena touched his chest where the robe gaped open. "How well are you?" she asked, sliding her hand down inside the garment.

His erection rose to stand at attention like a good soldier. She let it rub against her palm before sliding her hand down the length of him. She closed her fist around the base of his cock, watching his lids lower by half.

"Shall I ride you, my blonde stallion?" she whispered.

He nodded.

She loosened the tie of his robe, and it fell to the floor. The robe opened. She let go of him and watched his cock sway tantalizingly as he backed up toward the bed. He shrugged the robe off his shoulders as she eyed the tuft of blonde hair that his cock sprung from. The hair seemed to her very like the fur of a lion.

He lay on the bed on his back and turned his head to watch her undress. Argus was a fierce warrior, but in her bedroom he was as docile as a kitten. He'd learned early in their relationship that the strength of a goddess surpassed that of mortals. And Athena, a battle goddess, never allowed her lovers to conquer her. She always chose the position. And the time and place.

Athena slid out of her gown. She was naked underneath. Her full breasts hung heavily. They wanted sucking.

She strolled over to the bed and climbed atop it, straddling Argus' belly. She could feel the tip of his cock straining upward, but it wasn't time for that yet. She bent forward, her breasts over his face.

Argus' mouth opened hungrily, and took her in. He sucked heartily and bit lightly on her right nipple as she withdrew it.

"My love, how I've missed you," she murmured, feeding him the other breast. She closed her eyes and surrendered herself to the swirling motion of his tongue and then the deep suction as he pulled more of her soft flesh into his mouth.

"Mmm." She moved her hips, grinding her sex against him. As she rubbed, it became more inflamed. "You can move your hips," she said.

He suckled her and shook his head as he did so. She knew he wouldn't move his pelvis until she straddled it. He wanted to preserve all his lust for while he was inside her.

"Touch me, Argus," she said softly.

One hand moved to her free breast. The other tickled her clit.

She moaned and tossed her head back, braid falling down her back. He groaned, and she realized that the end of the heavy braid was swishing over his engorged rod.

He rubbed and sucked her in earnest, whipping her body into a frenzy. She pulled free of his mouth and inched back. She loved listening to him pant. She loved his hooded eyes.

She bit his nipple gently, causing him to groan again. The tip of his cock was just inside her wetness. He'd balled his hands into fists, trying to keep himself from moving.

She moved her hips backward sharply, gliding down onto his erection. She sat up and tightened her inner muscles, causing him to gasp. The tighter she became around him, the more frantic he became. She loved drawing the passion out of him. He'd once admitted that the place he felt most alive was in her arms.

She stared down at him as she raised herself up and then thrust back down on his cock. His eyes were closed now, his face a mask of concentration.

She tightened and leaned forward slightly to increase the pressure on her clit. Rubbing it against his pelvic bone created an absolutely exquisite sensation. Aphrodite had taught her that secret, among others. The goddess of love? Goddess of making love, more like, while she'd lived with Ares. For a moment, Athena pictured Ares and Aphrodite having sex, the god of war's fury channeled into pounding the prettiest vessel in the universe. Athena had seen Aphrodite naked, lying on a beach once with her legs open. After that day, Athena had never questioned the war god's obsession with her.

Suddenly Athena's body started to hum with excitement. She bent forward further, grabbing Argus' hands and leading them to her breasts. He squeezed them forcefully, connecting the sensation in her pussy with that in her nipples.

She tightened around him, moving up and down by small degrees, driving them both toward release.

She came as Argus roared. He thrust desperately, and their coupling grew wetter until finally he spurted inside her, and the hot seed leaked down onto him, coating her lips.

Afterward, she stretched out next to him.

"They say he's found a woman who reminds him of Aphrodite, and that you'll help him bring her here," Argus said.

Athena nodded.

"You shouldn't. He'll keep her prisoner and make her miserable."

"I've given my promise," she said running a fingertip over his chest.

"And I am not certain that Aphrodite was miserable with Ares."

"She ran from him."

"Yes, but that was perhaps so that he would chase her."

Argus shook his head. "It's wrong for you to help him in this way."

"Perhaps, but I did promise. Of course, I said that I would help him bring her here. I never said I would let him keep her."

Argus raised his eyebrows in surprise. "You'll rescue her?"

"If she wishes it."

# Chapter 6

Ares, over several weeks time, had become accustomed to treading between two worlds. Earth had once been his home, but he'd never missed it. While on Olympus, he'd been despised by most of the other gods, and he'd never collected a large following of worshippers. There had been a few epic wars, but he wasn't one for nostalgia.

On Elios, he was widely adored. Men became heroes in war and, as the war god, he enjoyed perpetually full temples. He'd drawn power from so many sources while on Elios that there he could do things, which on Earth had been inconceivable. The only thing he had not yet managed was to bring Estella to his new home. It was a source of constant aggravation. He wondered how Athena was progressing.

Ares was dragged from his thoughts by the scent of Estella. Vanilla. Always vanilla. His obsession for her had turned into something more than a desire for her body. He liked to see her face, hear her laugh, witness her kindness. He craved her presence more than he'd ever craved another being. Despite pressing matters on Elios, he could not stay away from Earth and Estella for long.

He was sitting invisibly in her small apartment on the worn sofa. She'd just come from the shower. It was too much of a torment to watch her there so he was waiting in another room for her to appear.

She'd trimmed her sleek hair so that the front only just reached her eyebrows and the rest swung above her shoulders. Aphrodite had had long, wavy butterscotch hair. He preferred the color of Estella's hair, but might like it longer. He remembered the feel of Aphrodite's hair on his skin when she leaned over him. He'd liked that. He'd noticed when he'd touched Estella's hair that it was even silkier than the goddess's. It would feel very good against his chest or stomach… or crotch.

That settled it then. When Estella got to Elios, he'd forbid her to cut it.

He was tempted to appear, but then he'd want sex, which would sap his energy too quickly. On Elios, he would be able to make love to her every hour of the day, but on Earth he wasn't as strong. Sometimes when he took human form on Earth, he felt himself less strong than even mortal men, which incensed him. He needed to gather strength and appear only when he had enough to make good use of his time in human form.

It had been two weeks since they'd been in the nightclub together, and he'd stopped disturbing her dreams because she'd become too exhausted from lack of sleep. He'd noticed that now, even though she was more rested, she spent more and more time trying to take naps. And she always sped along the stretch of road where he'd stopped her in the guise of a policeman. He was convinced that she wanted to be found again.

"Where are you?" she whispered now.

He stared at her, pleased.

"Where are you?" she asked again, looking around. Then she shook her head. "I'm going crazy."

He smiled. She missed him. She might not know it or fully accept it, but she was already his. Damn Athena for taking so long. If Estella grew old while he waited, he'd see Athena spending eternity in Tartarus.

Estella toweled her hair and picked up a scrap of paper from the cluttered pressboard desk. She walked over to the phone, carrying it. She sat on the couch next to him and set the phone on her lap.

She dialed the phone number written on the scrap and then waited for someone to pick up on the other end. Telephones were remarkable things.

"Hi, is Art there?"

*Art?*

"This is Estella, Sheila and Doug's friend."

She paused, tucking her damp hair behind her free ear.

"Right, they said you wanted me to call. I'm glad you're not holding a grudge after I had to cancel our other date."

Ares narrowed his eyes.

"Oh, they did?" She paused. "Um, I guess I look in pictures the way I really look." She paused again. "Oh, well, thanks. That's a very nice thing to say."

Ares rolled his eyes. *Telling her she's beautiful. Not particularly original.*

"So you're working on your doctorate?"

Ares leapt up, disappearing and then reappearing in human form in Estella's kitchen. He opened a cupboard, grabbed a glass, and dropped it.

It shattered on the floor. He changed form, invisible again.

A moment later, she came into the kitchen. She stared down at the broken glass and then looked around. He frowned. He'd been reduced to playing a disgruntled poltergeist. It was ridiculous for a god of his stature. He moved back to the living room. At least, she'd hung up on Art.

*Athena needs to hurry.*

Estella stopped to collect her mail before going into her home. She dropped her books on the table and flipped through the mail. There was a plain envelope, which she ripped open. It contained a plane ticket to Las Vegas in her name. She stared at it. It was for a Saturday morning departure. *This weekend.*

She pulled the envelope open further and peered inside. There was a note. She fished it out, reading.

*There will be a car waiting for you at the airport.*
*Come to me. A—*

She bit her lower lip. A. Aristotle. What was he doing in Las Vegas? How could he, on a bouncer's salary, afford to fly her there? Her heart started to pound at the thought of him.

*You can't go,* she told herself.

She sat down with a thump on the closest chair and bit her thumbnail nervously. Ari. The incredibly handsome, incredibly arrogant bouncer. Did she really want to see him again? She still didn't understand how she'd dreamt about him before she'd met him. Maybe she'd seen him someplace before they'd met and it hadn't registered to her conscious mind. But what about the cop? He'd looked so much like Ari. Were they the same guy? Was he stalking her?

*You can't go to Vegas. Remember what he said about getting taken prisoner? You might go there, and he'll drag you out into the desert never to be seen again... but I want to see him again.*

Her breathing, too quick and shallow, made her dizzy. She put her head down to her knees until she felt better. She shoved the note and ticket back in the envelope and set it on the table. She got up, took a slow deep breath and started to pace. Saturday was only a day and a half away.

She called Sheila, who answered sounding sleepy.

"Hey, you sound tired. I won't keep you long. Someone sent me a plane ticket."

"What?"

"Someone sent me a plane ticket to Las Vegas. Think I should go?"

"Who do you know in Vegas?"

"No one."

"No one." Sheila paused, then asked, "So this is some kind of secret admirer thing? Some guy that sends plane tickets instead of flowers? Sounds either rich or psycho or both."

"So I shouldn't go?"

"First off, even though it's a free ticket, when you get there you wouldn't have a place to stay, and it'd be too expensive."

"It's round trip. I'd be coming back on Sunday night. Only a one-night stay. I've never been there. It might be interesting."

"Stel, it's too crazy. Why would someone send you a ticket unless he wanted to get you out of your normal environment and to a place where you've got no friends?"

"Maybe there's a reason he's got to be there."

"Uh huh. What aren't you telling me?"

"What?"

"Out with it. You're trying to talk yourself into going by trying to convince me. You must have some idea who this guy is."

"It could be—it might be—" She winced. Why had she called Sheila?

"Who?"

"Remember that bouncer from The Domino Club?" *The gorgeous bouncer that I can not stop thinking about? The one with the dark eyes and the dark thoughts? With the big arms and long fingers.*

"What!"

Estella yanked the phone from her ear.

"That jerk? You gave him your address?"

She put the phone back against her head carefully. "No."

"I thought you never even told him your last name."

"I didn't, but you know Leslie knows the band that played there. They could've gotten my last name and given it to him." *And isn't it at least a good sign that he took the trouble?*

"I don't like this. That guy was so nasty that night. Asking all smug if he'd given your underwear back. Loud enough for everyone to hear! I wanted to clobber him."

"He was pretty awful at the end." *She's right. He's somewhat horrible. It doesn't matter that he makes my body tighten up in all the right places.*

Sheila said sternly, "Look, Estella, guys like that are trouble. They act nice part of the time, but then they're horrible, and it's not worth it."

"You're right. I'm not even sure it's him. He didn't seem like the kind of guy who'd go out of his way for a woman, like by buying plane tickets."

"Even if he did buy the ticket, it doesn't score any points with me and it shouldn't with you either. The guy's good-looking so he thinks he can get away with treating you the way he did. Tear up that ticket. Or better yet, cash it in."

Estella glanced over at the ticket envelope. "I don't know if I can do that. I didn't buy it."

"Well, just tear it up, honey. You can't go there alone."

"Uh-huh. And I guess there's no way I could talk you into going with me?"

"'Fraid not, sweetie."

"Think Les would go?"

"Check with her, but for the record, I think it's a terrible idea."

"I know. I won't go."

"Good girl."

Estella hung up and grabbed the ticket envelope.

Estella walked past the security checkpoints, still marveling at the fact that there were slot machines in the Las Vegas airport. Near the gates, she spotted a young brown-haired woman holding up a sign with her name on it.

"I'm Estella Eaton."

"Just that bag?" the woman asked, inclining her head at Estella's duffle bag.

"Yes, I'm only staying one night."

"He didn't mention it, but I guess that makes sense. Just here for the fight, huh?" she asked, waving for Estella to follow her.

"Fight?"

At the curb, the woman stopped in front of a black Lincoln Town Car and opened the back door for her. "Sure, he's fighting tonight."

"Who?"

"Ari O."

"Aristotle Onassis is dead." Even as Estella said it, she knew they were talking about the bouncer.

"Ari Odekkos. He sent a car for you and you don't even know his name? You'll fit right in around here."

"Where is he now?" *And when do I get to see him,* she thought, her heart racing in anticipation. She'd been thinking about him constantly since getting the ticket. Mental foreplay.

"Probably resting. He's got the big fight and all." The woman climbed into the front of the car and started it up.

"What fight?"

"You're kidding, right?"

Estella stared at her in the rearview mirror.

"The guy's getting paid a couple million dollars to fight tonight. If he wins, he'll be in contention, and that's where the real money comes in."

Estella gasped. "Two million dollars?" Estella leaned back, slumping in her seat as they drove along the strip. *So what was he doing working in that club? Nothing about him makes sense.*

*A boxer?* Her body shivered at the thought. He was built powerfully enough to be a fighter. She remembered the feel of his solid muscles when she'd touched him.

Estella looked up, surprised when they stopped in front of the Bellagio. The ride from the airport had been so short, she'd missed it, distracted by thoughts of Ari.

"Is he meeting me inside?" Estella asked, glancing down at her jeans. She wasn't sure how he was going to react to finding her in pants.

"I doubt it. Just go up to the desk. The room's already taken care of. You just check in."

"Okay. Let me get you something," Estella said, opening her purse.

"Honey," the driver said with a laugh. "He's making millions tonight. You let him pay."

"Right." Estella snapped her purse shut and sat, unmoving in the back seat.

"What's up?"

*I'm stalling. I don't know what the hell I'm doing here.* "Well, thanks for the ride." She climbed out, looking up and down the strip before she walked up to the hotel.

Inside, her stride slowed. It was incredible. She stopped under the ceiling of colored glass shells and swirls. It was an unlikely place for a coral reef, but it made as much sense as the rest of Vegas, where a medieval castle stood across the street from New York City skyscrapers and down the street from an Egyptian pyramid.

She checked in, and found that she was staying in a suite. It turned out to be bigger than her house. There were dark red roses in five different vases. She counted seven dozen.

She sat down on a couch and bit her lip. A plane ticket, a suite, and seven dozen roses. She shivered nervously. *Exactly what kind of sex is he expecting?*

# Chapter 7

Estella spent the day walking around from hotel to hotel. They were so big and full of interesting shops where she couldn't afford anything. She ate Chinese noodles and egg rolls for lunch and played some nickel slot machines. When she got back to the hotel, there was a dress waiting for her on the bed.

It was pale blue lace overlying an indigo lining, halter-style on top and body-hugging on bottom, very sexy and possibly the most beautiful dress she'd ever seen. She showered quickly and got ready, putting the dress on last.

"Cinderella's got nothing on me," she murmured as she slid it over her head. The lining was silk, and she'd been in beds that weren't as comfortable as the dress. She walked to the mirror and stared at herself. The top showed more skin than she normally did, but the dress was gorgeous, and she couldn't wait for him to see her in it.

She ran a finger along the edge of the material covering her chest. If she bent her neck forward, there was a little slack. She'd be able to get her hand inside it easily. Of course, his hands were huge. He might not have such an easy time. Knowing him though, he'd just make her take it off. She bit her lip. Why was she already contemplating stripping when she'd just gotten dressed?

She found shoes to match the dress in the closet next to the black sandals she'd brought from home. She slipped on the new shoes and took a deep breath. She was delivering herself like a pretty present right into his hands. In her head, it was a terrible idea. To the rest of her body, already tense with anticipation at seeing him, it made perfect sense.

An hour later, she was at the fight-site, taking her seat ringside. The other people in her row were looking her over, probably wondering who she was. She smoothed her skirt and then clasped her hands on her lap.

The announcer got in the ring, and booming music started overhead. The audience came to its feet. She looked around, realizing that the fighters were about to come in.

A moment later, she saw a tall figure cloaked in a deep burgundy satin hooded robe enter the arena. There were cheers, and everyone rose, Estella too. It was him. It had to be. He towered over the group around him.

He entered the ring like a king returning to his castle. He tossed the hood back, and she stared up at him. He'd shaved his beard and buzzed his hair. His face was still handsome, but the angles seemed sharper, almost brutal. She took a step back, but didn't realize it until her calves bumped into the chair behind her.

The opponent, Nolo Johnson, wasn't as tall, but he was just as muscular. Estella wasn't worried about Ari's fate, but as she retook her seat, she reassured herself that he was the stronger of the two fighters. Without the robe, his body was sculpted and powerful. A godlike body.

When the fight began, the two fighters pounded on each other viciously, locked in a violent dance. They both moved in a blur of speed, elegant in their footwork. She had never liked boxing as a sport, but there was something compelling about it, and she couldn't look away from Ari and his prey.

Finally, Nolo fell. His sweat and blood spattered with the impact, and she shuddered. The ten count seemed agonizingly slow. He pulled himself up, but not in time.

The bell rang and the referee grabbed Ari's arm and held it up in victory. He smiled as flashbulbs popped. And then as she stood watching him, he turned and looked directly at her and winked. She shook her head, but felt the corners of her mouth curve up. He pulled free of the men embracing him and stalked over to the ropes. Over the cheers of the crowd, he said, low and intimate, just for her, "Hello, princess."

Estella took a deep breath. "Congratulations."

"The driver will take you back to the hotel. I'll meet you there, and we'll celebrate." A trickle of blood oozed down his cheek, and he wiped it away.

"You're hurt."

"No." He dropped to one knee and reached through the ropes. His hand cupped the back of her head, and he pulled her mouth to his. He tasted like sweat and raw power. Her lips tingled from the force of the kiss. "You're beautiful."

She pulled away. "It's the dress. Thank you."

"It's not the dress. I have a surprise for you tonight."

She wiped a smudge of blood from his face. "Take your time. I'll wait if you need to let a doctor look at you."

"The only attention I need isn't medical." He stood, and she looked up at him for a moment, then she felt a hand on her arm. The driver had come through the crowd to collect her. She glanced back once, to see him in the center of the ring, then followed the driver out into the cool desert night. She rode back down the strip, feeling strange. She wouldn't have believed she could enjoy a boxing match, but she had—because he was the one doing the boxing.

When she walked into her hotel room, she was startled to hear running water. She hesitated until he walked out of the bathroom.

"You're back already?" she mumbled, staring at him. "It's not possible."

He grinned. "I don't suppose it is."

She took a couple steps back. What was happening to her? Was she going crazy?

"Come help me bathe." His voice was low and intimate.

"You don't look like you need help."

His muscles flexed as if to agree that they were perfectly capable of any task put before them. "I never said I needed help. What I need is your hands all over me."

Estella put her hand to her forehead. "I'm... there's something wrong with me. I think there is."

He moved closer to her. "There is nothing wrong with you. You're perfect. Come in here," he said, taking her hand and leading her into the bathroom.

"Stop." She yanked her hand free. "I'm frightened. I don't know if I'm dreaming or losing my mind or what. Things don't feel real."

"Let me wash while we talk." He nodded toward the shower. It was so deep that no curtain was necessary, like a dark hidden cave. "Take off your dress."

She shook her head. "Are you listening to me? I saw you in the middle of the ring as I left. You can't have beaten me here. I'm losing time... or something. And this isn't the first time. I'm dreaming about you before you show up, hearing your voice when you're not there. I'm—my mind is—"

"Relax," he said, taking her by the shoulders. "I took a shortcut. That's all. You're fine. Your mind is as flawless as the rest of you." He sounded completely sincere about the shortcut and not the least bit worried that she might be going crazy.

*I don't feel sick. Maybe I am okay.*

"Nothing's wrong," he said, brushing his lips across her temple. "Everything is exactly as it should be."

"What's gotten into you?"

"What?" he asked innocently.

"You're being sweet."

He laughed. "I'm in a pleasant mood. Things have gone my way tonight, and I expect that to continue." He slid down his shorts. She stared at him. He was magnificent.

He walked into the shower. "Come in here before I drag you in."

Her pulse pounded under her skin, her body moistening, ripening at the sight of him. She felt slightly dazed. Everything was happening so fast, too many emotions too quickly. Excitement, panic, now lust. She needed a minute to catch her breath. He didn't give it to her. He stepped out of the shower, water mixed with blood and sweat running over his body and onto the formerly pristine pale blue tile.

Her eyes widened. He grabbed her by the arms and lifted her.

"Wait," she gasped, but he ignored her and yanked her in next to him. Water sprayed down on them. "Oh, no," she groaned, as the water and his blood dripped on the beautiful lace.

"Gowns can be replaced," he growled. "Pay attention to me."

She looked up at him through the pounding water and smiled. "I am. How could anyone not?"

"The soap." He nodded his head at the bar of soap sitting in the dish.

"What about it?"

He handed it to her. "Wash me."

Her laughter bubbled just loud enough to be heard over the water. "You really are a prima donna in some ways, Ari." She took the soap from the disk and worked it into lather in her hands. "Do your trainers do this for you when I'm not around?"

"Not so far," he grumbled, "but if I'd known you would take so long, I might have considered asking them to."

She grinned. "Turn around and rinse the front of you first."

He turned, rinsing, and started to turn back.

"No." She put a hand on his back. "Stay that way for a minute." She set the soap down and reached for the tops of his shoulders, letting her slippery fingers caress him.

He tilted his head forward, and the water ran in rivulets down his neck and the middle of his back. Her gaze traveled down with the water, stopping at his muscular butt. It was tight and perfect. Things low in her body throbbed, ready for him.

She rubbed her hands over his slick skin and then lathered her hands again. He was perfectly still as if made of flesh-covered granite. It helped her to relax and concentrate on what she was doing. She scrubbed and kneaded his flesh, enjoying the feel of him under her fingertips. He really was a remarkable specimen of the male body. She could see the edges of his muscles even when he wasn't moving and causing them to ripple.

She bent down to wash the backs of his legs. She admired his poise. Her own knees would probably have buckled if someone had started washing them while she was naked.

When the only thing left to wash were his gorgeous buttocks, she hesitated.

"Do you want to do the rest yourself?" she asked.

"Finish what you started," he said in a rumbling baritone.

She took a small bracing breath and then put her hands on his ass. He moved his feet, widening his stance. She felt the heat in her body rise. She wasn't sure what he wanted her to do. She massaged suds into his lower back and butt, but carefully avoided the space between his cheeks.

She took a step back finally. "Done."

He looked over his shoulder at her, smirking. He stood up straighter, bringing his feet back together. "There are those who would undoubtedly chide you for not being bolder. There are plenty that have begged for access to that area of my body."

"Why do they want it?" she asked, blushing furiously.

He smiled. "I'm sure you can guess."

She looked down for a moment, thinking about gay guys propositioning him. Finally, she looked back up to meet his gaze. "Ever let anyone...?"

He shook his head. "So, you're finished with the back of me?"

"Yes."

"Sometime," he said, as he turned to face her, "when I put my fingers in places that feel uncomfortable at first, you'll have to remember that I offered you the same latitude."

"Just because you offered doesn't mean I will." She kept her eyes focused on his right shoulder.

"You don't need to offer. I'll do what I wish."

The stab of lust was so powerful her knees nearly buckled. He turned her on so much it worried her. "You talk like if I don't agree, you'll just rape me."

"I would never have to. When the time comes, I'll do what I want, and you'll enjoy it."

"There are some things I *won't* agree to."

He smiled again. Clearly he was skeptical of her resolve. "You can't foresee how things will end up between us. It's silly for you to predict what our relationship will entail."

"We may never see each other again after tonight," she said.

"Well, then, at least do a good job washing the front of me so that I can remember you fondly."

She got the distinct impression that he was mocking her. He took the soap and lathered up his hands and then rubbed them over his scalp.

"That's not for your head."

"It doesn't matter," he said tipping his head back to rinse it.

"Why did you cut your hair?"

"For the fight."

"Will you grow it back?"

"What length pleases you?" he asked.

"I liked the way you had it in the bar."

"I'll take that under advisement."

She watched as he lathered up again and washed his arms and then under them. His chest was so wide, the expanse of muscle so male, it took her breath away. When he said he would do what he wanted to her, she believed it. He looked utterly unstoppable.

He turned and rinsed and then turned back, handing her the soap. He rested his hands on top of his head as if surrendering his body back to her. She lathered up her hands and ran them over his chest, studying the way her fingers looked amidst his black hair. She rubbed a fingertip over his left nipple and then glanced up at his face.

"Are you sensitive to being touched here?" she asked.

"Sensitive isn't an adjective often used to describe me."

"You know what I mean." She dragged her fingernail over his right nipple.

"I find that having you touch me anywhere is stimulating." He glanced down at his nipple. "It makes it difficult for me to control myself."

She pulled her hand away.

"I didn't say you should stop."

"I'm not sure I'm ready to see you lose control."

"You're ready for more than you realize."

Again, lust sizzled through her. She washed his stomach. His abs were so tight that it was like running her hand over bone rather than muscle. She moved her hands outward and washed his hips and then she paused.

"Now what?" he said with a smirk. "Will you kneel to wash my legs?"

"No, I think you can do your own legs."

"As you wish, but you'll wash my groin. On that, I insist." He snagged the soap and washed his muscular thighs and calves and then his feet. He turned to rinse and then turned back, thrusting the soap out challengingly.

She wouldn't have minded washing his legs. They were nice and long and muscular. By refusing, she'd been trying to avoid coming to eye-level with his crotch and the temptation of sucking him to orgasm. This time she wanted them to take their time and their pleasure together.

"Take the soap, Estella," he commanded.

She took it and created some lather, glancing at the black hair funneling downward. Her gaze followed its trail.

His partially engorged cock was long and thick. She couldn't imagine how big it would get if he were fully erect. She remembered kneeling in front of the cop and how she could never get all of him in her mouth. Was it possible that Ari and the cop were two different men? With the same face? The same build? The same oversized package below the belt?

"Tell me the truth," she said, rubbing soap gently into his balls.

"About what?" he asked, a feral light shining in his eyes.

"The night at the club wasn't the first night we'd met. You were pretending to be a cop one night, right? You borrowed a uniform and car from some friend of yours or something?"

"Something like that."

"So it was you?"

"It was me."

She soaped up the tuft of hair at the base of his cock, twisting her fingers in it.

"I took you into the woods. You took me into your mouth," he said.

She ran the edge of the soap over his cock slowly. It was fully erect by the time she finished. She slid her hand around him. He was very, very big. She slip-dragged her fist up and down.

He tipped his head back, eyes closed. She ran a fingertip over the slit at the tip. There was a drop of thick fluid there. She smeared it over the head, hearing him moan.

She took her time, exploring him with her fingers while he kept his eyes closed. She stared up at his tense body, his muscles twitching in response to her grip on him. She stroked him, then bent forward to lick his tip. He growled softly, wolf-like.

She straightened up as he put his arms out, bracing himself against the walls of the shower. His breathing was ragged now. She watched his massive chest expand with each inhalation. She leaned forward, running her tongue across the ribs over his heart. She kissed his nipple and then sucked slowly, tantalizingly. She liked the clean taste of his skin. She bit his flesh gently.

"Estella," he rasped.

"Yes?" she whispered, tilting her mouth a few millimeters away from his chest.

He didn't respond with words. Instead, he began to thrust with more vigor. She brought her mouth back to him, licking, kissing, sucking.

Time passed. Finally, she was startled by the sound of his fist striking the tile. He roared her name and thick cum gushed from him splashing the front of her dress and over his naked stomach and chest.

He grabbed her and pulled her to him, kissing her fiercely.

"You last a long time," she said. "My skin's all pruned up."

"Imagine what it'll be like when I'm inside you. You'll come a dozen times before I do." He slid his hand down her lower back. She felt the dress being pulled up, his hand exploring her buttocks. He grabbed her panties and made a fist, causing them to ride up.

She squirmed.

"You wore them," he growled softly in her ear.

She twisted, trying to pull free.

"You're not going anywhere," he said and picked her up, throwing her over his shoulder.

"Hey!" She slapped his wet back as he carried her out of the shower. "Put me down, Conan."

He ignored her struggling and strode into the bedroom, dropping her onto the bed. He flipped her onto her stomach. She tried to scramble up, but he had a hold on her. She felt him yank the underwear up so that it was wedged in her cleft, and then he ripped it. When he let it go, it fell open at the crotch.

He moved so that his body was pinning her to the bed. Her heart hammered from the struggle and the adrenaline and lust. A moment later, she felt him nudging her legs apart.

"Ari!" she said, not liking the high pitch in her voice.

"You have such a beautiful ass," he said, squeezing it. He swatted her bottom firmly. "You are much too defiant." He slid an arm under her, then yanked her body upward so that she instinctively put her palms and knees down on the mattress.

She felt him flick aside the gaping material of her panties and then ease his fingers into her sex. He twisted them, penetrating further and further, startling and invading her. Her body flushed, moisture easing the way for his wickedly long fingers.

"Move your knees further apart," he commanded.

She rocked back against his hand, helping his fingers impale her deeper. She moved her knees apart, giving him the access he demanded.

"Good. Now arch your back."

She gasped, her face burning as he fingered her. He slid his hand away and pulled her up so that she was kneeling upright. He yanked her wet dress forcefully over her head and tossed it aside. Then he shoved her back down onto her palms.

He moved onto his hands and knees above her. His naked pelvis was pressed against hers. She could feel his cock, hard against her bottom.

He reached up, putting his big hands over her breasts, squeezing them firmly. She panted slowly, desperately. He rolled her tight nipples between his thumbs and forefingers.

She moaned, moving her knees further apart and pressing back into him.

He banged his pelvis against her, sending white-hot stabbing desire through her. Heat pooled inside her, and she wanted him to wet himself in it, to bury his cock where it belonged.

"Ari," she moaned.

"What?" he asked, banging harder.

She tried to balance on one hand because she wanted to reach back and guide him into her pulsing core, but his thrusting body was knocking her forward too forcefully.

"Ari, do it."

"What?" he asked.

"Come inside me," she groaned.

He ignored her for several minutes and then flipped her suddenly onto her back. She splayed her legs for him, staring up into his black eyes.

"You weren't supposed to wear underwear." He ran a finger between her deeply inflamed labia.

She arched, thrusting her hips toward his hand.

He shook his head at her. "If I make you come, you'll be encouraged to defy me again in the future."

He grabbed her hand and yanked it down, pressing it over her wetness.

"Ari," she said, writhing.

"What?" he asked, bending his head. He bit her nipple, causing her to cry out.

"Please."

"You've got fingers," he said ruthlessly. He pushed down on her hand so that her own palm was ground over her clit.

She moaned deeply. "Yours are longer. Please, Ari."

He frowned and shook his head. "I shouldn't indulge you."

She panted, writhing helplessly as he continued to grind her hand against her wildly aroused body. She curled her hand, dipping a couple fingers inside. She spread her thighs wider.

He sat up, removing his hand from on top of hers. She whimpered at the immediate loss of pressure. His hand was so much stronger than hers. Even adding a finger didn't feel as good as when his hand had been on top of hers.

"Put your hand back," she begged.

"What are you going to do the next time I tell you to do something?"

"Ari, come on," she said, rubbing herself.

"Going to obey me?" he asked.

She bit her lip stubbornly trying not to say the words that threatened to spill forth. He flicked his tongue lazily over a nipple.

"Yes."

"Yes what?" he asked, raising his eyes to study her face.

"Yes, next time I'll do what you say."

"Then next time, I'll make you come. Hard." He rolled over onto his back, putting his big hands behind his head.

She screamed in frustration and heard him chuckle. She took a couple of deep breaths and then concentrated on trying to pleasure herself, but she couldn't seem to come any closer to orgasm. He was too much of a temptation and distraction, lying next to her. She pulled her hand free.

"That was a poor attempt at pleasuring yourself."

"Shut up, damn you."

She sat up and started to get out of the bed when he grabbed her and pulled her back, curling her body against his. She tried to wrench loose. She was frustrated and wanted him to know it, but she couldn't break free of his iron grasp.

"Be still. You can't escape."

"Unless you're going to make yourself useful, I want to get up."

"Too bad," he teased. His hand moved between her thighs. He stared into her eyes as his fingers moved inside her, strong and deep. She closed her eyes and arched her back. His mouth was warm on her neck, his thumb finding her clit and working it. She clutched his shoulders.

"Oh, please. Oh!" And then her body exploded into orgasm as she cried out.

He kissed her gently on the mouth and wrapped his arms around her tightly.

"Ares," he said.

"What?"

"My name is Ares. You summoned me, and I came."

She blinked. The blood was still rushing in her ears. *What is he saying?*

"I'll come back to you over and over until the day I come and take you from this place."

"What are you talking about?"

"I'm not mortal. I'm a god, and you belong to me. One day, I'll keep you forever."

She opened her mouth to scoff, but he suddenly wasn't there. She sat up and looked around.

"What the hell?"

She was alone in the room.

"I have gone *completely* crazy."

# *Chapter 8*

Ares stood at the gate to Athena's palace. The sentry spotted him and opened the gate, bidding him a fair morning and sending him, with an escort, up to the palace. The stone floors inside it were slightly coarse and pale, in contrast to the floors of his palace.

He allowed himself to be led across a blooming courtyard where winged creatures both great and small seemed to be cohabitating peacefully. A griffin landed nearby and circled him curiously. Its paw swiped the air as if testing its consistency.

Ares's power was tightly coiled inside him, but animals were always dangerously intuitive. He walked past a tree bearing ruby-colored fruit and noticed an owl blinking large eyes at him. Ares scowled at the owl, but it didn't retreat. Its feathers, the color of sepia and umber, twitched twice, but didn't ruffle.

When Ares finally reached the corridor outside Athena's suite of rooms, he recognized the boy standing guard at the door.

"Waiting to be invited in?" Ares asked dryly.

The boy didn't answer, but he frowned. Ares smirked. Clearly the invitation was exactly what interested the boy.

The door opened and Athena, dressed in an opalescent gown the color of the frothing sea, stepped forward.

"Ares, it is you. Come in."

Ares looked at the boy and said in a low voice, "You wait here. I'll let you know how she is."

The youth clenched his teeth, taking a step into the doorway directly behind Ares.

"Doran," Athena began. "Why are you on guard duty?"

"I volunteered," he said impassively.

"He's looking for goddess milk," Ares said.

Doran's sword slid free and sliced the air toward Ares's throat. It clanged against the god's sword, which Ares barely got up in time. Ares shot his free hand forward to grab the boy by the throat and lift him off the ground.

"Ares, release him," Athena said with a sigh.

Ares waited until Doran's face turned dusky before he dropped the boy. Doran gasped to recover his breath. Ares wondered if it were youth or poor training that compelled the young man to engage a god in battle. Whatever caused the poor judgment, Doran needed to be broken of it or he wouldn't last long on a battlefield.

Athena frowned at Ares, who shrugged. Soldiers needed harsh training. He doubted Athena ruled them hard enough.

"Your soldiers are quick and brave, but foolish," Ares said when she'd walked over to him.

"What possible pleasure can you have from baiting one so young?"

He folded his arms across his chest. "Males like to show off in front of females. It's the way of the universe."

"Was that supposed to impress me?" she asked with a laugh. "As if I didn't know that as a god you're stronger than a boy? You felt the need to show me?"

"Impulse," he said with a shrug. "Enough of this. Speak to me of getting Estella to Elios."

"You're convinced she has the essence of Aphrodite?"

He nodded. "I'm sure of it."

"Are you willing to risk her life?"

"Why?" Ares asked darkly.

"I have a way that may work, but it's dangerous."

He frowned. He didn't want to risk Estella. "I want her here. My powers are too diminished on Earth. I don't wish to spend my time there." He cocked his head. "But I don't want to risk her life. I don't want her hurt."

Athena's eyebrows rose in surprise.

"Can you draw on my power?" he asked. "Wound me or use me to bring her here without hurting her?"

Her pale gray eyes bored into him. "You offer to let me injure you?" she asked incredulously.

He spread his arms as if to show he wasn't concealing anything. "She's fragile. I can tolerate pain without real damage. I don't want to forfeit any of her life."

"You care for her."

*Yes.* "I care about possessing what I want for as long as possible," he said, trying to keep any sentiment from his voice. Estella was far more than a plaything, but Athena need not know that the ferocious god of war was in love with a mortal woman.

"All right," Athena said, sitting down on a cushioned bench. "You want her to serve your lust, and she has Aphrodite's essence, so we'll use those things in a ritual. We'll need a surrogate for you and for Aphrodite. They'll couple in Aphrodite's temple."

"Surrogates?" he echoed.

"Yes. Aphrodite's small temple isn't dormant. There are virgin priestesses there who still worship. They want their goddess back. I could probably convince one of them to participate under the guise of drawing her spirit here."

"Fine," he said.

"You'll need a surrogate for you."

"Done."

"You'll need to forge a bond with the surrogate… to give a drop or two of blood and power to him."

He nodded. "When can it be done?"

"Anytime, once we get the surrogates, but Aphrodite's followers blame you for her departure. I doubt her priestesses will agree to help you in anything. It may take me time to convince them."

"Tonight then."

"You are very impatient."

"I don't deny it," he snapped. "And I want the coupling in my temple."

"No priestess loyal to Aphrodite will come willingly to your temple."

"So be it. I'll bring one unwillingly."

Athena shook her head. "Ares, it's not wise to mix violence into the ritual."

"Then convince a priestess to come of her own accord." He'd felt Aphrodite's essence rising up in Estella. He wouldn't risk her gaining too much of the goddess's power. She must be brought to his temple, so that once he got her to Elios, she would be completely within his control.

Upon his return from Athena's, Ares had announced to the toughest of his soldiers that they should choose among themselves one worthy to receive his power and act as surrogate. Four hours later, Rhodes entered the great hall. His lip was split and there were bruises on his bare back and chest. Ares said nothing, but waved for him to follow him to the temple.

The torches in the corridor were burning low as they passed. Rhodes's hands hung at his sides, fists clenched as if getting ready for battle. The temple was cool and dim. A single war priest in a crimson robe waited for them. He lit some tall candles as they entered.

Ares smiled, noting that Rhodes's eyes had fixated on the thick mat at the foot of the altar. It was covered with a black satin sheet and pillows.

The altar was dressed in blood-red silk. Ares's eyes flicked to it and then back to the mat. He had assembled the best healers loyal to him. If Estella had even a faintly beating heart when she appeared, they would help her recover.

He wondered for a moment if he could trust Athena. She might not want him to have even a piece of Aphrodite. Perhaps she was drawing him into the ritual so that Estella would die and release the essence so Aphrodite could reclaim it. He gritted his teeth at the thought. *She must not die.* She meant the universe to him.

People filed in and lined the walls and aisles. Rhodes' dark eyes glanced around, but if he was nervous about performing in front of a crowd, it didn't show.

The metal doors inlaid with black diamonds opened. Several minstrels paraded in with lyres and flutes followed by a procession of girls in sheer gowns and pink ribbons. Finally, a woman strode in wearing a crown of vibrant flowers. *Aphrodite's crown.*

The woman wore a white shift of thin material. She had a full figure, like the goddess of love. Her hair, however, was a dull brown and her face, Ares could tell, would never start wars of jealousy between men.

Ares glanced to Rhodes, who watched her approach. With a thought, Ares was at the side of Rhodes's chair. The mortal man showed no surprise at Ares's sudden appearance.

"Are you ready?" Ares asked.

Rhodes nodded.

"Remember the timing."

"I will not fail you," Rhodes said. Ares noted that his captain's dark brown eyes were rimmed with hazel. He had never noticed it before and wondered if the additional power Ares had given him had transformed him physically.

The surrogate woman, who appeared to be in her mid-twenties, stood in front of the altar. The war priest was at the edge of the stage, and everyone became silent when he began to recite lines.

Rhodes rose and walked to the altar. He let the black wrap around his waist slide into a slick pile on the floor. He was naked and erect. There was a murmur of wonder by the revelers. Ares guessed they were noticing Rhodes's back. Spanning from the right shoulder to left hip was a leathery scar in the shape of a crescent.

Even from a distance, Ares could see that the woman was trembling at the sight of Rhodes's body. The mortal was tall and muscular, and his cock was impressively long and thick.

The captain walked to the woman, studying her. Then Rhodes gripped the top of her shift in his meaty hands and pulled, tearing the fabric. The woman stood perfectly serene even amongst the anxious murmurs of the onlookers. Her heavy breasts had rosy pink nipples capping them, like foam on the ocean.

The words of the priest became louder and more urgent. The woman's eyes stayed fixed on Rhodes's face, and the warrior grasped the woman under the arms and lifted her so that she was sitting on the altar in full view. She blushed, reminding him of Estella. Ares felt himself stiffen. The crowd too was becoming aroused. Both Rhodes and the woman had well-made bodies, and the captain of the guard looked prepared to enjoy himself.

Rhodes laid the surrogate back. All eyes focused on her naked, trembling body. Her breasts jiggled attractively. The crowd leaned forward, waiting for a glimpse of the virgin territory between her pale legs.

Rhodes popped up on the altar, kneeling at the edge of it. He separated her thighs, moving between them. The tightly muscled ass of the captain twitched as he bent forward, testing the woman's maidenhood.

The woman stretched herself out on the altar like a perfect sacrifice. She was beautiful, ripe and willing. The audience pressed inward, hungry for Rhodes to take her. Rhodes poised himself at the entrance to her body, spreading the woman's plump labia with one hand and holding himself with the other. Ares waited. The room waited.

Then the captain moved, and she gasped, tipping her head back, the picture of exquisite arousal and distress. Rhodes grunted with pleasure as he pushed inside, holding her hips so that she couldn't inch away. Ares, like so many men in the room, was rock hard, but he couldn't stay and watch. He disappeared.

When he appeared on Earth, he found Estella conveniently asleep in her bed. He crawled under the covers with her. Her soft, sweet-smelling body curled toward his. He slid his arms around her carefully. She purred in her sleep, and he was tempted to bury his fingers inside her and cajole her from sleep with desire. Instead, he hugged her body to his and disappeared.

The darkness between worlds was pierced by a burning whiteness. She shrieked in his arms. He faltered at her anguish and considered taking her back to Earth, but, instead, pulled her tight against him.

Then they were in his temple on Elios. Estella was drenched with sweat and lay unconscious on the coverlet at the foot of the altar, her naked body limp and barely breathing. The healer rushed forward, wrapping her in a warm fleece blanket. Many of the revelers had been distracted by his appearance with Estella, but Rhodes was still rutting, and now the surrogate clutched him too in the throes of passion. The surrogate cried out as they finished.

There were cheers from around the temple. Rhodes pushed up and smiled at the surrounding people, his fallen cock covered with blood and semen. The priestess's mouth curled softly in a sated smile. She had done her duty. She turned her head to look at Estella as Ares's priest and the women of the procession stepped forward to cover the surrogate.

She shivered. "She has come back. Let me see her," she said, sitting up. She crawled to the edge of the altar and looked down. "She looks very different." She hesitated as if trying to put her finger on what was different. "This isn't our goddess. You've tricked us."

"Not I. It's Aphrodite's trick," Ares said with a shrug as the priestesses started to curse at him.

Estella was spirited inside the palace surrounded by healers and members of the guard, but Rhodes volunteered to stay behind and see to the crowd.

Ares appeared in the room that had been prepared for her. Ivory silk bedding. A ceiling painted like the Earth sky and murals on the walls with scenes of meadows of flowers. It seemed to Ares the sort of room that a mortal woman from a green planet would like.

Ares looked up at the sound of thunder. He strode to a nearby window overlooking the black ocean. There were streaks of lightning cracking the water. Gusts of wet wind gathered.

"The storm will be bad. Tell Rhodes to prepare the palace," Ares commanded.

The guards left quickly.

The war priest stood near the doorway, staring at Estella's unconscious body. "We've upset nature's order."

"Nature will smooth the ripples we've created," Ares said. "Hurry and give her the elixir.

The healer dripped the shimmering cobalt liquid into Estella's mouth. Ares smoothed Estella's hair back from her face.

"Now she is mine. And nothing can separate us."

## *Chapter 9*

Estella woke feeling lighter than usual and refreshed after a dreamless sleep. She rolled over, reaching for the lamp. The first thing she noticed was that there was no lamp, then she realized she wasn't in her house.

"Where am I?" Estella mumbled, glancing to the floor, which looked like polished ivory.

"The queen's room. Because you are queen."

Estella looked up to find Aristotle, looking as handsome and ferocious as ever with a lethal-looking sword hanging from his waist.

"What? Whose queen?"

"Mine."

"Where am I?"

"My palace on Elios."

She stared at him, bewildered.

Ari started to explain, but his explanation made no sense. He said that the gods of ancient Greece had relocated, that she was carrying some partial spirit of Aphrodite, and that he'd kidnapped her from Earth seven days earlier.

"The herd never gathers in the West, but they're here again now that you're in the palace."

She was sure her confusion showed because the delusional man, formerly known as Aristotle, spoke again. "The winged horses. They loved Aphrodite. She left Elios and they scattered, never returning to the western quarter of the world until now."

"Winged horses," she said with a laugh, climbing from the bed. She paused when she found that her dress was nearly translucent. She snatched the thin silk coverlet and wrapped it around her. She turned to Ari. "Okay, if you want me not to press charges against you over this little joke then you'd better take me home right now."

"This is your home." He looked her over in a predatory manner.

"Don't look at me like that."

He smiled. "I have to oversee a battle. I'll be back soon." He vanished, just disintegrating before her eyes.

"That is not possible!" She stomped her foot in protest. She remembered his disappearance in Las Vegas and frowned. She'd told herself it had been some sort of magician's trick, but now...

*Not real,* she thought firmly.

Estella searched the room, finding a closet full of gowns. Lots of silk cut to drape like sarongs. She turned and looked around the room. No dressers. She walked to a finely carved trunk and opened it, finding it lined with quilted satin and full of lush slips. Other trunks contained slippers and sandals. There were boxes full of jewelry. There were no jeans, no trousers, no shorts.

She tossed off the nightgown she was wearing and put on a deep blue-green dress. Donning sandals, she twisted the strips of fabric around her calves, feeling like she was on a movie set. Where had he gotten all the costumes?

She was dressed and just ready to make her escape when the door was opened by a young girl with coarse dark hair and a big smile.

"Mistress Estella, you are awake. I'm so happy to find you so. I'm Semele."

"Hello. I was just about to go for a walk."

Semele shook her head. "Mistress, there is no time. Master Ares will hurry to return. When he arrives he will want you ready."

"Ready?"

"For him."

"I need to get out of here," Estella said, feeling the panic rise. She shoved past the startled girl and through the open doorway. She managed to get five steps out of the room before her path was blocked by three very large men in S&M style leather outfits that matched the one that Ari had been wearing.

She gaped at them. They appraised her closely, making her blush.

"Mistress," Semele said breathlessly and grabbed her arm. "You must come with me. You mustn't wander. The palace can be a dangerous place for a young woman alone. Not everyone knows you're here, and Master Ares would certainly burn us alive for allowing some other man to have you."

Estella felt her face fall. Surely the woman exaggerated. Even if Aristotle really were Ares as he'd said, ancient god of war, surely he wouldn't kill loyal servants for her defiance... or would he?

Estella clutched Semele's arm. "Please. I have to get home. Can you help me? You can come with me. I live in a place where women are free."

"I would like to know please: free to do what?" Semele asked.

"Well, anything. Anything a man's free to do," Estella said.

Semele laughed. "Why would a woman want to do what men do? Come this way please. We must hurry."

"There's no need to hurry," Estella said stubbornly. Then she caught sight of the men following them and picked up her pace.

They walked past a beautiful courtyard full of fruit trees, and Estella stopped suddenly at the most fantastic sight she'd ever seen. A herd of winged horses pranced around in the open air.

"Like Pegasus," she whispered.

Her voice had been so soft that she almost hadn't heard it herself, but the horses turned their heads. The first one that made eye contact with her had turquoise eyes and a coat the color of an opal. It was utterly beautiful and vaguely familiar.

Other horses, like the first, turned to look at her, and they cantered over to the door leading from the palace to the courtyard. She reached for the handle, wanting nothing in the world more than to open it and run out to them.

Semele grabbed her arm and pulled her along. "You mustn't think of riding away. He'll hunt them down and slaughter the herd. You don't understand yet what he went through to bring you here. He won't let you go. You belong to him."

"I'm a person. I don't belong to anyone. There's no slavery anymore."

"Come, come. You'll have a bath. You'll feel soothed."

"Why? Are you going to soak me in valium?"

"Come along. Oh, he'll be so delighted to see you awake and well. In the early hours he was frantic. None of us has ever seen him so. He was so worried you would be lost. He paced until the straps of his shoes snapped. Then he paced in bare feet."

Estella was propelled forward by Semele's momentum, still startled at the thought of Ari worrying about her. After what seemed an endless series of lovely corridors deeper into the palace, she was taken outside. On a balcony overlooking the ocean, there was a basin of water under a fountain.

"We begin here, Mistress. First the sea foam."

Estella looked at Semele quizzically.

"You should bid a greeting to the sea first."

"Greet the sea?" Estella said with an arch of her eyebrow.

She froze as Semele knelt down, carefully grasping the hem of Estella's gown and lifting it slowly, baring her ankles then calves, then thighs. Estella grabbed the material to keep it from rising further.

"What are you doing?"

"Helping you," Semele said, twisting and pulled the fabric until it was wrenched free of Estella's grasp. "Mistress, you have no cause for shyness. I am the Queen's lady. Master Ares told me so on the night you arrived, and I will attend you."

"I don't need help," Estella said. She glanced down and saw herself in a reflective pool of still water. Her eyes glowed a strangely vibrant blue-green against her now-alabaster skin and her hair hung several inches below her shoulder. "Good grief." He'd kidnapped her to another world.

She tugged her hair. It was real. Everything was real. Servants and winged horses and disappearing ancient war gods. These were not special effects. She was trapped.

Semele moved forward and pulled her gown and underclothes off. Estella shivered as Semele ushered her into the basin of foamy salt water. She sat on a smooth bench as the girl took a slightly rough stone and buffed her skin until Estella's body felt soft and smooth.

Semele wrapped her in a robe and took her inside. They walked through a passageway leading down. The only light came from candles burning on each step. A floral scent, something like gardenias, floated up and enveloped them.

"It's dark down here. Where are we going?"

"The hot springs for your bath."

"Hot springs. How nice," Estella said, inhaling deeply. It was odd to be treated like a queen, but she should enjoy it while she could, and the place really was beautiful. At the bottom of the steps, they walked into an open chamber that was at least two thousand square feet. There were benches and pools big enough for six or seven. There were also other women in various states of undress. Some had damp hair wound with jewels and beads and were dressed in robes. Others were naked and testing the water or scrubbing their bodies. No one seemed particularly modest.

A nubile girl with hair the color of a black cherry strolled over. She carried a jar in her hands.

"Mistress Estella, this is Kira who is in charge of the bath," Semele said.

"Hello," Estella said, politely extending her hand.

"Let me see her," Kira said to Semele.

"She's quite lovely."

*I'm not a lamb chop.* Estella started to fold her arms across her chest, but Semele quickly snagged the edges of her robe and pulled it open, sliding it off her shoulders.

Kira stepped forward. "Not as lush as our lady, Aphrodite," Kira said, cupping Estella's breasts as if to weigh them.

"Hey," Estella sputtered indignantly, taking a step back. She glared down at her nipples, which had tightened instinctively.

"She excites easily," Kira commented, pinching one of her Estella's taut buds. "Ares must love that. Bring her. Backside first."

Estella tried to dig her heels in, but Semele was surprisingly strong, and she forced Estella into a bubbling pool of hot water. They dunked her and pulled her up so that she was completely saturated. Then they scrubbed her with a soft cloth that was thick with a slightly spicy-smelling soap.

Estella's heart raced as they massaged the suds under her arms and over her breasts. Each girl seemed to hold her a little longer at each pass, making her feel breathless. A few moments later, they moved her to a bench that was just submerged in the water and pressed her into a kneeling position. Her naked body shivered, though the air was quite warm.

Her eyes darted around. The other women didn't seem to be watching her as Semele soaped her back and butt. Kira moved Estella's ankles apart and reached right between her legs with the cloth. The warm sudsy water coated her clit and lips, making them twitch and pucker. Her whole body convulsed at the sensation and then shivered.

After a few seconds, she whispered discreetly that she'd like to rinse herself. They ignored her. Semele came with a pitcher and poured water over her to wash away the soap and then went to work rubbing her with soap again. Belly, between her cheeks, between her lips. Her lower body was on fire.

Finally, when her legs were wobbly, they dipped her into the hot water and then floated her through a channel to a pool of cooler water. She rested on their hands, helplessly, her legs slightly open, letting the cool liquid caress her.

She bit her lip with nervousness when she spotted Kira smiling above her. She quickly closed her legs as they slid her over the smooth lip of the pool and onto the floor. She lay limp for a few moments before Semele helped her up.

"Oiling comes after washing," Semele said.

The smell of vanilla filled the air, and Estella felt warm slippery liquid being drizzled over her.

"Oil infused with vanilla. Specially prepared for you by Ares's command. He said it is your favorite," Semele whispered.

*By Ares's command. They all believe he's the god of war. This is either the biggest delusion of all time... or I'm in big trouble.*

❧⟨ᴗ⟩☙

"You smell good," Ares said when he appeared and found her stretched out in his bed atop burgundy satin-covered pillows. He was dressed in war garb at first, and then he wasn't. In an instant he was nude, and what a body he had, all bulging muscles and bulging other things. She blinked at the sight of his huge erection. Her mouth watered, and she swallowed slowly.

"You have lust in your eyes." He glanced her over. "And on your thighs." He sauntered toward her with a smile, graceful as a panther and every bit as predatory.

She never took her eyes off his body.

"Estella," he said, crawling onto the bed with her. She stared at him, unspeaking, his body warming hers.

"The first time will be fast and rough. Then we'll take our time." With one hand he reached down and spread her curls, opening her wide. She arched her back as the motion made her breathless with anticipation.

With his free hand, he guided the tip of his cock to her willing pussy and sunk down into her an inch. She writhed against the pillows, lifting her hips. For a split second she saw the triumph in his eyes, then she felt the hardest, longest, thickest cock in existence bury itself into her soft drenched folds.

The oil and her desire made it slide in easier, but she was impossibly stretched. She moaned from pain and pleasure as he rocked forward. A second later, he started to move. A few slow jabs, then fast sure strokes in and out. She could feel him deep inside, like he was moving up to her ribs.

Her body burned from the friction as his sweat rained down on her. She was jarred by his thrusts. Her legs tried to wrap around him, but he pulled them free so that he could move in his own rhythm.

He grabbed her hips, stabilizing her while he pushed inside, the penetration sharp and complete. Her back bowed as one of his thumbs found her pulsing clit and pressed against it. He rubbed incessantly while his cock burrowed deep into her body. She caught fire, awash with his heat, her desire.

She screamed when she came, startling herself. He laughed softly, pressing deeper into her body. She squirmed under him. The sensations were so intense they burned. She needed to catch her breath, but he didn't let her escape. His mouth silenced hers, and he pinned her under him. It went on and on and on.

She lost count of her orgasms and half-lost her mind, crying and shaking through the last hour. When he finally withdrew, he was only partially flaccid after spilling his seed. She felt like he'd left a gaping hole in his wake. In some respects, he had. She touched her sore lower lips gingerly.

He was upright on his knees. A jug of water appeared in his hand. He poured some over his head, apparently to cool himself, and then splashed some over her fevered body. Then he pressed the pitcher to her mouth, and she drank several gulps before falling back down to the pillow.

"Yes, rest for a few moments before we resume."

"Before we what?" she gasped. She looked down and found that he was fully erect again.

"I'm not as hard as I first was, but when I get inside you, I'll thicken up."

"We're—I'm done for the night." She pulled her legs up to roll away from him.

"We've only gotten started," he said, drinking from the pitcher.

She staggered from bed, not even bothering with her sheet. She snatched her robe from the hook by the door and pulled it on. She grabbed the door handle and tried to turn it, but it didn't budge. She fiddled with it, making no progress.

"Come back to bed," he said lazily.

She ignored him, pulling with all her might.

An instant later her robe was gone, evaporated in the air. She looked over her shoulder.

"Kiss me," he said.

"Let me out."

He shook his head with a smile.

She put her frustrated head to the door and shut her eyes. All of this was impossible. Then she felt herself being lifted, and she opened her eyes. She was in his arms, cradled several feet above the floor.

"I'm tired, and I'm sore," she said.

He bent his head and sucked on her lip slowly. When he let it go, they were lying on the bed again. "I want to be between your legs, inside you, at least once more tonight. Indulge me."

"No."

He laughed, stroking her cheek. "You're like a farmer with a shovel telling an army it can not pass."

"We've had a lot of sex tonight."

"And I want more." He coaxed her legs open. He slipped a finger gently inside her. "Still wet."

"That's your wetness, leftover."

"It provides the same function. I'll be very gentle. You'll barely know I'm there."

"Right," she said with a derisive laugh.

He kissed her slowly. "Let me," he whispered against her mouth. She didn't struggle as he eased inside her. "You're so warm and swollen, so tight around me."

He moved his body so that his pelvic bone rubbed against her achingly sensitive clit. It stung and felt good at the same time. Her back arched. She couldn't believe she wanted him again.

"That's it. That's my little goddess." His rhythm picked up but was still gentle. Soon, a succulent tension built inside her, floating on top of the pain.

She dug her nails into his arms, dragging her hands down. She wanted him to hurt too, to be marked and as sore as she was. Moments later she exploded, and he came soon after, his warmth filling her inside. It was only afterward that she was shocked by her violent impulse.

He lay next to her, vibrating with hot strength. She opened her eyes and found blood dotting the scratches she'd made on him. She dabbed them with her fingertips. "You're bleeding."

One of his heavy arms slid across her body. The weight of it pinned her to the bed next to him.

"No pain you could inflict during sex would be more than I can handle. You're welcome to do your worst whenever you want."

"I don't want to hurt you. Our goal shouldn't be to damage each other when we make love."

"Well-spoken." He pulled her against his body and curled them together like spoons. "I have waited so long to sleep with you in my arms. Never leave me."

Her head swam at the feeling that things were spinning out of control. How could she leave him? Where would she go? Her pulse raced. It was a very important question that she would need to answer. The sex with him was amazing, but she couldn't possibly be expected to never go home.

"That's an unfair thing to ask. You kidnapped me."

"I never claimed to be fair," he said. "But I will give you happiness and everything a mortal woman could want. Give me your promise that you will stay."

"I can't," she stammered. It was hard to refuse him. He was so handsome, such a powerful presence, but she did have a life of her own. She'd worked hard in graduate school and was proud of her accomplishments. There was no way she could just be a concubine to some testosterone-crazed man until he tired of her, no matter how irresistibly attracted to him she was.

He kissed the side of her face and then whispered in her ear, "If you escape, I'll find you, sooner or later, because you are what I want. And on Elios, I always get what I want." His hand slid down to her belly making it clench in anticipation and desire.

In a show of defiance, she tried to untangle herself from his arms, but couldn't. She finally stopped struggling and sighed. She held little hope of ever leaving his world when she couldn't even escape from his bed.

# *Chapter 10*

Ares returned from the battlefield on the eastern edge of his territories. Most of the army rode home with him as the local troops had things well in hand. The men were anxious to get to their women, and he felt the same way. As the weeks had passed, he'd become used to appearing in his bedroom to make love to Estella and then to talk to her most of the night before he left to return to the battle. She always improved his mood, even when it didn't need improving.

But today he didn't find Estella in her rooms or his. He found her in the children's courtyard, playing games with dozens of them. Their high-pitched laughter rang through the air as they raced back and forth, watching Estella's delighted reaction.

Many of the warriors and the palace girls had children together. The daughters grew up and sometimes married outside the palace. The sons largely became warriors and continued to live in the fortress, though once they were of age they moved to the soldiers' quarters rather than staying with the women and children.

Estella's skin glowed golden-pink under the large red sun. When Ares made himself visible, the children scattered, leaving Estella standing alone.

"What are you doing here?" he asked.

"An excellent question. What *am* I doing here?"

"I meant in this courtyard."

"I was making myself useful, babysitting and playing with the children so that the women can rest before putting in their hours with your warriors."

"You sound as though you don't approve."

"These girls are sex slaves."

"Actually, you're the only real sex slave here. All the others can leave at will," he teased, but she didn't smile. He sighed. "Do they say they're mistreated? Do they tell you they don't like bedding my warriors?

"No," she admitted.

"Then what is the problem?"

"You've seen to it that their families and friends won't take them in if they leave. They're as good as prisoners."

"In these walls, they have everything they need and want. Male attention. Protection. An endless supply of food and flowers. Their children can play instead of work. This place is paradise."

"According to you," she said, rolling her eyes.

"Ask them if they disagree with me."

"Master Ares," Semele said, entering the courtyard. "A word?"

"Yes, what is it?"

"Captain Rhodes' new girl is missing."

"What new girl?"

"A farmer's daughter. The captain and five men defended his farm from a force of forty who are loyal to Apollo. The farmer brought his daughter Jemdine as a gift for the captain since he'd shown an interest in her when he dined with them."

"And the girl is missing?"

Semele nodded. "The captain is quite angry. She was in his rooms and when he returned from training the young warriors, she was gone."

"Someone let her out." Ares glanced at Estella suspiciously. She was the only person he could imagine doing such a thing.

"So it seems," Semele agreed.

"Where do you think she is, Semele?" Ares asked. Semele hesitated, clearly trying to avert Rhodes' rage without implicating her mistress.

"I wouldn't know, but since you could find her easily, I thought to bring the matter to your attention before Captain Rhodes becomes too angry, and the girl suffers for it." The servant woman cast a meaningful look at Estella, who folded her arms across her chest.

"Didn't you just say the girls are free to leave?" Estella demanded.

"They're free once they'd done their duty. This girl hasn't yet."

"Why is it her duty?" Estella snapped, flinging her shimmering hair over her shoulder. "Your men saved the girl's father's farm. He should pay money or homage or whatever, not sell his daughter!"

"You're an outsider. You wouldn't understand," Ares said, watching the fabric of Estella's deep green gown stretch over her breasts as she took a deep breath.

"I understand it perfectly."

He waved a dismissive hand and glanced back at the servant. "You show very good judgment, Semele. I'll get the girl and take her back—"

"Ares, no." Estella had stepped forward and placed a hand on his arm. "She's too young."

He glanced at Semele, who shook her head almost imperceptibly. "She has a woman's body, doesn't she?"

"She's past puberty, yes, but she's young and terrified. Give her some time to grow up and get used to the idea."

Whenever Estella asked him for anything, it was difficult to refuse her. On Earth, he'd been obsessed with his lust for her, but now he also enjoyed her good humor. He didn't like to quarrel with her. "Rhodes has a bad temper. It'll not improve his demeanor to make him wait."

"Then he shouldn't have her at all. You could tell him that he can't."

"Why would I do that?"

"Because you're in charge, and she's in your lands. You should protect her. It's the right thing to do."

"The right thing to do is to give my captain of the guard what is due him. She wasn't a gift to me. She belongs in his bed."

"It's her choice."

"Listen, the men are not cruel. He'll be gentle with her. Rhodes's women all fall in love with him eventually."

Her blue eyes snapped with fury. "After he rapes them, you mean? Maybe they convince themselves it's love so they can stand it."

"Don't stir up trouble among the women, Estella."

"Or what?"

"Or I won't let you socialize with them."

Her eyes narrowed, but then her expression went blank. "Fine. Then keep me away from them," she said, but he knew that wasn't the end of the argument, by any means. He also knew that keeping Estella away from the other women was easier said than accomplished, with her living in the palace and him gone much of the time.

He sighed. She was as irritating as she was beautiful, and he wanted to roar at her, but doubted it would bring any good outcome. He wondered why it was so difficult to harden his heart against her. Just looking at her made him want to relent and tell Rhodes he couldn't have the spoils of war that he'd earned, but Ares knew that wouldn't be wise. There was an order to things. He couldn't let anyone destroy that natural order, not even the woman he loved.

"I don't seek to punish you, Estella, but I won't let you disrupt the peace. The men need the women to praise and soothe them after battle, and the women need the men to cherish them. It's the way of things. The other gods are all considered more yielding than I am, but it's the same in their camps. Men and women fight and struggle, but there is a passion between them that must be sated for the good of everyone concerned. You must feel it and understand it. It's the same passion that exists between us. You don't bar me from your bed, even in anger. And when I'm wounded, it eases me to have you stroke my hair and whisper to me. This is the nature of what men and women offer to each other."

He waited, but she didn't answer him. She went instead to the courtyard's edge and looked out at the sea. He struggled with his frustration, clenching his jaw against the angry words that threatened to burst forth. She could be so unreasonable.

"She remembers a different life," Semele observed.

"I know, but she must forget it. I am her life now."

*And she is mine.*

Estella set aside the parchment she'd been writing on. She had lists of lessons on science and mathematics that she'd been teaching the women and children. Ares hadn't been enthusiastic about her educating the people, but he hadn't forbidden it. And he'd given Rhodes a dozen oversexed dancing girls in exchange for the young virgin Jemdine, who wasn't returned to him.

Estella supposed that she'd won in many ways, but a part of her heart still resisted him… the part that remembered that she'd been brought here without a choice. That she lived as a prisoner, a pampered and indulged prisoner, but a prisoner nonetheless.

There had been invitations for her to travel. An offer of a temporary peace had been made so that the gods could gather for a feast and so that Estella, Ares's new queen, could meet Apollo and Athena. But Ares refused. And he forbade the guards to let her outside the walls of the fortress or to admit any other gods' ambassadors. It was terribly frustrating to Estella.

*But just maybe this is what I was born to do,* she told herself. *To educate these people. To elevate the status of women in the most powerful nation on Elios.*

Everyone seemed to agree that she was good for Ares and his provinces. He was apparently happier and more good-humored than he'd been in years. Still, she wasn't content.

Estella adjusted her shift. Her body had changed. She had fuller breasts, wider hips. At first, she'd thought she was pregnant, but that theory had been disproved time and again. The world was just different and so was she. She sometimes had daydreams of Elios in past times, as if she'd lived before and as if the people of Elios were her own. Earth seemed a distant memory most days.

She glanced to where Ares slept. His loose black curls fell to his broad shoulders. His wide chest was covered with such hard muscle that it almost looked like armor. The bandage, over a wound made recently by one of Apollo's arrows, had slipped down and showed a circular defect in Ares' upper left arm. If the pain troubled him, he never showed it. Like all his soldiers, he was strong, fierce, and virile.

The slow thud of her heart echoed in her ears. For the thousandth time she wondered if she loved him or only lusted after him. She moved to the bed, knowing the answer wouldn't be found there, but unable to resist the impulse to join him in it.

She leaned over him. "Wake up."

His mouth twitched, and then his eyes opened slowly. "What do you want of me?"

"Your body."

He smiled and stretched slowly. "It's yours." He pulled her next to him. "I'd like to break you of the habit of wearing shifts. You've a magnificent body. You should let all of Elios see it."

"I don't think so."

His hand slid along her silky thigh, finding the soft curls of her mound. "You've gotten used to wearing nothing underneath."

"I wouldn't want to slow you down," she said with a hint of sarcasm in her voice.

He smiled. "I'm glad."

He rubbed the tip of his cock over her cleft where the finest sheen of moisture had started to collect. He pushed into her a fraction of an inch, and she slid her leg up so that her heel dug gently into the back of his thigh. His stomach muscles contracted violently at her invitation.

"I wish I could make you beg, but this early in the day, I don't have the patience," he mumbled with his mouth over hers.

She dragged her hands over his sides, pulling him to her. She wanted him deep inside her, with long hard strokes that took her breath and her thoughts away.

He rocked forward, plunging into her velvet folds. She arched her back, making her breasts jut upward. He bent his head, tonguing one and then the other.

She tightened her pelvic muscles around him, making him roar with pleasure. She tilted her head back, exposing her long neck. He bent his head and sucked on the pulse beating frantically under her skin, the soft vibration of her moans against his mouth.

"Ares," she breathed.

His name from her lips was like a siren song to the war god. While buried inside her, licking her vanilla-scented skin, Ares wanted nothing more than to give her anything and everything she desired. And when she arched her body beneath him and purred his name, he felt almost dazed.

She dug her nails into his back. "More."

At her beckoning, he thrust wildly. No beast had ever fucked his mate with more furor. Moments later, while she was shrieking the word *yes*, he poured his seed into her.

Afterward, he collapsed onto her and caught his breath slowly, with his mouth open. He was surprised when she started licking his lips and letting her tongue lazily court his. Usually, after the first time he fucked her in the morning, she disappeared to soak in a soothing bath and afterward rubbed medicinal ointment over her sore body. Letting her body recover from the roughest coupling of the day was the only way she could manage to let him take her body over and over without being reduced to tears by nightfall. But she was stronger now than when she'd first arrived on Elios. He tried not to think about what that might mean. He ran a finger over her hair, golden silk shimmering through his fingers.

Estella looked forward to the winter. Ares had said that his troops had advanced as far as he wanted them to for the year. He would not go to battle over the coming months. Things would be calm, and they would enjoy the closeness that had been growing between them. She hated to admit it to him, but she longed to see him when he was gone. She loved to tease him and make him laugh. She loved to see him playful with the children when he found her in the courtyard. All of Elios had noted the change in its fierce war god. And Estella had to admit that she had changed too. Not that there weren't still problems. Ares continued to find it difficult to compromise. He would lay jewels at her feet, name newly discovered flowers after her, and give her any gift she wanted, but he did not trust her to wander free.

"Stop!" A loud voice called in the corridor.

Estella looked up from her cushioned seat on the balcony. A girl ran in and slammed the door on Semele, who shouted at her again to stop.

Estella recognized the girl, and Estella widened her eyes as her bedroom door was locked with the heavy latch that Ares had had placed so that Estella could bolt the door if she wanted to.

The young girl, Jemdine, turned with a forced exhalation that was very like a sob.

"What is it?"

"Master Rhodes has taken Tholipsios."

"Apollo's stronghold? That's wonderful. Ares will be—what's wrong?"

The girl's face crumpled. "He demanded a reward. Me."

Estella's mouth fell open. "Who said so?"

Huge tears welled in Jemdine's eyes and spilled over. "The first soldiers are back from the battle. Kira said so. Her man was there when Ares made the promise."

"He couldn't have." Estella's heart plummeted.

"I'm sorry. I'm sorry. I shouldn't ask for your mercy and help again." The girl slid across the tile and fell prostrate before Estella, her dark curls falling like satin over Estella's feet.

"They say you are Aphrodite in disguise. I beg you, my lady. I beg you to help me. I love another. I do not want to be the captain's whore. Please."

Estella's back stiffened, and she felt something inside her turn cold. Ares had betrayed her, and he had promised an innocent fifteen-year-old girl to his forty-year-old captain-at-arms who would use and forget her.

In an instant, Estella remembered ancient betrayals, and old wounds opened again. Ares would always choose war over love. He would always reward violence above tenderness. It was his nature. But it wasn't her nature. It never had been.

Estella's touched the girl's head. "Calm yourself."

The girl looked up with hope shining in her damp eyes. "Mistress?"

"Wipe your eyes, and I will tell you exactly what you must do."

"What do you mean, gone?" Ares roared. The day he had feared had apparently come.

Semele cowered in the corner as the tower sentry knelt, shaking, before the war god. "She was on the balcony overlooking the sea. And then we saw the herd. She called to them and jumped. The pearly-white stallion dove into the sea and when he emerged, she rode him."

Ares cursed and smashed the bedstand. "I should have slaughtered that herd after the first time!" He paced to the balcony and looked out at the ocean. "But I didn't expect this. It wasn't like before. We haven't quarreled. She wanted to be here with me. She said so." He glanced at the bed where Estella had lied to him.

"Master," Semele said, her voice a faint whisper.

"What?" Ares demanded, whirling to face the woman.

"I think she felt she had reason to go."

"What reason?" Ares said, his muscles tightening. Had someone threatened her? Hurt her in some way while he was gone? Who would dare?

"She had word that you promised Jemdine to Rhodes."

"From who?" he shouted. He'd given specific instructions that the girl was not to be allowed to talk to Estella. He'd known Estella wouldn't approve. She was too tender-minded about such things. But Rhodes had done what no one else had been able to do in seventy years. He had taken Tholipsios. He had to be rewarded.

"She took the girl and a young soldier when she left. Jemdine and Dimaris have been seen talking together. The boy is fifteen."

"What would a young woman want with a fifteen-year-old?" Ares said.

"Jemdine is newly fifteen herself," Semele said.

"Fifteen?" Ares asked, bemused. Ares had seen her. She looked older than that. But that was the way of things. Children turned into adults when he blinked.

Ares turned to the sentry. "Athena or Apollo?"

"Master?"

"The herd," Ares snapped. "In which direction did they fly?" Only a god's palace or temple could act as sanctuary against the other gods. Anywhere else, he could enter and simply recover Estella instantly. She would know that and plan accordingly.

"Apollo."

Ares frowned.

"We have heard that Athena and her ambassadors have ridden in that direction too. Last night."

Ares grimaced. "Perfect," he muttered through his teeth. "Tell Rhodes to assemble his men. We ride in two hours."

Estella smudged oil onto Jemdine's forehead and wrists. "You are bound into the service of Aphrodite. No other god may claim you, but you must serve two years in her temple under the supervision of her priestesses and pay tribute daily. When the two years have passed, you will be free to marry as you choose."

Jemdine smiled, casting a glance at the boy, who was, to Estella's eyes, impossibly young and earnest. Dimaris had sworn his allegiance to Athena, forsaking his family and friends to become one of her soldiers. It couldn't be helped, Estella knew. There was no way to protect him from Rhodes if he lived in Ares's fortress. And somehow she doubted that the proud Rhodes would favor the boy with mercy for the sake of love.

"My lady," Jemdine said, kissing the back of Estella's hands.

Estella smiled at her. "Two years."

"I will pay the best tribute because my heart is the most grateful of all Aphrodite's worshippers."

Estella nodded, lifting the hood of the girl's pink cloak. "Say goodbye to your young man now."

Jemdine shuffled to the boy and beamed at him.

His voice cracked slightly, but he didn't falter as he spoke. "They tell me that the first training is six months without interruption, but when I am free to ride alone, I will come as far as the north edge of Aphrodite's temple. You'll know my arrow by its green shaft. I'll paint it myself, the color of your eyes. Look for it among the rocks."

Estella smiled. Now, why couldn't Ares ever say anything romantic like that to her? She glanced over at Apollo, stunningly handsome and golden. His bright blue tunic hung to his narrow waist and made his eyes reflect like sapphires. He wasn't as tall as Ares, or as menacing. She couldn't imagine him on a battlefield against the god of war. Still, he had an easy confidence to him. Apollo had flirted with her since her arrival, and she wondered if he wanted her for herself or for what she represented.

Athena strode into the room, causing everyone to look at her. "Ares has been spotted. He rides with an army. We must get Jemdine and Dimaris out now if they're to reach protected places."

Dimaris stood tall. "We are ready, my lady."

Athena nodded and waved for them to go to the main hall. Athena turned then to Estella. "And what of you, my lady? Will you shelter with me? Or stay with Apollo?"

"What do you recommend?" Estella asked.

"Do you wish to anger Ares? Or only to avoid him?"

Estella blinked. She hadn't really thought over what she wanted, beyond helping Jemdine to escape safely.

"Knowing Ares, he'll be angry no matter what," Apollo said.

"True, but you know which will make him angrier," Athena said mildly.

Apollo declared, "My fortress is closest to the palace of Aphrodite. If Estella is to reach her full potential, she should be close to it."

Athena looked at Estella. "He's right about that."

"I'll stay here then," Estella said.

"Have a care though with Ares's feelings," Athena warned. "If you have an affair with Apollo, you should conceal it and never speak of it when you return to Ares. His pride is never wounded without revenge."

Estella raised her eyebrows. "What makes you think I'll ever go back to Ares?"

Athena shrugged lean muscled shoulders. "History." Athena strolled out of the small temple room.

"Where is she going?" Estella asked.

Apollo replied, "Home. Ares will surround this fortress on three sides and the ocean is the fourth barrier. Athena has to lead her men out now, or they'll be trapped here while we're under siege."

"Under siege," Estella echoed with a shiver. "Are you sure you want me to stay?"

Apollo smiled, a ray of sunshine in the dark room. "Oh, yes, I'm sure."

# *Chapter 11*

Estella stood near the window watching the rain pour down. Ares's army huddled in their tents a mile away from the fortress. It had been two months of clouds and sleet, and she worried about Ares's men. She'd heard that some had fallen ill with fever, probably pneumonia. Still, Ares stayed exactly where he was, fires burning nightly in the stone hearths that they had built.

Ares had sent no ambassadors to Apollo's gates nor any messengers. His message was clear by his presence, by his constant vigil. "Come back to me," it said. And she felt his pull through freezing rain and stone. Apollo's flirtations were friendly and sweet, but she was never truly tempted by his perfect beauty. And he never pressed her. She suspected his interests lay elsewhere, but she couldn't sort out where, nor did she care to. Ares consumed her thoughts.

She kept recalling their last week together before she'd left. One night, he'd tossed a pallet onto the terrace and made love to her over the ocean, kissing her slowly as though they had all the time in the world. "Before I met you, my only joy was on the battlefield," he'd whispered, thrusting deep inside her. "You surprise me, Estella. You make me love something more than war."

"I love you too," she whispered onto the wind, hoping he'd sense that she missed him and come to Apollo's palace to negotiate.

She pulled the cord tightly around her emerald green robe and walked across the room. She'd been reading and missed lunch. Now she was famished and restless. After dinner she would raise the subject again with Apollo about beginning science classes among his followers. He'd told her to wait, saying they weren't ready for complex lessons, but she suspected that he was the one who wasn't ready. And she wondered why he wouldn't want them educated. Maybe ignorance made them easier to control.

She walked down the hall and heard low voices arguing.

"Put her out, I say. She'll be the death of us all."

Estella cocked her head and walked toward the voices. Could they be talking about her? She turned a corner and saw a pair of very thin women washing the floor near a far stone doorway that the wind often blew in.

"Excuse me," she said.

The women went silent and pale at the sight of her. *So they were talking about me.*

They stood and bowed low. She could see their jutting collarbones as they bent forward. She grimaced and turned back. She'd noticed that the food had gotten less splendid in the past month at Apollo's table. How was the rest of the fortress faring if the god's dinner was suffering?

She went into the main banquet hall, which was swathed in sumptuous jewel-tone fabrics. Apollo sat at the head table talking to his advisors. There was an empty chair next to him, where she always sat at dinner. The conversation died as she approached.

"May I speak to you alone?" she asked.

Apollo nodded and stood. They walked to a far corner of the room.

"You told me there was plenty of food in storage for the winter. Is that true?"

He frowned and looked away.

"Tell me the truth."

"We have a herd that supplies meat for the fortress, but some have died, more than expected. And the first frost came early."

"So the gardens were destroyed before the harvest?"

"On Earth, I could force the sun to shine, but this place is different. It takes more effort here because my temple isn't as well attended as it should be. And if I ride into the clouds, Ares will meet me there. My arrows would certainly stop him, but only if I saw him in time. This weather is a curse."

"Well," she said, forcing a bright smile, "it's a good thing that he'll go away soon."

"He won't go. He fights year round when it suits him. He rewards his men for their grit. The harder things are, the more they like it. They're as mad as he is."

"That is a problem. Well, maybe we'll think of something."

Apollo nodded, but she didn't miss the way his eyebrows drew together with worry.

The opal-winged horse came every day. He flew over the sea, too fast to be caught by soldiers. Estella tied rolled messages in his mane and sent them to Aphrodite's temple each week and received messages in return. The priestesses were content, and Jemdine was doing very well in her duties.

On the night of the crescent moon, however, Estella didn't send a message because the temple had been emptied on her orders. Aphrodite's priestesses and followers were safely in Athena's palace.

Estella ran a hand over the horse's sleek flank and then stepped off the balcony, sliding down on the horse's back. "This will be our last ride for awhile," she whispered. Aphrodite's temple was land-locked, and Estella wouldn't risk the horse once Ares's army surrounded it.

The horse rose, majestic wings flapping with mesmerizing strength. The cold blistered Estella's cheeks, but the ride was no less exhilarating than usual. She stretched her arms out against the wind, feeling light and free, her nipples tight, her thighs taut.

There was no question that Ares would follow her. She could feel his need for her burning in the night with the fires. He wanted to see her as much as she wanted to see him. And they needed to meet to settle things once and for all.

If she lived or if she died didn't so much matter. She understood that now. A sliver of her soul was Aphrodite's, and Aphrodite was a goddess. She could not be held prisoner, not even by a god.

The opal landed light-footed, and she slipped from its back. She pressed a kiss on its neck and then walked into the empty white marble temple. She lit a fire and waited.

The knock came two hours later. Just after her message had been delivered, she realized. He'd wasted no time in coming then.

"Come in," she called. She sat on a stone bench next to the flames and watched him approach. His hard body emerged from the darkness. He wore black pants, but was shirtless despite the cold. A black cord wrapped his bulging left bicep, a warrior's mark. His hair spilled black over his shoulders. He was temptation made flesh, and she was sure he'd intended exactly that.

His voice was deep and rough-edged. "You asked for me. Here I am."

"Is your army on its way too?"

He shook his head. "One of my armies surrounds Apollo's fortress. The other blocks the only road that Athena's troops could use to get to this temple. I don't need an army here." He leaned against the altar, studying her.

"This temple is protected like the palaces of Apollo and Athena, like your own. You can't drag me from here."

"I know that."

"So what are we going to do?" she asked.

"About what?"

"I don't want you to starve Apollo's women and children to death."

He narrowed his eyes. "Why? Because you love Apollo so much?"

"No."

"Because you've taken his people as your own?"

"No."

"Then why?"

"Because I'm mortal and so are they. I know what it is to be hungry, and I don't want anyone to starve, especially not on my account."

"So you want to bargain with me? Good. I want something too," he said, looking her body over. She felt the impact of his lust, fierce and raw. A throb began deep inside her womb and spread outward, belly and pussy contracting with need. As always, she wanted him to intensify that feeling by planting his cock at its origin.

"We can barter," he said.

She was tempted, so impossibly tempted, just looking at him. "I don't think so."

He strode to her, looming over her. "Why not?"

"Because your bargains are too temporary for my taste. You took Jemdine out of Rhodes's hands at my request and then planned to give her back to him when new circumstances arose."

He gnashed his teeth. "She was given to him, and beyond that, she was born in my lands. The daughter of a father loyal to me and to my men. You had no right to interfere in the first place."

Estella smiled mirthlessly. "I know. Because I have no rights in your palace. I was just a prisoner."

He shook his head bitterly, but then stopped. His mouth was a hard line, his fists clenched. "You know, you're right. You were my prisoner, and you will be again. And the next time Apollo is under my sword on a battlefield will be the last time."

"I don't love Apollo. I never made love to him. You can be angry that he gave me shelter, but don't be jealous. There's no cause for that."

He exhaled slowly, and his fists uncurled. "Still, this game *is* over. Come with me now."

Her heart beat painfully. She so wanted to go with him anywhere, to lie beneath him again. *Be strong,* she thought fiercely and shook her head.

"You can't stay here. There's no food. And there's no one to rescue you."

"I don't need to be rescued, and I don't need food either."

"You'll die without food. You said so yourself."

"I know. That's what I plan to do."

His mouth dropped open in shock, and he raised his eyebrows. "What? You wouldn't do that. Mortals cherish their lives. You wouldn't waste it."

"No, I wouldn't. I don't consider it a waste. Aphrodite took a stand and entrusted me with something of herself. I intend to take a stand too."

"I won't let you do it."

"How will you stop me?"

His eyes darted around temple. She could feel him calculating.

He sighed in frustration. "What do you want?"

"Freedom."

"You want me to take you back to Earth, is that it? I couldn't if I wanted to, and I don't want to. If you want to be free of me, maybe death is your only option."

She put her palm against his cheek. He closed his eyes, seemingly caught in the sensation. "I don't want to be free of you," she whispered.

His eyes fluttered open, anger and desire burning behind them. "Then speak plainly. Give me your terms."

She took a deep breath and exhaled slowly. "Share your power. Let me be your partner, not your prisoner. And let men and women share the same freedom, the same choices. Don't crush the spirit of one to exalt the other. People can't be the property of other people."

"Share my power with you?" he echoed, turning away from her. "I've fought thousands of years to conquer this world, wrestling it away from the other gods. Now you want me to yield half to you, when you've never had to raise an army, never had to lift a sword to earn it. The blood of my men has soaked battlefields from one ocean to the other. How can you ask me to make them bow to you when you've never earned the right to have them do so?"

"I don't earn things with a sword. I'm not the goddess of war. And I don't want to be. But I'm not a slave either. And I won't stand and watch women be traded like cattle. I'd rather die alone in this temple."

"I don't believe you. You won't do it."

"You don't know me," she said, her voice as hard as the stone under her feet. She felt slightly euphoric. It might have been from lack of food and water, but it might too have been from sensing that she'd found the heart of her life's purpose. "I've sent a message to your palace. Maybe it won't mean anything to the women there. But maybe it will. I've told them that when I come home they'll be free, or I won't come home at all because I've died of hunger standing in defiance of your army."

He looked stunned for a moment and then tipped his head back and laughed. "You are worse than she ever was. Aphrodite played matchmaker with mortals for her own amusement, but she never concerned herself with any mortals' rights. She and I fought mostly because she wanted me to force larger numbers of women to be virgin priestesses in her temple. She wanted more power for herself, not for mortal women."

"Well, I'm not a goddess. I'm just a woman. And you have my terms." She walked to the bench and sat down.

He stared at her with such intensity that she worried he'd scorch the clothes from her body. And she ached for him to do just that, but she hid it from him.

"You would do well to watch your step. Put a toe outside this temple, and I'll have you. I may care for you, but it won't stop me from stretching your body out on the stones and taking you outside your temple door."

Her body spasmed inwardly, lusting for just such a thing. Moisture coated her lower lips, and she fought to keep still so Ares wouldn't figure out just how weak she was for him.

"Spoken like a war god," she said with a smile.

He moved close to her. "Give me a kiss."

She couldn't resist it. She grazed her lips roughly over his mouth, bruising them both. He shuddered and fisted his hands, struggling for control.

"Answer me one thing. During our time apart, have you missed me?"

"Yes, I've missed you."

His eyes closed for a moment, then looked at her with a hooded expression. "My men will bring you supplies. You'll eat and drink and stay alive until you and I have settled this."

"That's acceptable."

He rolled his eyes. "You may not be a goddess, but you act like one."

Two days later, Ares returned. She was eating roast fowl by the fire when he arrived.

"I see my hunters have had a successful day," he said.

She nodded, setting aside a glazed-clay tray and rinsing her hands.

"You've had a successful day too," Ares said. "When I visited the women in the palace, they were collectively more agitated than I've ever seen them. They calmed some when I told them that you were still alive."

"I'm glad they're pleased that I'm alive. Am I going to stay that way?"

He nodded.

"So you're meeting my terms? Just like that?"

"Well, there are conditions—"

"I—"

"Wait until you've heard me out."

She clamped her lips closed.

"I've talked it over with the women, and they agree with me that while they're free beginning today, the men can't know it."

Estella stared at him. "What? What good is freedom if no one knows you have it? It's not really freedom. You tricked them into agreeing to that."

"Listen, if you want the men to come around, they have to be worked on slowly. And often. Preferably by women who are naked and willing to spread their legs to drain a man's fighting spirit. The women are convinced that's the way to go about it."

"That's ridiculous."

"Why? It worked for you."

She laughed. "Is that what you told them?"

"No, that's what they told me."

She laughed again, but shook her head. "And what happens when some farmer gives his unwilling daughter to the captain of the guard? Are the other women going to tell her to take one for the team? So that the men don't have to face an unpleasant reality?"

"Something will be worked out."

"Something that doesn't involve the girl being raped?"

"Yes."

She stared at him, not quite believing.

He leaned forward. "Yes," he repeated. "You have my word."

So she'd won. It was hard to get her mind around that fact. And she wondered how her victory would affect the two of them as lovers. Ares was not used to losing, nor known for doing it gracefully. Would he resent it? Did he already?

"Are you angry?" she asked.

He shook his head. "I brought you here without your permission and held you on Elios against your will. But it didn't satisfy me. I realized I wanted to win you, not enslave you. And, over time, I began to feel that you wanted to be with me, and I cherished that." He smiled at her. "When you left me, I understood the reason, but I still hoped that part of you loved me, that I would have you back after you punished me. When you said you'd sacrifice your life for what you believe in, I knew that you are not like the selfish goddess I once knew. You are as fierce as any warrior I could ever hope to train. I respect you."

She couldn't reply.

He ran a finger along her jaw and touched a strand of her hair. "I once promised that I would give you happiness. If this bargain will do that, so be it. For there is no prison a man in love can create that a woman cannot escape, nor should any man try to build one. I would have you stay with me forever, but, more importantly, I would have you stay as long as you want to. And perhaps my men, whom I train in my image, should learn that lesson from me."

She threw her arms around his neck and kissed him. "Take me home."

Estella walked into Ares's suite of rooms and found him looking over a map while five musicians played a small concert. He looked up when he heard her approach.

"Can they come back later?" she asked.

He glanced at the men. "Why?"

"I want you."

"Get out," Ares barked at the musicians.

They shuffled out with their instruments in hand. An instant later, she and Ares were both naked.

*Wasting no time,* she thought, but smiled. Her body was already tender from all the ways he'd pounded into her over the past few days, but despite the soreness, she still wanted him.

He strode over, magnificent buttocks twitching in the cool air. Estella opened one of the doors to the balcony, bending forward to inhale deeply of the sea and also to give him a good look at her body. He growled impatiently. She liked the way he always wanted her in the most primitive way.

She turned and looked at him, touching her breasts slowly, tweaking the nipples.

"Come here," he commanded.

She stretched, sliding her fingers amidst the sleek blonde strands and lifting them over her head. Her breasts rose, nipples pointing at the ceiling. She could feel his gaze scorching her.

"Estella, come to me right now."

She knew that if he was really too impatient to wait for her to walk over he'd have disappeared and reappeared right next to her in an instant and tossed her to the floor.

She let her arms fall back to her sides and put her foot up on a bench, still stretching.

He stared at her swollen labia, which were deep pink and plump with arousal. She watched Ares lick his lips like the predator he was.

She put her foot down and crossed the distance to stand in front of him. She ran her fingertips over his nipples. He grabbed her arms, yanking her toward him roughly.

He bit her lip firmly, holding her flesh between his teeth for several seconds, making her heart pound as they stared into each other's eyes with dizzying closeness.

He finally opened his mouth, releasing her lip, and she sucked the sore spot where he'd softly bruised it. He was so often pure animal lust and fury, always inflicting a drop of pain into their passion.

She bit his nipple, hard enough to make him hiss. She licked the surrounding teeth marks. Her hand slipped down to stroke his cock. It was hard enough to hammer stone. She smoothed the drop of juice over the tip.

He groaned and lifted her off the floor. She wrapped her legs around his waist, and her hand circled his stiff member and guided it into her slick wetness. He lowered her until she was fully impaled.

He moved to the wall, squeezing her between him and it, leaving her breathless. He thrust slowly, big and thick, filling every bit of space within her. His cock was buried so deep that her insides had to recede to receive him. It caused her lower belly to cramp and shudder.

"Oh. That's really deep," she gasped. "That's so deep." She gripped his shoulders, circling her hips to grind down on him.

Ares panted. "Be quiet for moment," he said and kissed her.

In a shimmer of velvet and vanilla, she melted to nothing and then reformed. They were in an alcove behind a heavy burgundy drape. Ares continued to thrust into her slowly. Now she could smell candle smoke and hear men and women making love.

"What?" she gasped in a harsh whisper.

"I thought you might like to hear how the negotiations are going between the men and the women."

He grinned and thrust deeper, and her fear of discovery spiked her blood with even more arousal. She loved the uncomfortable but exquisite way he felt inside her.

"Oh, Ares," she whimpered as her clit caught fire. She rubbed it frantically against his body, while his stony cock was still trapped inside her, throbbing like a heartbeat. Her moisture dripped slowly to coat the base of him where they were joined.

Ares groaned softly.

"Shh," she moaned, licking at his salty neck. "Oh, yes. Ares, yes." When she came, she knew he could feel it as she pulsated all around him, suffocating him.

"Estella," he groaned. "I love you."

She collapsed against him, panting. "I know."

In a ripple of energy, they were alone on the sand near the water. "Say it," he said, thrusting hard and fast.

Another orgasm crashed over her as a wave of salt water swallowed their feet. She felt herself being pulled under. She thrust her hips up to meet him and gasped at the force as he knocked her body back down.

"Tell me," he growled.

She stared into his eyes. "I love you too."

He roared, his arms crushing her against him. She felt his cock empty inside her. "Stay with me," he said. "Just stay with me forever."

"I will," she whispered. "Always."

## *About the Author:*

*Alexa Aames likes to spend her free time buried in books with her toes in the sand and the sound of the ocean nearby. She loves the variety of the Secrets stories and is happy to be able to contribute to the latest collection.*

*She loves hearing from readers at* alexa_aames@hotmail.com, *and you can learn about her other available stories at* alexaaames.com.

# Men you've been dreaming about!

## *Secrets*

*Satisfy your desire for more.*

*F*eel the wild adventure, fierce passion and the power of love in every **Secrets** Collection story. Red Sage Publishing's romance authors create richly crafted, sexy, sensual, novella-length stories. Each one is just the right length for reading after a long and hectic day.

Each volume in the **Secrets** Collection has four diverse, ultra-sexy, romantic novellas brimming with adventure, passion and love. More adventurous tales for the adventurous reader. The **Secrets** Collection are a glorious mix of romance genre; numerous historical settings, contemporary, paranormal, science fiction and suspense. We are always looking for new adventures.

Reader response to the **Secrets** volumes has been great! Here's just a small sample:

> *"I loved the variety of settings. Four completely wonderful time periods, give you four completely wonderful reads."*

> *"Each story was a page-turning tale I hated to put down."*

> *"I love **Secrets**! When is the next volume coming out? This one was Hot! Loved the heroes!"*

**Secrets** have won raves and awards. We could go on, but why don't you find out for yourself—order your set of **Secrets** today! See the back for details.

# Secrets, Volume 1

*A Lady's Quest* by Bonnie Hamre
Widowed Lady Antonia Blair-Sutworth searches for a lover to save her from the handsome Duke of Sutherland. The "auditions" may be shocking but utterly tantalizing.

*The Spinner's Dream* by Alice Gaines
A seductive fantasy that leaves every woman wishing for her own private love slave, desperate and running for his life.

*The Proposal* by Ivy Landon
This tale is a walk on the wild side of love. *The Proposal* will taunt you, tease you, and shock you. A contemporary erotica for the adventurous woman.

*The Gift* by Jeanie LeGendre
Immerse yourself in this historic tale of exotic seduction, bondage and a concubine's surrender to the Sultan's desire. Can Alessandra live the life and give the gift the Sultan demands of her?

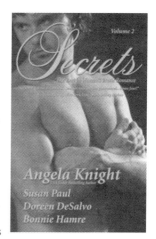

# Secrets, Volume 2

*Surrogate Lover* by Doreen DeSalvo
Adrian Ross is a surrogate sex therapist who has all the answers and control. He thought he'd seen and done it all, but he'd never met Sarah.

*Snowbound* by Bonnie Hamre
A delicious, sensuous regency tale. The marriage-shy Earl of Howden is teased and tortured by his own desires and finds there is a woman who can equal his overpowering sensuality.

*Roarke's Prisoner* by Angela Knight
Elise, a starship captain, remembers the eager animal submission she'd known before at her captor's hands and refuses to become his toy again. However, she has no idea of the delights he's planned for her this time.

*Savage Garden* by Susan Paul
Raine's been captured by a mysterious and dangerous revolutionary leader in Mexico. At first her only concern is survival, but she quickly finds lush erotic nights in her captor's arms.

**Winner of the Fallot Literary Award for Fiction!**

# Secrets, Volume 3

*The Spy Who Loved Me* by Jeanie Cesarini
Undercover FBI agent Paige Ellison's sexual appetites
rise to new levels when she works with leading man
Christopher Sharp, the cunning agent who uses all his
training to capture her body and heart.

*The Barbarian* by Ann Jacobs
Lady Brianna vows not to surrender to the barbaric
Giles, Earl of Harrow. He must use sexual arts
learned in the infidels' harem to conquer his bride. A
word of caution—this is not for the faint of heart.

*Blood and Kisses* by Angela Knight
A vampire assassin is after Beryl St. Cloud. Her only
hope lies with Decker, another vampire and ex-merce-
nary. Broke, she offers herself as payment for his services. Will his seductive powers
take her very soul?

*Love Undercover* by B.J. McCall
Amanda Forbes is the bait in a strip joint sting operation. While she performs, fellow
detective "Cowboy" Cooper gets to watch. Though he excites her, she must fight the
temptation to surrender to the passion.

**Winner of the 1997 Under the Covers Readers Favorite Award**

# Secrets, Volume 4

*An Act of Love* by Jeanie Cesarini
Shelby Moran's past left her terrified of sex. International film star Jason Gage must gently coach the young
starlet in the ways of love. He wants more than an act—
he wants Shelby to feel true passion in his arms.

*Enslaved* by Desirée Lindsey
Lord Nicholas Summer's air of danger, dark passions,
and irresistible charm have brought Lady Crystal's
long-hidden desires to the surface. Will he be able to
give her the one thing she desires before it's too late?

*The Bodyguard* by Betsy Morgan & Susan Paul
Kaki York is a bodyguard, but watching the wild,
erotic romps of her client's sexual conquests on the
security cameras is getting to her—and her partner, the ruggedly handsome James
Kulick. Can she resist his insistent desire to have her?

*The Love Slave* by Emma Holly
A woman's ultimate fantasy. For one year, Princess Lily will be attended to by three
delicious men of her choice. While she delights in playing with the first two, it's the
reluctant Grae, with his powerful chest, black eyes and hair, that stirs her desires.

## Secrets, Volume 5

*Beneath Two Moons* by Sandy Fraser
Step into the future and find Conor, rough and masculine like frontiermen of old, on the prowl for a new conquest. In his sights, Dr. Eva Kelsey. She got away before, but this time Conor makes sure she begs for more.

*Insatiable* by Chevon Gael
Marcus Remington photographs beautiful models for a living, but it's Ashlyn Fraser, a young exec having some glamour shots done, who has stolen his heart. It's up to Marcus to help her discover her inner sexual self.

*Strictly Business* by Shannon Hollis
Elizabeth Forrester knows it's tough enough for a woman to make it to the top in the corporate world. Garrett Hill, the most beautiful man in Silicon Valley, has to come along to stir up her wildest fantasies. Dare she give in to both their desires?

*Alias Smith and Jones* by B.J. McCall
Meredith Collins finds herself stranded at the airport. A handsome stranger by the name of Smith offers her sanctuary for the evening and she finds those mesmerizing, green-flecked eyes hard to resist. Are they to be just two ships passing in the night?

## Secrets, Volume 6

*Flint's Fuse* by Sandy Fraser
Dana Madison's father has her "kidnapped" for her own safety. Flint, the tall, dark and dangerous mercenary, is hired for the job. But just which one is the prisoner—Dana will try *anything* to get away.

*Love's Prisoner* by MaryJanice Davidson
Trapped in an elevator, Jeannie Lawrence experienced unwilling rapture at Michael Windham's hands. She never expected the devilishly handsome man to show back up in her life—or turn out to be a werewolf!

*The Education of Miss Felicity Wells* by Alice Gaines
Felicity Wells wants to be sure she'll satisfy her soon-to-be husband but she needs a teacher. Dr. Marcus Slade, an experienced lover, agrees to take her on as a student, but can he stop short of taking her completely?

*A Candidate for the Kiss* by Angela Knight
Working on a story, reporter Dana Ivory stumbles onto a more amazing one—a sexy, secret agent who happens to be a vampire. She wants her story but Gabriel Archer wants more from her than just sex and blood.

# Secrets, Volume 7

*Amelia's Innocence* by Julia Welles
Amelia didn't know her father bet her in a card game
with Captain Quentin Hawke, so honor demands a
compromise—three days of erotic foreplay, leaving
her virginity and future intact.

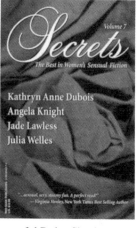

*The Woman of His Dreams* by Jade Lawless
From the day artist Gray Avonaco moves in next door,
Joanna Morgan is plagued by provocative dreams.
But what she believes is unrequited lust, Gray sees
as another chance to be with the woman he loves. He
must persuade her that even death can't stop true love.

*Surrender* by Kathryn Anne Dubois
Free-spirited Lady Johanna wants no part of the bind-
ing strictures society imposes with her marriage to the powerful Duke. She doesn't
know the dark Duke wants sensual adventure, and sexual satisfaction.

*Kissing the Hunter* by Angela Knight
Navy Seal Logan McLean hunts the vampires who murdered his wife. Virginia Hart
is a sexy vampire searching for her lost soul-mate only to find him in a man determined to kill her. She must convince him all vampires aren't created equally.

**Winner of the Venus Book Club Best Book of the Year**


# Secrets, Volume 8

*Taming Kate* by Jeanie Cesarini
Kathryn Roman inherits a legal brothel. Little does
this city girl know the town wants her to be their new
madam so they've charged Trey Holliday, one very
dominant cowboy, with taming her.

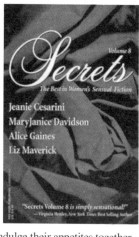

*Jared's Wolf* by MaryJanice Davidson
Jared Rocke will do anything to avenge his sister's
death, but ends up attracted to Moira Wolfbauer, the
she-wolf sworn to protect her pack. Joining forces to
stop a killer, they learn love defies all boundaries.

*My Champion, My Lover* by Alice Gaines
Celeste Broder is a woman committed for having a sexy
appetite. Mayor Robert Albright may be her champion—
if she can convince him her freedom will mean they can indulge their appetites together.

*Kiss or Kill* by Liz Maverick
In this post-apocalyptic world, Camille Kazinsky's military career rides on her ability to make a choice—whether the robo called Meat should live or die. Can he prove
he's human enough to live, man enough… to make her feel like a woman.

**Winner of the Venus Book Club Best Book of the Year**

# Secrets, Volume 9

*Wild For You* by Kathryn Anne Dubois
When college intern, Georgie, gets captured by a
Congo wildman, she discovers this specimen of male
virility has never seen a woman. The research pos-
sibilities are endless!

*Wanted* by Kimberly Dean
FBI Special Agent Jeff Reno wants Danielle Carver.
There's her body, brains—and that charge of treason
on her head. Dani goes on the run, but the sexy Fed is
hot on her trail.

*Secluded* by Lisa Marie Rice
Nicholas Lee's wealth and power came with a price—
his enemies will kill anyone he loves. When Isabelle
steals his heart, Nicholas secludes her in his palace for a lifetime of desire in only a
few days.

*Flights of Fantasy* by Bonnie Hamre
Chloe taught others to see the realities of life but she's never shared the intimate
world of her sensual yearnings. Given the chance, will she be woman enough to
fulfill her most secret erotic fantasy?

# Secrets, Volume 10

*Private Eyes* by Dominique Sinclair
When a mystery man captivates P.I. Nicolla Black
during a stakeout, she discovers her no-seduction rule
bending under the pressure of long denied passion.
She agrees to the seduction, but he demands her total
surrender.

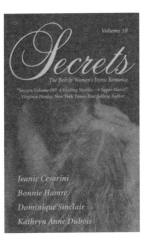

*The Ruination of Lady Jane* by Bonnie Hamre
To avoid her upcoming marriage, Lady Jane Ponson-
by-Maitland flees into the arms of Havyn Attercliffe.
She begs him to ruin her rather than turn her over to
her odious fiancé.

*Code Name: Kiss* by Jeanie Cesarini
Agent Lily Justiss is on a mission to defend her country
against terrorists that requires giving up her virginity as a sex slave. As her master
takes her body, desire for her commanding officer Seth Blackthorn fuels her mind.

*The Sacrifice* by Kathryn Anne Dubois
Lady Anastasia Bedovier is days from taking her vows as a Nun. Before she denies
her sensuality forever, she wants to experience pleasure. Count Maxwell is the perfect man to initiate her into erotic delight.

# Secrets, Volume 11

*Masquerade* by Jennifer Probst
Hailey Ashton is determined to free herself from her
sexual restrictions. Four nights of erotic pleasures
without revealing her identity. A chance to explore her
secret desires without the fear of unmasking.

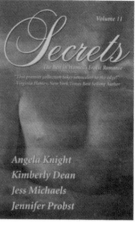

*Ancient Pleasures* by Jess Michaels
Isabella Winslow is obsessed with finding out what
caused her husband's death, but trapped in an Egyptian concubine's tomb with a sexy American raider,
succumbing to the mummy's sensual curse takes over.

*Manhunt* by Kimberly Dean
Framed for murder, Michael Tucker takes Taryn
Swanson hostage—the one woman who can clear him.
Despite the evidence against him, the attraction is strong. Tucker resorts to uncon-
ventional, yet effective methods of persuasion to change the sexy ADA's mind.

*Wake Me* by Angela Knight
Chloe Hart received a sexy painting of a sleeping knight. Radolf of Varik has been
trapped there for centuries, cursed by a witch. His only hope is to visit the dreams of
women and make one of them fall in love with him so she can free him with a kiss.

# Secrets, Volume 12

*Good Girl Gone Bad* by Dominique Sinclair
Setting out to do research for an article, nothing could
have prepared Reagan for Luke, or his offer to teach
her everything she needs to know about sex. Licen-
tious pleasures, forbidden desires… inspiring the best
writing she's ever done.

*Aphrodite's Passion* by Jess Michaels
When Selena flees Victorian London before her evil
stepchildren can institutionalize her for hysteria,
Gavin is asked to bring her back home. But when he
finds her living on the island of Cyprus, his need to
have her begins to block out every other impulse.

*White Heat* by Leigh Wyndfield
Raine is hiding in an icehouse in the middle of nowhere from one of the scariest men
in the universes. Walker escaped from a burning prison. Imagine their surprise when
they find out they have the same man to blame for their miseries. Passion, revenge
and love are in their future.

*Summer Lightning* by Saskia Walker
Sculptress Sally is enjoying an idyllic getaway on a secluded cove when she spots a
gorgeous man walking naked on the beach. When Julian finds an attractive woman
shacked up in his cove, he has to check her out. But what will he do when he finds
she's secretly been using him as a model?

# Secrets, Volume 13

*Out of Control* by Rachelle Chase
Astrid's world revolves around her business and she's
hoping to pick up wealthy Erik Santos as a client. He's
hoping to pick up something entirely different. Will
she give in to the seductive pull of his proposition?

*Hawkmoor* by Amber Green
Shape-shifters answer to Darien as he acts in the name
of long-missing Lady Hawkmoor, their ruler. When
she unexpectedly surfaces, Darien must deal with a
scrappy individual whose wary eyes hold the other half
of his soul, but who has the power to destroy his world.

*Lessons in Pleasure* by Charlotte Featherstone
A wicked bargain has Lily vowing never to yield to the
demands of the rake she once loved and lost. Unfortunately, Damian, the Earl of St.
Croix, or Saint as he is infamously known, will not take 'no' for an answer.

*In the Heat of the Night* by Calista Fox
Haunted by a curse, Molina fears she won't live to see her 30th birthday. Nick, her for-
mer bodyguard, is re-hired to protect her from the fatal accidents that plague her family.
Will his passion and love be enough to convince Molina they have a future together?

# Secrets, Volume 14

*Soul Kisses* by Angela Knight
Beth's been kidnapped by Joaquin Ramirez, a sadistic
vampire. Handsome vampire cousins, Morgan and
Garret Axton, come to her rescue. Can she find happiness with two vampires?

*Temptation in Time* by Alexa Aames
Ariana escaped the Middle Ages after stealing a kiss
of magic from sexy sorcerer, Marcus de Grey. When
he brings her back, they begin a battle of wills and a
sexual odyssey that could spell disaster for them both.

*Ailis and the Beast* by Jennifer Barlowe
When Ailis agreed to be her village's sacrifice to the
mysterious Beast she was prepared to sacrifice her vir-
tue, and possibly her life. But some things aren't what they seem. Ailis and the Beast
are about to discover the greatest sacrifice may be the human heart.

*Night Heat* by Leigh Wynfield
When Rip Bowhite leads a revolt on the prison planet, he ends up struggling to
survive against monsters that rule the night. Jemma, the prison's Healer, won't allow
herself to be distracted by the instant attraction she feels for Rip. As the stakes are
raised and death draws near, love seems doomed in the heat of the night.

# Secrets, Volume 15

*Simon Says* by Jane Thompson
Simon Campbell is a newspaper columnist who panders to male fantasies. Georgina Kennedy is a respectable librarian. On the surface, these two have nothing in common... but don't judge a book by its cover.

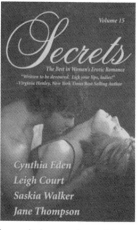

*Bite of the Wolf* by Cynthia Eden
Gareth Morlet, alpha werewolf, has finally found his mate. All he has to do is convince Trinity to join with him, to give in to the pleasure of a werewolf's mating, and then she will be his... forever.

*Falling for Trouble* by Saskia Walker
With 48 hours to clear her brother's name, Sonia Harmond finds help from irresistible bad boy, Oliver Eaglestone. When the erotic tension between them hits fever pitch, securing evidence to thwart an international arms dealer isn't the only danger they face.

*The Disciplinarian* by Leigh Court
Headstrong Clarissa Babcock is sent for instruction in proper wifely obedience. Disciplinarian Jared Ashworth uses the tools of seduction to show her how to control a demanding husband, but her beauty, spirit, and uninhibited passion make Jared hunger to keep her—and their darkly erotic nights—all for himself!

# Secrets, Volume 16

*Never Enough* by Cynthia Eden
Abby McGill has been playing with fire. Bad-boy Jake taught her the true meaning of desire, but she knows she has to end her relationship with him. But Jake isn't about to let the woman he wants walk away from him.

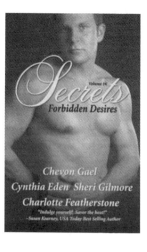

*Bunko* by Sheri Gilmoore
Tu Tran must decide between Jack, who promises to share every aspect of his life with her, or Dev, who hides behind a mask and only offers nights of erotic sex. Will she gamble on the man who can see behind her own mask and expose her true desires?

*Hide and Seek* by Chevon Gael
Kyle DeLaurier ditches his trophy-fiance in favor of a tropical paradise full of tall, tanned, topless females.
Private eye, Darcy McLeod, is on the trail of this runaway groom. Together they sizzle while playing Hide and Seek with their true identities.

*Seduction of the Muse* by Charlotte Featherstone
He's the Dark Lord, the mysterious author who pens the erotic tales of an innocent woman's seduction. She is his muse, the woman he watches from the dark shadows, the woman whose dreams he invades at night.

## Secrets, Volume 17

*Rock Hard Candy* by Kathy Kaye
Jessica Hennessy, descendent of a Voodoo priestess, decides it's time for the man of her dreams. A dose of her ancestor's aphrodisiac slipped into the gooey center of her homemade bon bons ought to do the trick.

*Fatal Error* by Kathleen Scott
Jesse Storm must make amends to humanity by destroying the software he helped design that's taken the government hostage. But he must also protect the woman he's loved in secret for nearly a decade.

*Birthday* by Ellie Marvel
Jasmine Templeton's been celibate long enough. Will a wild night at a hot new club with her two best friends ease the ache or just make it worse? Considering one is Charlie and she's been having strange notions about their relationship of late… It's definitely a birthday neither she nor Charlie will ever forget.

*Intimate Rendezvous* by Calista Fox
A thief causes trouble at Cassandra Kensington's nightclub and sexy P.I. Dean Hewitt arrives to help. One look at her sends his blood boiling, despite the fact that his keen instincts have him questioning the legitimacy of her business.

## Secrets, Volume 18

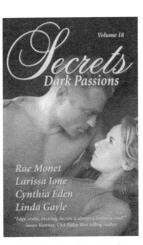

*Lone Wolf Three* by Rae Monet
Planetary politics and squabbling drain former rebel leader Taban Zias. But his anger quickly turns to desire when he meets, Lakota Blackson. She's Taban's perfect mate—now if he can just convince her.

*Flesh to Fantasy* by Larissa Ione
Kelsa Bradshaw is a loner happily immersed in a world of virtual reality. Trent Jordan is a paramedic who experiences the harsh realities of life. When their worlds collide in an erotic eruption can Trent convince Kelsa to turn the fantasy into something real?

*Heart Full of Stars* by Linda Gayle
Singer Fanta Rae finds herself stranded on a lonely Mars outpost with the first human male she's seen in years. Ex-Marine Alex Decker lost his family and guilt drove him into isolation, but when alien assassins come to enslave Fanta, she and Decker come together to fight for their lives.

*The Wolf's Mate* by Cynthia Eden
When Michael Morlet finds "Kat" Hardy fighting for her life, he instantly recognizes her as the mate he's been seeking all of his life, but someone's trying to kill her. With danger stalking them, will Kat trust him enough to become his mate?

# Secrets, Volume 19

*Affliction* by Elisa Adams
Holly Aronson finally believes she's safe with sweet
Andrew. But when his life long friend, Shane, arrives, events begin to spiral out of control. She's
inexplicably drawn to Shane. As she runs for her life,
which one will protect her?

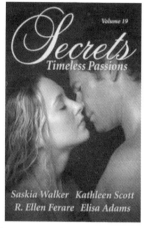

*Falling Stars* by Kathleen Scott
Daria is both a Primon fighter pilot and a Primon
princess. As a deadly new enemy faces appears, she
must choose between her duty to the fleet and the
desperate need to forge an alliance through her marriage to the enemy's General Raven.

*Toy in the Attic* by R. Ellen Ferare
Gabrielle discovers a life-sized statue of a nude man. Her unexpected roommate
reveals himself to be a talented lover caught by a witch's curse. Can she help him
break free of the spell that holds him, without losing her heart along the way?

*What You Wish For* by Saskia Walker
Lucy Chambers is renovating her historic house. As her dreams about a stranger
become more intense, she wishes he were with her. Two hundred years in the past, the
man wishes for companionship. Suddenly they find themselves together—in his time.

# Secrets, Volume 20

*The Subject* by Amber Green
One week Tyler is a game designer, signing the deal
of her life. The next, she's running for her life. Who
can she trust? Certainly not sexy, mysterious Esau,
who keeps showing up after the hoo-hah hits the fan!

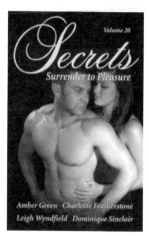

*Surrender* by Dominique Sinclair
Agent Madeline Carter is in too deep. She's slipped
into Sebastian Maiocco's life to investigate his Sicil-
ian mafia family. He unearths desires Madeline's
unable to deny, conflicting the duty that honors her.
Madeline must surrender to Sebastian or risk being
exposed, leaving her target for a ruthless clan.

*Stasis* by Leigh Wyndfield
Morgann Right's Commanding Officer's been drugged with Stasis, turning him into
a living statue she's forced to take care of for ten long days. As her hands tend to
him, she sees her CO in a totally different light. She wants him and, while she can
tell he wants her, touching him intimately might come back to haunt them both.

*A Woman's Pleasure* by Charlotte Featherstone
Widowed Isabella, Lady Langdon is yearning to discover all the pleasures denied her
in her marriage, she finds herself falling hard for the magnetic charms of the mysterious and exotic Julian Gresham—a man skilled in pleasures of the flesh.

# Secrets, Volume 21

*Caged Wolf* by Cynthia Eden
Alerac La Morte has been drugged and kidnapped. He realizes his captor, Madison Langley, is actually his destined mate, but she hates his kind. Will Alerac convince her he's not the monster she thinks?

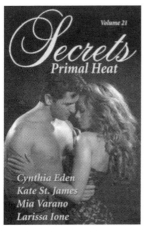

*Wet Dreams* by Larissa Ione
Injured and on the run, agent Brent Logan needs a miracle. What he gets is a boat owned by Marina Summers. Pursued by killers, ravaged by a storm, and plagued by engine troubles, they can do little but spend their final hours immersed in sensual pleasure.

*Good Vibrations* by Kate St. James
Lexi O'Brien vows to swear off sex while she attends grad school, so when her favorite out-of-town customer asks her out, she decides to indulge in an erotic fling. Little does she realize Gage Templeton is moving home, to her city, and has no intention of settling for a short-term affair..

*Virgin of the Amazon* by Mia Varano
Librarian Anna Winter gets lost on the Amazon and stumbles upon a tribe whose shaman wants a pale-skinned virgin to deflower. British adventurer Coop Daventry, the tribe's self-styled chief, wants to save her, but which man poses a greater threat?

# Secrets, Volume 22

*Heat* by Ellie Marvel
Mild-mannered alien Tarkin is in heat and the only compatible female is a Terran. He courts her the old fashioned Terran way. Because if he can't seduce her before his cycle ends, he won't get a second chance.

*Breathless* by Rachel Carrington
Lark Hogan is a martial arts expert seeking vengeance for the death of her sister. She seeks help from Zac, a mercenary wizard. Confronting a common enemy, they battle their own demons as well as their powerful attraction, and will fight to the death to protect what they've found.

*Midnight Rendezvous* by Calista Fox
From New York to Cabo to Paris to Tokyo, Cat Hewitt and David Essex share decadent midnight rendezvous. But when the real world presses in on their erotic fantasies, and Cat's life is in danger, will their whirlwind romance stand a chance?

*Birthday Wish* by Elisa Adams
Anna Kelly had many goals before turning 30 and only one is left—to spend one night with sexy Dean Harrison. When Dean asks her what she wants for her birthday, she grabs at the opportunity to ask him for an experience she'll never forget.

# Secrets, Volume 23

*The Sex Slave* by Roxi Romano
Jaci Coe needs a hero and the hard bodied man in black meets all the criteria. Opportunistic Jaci takes advantage of Lazarus Stone's commandingly protective nature, but together, they learn how to live free... and love freely.

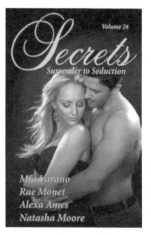

*Forever My Love* by Calista Fox
Professor Aja Woods is a 16th century witch... only she doesn't know it. Christian St. James, her vampire lover, has watched over her spirit for 500 years. When her powers are recovered, so too are her memories of Christian—and the love they once shared.

*Reflection of Beauty* by Bonnie Dee
Artist Christine Dawson is commissioned to paint a portrait of wealthy recluse, Eric Leroux. It's up to her to reach the heart of this physically and emotionally scarred man. Can love rescue Eric from isolation and restore his life?

*Educating Eva* by Bethany Michaels
Eva Blakely attends the infamous Ivy Hill houseparty to gather research for her book *Mating Rituals of the Human Male*. But when she enlists the help of research "specimen" and notorious rake, Aidan Worthington, she gets some unexpected results.

# Secrets, Volume 24

*Hot on Her Heels* by Mia Varano
Private investigator Jack Slater dons a g-string to investigate the Lollipop Lounge, a male strip club. He's not sure if the club's sexy owner, Vivica Steele, is involved in the scam, but Jack figures he's just the Lollipop to sweeten her life.

*Shadow Wolf* by Rae Monet
A half-breed Lupine challenges a high-ranking Solarian Wolf Warrior. When Dia Nahiutras tries to steal Roark D'Reincolt's wolf, does she get an enemy forever or a mate for life?

*Bad to the Bone* by Natasha Moore
At her class reunion, Annie Shane sheds her good girl reputation through one wild weekend with Luke Kendall. But Luke is done playing the field and wants to settle down. What would a bad girl do?

*War God* by Alexa Aames
Estella Eaton, a lovely graduate student, is the unwitting carrier of the essence of Aphrodite. But Ares, god of war, the ultimate alpha male, knows the truth and becomes obsessed with Estelle, pursuing her relentlessly. Can her modern sensibilities and his ancient power coexist, or will their battle of wills destroy what matters most?

# The Forever Kiss
## by Angela Knight

### Listen to what reviewers say:

"*The Forever Kiss* flows well with good characters and an interesting plot. ... If you enjoy vampires and a lot of hot sex, you are sure to enjoy *The Forever Kiss*."

—*The Best Reviews*

"Battling vampires, a protective ghost and the ever present battle of good and evil keep excellent pace with the erotic delights in Angela Knight's *The Forever Kiss*—a book that absolutely bites with refreshing paranormal humor." **4½ Stars, Top Pick**

—*Romantic Times BOOKclub*

"I found *The Forever Kiss* to be an exceptionally written, refreshing book. ... I really enjoyed this book by Angela Knight. ... 5 angels!"

—*Fallen Angel Reviews*

"*The Forever Kiss* is the first single title released from Red Sage and if this is any indication of what we can expect, it won't be the last. ... The love scenes are hot enough to give a vampire a sunburn and the fight scenes will have you cheering for the good guys."

—*Really Bad Barb Reviews*

### In *The Forever Kiss*:

For years, Valerie Chase has been haunted by dreams of a Texas Ranger she knows only as "Cowboy." As a child, he rescued her from the nightmare vampires who murdered her parents. As an adult, she still dreams of him— but now he's her seductive lover in nights of erotic pleasure.

Yet "Cowboy" is more than a dream—he's the real Cade McKinnon—and a vampire! For years, he's protected Valerie from Edward Ridgemont, the sadistic vampire who turned him. Now, Ridgmont wants Valerie for his own and Cade is the only one who can protect her.

When Val finds herself abducted by her handsome dream man, she's appalled to discover he's one of the vampires she fears. Now, caught in a web of fear and passion, she and Cade must learn to trust each other, even as an immortal monster stalks their every move.

Their only hope of survival is... *The Forever Kiss*.

**Romantic Times Best Erotic Novel of the Year**

# It's not just reviewers raving about *Secrets*. See what readers have to say:

"When are you coming out with a new Volume? I want a new one next month!" via email from a reader.

"I loved the hot, wet sex without vulgar words being used to make it exciting." after *Volume 1*

"I loved the blend of sensuality and sexual intensity—HOT!" after *Volume 2*

"The best thing about *Secrets* is they're hot and brief! The least thing is you do not have enough of them!" after *Volume 3*

"I have been extremely satisfied with *Secrets*, keep up the good writing." after *Volume 4*

"Stories have plot and characters to support the erotica. They would be good strong stories without the heat." after *Volume 5*

"*Secrets* really knows how to push the envelop better than anyone else." after *Volume 6*

"These are the best sensual stories I have ever read!" after *Volume 7*

"I love, love, love the *Secrets* stories. I now have all of them, please have more books come out each year." after *Volume 8*

"These are the perfect sensual romance stories!" after *Volume 9*

"What I love about *Secrets Volume 10* is how I couldn't put it down!" after *Volume 10*

"All of the *Secrets* volumes are terrific! I have read all of them up to *Secrets Volume 11*. Please keep them coming! I will read every one you make!" after *Volume 11*

# Finally, the men you've been dreaming about!

## Give the Gift of Spicy Romantic Fiction

Don't want to wait? You can place a retail price ($12.99) order
for any of the *Secrets* volumes from the following:

① online at **eRedSage.com**

② **Waldenbooks, Borders, and Books-a-Million Stores**

③ **Amazon.com** or **BarnesandNoble.com**

④ or buy them at your local bookstore or online book source.

Bookstores: Please contact Baker & Taylor Distributors, Ingram Book Distributor,
or Red Sage Publishing, Inc. for bookstore sales.

## Order by title or ISBN #:

**Vol. 1:**   0-9648942-0-3
ISBN #13 978-0-9648942-0-4

**Vol. 2:**   0-9648942-1-1
ISBN #13 978-0-9648942-1-1

**Vol. 3:**   0-9648942-2-X
ISBN #13 978-0-9648942-2-8

**Vol. 4:**   0-9648942-4-6
ISBN #13 978-0-9648942-4-2

**Vol. 5:**   0-9648942-5-4
ISBN #13 978-0-9648942-5-9

**Vol. 6:**   0-9648942-6-2
ISBN #13 978-0-9648942-6-6

**Vol. 7:**   0-9648942-7-0
ISBN #13 978-0-9648942-7-3

**Vol. 8:**   0-9648942-8-9
ISBN #13 978-0-9648942-9-7

**Vol. 9:**   0-9648942-9-7
ISBN #13 978-0-9648942-9-7

**Vol. 10:**   0-9754516-0-X
ISBN #13 978-0-9754516-0-1

**Vol. 11:**   0-9754516-1-8
ISBN #13 978-0-9754516-1-8

**Vol. 12:**   0-9754516-2-6
ISBN #13 978-0-9754516-2-5

**Vol. 13:**   0-9754516-3-4
ISBN #13 978-0-9754516-3-2

**Vol. 14:**   0-9754516-4-2
ISBN #13 978-0-9754516-4-9

**Vol. 15:**   0-9754516-5-0
ISBN #13 978-0-9754516-5-6

**Vol. 16:**   0-9754516-6-9
ISBN #13 978-0-9754516-6-3

**Vol. 17:**   0-9754516-7-7
ISBN #13 978-0-9754516-7-0

**Vol. 18:**   0-9754516-8-5
ISBN #13 978-0-9754516-8-7

**Vol. 19:**   0-9754516-9-3
ISBN #13 978-0-9754516-9-4

**Vol. 20:**   1-60310-000-8
ISBN #13 978-1-60310-000-7

**Vol. 21:**   1-60310-001-6
ISBN #13 978-1-60310-001-4

**Vol. 22:**   1-60310-002-4
ISBN #13 978-1-60310-002-1

**Vol. 23:**   1-60310-164-0
ISBN #13 978-1-60310-164-6

**Vol. 24:**   1-60310-166-7
ISBN #13 978-1-60310-166-0

**The Forever Kiss:**
0-9648942-3-8
ISBN #13
978-0-9648942-3-5 ($14.00)

# Check out our hot eBook titles available online at eRedSage.com!

**Visit the site regularly as we're always adding new eBook titles.**

**Here's just some of what you'll find:**

*A Christmas Cara* by Bethany Michaels

*A Damsel in Distress* by Brenda Williamson

*Blood Game* by Rae Monet

*Fires Within* by Roxana Blaze

*Forbidden Fruit* by Anne Rainey

*High Voltage* by Calista Fox

*Master of the Elements* by Alice Gaines

*One Wish* by Calista Fox

*Quinn's Curse* by Natasha Moore

*Rock My World* by Caitlyn Willows

*The Doctor Next Door* by Catherine Berlin

*Unclaimed* by Nathalie Gray

# *Red Sage Publishing* Order Form:
(Orders shipped in two to three days of receipt.)

Each volume of *Secrets* retails for $12.99, but you can get it direct via mail order for only $10.99 each. The novel *The Forever Kiss* retails for $14.00, but by direct mail order, you only pay $12.00. Use the order form below to place your direct mail order. Fill in the quantity you want for each book on the blanks beside the title.

| | | |
|---|---|---|
| _____ *Secrets* Volume 1 | _____ *Secrets* Volume 10 | _____ *Secrets* Volume 19 |
| _____ *Secrets* Volume 2 | _____ *Secrets* Volume 11 | _____ *Secrets* Volume 20 |
| _____ *Secrets* Volume 3 | _____ *Secrets* Volume 12 | _____ *Secrets* Volume 21 |
| _____ *Secrets* Volume 4 | _____ *Secrets* Volume 13 | _____ *Secrets* Volume 22 |
| _____ *Secrets* Volume 5 | _____ *Secrets* Volume 14 | _____ *Secrets* Volume 23 |
| _____ *Secrets* Volume 6 | _____ *Secrets* Volume 15 | _____ *Secrets* Volume 24 |
| _____ *Secrets* Volume 7 | _____ *Secrets* Volume 16 | _____ *The Forever Kiss* |
| _____ *Secrets* Volume 8 | _____ *Secrets* Volume 17 | |
| _____ *Secrets* Volume 9 | _____ *Secrets* Volume 18 | |

Total _____ *Secrets* Volumes @ $10.99 each = $_____

Total _____ *The Forever Kiss* @ $12.00 each = $_____

**Shipping & handling (in the U.S.)**                                      $_____

US Priority Mail:
 1–2 books .................. $  5.50
 3–5 books ................... $11.50
 6–9 books ................... $14.50
 10–24 books ............... $19.00

UPS insured:
 1–4 books ...................... $16.00
 5–9 books ...................... $25.00
 10–24 books .................. $29.00

SUBTOTAL  $_____

Florida 6% sales tax (if delivered in FL)  $_____

TOTAL AMOUNT ENCLOSED  $_____

*Your personal information is kept private and not shared with anyone.*

**Name:** (please print) _____

**Address:** (no P.O. Boxes) _____

**City/State/Zip:** _____

**Phone or email:** (only regarding order if necessary) _____

You can order direct from **eRedSage.com** and use a credit card or you can use this form to send in your mail order with a check. Please make check payable to **Red Sage Publishing**. Check must be drawn on a U.S. bank in U.S. dollars. Mail your check and order form to:

**Red Sage Publishing, Inc.  Department S24   P.O. Box 4844   Seminole, FL 33775**